At His Gates by Margaret Oliphant

In Three Volumes

Margaret Oliphant Wilson was born on April 4th, 1828 to Francis W. Wilson, a clerk, and Margaret Oliphant, at Wallyford, near Musselburgh, East Lothian.

Her youth was spent in establishing a writing style and by 1849 she had her first novel published: Passages in the Life of Mrs. Margaret Maitland.

Two years later, in 1851 Caleb Field was published and also an invitation to contribute to Blackwood's Magazine; the beginning of a life time business relationship.

In May 1852, Margaret married her cousin, Frank Wilson Oliphant. Their marriage produced six children but, tragically, three died in infancy. When her husband developed signs of the dreaded consumption (tuberculosis) they moved to Florence, and then to Rome where, sadly, he died.

Margaret was naturally devastated but was also now left without support and only her income from writing to support the family. She returned to England and took up the burden of supporting her three remaining children by her literary activity.

Her incredible and prolific work rate increased both her commercial reputation and the size of her reading audience. Tragedy struck again in January 1864 when her only remaining daughter Maggie died.

In 1866 she settled at Windsor to be closer to her sons, who were being educated at near-by Eton School.

For more than thirty years she pursued a varied literary career but family life continued to bring problems. Cyril Francis, her eldest son, died in 1890. The younger son, Francis, who she nicknamed 'Cecco', died in 1894.

With the last of her children now lost to her, she had little further interest in life. Her health steadily and inexorably declined.

Margaret Oliphant Wilson Oliphant died at the age of 69 in Wimbledon on 20th June 1897. She is buried in Eton beside her sons.

Index of Contents

CHAPTER I

Mr and Mrs Robert Drummond lived in a pretty house in the Kensington district; a house, the very external aspect of which informed the passer-by who they were, or at least what the husband was. The house was embowered in its little garden; and in spring, with its lilacs and laburnums, looked like a great bouquet of bloom—as such houses often do. But built out from the house, and occupying a large slice of the garden at the side, was a long room, lighted with sky windows, and not by any means charming to look at outside, though the creepers, which had not long been planted, were beginning to climb upon the walls. It was connected with the house by a passage which acted as a conservatory, and was full of flowers; and everything had been done that could be done to render the new studio as beautiful in aspect as it was in meaning. But it was new, and had scarcely yet begun, as its proprietor said, to 'compose' with its surroundings. Robert Drummond, accordingly, was a painter, a painter producing, in the mean time, pictures of the class called genre; but intending to be historical, and to take to the highest school of art as soon as life and fame would permit. He was a very good painter; his subjects were truly 'felt' and exquisitely manipulated; but there was no energy of emotion, no originality of genius about them. A great many people admired them very much; other painters lingered over them lovingly, with that true professional admiration of 'good work' which counteracts the jealousy of trade in every honest mind. They were very saleable articles, indeed, and had procured a considerable amount of prosperity for the young painter. It was almost certain that he would be made an Associate at the next vacancy, and an Academician in time. But with all this, he was well aware that he was no genius, and so was his wife.

The knowledge of this fact acted upon them in very different ways; but that its effect may be fully understood, the difference in their characters and training requires to be known. Robert Drummond had never been anything but a painter; attempts had been made in his youth to fix him to business, his father having been the senior clerk, much respected and utterly respectable, of a great City house; and the attempt might have been successful but that accident had thrown him among artists, a kind of society very captivating to a young man, especially when he has a certain command of a pencil. He threw himself into art, accordingly, with all his soul. He was the sort of man who would have thrown himself into anything with all his soul; not for success or reward, but out of an infinite satisfaction in doing good work, and seeing beautiful things grow under his hand. He was of a very sanguine mind, a mind which seldom accepted defeat, but which, with instinctive unconscious wisdom, hesitated to dare the highest flights, and to put itself in conflict with those final powers which either vanquish a man or assure his triumph. Perhaps it was because there was some hidden possibility of wild despair and downfall in the man's mind, of which only himself was aware, that he was thus cautious of putting his final fortune to the touch. But the fact was that he painted his pictures contentedly, conscientiously, doing everything well, and satisfied with the perfection of his work as work, though he was not unaware of the absence from it of any spark of divinity. He did not say it in so many words, but the sentiment of his mind was this:—'It is good work, work no man need be ashamed of. I am not a Raphael, alas! and I cannot help it. What is the good of being unhappy about a thing I cannot mend? I am doing my best; it is honest work, which I know I don't slight or do carelessly; and I can give her everything she wants except that. I should be too happy myself if she were but content.' But she was not content, and thus his happiness was brought down to the moderate pitch allowed to mortal bliss.

She was very different from her Robert. She had been a young lady of very good connections when she first met the rising young artist. I do not say that her connections were splendid, or that she made an absolute mésalliance, for that would be untrue. Her people, however, had been rich people for several generations. They had begun in merchandise, and by merchandise they had kept themselves up; but to have been rich from the time of your great-grandfather, with never any downfall or even break in the wealth, has perhaps more effect on the mind than that pride which springs from family. Well-descended people are aware that every family now and then gets into trouble, and may even fall into poverty without sacrificing any of its pretensions. But well-off people have not that source of enlightenment. When they cease to be very well off, they lose the great point of eminence on which they have taken their stand; and, consequently, success is more absolutely necessary to them than it is to any other class in the community. Helen Burton besides was very proud, very ambitious, and possessed of that not unusual form of amour propre which claims distinction as a right—though she had not anything particular in herself to justify her claim. She had, or believed she had, an utter contempt for that money which was the foundation of her family pride; and she was, at the same time, too well endowed in mind, and too generous in temper, to be able to give herself up sincerely to worship of that rank, which, as their only perpetual superior, tantalizes the imagination of the plebeian rich, and thrusts itself constantly before them. Helen could have married the son of a poor lord, and become the Honourable Mrs Somebody, with her mother's blessing, had she so willed. But as her will took a totally different direction, she had defied and alienated her mother, who was also a woman of high spirit, and only some seventeen years older than her only child; the consequence was that when Mrs Burton found herself abandoned and left alone in the world, she married too, as truly out of pique as a girl sometimes does when deserted by her lover; and at her death left everything she had to her husband and the two small babies, one of them younger than Helen's little Norah, whom she left behind. So that a little tragedy, of a kind not much noted by the world, had woven itself around the beginning of her married life. The mother's second marriage had not been a success, but was Helen to blame for that? Nobody said she was, no one around her; but sometimes in the silence of the night, when she alone was awake, and all her household slept so peacefully—Robert, good Robert, was not a success either, not such a man as she had hoped. She loved him sincerely, was grateful to him for his love, and for his constant regard to her wishes. But yet, in the depths of her heart,—no, not despised him, the expression is too strong,— but felt a minute shade of indignation mingled in her disappointment with him for not being a great genius. Why was he not a Raphael, a Titian? She had married him with the full understanding that he was such, that he would bring her sweet fame and distinction. And why had not he done it? Every time she looked out his pictures she found out the want of inspiration in them. She did not say anything. She was very kind, praising the pretty bits of detail, the wonderful perfection of painting; but Robert felt that he would rather have the President and all the Hanging Committee to pass judgment on his pictures than his wife. Her sense that he had somehow defrauded her by not mounting at once to the very height of his profession, seemed to endow her with a power of judgment a hundred-fold more than was justified by her knowledge of art. She saw the want of any soul in them at the first glance, from under her half-closed eyelids—and it seemed to Robert that in her heart she said: 'Another pretty piece of mediocrity, a thing to sell, not to live—with no genius, no genius in it.' These were the words Robert seemed to himself to hear, but they were not the real words which, in her heart, Helen uttered. These were rather as follows:—'It is just the same as the last. It is no better, no better. And now everybody says he is at his best. Oh! when his worst begins to come, what will become of us?' But she never said an uncivil word. She praised what she could, and she went her way languidly into the drawing-room. She had come down out of her sphere to give herself to him, and he had not repaid her as she expected. He had given her love—oh, yes; but not fame. She was Mrs Drummond only; she was not pointed out where she went as the wife of the great painter. 'Her husband is an artist' was all that anybody ever said.

The effect of this upon poor Robert, however, was much worse even than it was upon his wife. Some time elapsed, it is true, before he discovered it. It took him even years to make out what it was that shadowed his little household over and diminished its brightness. But gradually a sense of the absence of that sympathetic backing up which a man expects in his own house, and without which both men and women who have work to do are so apt to pine and faint, stole over him like a chill. When anything was said against his pictures outside, a gloom in his wife's face would show him that worse was thought within. He had no domestic shield from adverse criticism. It was not kept in the outer circle of his mind, but was allowed to penetrate down to his heart, and envelop him in a heavy discouragement. Even applause did not exhilarate him. 'She does not think I deserve it,' was what he would say to himself; and the sense of this criticism which never uttered a word weighed upon the poor fellow's soul. It made his hand unsteady many a day when his work depended on a firm touch—and blurred the colours before his eyes, and dulled his thoughts. Two or three times he made a spasmodic effort to break through his mediocrity, and then the critics (who were very well pleased on the whole with his mediocrity) shook their heads, and warned him against the sensational. But Helen neither approved nor condemned the change. To her it was all alike, always second-rate. She did her very best to applaud, but she could not brighten up into genuine admiration the blank composure in her eyes. What could she do? There was something to be said for her, as well as for him. She could not affect to admire what she felt to be commonplace. Nature had given her a good eye, and intense feeling had strengthened and corrected it. She saw all the weakness, the flatness, with fatal certainty. What, then, could she say? But poor Robert, though he was not a great artist, was the most tender-hearted, amiable, affectionate of men; and this mode of criticism stole the very heart out of him. There is no such want in the world as that want of backing up. It is the secret of weakness and failure, just as strong moral support and sympathy is the very secret of strength. He stood steady and robust to the external eye, painting many pictures every year, getting very tolerable prices, keeping his household very comfortable, a man still under forty, healthy, cheerful, and vigorous; but all the time he was sapped at the foundations. He had lost his confidence in himself, and it was impossible to predict how he would have borne any sudden blow.

It was about this time that Mr Reginald Burton, a cousin of Helen's, who had once, it was supposed, desired to be something nearer to her, found out the house in Kensington, and began to pay them visits. The circumstances of her marriage had separated her from her own people. The elder among them had thought Helen unkind to her mother; the younger ones had felt that nothing had come of it to justify so romantic a story. So that when Reginald Burton met the pair in society it was the reopening of an altogether closed chapter of her life. Mr Burton was a man in the City in very extensive business. He was chairman of ever so many boards, and his name, at the head of one company or another, was never out of the newspapers. He had married since his cousin did, and had a very fine place in the country, and was more well off still than it was natural for the Burtons to be. Helen, who had never liked him very much, and had not even been grateful to him for loving her, received his visits now without enthusiasm; but Drummond, who was open-hearted like his kind, and who had no sort of jealousy about 'Helen's friends,' received him with a cordiality which seemed to his wife much too effusive. She would not accept the invitation which Mrs Burton sent to pay a long visit to Dura, their country place; but she could not be less than civil to her cousin when he insisted upon calling, nor could she openly resist when he carried off her husband to City dinners, or unfolded to him the benefits of this or that new society. Drummond had done very well in his profession, notwithstanding Helen's dissatisfaction with his work; and also notwithstanding her dissatisfaction, she was a good housewife, doing her duty wisely. She had a hundred a year of her own, which Drummond had taken care to have settled upon herself; but since they had grown richer he had insisted upon letting this accumulate as 'a portion for Norah,' and the two had laid by something besides. For painter-folk it will be readily seen they were at the very height of comfort—a pretty house, one pretty child, a little reserve of money, slowly but pleasantly accumulating. And money, though it is an ignoble thing, has so much to do with happiness! Drummond, who had been quite content to think that there was a portion saving up for Norah, and to whom it had not occurred that his little capital could be made use of, and produce twenty and a hundred-fold, gradually grew interested, without being aware of it, in the proceedings of Mr Burton. He began to talk, half laughingly, half with intention, of the wonderful difference between the slowly-earned gains of labour and those dazzling results of speculation. 'These fellows seem simply to coin money,' he said, 'half in jest and whole in earnest;' 'everything they touch seems to become gold. It looks incredible—' and he wound up with a nervous laugh, in which there was some agitation. Helen had all a woman's conservatism on this point.

'It is incredible, you may be sure,' she said. 'How can they invent money? Some one will have to pay for it somewhere;' which was a sentence of profound wisdom, much deeper than she thought.

'So one would say,' said Drummond, still laughing; 'but nobody seems to suffer. By Jove! as much as—not to say I, who am one of the rank and file—but as Welby or Hartwell Home get for one of their best pictures, your cousin will clear in five minutes, without taking the slightest trouble. When one sees it, one feels hugely tempted'—he added, looking at her. He was one of those men who like to carry their people's sympathy with them. He wanted not acquiescence simply, but approval; and notwithstanding that he was very well used to the absence of it, sought it still. She would not—could not, perhaps—enter warmly into the subject of his pictures; but here was a new matter. He looked up at her with a certain longing—ready, poor fellow, to plunge into anything if she would but approve.

'I hope you won't let yourself be tempted to anything, Robert, that you don't see the end of,' she said; but so gently that her husband's heart rose.

'Trust me for that,' he said joyously, 'and you shall have the first fruits, my darling. I have not as fine a house for you as your cousin can give to his wife, but for all that—'

'For all that,' she said, laughing, 'I would not change with Mrs Reginald Burton. I am not tempted by the fine house.'

'I have thought how we can make this one a great deal better,' he said, as he stooped to kiss her before he went out. He looked back upon her fondly as he left the room, and said to himself that if he wished for gain it was for her sake—his beautiful Helen! He had painted her furtively over and over again, though she never would sit to him. A certain shadow of her was in all his pictures, showing with more or less distinctness according as he loved or did not love his temporary heroine: but he knew that when this was pointed out to her she did not like it. She was anxious that everybody should know she did not sit to him. She was very indignant at the idea that a painter's wife might serve her husband as a model. 'Why should a painter's profession, which ought to be one of the noblest in the world, be obtruded upon the outer world at every step?' she said. But yet as he was a painter, every inch of him, his eye caught the pose of her head as she moved, and made a mental note of it. And yet she was not, strictly speaking, a beautiful woman. She was not the large Juno, who is our present type of beauty; she was not blazing with colour—red, and white, and golden—like the Rubens-heroines of the studio; nor was she of the low-browed, sleepy-eyed, sensuous, classic type. She was rather colourless on the contrary. Her hair was olive brown, which is so harmonious with a pale complexion; her eyes hazel-grey; her colour evanescent, coming and going, and rarely at any time more than a rose tint; her very lips, though beautifully formed, were only rose—not scarlet—and her figure was slight and deficient in 'grand curves.' Her great characteristic was what the French call distinction; a quality to which in point of truth she had no claim—for Helen, it must be remembered, was no long-descended lady. She was the produce of three generations of money, and a race which could be called nothing but Philistine; and from whence came her highbred look, her fanciful pride, her unrealisable ambition, it would be difficult to say.

She went over the house with a little sigh after Robert was gone, professedly in the ordinary way of a housewife's duty, but really with reference to his last words. Yes, the house might be made a great deal better. The drawing-room was a very pretty one—quite enough for all their wants—but the dining-room was occupied by Drummond as his studio, according to an arrangement very common among painters. This, it will be perceived, was before the day of the new studio. The dining-room was thus occupied, and a smaller room, such as in most suburban houses is appropriated generally to the often scanty books of the family, was the eating-room of the Drummonds. It was one of those things which made Helen's pride wince—a very petty subject for pride, you will say—but, then, pride is not above petty things; and it wounded her to be obliged to say apologetically to her cousin—'The real dining-room of the house is Mr Drummond's studio. We content ourselves with this in the mean time.' 'Oh, yes; I see; of course he must want space and light,' Reginald Burton had replied with patronising complacency, and a recollection of his own banqueting-hall at Dura. How Helen hated him at that moment, and how much aggravated she felt with poor Robert smiling opposite to her, and feeling quite comfortable on the subject! 'We painters are troublesome things,' he even said, as if it was a thing to smile at. Helen went and looked in at the studio on this particular morning, and made a rapid calculation how it could be 'made better.' It would have to be improved off the face of the earth, in the first place, as a studio; and then carpeted, and tabled, and mirrored, and ornamented to suit its new destination. It would take a good deal of money to do it, but that was not the first consideration. The thing was, where was Robert to go? She, for her part, would have been reconciled to it easily, could he have made up his mind to have a studio apart from the house, and come home when his work was done. That would be an advantage in every way. It would secure that in the evening, at least, his profession should be banished. He would have to spend the evening as gentlemen usually do, yawning his head off if he pleased, but not professional for ever. It would no longer be possible for him to put on an old coat, and steal away into that atmosphere of paint, and moon over his effects, as he loved to do now. He liked Helen to go with him, and she did so often, and was tried almost beyond her strength by his affectionate lingerings over the canvas, which, in her soul, she felt would never be any better, and his appeals to her to suggest and to approve. Nothing would teach him not to appeal to her. Though he divined what she felt, though it had eaten into his very life, yet still he would try again. Perhaps this time she might like it better—perhaps—

'If he would only have his studio out of doors,' Helen reflected. She was too sure of him to be checked by the thought that his heart might perhaps learn to live out of doors too as well as his pictures, did she succeed in driving them out. No such doubt ever crossed her mind. He loved her, and nobody else, she knew. His mind had never admitted another idea but hers. She was a woman who would have scorned to be jealous in any circumstances—but she had no temptation to be jealous. He was only a moderate painter. He would never be as splendid as Titian, with a prince to pick up his pencil—which is what Helen's semi-Philistine pride would have prized. But he loved her so as no man had ever surpassed. She knew that, and was vaguely pleased by it; yet not as she might have been had there ever been any doubt about the matter. She was utterly sure of him, and it did not excite her one way or another. But his words had put a little gentle agitation in her mind. She put down her calculation on paper when she went back to the drawing-room after her morning occupations were over, and called Norah to her music. Sideboard so much, old carved oak, to please him, though for herself she thought it gloomy; curtains, for these luxuries he had not admitted to spoil his light; a much larger carpet—she made her list with some pleasure while Norah played her scales. And that was the day on which the painter's commercial career began.

Drummond's first speculations were very successful, as is so often the case with the innocent and ignorant dabbler in commercial gambling. Mr Burton instructed him what to do with his little capital, and he did it. He knew nothing about business, and was docile to the point of servility to his disinterested friend, who smiled at his two thousand pounds, and regarded it with amused condescension. Two thousand pounds! It meant comfort, ease of mind, moral strength, to Drummond. It made him feel that in the contingency of a bad year, or a long illness, or any of the perils to which men and artists are liable, he would still be safe, and that his wife and child would not suffer; but to the rich City man it was a bagatelle scarcely worth thinking of. When he really consented to employ his mind about it, he made such use of it as astonished and delighted the innocent painter. All that his simple imagination had ever dreamed seemed likely to be carried out. This was indeed money-making he felt— Trade spelt with a very big capital, and meaning something much more splendid than anything he had hitherto dreamt of. But then he could not have done it by himself or without instruction. Burton could not have been more at a loss in Drummond's studio than he would have felt in his friend's counting-house. Mr Burton was 'a merchant;' a vague term which nevertheless satisfied the painter's mind. He was understood to be one of the partners in Rivers's bank, but his own business was quite independent of that. Money was the material he dealt in—his stock-in-trade. He understood the Funds as a doctor understands a patient whose pulse he feels every day. He could divine when they were going to rise and when they were going to fall. And there were other ways in which his knowledge told still more wonderfully. He knew when a new invention, a new manufacture, was going to be popular, by some extraordinary magic which Drummond could not understand. He would catch a speculation of this sort at its tide, and take his profit from it, and bound off again uninjured before the current began to fall. In all these matters he was knowing beyond most men; and he lent to his cousin's husband all the benefit of his experience. For several years Drummond went on adding to his store in a manner so simple and delightful, that his old way of making money, the mode by which months of labour went to the acquisition of a few hundred pounds, looked almost laughable to him. He continued it because he was fond of his art, and loved her for herself alone; but he did it with a sort of banter, smiling at the folly of it, as an enlightened old lady might look at her spinning-wheel. The use of it? Well, as for that, the new ways of spinning were better and cheaper; but still not for the use, but for the pleasure of it!—So Drummond clung to his profession, and worked almost as hard at it as ever. And in the additional ease of his circumstances, not needing to hurry anything for an exhibition, or sacrifice any part of his design for the fancy of a buyer, he certainly painted better than usual, and was made an Associate, to the general satisfaction of his brethren. These were the happy days in which the studio was built. It was connected with the house, as I have said, by a conservatory, a warm, glass-covered, fragrant, balmy place, bright with flowers. 'There must always be violets, and there must always be colour!' he had said to the nurseryman who supplied and kept his fairy palace in order, after the fashion of London. And if ever there was a flowery way contrived into the thorny haunts of art it was this. It would perhaps be rash to say that this was the happy time of Drummond's married life, for they had always been happy, with only that one drawback of Helen's dissatisfaction with her husband's work. They had loved each other always, and their union had been most true and full. But the effect of wealth was mollifying, as it so often is. Prosperity has been railed at much, as dangerous and deadening to the higher being; but prosperity increases amiability and smooths down asperities as nothing else can. It did not remove that one undisclosed and untellable grievance which prevented Mrs Drummond's life from attaining perfection, but it took away ever so many little points of irritation which aggravated that. She got, for one thing, the dining-room she wanted—a prosaic matter, yet one which Helen considered important— and she got, what she had not bargained for, that pretty conservatory, and a bunch of violets every day—a lover-like gift which pleased her. Things, in short, went very well with them at this period of their existence. Her discontents were more lulled to sleep than they had ever been before. She still saw the absence of any divine meaning in her husband's pictures; but she saw it with gentler eyes. The pictures did not seem so entirely his sole standing-ground. If he could not grow absolutely illustrious by that or any personal means of acquiring fame, he might still hold his own in the world by other means. Helen sighed over her Titian-dream, but to a great extent she gave it up. Greatness was not to be; but comfort and even luxury were probable. Her old conditions of life seemed to be coming back to her. It was not what she had dreamed of; but yet it was better to have mediocrity with ease and modest riches, and pleasant surroundings, than mediocrity without those alleviations. To do her justice, had her husband been a great unsuccessful genius, in whom she had thoroughly believed, she would have borne privation proudly and with a certain triumph. But that not being so, she returned to her old starting-ground with a sigh that was not altogether painful, saying to herself that she must learn to be content with what she had, and not long for what she could not have.

Thus they were happier, more hopeful, more at their ease. They went more into society, and received more frequent visits from their friends. The new studio made many social pleasures possible that had not been possible. Of itself it implied a certain rise in the world. It gave grace and completeness to their little house. Nobody could say any longer that it was half a house and half a workshop, as Helen, under her breath, in her impatience, had sometimes declared it to be. The workshop phase was over, the era of self-denial gone—and yet Robert was not driven from the art he loved, nor prevented from putting on his old coat and stealing away in the evenings to visit the mistress who was dearer to him than anything else except his wife.

This was the state of affairs when the painter one day entered Helen's drawing-room in a state of considerable excitement. He was full of a new scheme, greater than anything he had as yet been engaged in. Rivers's bank, which was half as old as London, which held as high repute as the Bank of England, which was the favourite depository of everybody's money, from ministers of state down to dressmakers, was going to undergo a revolution. The Riverses themselves had all died out, except, indeed, the head of the house, who was now Lord Rivers, and had no more than a nominal connection with the establishment which had been the means of bringing him to his present high estate. The other partners had gradually got immersed in other business. Mr Burton, for instance, confessed frankly that he had not time to attend to the affairs of the bank, and the others were in a similar condition:— they had come in as secondaries, and they found themselves principals, and it was too much for them. They had accordingly decided to make Rivers's a joint-stock bank. This was the great news that Drummond brought home to his wife. 'I will put everything we have into it,' he said in his enthusiasm, 'unless you object, Helen. We can never have such another chance. Most speculations have a doubtful element in them. But this is not at all doubtful. There is an enormous business ready made to our hands, and all the traditions of success and the best names in the City to head our list—for of course the old partners hold shares, and will be made directors of the new company—And—you will laugh, Helen, but for you and the child I feel able to brave anything—I am to be a director too.'

'You!' cried Helen, with a surprise which had some mixture of dismay. 'But you don't know anything about business. You can't even—'

'Reckon up my own accounts,' said the painter placidly—'quite true; but you see it is a great deal easier to calculate on a large scale than on a small scale. I assure you I understand the banking system—at least, I shall when I have given my mind to it. I shouldn't mind even,' he said laughing, 'making an effort to learn the multiplication table. Norah might teach me. Besides, to speak seriously, it doesn't matter in the least: there are clerks and a manager to do all that, and other directors that know all about it, and I shall learn in time.'

'But, then, why be a director at all?' said Helen. She said this more from a woman's natural hesitation at the thought of change, than from any dislike of the idea; for she belonged to the race from which directors come by nature. Poor Drummond could not give any very good reason why he desired this distinction; but he looked very wise, and set before her with gravity all the privileges involved.

'It brings something in,' he said, 'either in the way of salary, or special profits, or something. Ask your cousin. I don't pretend to know very much about it. But I assure you he is very great upon the advantages involved. He says it will be the making of me. It gives position and influence and all that—'

'To a painter!' said Helen: and in her heart she groaned. Her dream came back like a mist, and wove itself about her head. What distinction would it have given to Raphael or to Titian, or even to Gainsborough or Sir Joshua Reynolds, to be made directors of a bank? She groaned in her heart, and then she came back to herself, and caught her husband's eyes looking at her with that grieved and wondering look, half aware of the disappointment he had caused her, humbled, sorry, suspicious, yet almost indignant, the look with which he had sometimes regarded her from among his pictures in the day when art reigned alone over his life. Helen came abruptly to herself when she met that glance, and said hurriedly, 'It cannot change your position much, Robert, in our world.'

'No,' he said, with a glance of sudden brightness in his eyes which she did not understand; 'but, my darling, our world may expand. I should like you to be something more than a poor painter's wife, Helen—you who might be a princess! I should not have ventured to marry you if I had not hoped to make you a kind of princess; but you don't believe I can; do you?' Here he paused, and, she thought, regarded her with a wistful look, asking her to contradict him. But how could she contradict him? It was true. The wife of a pleasant mediocre painter, Associate, or in time Academician—that was all. Not a thorough lady of art such as—such as—Such as whom? Poor Andrea's Lucrezia, who ruined him? That was the only painter's wife that occurred to Helen.

'Dear Robert,' she said earnestly, 'never mind me: so long as I have you and Norah, I care very little about princesses. We are very well and very happy as we are. I think you should be careful, and consider well before you make any change.'

But by this time the brightness that had been hanging about him came back again like a gleam of sunshine. He kissed her with a joyous laugh. 'You are only a woman,' he said, 'after all. You don't understand what it is to be a British director. Fancy marching into the bank with a lordly stride, and remembering the days when one was thankful to have a balance of five pounds to one's credit! You don't see the fun of it, Helen; and the best of the whole is that an R.A. on the board of directors will be an advantage, Burton says. Why, heaven knows. I suppose he thinks it will conciliate the profession. We painters, you see, are known to have so much money floating about! But anyhow, he thinks an R.A.—'

'But, Robert! you are not an R.A.'

'Not yet. I forgot to tell you,' he added, lowering his voice, and putting on a sudden look of gravity, which was half real, half innocently hypocritical. 'Old Welby died last night.'

Then there was a little pause. They were not glad that old Welby was dead. A serious shade came over both their faces for the moment—the homage, partly natural, partly conventional, that human nature pays to death. And then they clasped each other's hands in mutual congratulation. The vacant place would come to Drummond in the course of nature. He was known to be the first on the list of Associates. Thus he had obtained the highest honours of his profession, and it was this and not the bank directorship which had filled him with triumph. His wife's coldness, however, checked his delight. His profession and the public adjudged the honour to him; but Helen had not adjudged it. If the prize had been hers to bestow, she would not have given it to him. This made his heart contract even in the moment of his triumph. But yet he was triumphant. To him it was the highest honour in the world.

'Poor old Welby!' he said. 'He was a great painter; and now that he is dead, he will be better understood. He was fifty before he entered the Academy,' the painter continued, with half-conscious self-glorification. 'He was a long time making his way.'

'And you are more than ten years younger,' said Helen. Surely that might have changed her opinion if anything could. 'Robert, are you to be put upon this bank because you are an R.A.?'

'And for my business talents generally,' he said, with a laugh. His spirits were too high to be subdued. He would not hear reason, nor, indeed, anything except the confused delightful chatter about his new elevation, in which the fumes of happiness get vent. He plunged into an immediate revelation of what he would do in his new capacity. 'It will be odd if one can't make the Hanging Committee a little more reasonable,' he said. 'I shall set my face against that hideous habit of filling up "the line" with dozens of bad pictures because the men have R.A. at their names. Do you remember, Helen, that year when I was hung up at the ceiling? It nearly broke my heart. It was the year before we were married.'

'They were your enemies then,' said Helen, with some visionary remnant of the old indignation which she had felt about that base outrage before she was Robert Drummond's wife. She had not begun to criticise him then—to weigh his pictures and find them wanting; and she could still remember her disgust and hatred of the Hanging Committee of that year. Now no Hanging Committee could do any harm. It had changed its opinion and applauded the painter, but she—had changed her opinion too. Then this artist-pair did as many such people do. By way of celebrating the occasion they went away to the country, and spent the rest of the day like a pair of lovers. Little Norah, who was too small to be carried off on such short notice, was left at home with her governess, but the father and mother went away to enjoy the bright summer day, and each other, and the event which had crowned them with glory. Even Helen's heart was moved with a certain thrill of satisfaction when it occurred to her that some one was pointing her husband out as 'Drummond the painter—the new R.A.' He had won his blue ribbon, and won it honestly, and nobody in England, nobody in the world, was above him in his own profession. He was as good as a Duke, or even superior, for a Duke (poor wretch!) cannot help himself, whereas a painter achieves his own distinction. Helen let this new softness steal into her soul. She even felt that when she looked at the pictures next time they would have a light in them which she had not yet been able to perceive. And the bank, though it was so much more important, sank altogether into the background, while the two rowed down the river in the summer evening, with a golden cloud of pleasure and glory around them. They had gone to Richmond, where so many happy people go to realise their gladness. And were the pair of lovers new betrothed, who crossed their path now and then without seeing them, more blessed than the elder pair? 'I wonder if they will be as happy ten years hence?' Helen said, smiling at them with that mingling of sweet regret and superiority with which we gaze at the reflection of a happiness we have had in our day. 'Yes,' said the painter, 'if she is as sweet to him as my wife has been to me.' What more could a woman want to make her glad? If Helen had not been very happy in his love, it would have made her heart sick to think of all her failures towards him; but she was very happy; and happiness is indulgent not only to its friends, but even to itself.

CHAPTER III

Mr Burton, however, was soon restored to pre-eminence in the affairs of the Drummonds. The very next day he dined with them, and entered on the whole question. The glory which the painter had achieved was his own affair, and consequently its interest was soon exhausted to his friend, who, for his part, had a subject of his own, of which the interest was inexhaustible. Mr Burton was very explanatory, in his genial, mercantile way. He made it clear even to Helen, who was not above the level of ordinary womankind in her understanding of business. He had no difficulty in convincing her that Robert Drummond, R.A., would be an addition to the list of directors; but it was harder to make the reasons apparent why 'Rivers's' should change its character. If it was so firmly established, so profitable, and so popular, why should the partners desire to share their good fortune with others? Mrs Drummond asked. Her husband laughed with the confidence of a man who knew all about it, at the simplicity of such a question, but Mr Burton, on the contrary, took the greatest pains to explain all. He pointed out to her all the advantages of 'new blood.' The bank was doing well, and making enormous profits; but still it might do better with more energetic management. Mr Burton described and deplored pathetically his own over-burdened condition. Sometimes he was detained in the City while the guests at a state dinner-party awaited him at home. His carriage had waited for him for two hours together at the railway, while he was busy in town, toiling over the arrears of work at Rivers's. 'We have a jewel of a manager,' he said, 'or we never could get on at all. You know Golden, Drummond? There never was such a fellow for work—and a head as clear as steel; never forgets anything; never lets an opportunity slip him. But for him, we never could have got on so long in this way. But every man's strength has its limits. And we must have "new blood."'

Thus Helen gradually came to an understanding of the whole, or at least thought she did. At all events, she understood about the 'new blood.' Her own Robert was new blood of the most valuable kind. His name would be important, for the business of 'Rivers's' was to a considerable extent a private business. And his good sense and industry would be important too.

'Talk about business talent,' Mr Burton said; 'business talent means good sense and prudence. It means the capacity to see what ought to be done, and the spirit to do it; and if you add to this discretion enough not to go too far, you have everything a man of business needs. Of course, all technical knowledge has to be acquired, but that is easily done.'

'But is Robert so accomplished as all this?' Helen said, opening her eyes. She would not, for all England, have disclosed to her cousin that Robert, in her eyes, was anything less than perfect. She would not, for her life, have had him know that her husband was not the first of painters and of men; but yet an exclamation of wonder burst from her. She was not herself so sure of his clear-sightedness and discretion. And when Robert laughed with a mixture of vanity and amusement at the high character imagined for him, Helen flushed also with something between anger and shame.

'Your own profession is a different thing,' she said hastily. 'You have been trained for that. But to be an R.A. does not make you a man of business—and painting is your profession, Robert. More will be expected from you now, instead of less.'

'But we are not going to interfere with his time, my dear Helen,' said her cousin cheerfully. 'A meeting of directors once a week or so—a consultation when we meet—his advice, which we can always come to ask. Bless my soul, we are not going to sweep up a great painter for our small concern. No, no; you may make yourself quite easy. In the mean time Drummond is not to give us much more than the benefit of his name.'

'And all his money,' Helen said to herself as she withdrew to the drawing-room, where her little Norah awaited her. His money had increased considerably since this new era in their lives began. It was something worth having now—something that would make the little girl an heiress in a humble way. And he was going to risk it all. She went into the conservatory in the twilight and walked up and down and pondered—wondering if it was wise to do it; wondering if some new danger was about to swallow them up. Her reasonings, however, were wholly founded upon matters quite distinct from the real question. She discussed it with herself, just as her husband would discuss it with himself, in a way common to women, and painters, and other unbusiness-like persons, on every ground but the real one. First, he had followed Reginald Burton's advice in all his speculations, and had gained. Would it be honourable for him to give up following his advice now, especially in a matter which he had so much at heart? Secondly, by every means in his power, Reginald Burton took occasion to throw in her face (Helen's) the glories and splendour of his wife, and of the home he had given her, and all her high estate. Helen herself was conscious of having refused these glories and advantages. She had chosen to be Robert Drummond's wife, and thrown aside the other; but still the mention of Mrs Burton and her luxuries had a certain stinging and stimulating effect upon her. She scorned, and yet would have been pleased to emulate that splendour. The account of it put her out of patience with her own humility, notwithstanding that she took pride in that humility, and felt it more consistent with the real dignity of her position than any splendour. And then, thirdly, the thought would come in that even the magic title of R.A. had not thrown any celestial light into Robert's pictures. That very morning she had stood for half an hour, while he was out, in front of the last, which still stood on his easel, and tried to reason herself into love of it. It was a picture which ought to have been great. It was Francesca and Paolo, in the story, reading together at the crisis of their fate. The glow and ardour of suppressed passion had somehow toned down in Drummond's hands to a gentle light. There was a sunset warmth of colour about the pair, which stood in place of that fiercer illumination; and all the maze of love and madness, all the passion and misery and delight, all the terror of fate involved, and shadow of the dark, awful world beyond, had sunk into a tender picture of a pair of lovers, innocent and sweet. Helen had stood before it with a mixture of discouragement and longing impossible to put into words. Oh, if she could but breathe upon it, and breathe in the lacking soul! Oh, if she could but reflect into Drummond's eyes the passion of humiliation and impatience and love which was in her own! But she could not. As Helen paced up and down the pretty ornamented space, all sweet with flowers, which her husband's love had made for her, this picture rose before her like a ghost. He who painted it was an R.A. It was exquisitely painted—a very miracle of colour and manipulation. There was not a detail which could be improved, nor a line which was out of drawing. He would never do anything better, never, never! Then why should he go on trying, proving, over and over, how much he could, and how much he could not do? Better, far better, to throw it aside for ever, to grow rich, to make himself a name in another way.

Thus Helen reasoned in the vehemence of her thoughts. She was calm until she came to this point. She thought she was very calm, reasonable to the highest pitch, in everything; and yet the blood began to boil and course through her veins as she pursued the subject. Sometimes she walked as far as the door of the studio, and pausing to look in, saw that picture glimmering on the easel, and all the unframed canvases about upon the walls. Many of them were sketches of herself, made from memory, for she never would sit—studies of her in her different dresses, in different characters, according as her husband's fond fancy represented her to himself. She could not see them for the darkness, but she saw them all in her heart. Was that all he could do? Not glorify her by his greatness, but render her the feeble homage of this perpetual, ineffectual adoration. Why was not he like the other painters; like— Her memory failed her for an example; of all the great painters she could think of only Rubens' bacchanalian beauties and that Lucrezia would come to her mind. It was about the time of Mr Browning's poem, that revelation of Andrea del Sarto, which elucidates the man like a very ray from heaven. She was not very fond of poetry, nor anything of a critic; but the poem had seized upon her, partly because of her intense feeling on the subject. Sometimes she felt as if she herself was Andrea— not Robert, for Robert had none of that heart-rending sense of failure. Was she Lucrezia rather, the wife that goaded him into misery? No, no! she could not so condemn herself. When her thoughts reached this point she forsook the studio and the conservatory, and rushed back to the drawing-room, where little Norah, with her head pressed close against the window to take advantage of the last glimmer of light, was reading a book of fairy tales. Great painters had not wives. Those others—Leonardo, and Angelo, and the young Urbinese—had none of them wives. Was that the reason? But not to be as great as Michel Angelo, not to win the highest honours of art, would Robert give up his wife and his child. Therefore was it not best that he should give up being a painter, and become a commercial man instead, and grow rich! Helen sat down in the gathering darkness and looked at the three windows glimmering with their mist of white curtains, and little Norah curled up on the carpet, with her white face and her brown curls relieved against the light. Some faint sounds came in soft as summer and evening made them, through the long casement, which was open, and with it a scent of mignonette, and of the fresh earth in the flower-beds, refreshed by watering and dew. Sometimes the voices of her husband and cousin from the adjoining room would reach her ear; but where she was all was silent, nothing to disturb her thoughts. No, he would never do better. He had won his crown. Helen was proud and glad that he had won it; but in her heart did not consent. He had won and he had not won. His victory was because he had caught the banal fancy of the public, and pleased his brethren by his beautiful work; but he had failed because—because—Why had he failed? Because he was not Raphael or Leonardo—nor even that poor Andrea—but only Robert Drummond, painting his pictures not out of any inspiration within him, but for money and fame. He had gained these as men who seek them frankly so often seem to do. But it was better, far better, that he should make money now, by legitimate means, without pursuing a profession in which he never could be great.

These were not like a wife's reasonings; but they were Helen's, though she was loyal to her husband as ever woman was. She would have liked so much better to worship his works and himself, as most women do; and that would have done him good more than anything else in earth or heaven. But she could not. It was her hard fate that made her eye so keen and so true. It felt like infidelity to him, to come to such a conclusion in his own house, with his kind voice sounding in her ear. But so it was, and she could not make it different, do what she would. He was so pleased when he found she did not oppose his desires, so grateful to her, so strongly convinced that she was yielding her own pleasure to his, that his thanks were both lavish and tender. When their visitor had left them, and they were alone, he poured out his gratitude like a lover. 'I know you are giving in to me,' he said, 'my love, my self-forgetting Helen! It is like you. You always have given up your pleasure to mine. Am I a brute to accept it, and take my own way?'

'I am not making any sacrifice, Robert. Don't thank me, please. It is because I think you have judged right, and this is best.'

'And you think I am so blind and stupid not to see why you say that,' he said in his enthusiasm. 'Helen, I often wonder what providence was thinking of to give you only such a poor fellow as I am. I wish I was something better for your sake, something more like you; but I have not a wish or a hope in the world, my darling, except for you. If I want to be rich, Helen, it is only for you. You know that, at least.'

'And for Norah,' she said, smiling.

'For Norah, but most for Norah's mother, who trusted me when I was nobody, and gave me herself when I had little chance of being either rich or great,' said Drummond. He said it, poor fellow, with a swelling of his heart. His new dignity had for the moment delivered him even from the chill of his wife's unexpressed indifference to his work. With a certain trustful simplicity, which it would have been impossible to call vanity, he accepted the verdict of his profession—even though he had doubts himself as to his own eminence, they must know. He had won the greatness he wanted most, he had acquired a distinction which could not but vanquish his own doubts and hers. And as he was now, he would not change positions with any man in England. He was great, and please God, for Helen's sake, he would be rich too. He put his arm round his wife and drew her into the open conservatory. The moon was up, and shone down upon them, lighting up with a wan and spiritual light the colourless silent flowers. It was curious to see them, with all their leaves silvered, and all their identity gone, yet pouring forth their sweet scents silently, no one noting them. 'How sweet it is here,' said the painter, drawing a long breath in his happiness. It was a moment that lived in his mind, and remained with him, as moments do which are specially happy, detaching themselves from the common tenor of life with all the more distinctness that they are so few.

'Yes, it is the place I love best,' said Helen, whose heart was touched too, 'because you made it for me, Robert. The rest is ordinary and comfortable, but this is different. It is your sonnet to me, like that we were reading of—like Raphael's sonnet and Dante's angel.' This she said with a little soft enthusiasm, which perhaps went beyond the magnitude of the fact. But then she was compunctious about her sins towards him; and his fondness, and the moonlight, and the breath of the flowers, moved her, and the celestial fumes of Mr Browning's book of poetry had gone to Helen's head, as the other influences went to her heart.

'My darling! it will be hard upon me if I don't give you better yet,' he said. And then with a change in his voice—cheerful, yet slightly deprecating, 'Come and have a look at "Francesca,"' he said.

It was taking an unfair advantage of her; but she could not refuse him at such a moment. He went back to the drawing-room for the lamp, and returned carrying it, drawing flecks of colour round him from all the flowers as he passed flashing the light on them. Helen felt her own portrait look at her reproachfully as she went in with reluctant steps following him, wondering what she could say. It made her heart sick to look at his pet picture, in its beauty and feebleness; but he approached it lovingly, with a heart full of satisfaction and content. He held up the lamp in his hand, though it was heavy, that the softened light might fall just where it ought, and indicated to her the very spot where she ought to stand to have the full advantage of all its beauties. 'I don't think there is much to find fault with in the composition,' he said, looking at it fondly. 'Give me your honest opinion, Helen. Do you think it would be improved by a little heightening of those lights?'

Helen gazed at it with confused eyes and an aching heart. It was his diploma picture, the one by which most probably he would be known best to posterity, and she said to herself that he, a painter, ought to know better than she did. But that reflection did not affect her feelings. Her impulse was to snatch the lamp from his hand, and say, 'Dear Robert, dearest husband, come and make money, come and be a banker, or sweep a crossing, and let Francesca alone for ever!' But she could not say that. What she did say faltering was—'You must know so much better than I do, Robert; but I think the light is very sweet. It is best not to be too bright.'

'Do you think so?' he said anxiously. 'I am not quite sure. I think it would be more effective with a higher tone just here; and this line of drapery is a little stiff—just a little stiff. Could you hold the lamp for a moment, Helen? There! that is better. Now Paolo's foot is free, and the attitude is more distinct. Follow the line of the chalk and tell me what you think. That comes better now?'

'Yes, it is better,' said Helen; and then she paused and summoned all her courage. 'Don't you think,' she faltered, 'that Francesca—is—almost too innocent and sweet?'

'Too innocent!' said poor Robert, opening his honest eyes. 'But, dear, you forget! She was innocent. Why, surely, you are not the one to go in for anything sensational, Helen! This is not Francesca in the Inferno, but Francesca in the garden, before any harm had come near her. I don't like your impassioned women.' He had grown a little excited, feeling, perhaps, more in the suggestion than its mere words; but now he came to a stop, and his voice regained its easy tone. 'The whole thing wants a great deal of working up,' he said; 'all this foreground is very imperfect—it is too like an English garden. I acknowledge my weakness; my ideal always smacks of home.'

Helen said no more. How could she. He was ready laughingly to allow that England came gliding into his pencil and his thoughts when he meant to paint Italy: a venial, kindly error. But candid and kind as he was, he could not bear criticism on the more vital points. She held the lamp for him patiently, though it strained her arm, and tried to make what small suggestions she could about the foreground; and in her heart, as she stood trembling with pain and excitement, would have liked to thrust the flame through that canvas in very love for the painter. Perhaps some painter's wife who reads this page, some author's wife, some woman jealous and hungry for excellence in the productions of those she loves, will understand better than I can describe it how Helen felt.

When he had finished those fond scratches of chalk upon the picture, and had taken the lamp from her hand to relieve her, Drummond was shocked to find his wife so tremulous and pale. He made her sit down in his great chair, and called himself a brute for tiring her. 'Now let us have a comfortable talk over the other matter,' he said. The lamp, which he had placed on a table littered with portfolios and pigments, threw a dim light through the large studio. There were two ghostly easels standing up tall and dim in the background, and the lay figure ghostliest of all, draped with a gleaming silvery stuff, pale green with lines of silver, shone eerily in the distance. Drummond sat down by his wife, and took her hand in his.

'You are quite chilly,' he said tenderly; 'are you ill, Helen? If it worries you like this, a hundred directorships would not tempt me. Tell me frankly, my darling—do you dislike it so much as this?'

'I don't dislike it at all,' she said eagerly. 'I am chilly because the night is cold. Listen how the wind is rising! That sound always makes me miserable. It is like a child crying or some one wailing out of doors. It affects my nerves—I don't know why.'

'It is nothing but the sound of rain,' he said, 'silly little woman! I wonder why it is that one likes a woman to be silly now and then? It restores the balance between us, I suppose; for generally, alas! Helen, you are wiser than I am, which is a dreadful confession for a man to make.'

'No, no, it is not true,' she said with indescribable remorse. But he only laughed and put his arm round her, seeing that she trembled still.

'It is quite true; but I like you to be silly now and then—like this. It gives one a glimmer of superiority. There! lean upon me and feel comfortable. You are only a woman after all. You want your husband's arm to keep you safe.'

'What is that?' said Helen with a start. It was a simple sound enough; one of the many unframed, unfinished drawings which covered the walls had fallen down. Robert rose and picked it up, and brought it forward to the light.

'It is nothing,' he said; and then with a laugh, looking at it, added, 'Absit omen! It is my own portrait. And very lucky, too, that it was nothing more important. It is not hurt. Let us talk about the bank.'

'Oh, Robert, your portrait!' she said with sudden unreasonable terror, clutching at it, and gazing anxiously into the serene painted face.

'My portrait does not mind in the least,' he said, laughing; 'and it might have been yours, Helen. I must have all those fastenings seen to to-morrow. Now, let us talk about the bank.'

'Oh, Robert,' she said, 'let us have nothing to do with it. It is an omen, a warning. We are very well as we are. Give up all these business things which you don't understand. How can you understand them? Give it up, and let us be as we are.'

'Because a nail has come out of the wall?' he said. 'Do you suppose the nail knew, Helen, or the bit of painted canvas? Nonsense, dear. I defy all omens for my part.'

And just then the wind rose and gave a wailing cry, like a spirit in pain. Helen burst into tears which she could not keep back. No; it was quite true, the picture could not know, the wind could not know what was to come. And yet—

Drummond had never seen his wife suffer from nerves or fancies, and it half-amused, half-affected him, and went to his heart. He was even pleased, the simple-minded soul, and flattered by the sense of protection and strength which he felt in himself. He liked nothing better than to caress and soothe her. He took her back to the drawing-room and placed her on a sofa, and read the new book of poetry to her which she had taken such a fancy to. Dear foolishness of womankind! He liked to feel her thus dependent upon his succour and sympathy; and smiled to think of any omen that could lie in the howling of the wind, or the rising of a summer storm.

CHAPTER IV

It is needless to say that Helen's superstition about the fall of the picture and the sighing of the wind vanished with the night, and that in the morning her nervousness was gone, and her mind had returned to its previous train of thought. Her passing weakness, however, had left one trace behind. While he was soothing her fanciful terrors, Robert had said, in a burst of candour and magnanimity, 'I will tell you what I will do, Helen. I will not act on my own judgment. I'll ask Haldane and Maurice for their advice,' 'But I do not care for their advice,' she had said, with a certain pathos. 'Yes, to be sure,' Robert had answered; for, good as he was, he liked his own way, and sometimes was perverse. 'They are my oldest friends; they are the most sensible fellows I know. I will tell them all the circumstances, and they will give me their advice.'

This was a result which probably would have come whether Helen had been nervous or not; for Haldane and Maurice were the two authorities whom the painter held highest after his wife. But Helen had never been able to receive them with her husband's faith, or to agree to them as sharers of her influence over him. It said much for her that she had so tolerated them and schooled herself in their presence that poor Drummond had no idea of the rebellion which existed against them in her heart. But both of them were instinctively aware of it, and felt that they were not loved by their friend's wife. He made the same announcement to her next morning with cheerful confidence, and a sense that he deserved nothing but applause for his prudence. 'I am going to keep my promise,' he said. 'You must not think I say anything to please you which I don't mean to carry out. I am going to speak to Haldane and Maurice. Maurice is very knowing about business, and as for Stephen, his father was in an office all his life.'

'But, Robert, I don't want you to ask their advice. I have no faith in them. I would rather a hundred times you judged for yourself.'

'Yes, my darling,' said Robert; 'they are the greatest helps to a man in making such a decision. I know my own opinion, and I know yours; and our two good friends, who have no bias, will put everything right.'

And he went out with his hat brushed and a new pair of gloves, cheerful and respectable as if he were already a bank director, cleansed of the velvet coats and brigand hats and all the weaknesses of his youth. And his wife sat down with an impatient sigh to hear Norah play her scales, which was not exhilarating, for Norah's notions of time and harmony were as yet but weakly developed. While the child made direful havoc among the black notes, Helen was sounding a great many notes quite as black in her inmost mind. What could they know about it? What were they to him in comparison with herself? Why should he so wear his heart upon his sleeve? It raised a kind of silent exasperation within her, so good as he was, so kind, and tender, and loving; and yet this was a matter in which she had nothing to do but submit.

These two cherished friends of Robert's were not men after Helen's heart. The first, Stephen Haldane, was a Dissenting minister, a member of a class which all prejudices were in arms against. It was not that she cared for his religious opinions or views, which differed from her own. She was not theological nor ecclesiastical in her turn of mind, and, to tell the truth, was not given to judging her acquaintances by an intellectual standard, much less a doctrinal one. But she shrank from his intimacy because he was a Dissenter—a man belonging to a class not acknowledged in society, and of whom she understood vaguely that they were very careless about their h's, and were not gentlemen. The fact that Stephen Haldane was a gentleman as much as good manners, and good looks, and a tolerable education could make him, did not change her sentiments. She was too much of an idealist (without knowing it) to let proof invalidate theory. Accordingly, she doubted his good manners, mistrusted his opinions, and behaved towards him with studied civility, and a protest, carefully veiled but never forgotten, against his admission to her society. He had no right to be there; he was an intruder, an inferior. Such was her conclusion in a social point of view; and her husband's inclination to consult him on most important matters in their history was very galling to her. The two had come to know each other in their youth, when Haldane was going through the curious incoherent education which often leads a young man temporarily to the position of Dissenting minister. He had started in life as a Bluecoat boy, and had shown what people call 'great talent,' but not in the academical way. As a young man he had loved modern literature better than ancient. Had he been born to an estate of ten thousand a year, or had he been born in a rank which would have secured him diplomatic or official work, he would have had a high character for accomplishments and ability; but he was born only of a poor Dissenting family, without a sixpence, and when his school career was over he did not know what to do with himself. He took to writing, as such men do, by nature, and worked his way into the newspapers. Thus he began to earn a little money, while vaguely playing with a variety of careers. Once he thought he would be a doctor, and it was while in attendance at an anatomical class that he met Drummond. But Haldane was soon sick of doctoring. Then he became a lecturer, getting engagements from mechanics' institutions and literary societies, chiefly in the country. It was at one of these lectures that he fell under the notice of a certain Mr Baldwin, a kind of lay bishop in a great Dissenting community. Mr Baldwin was much 'struck' by the young lecturer. He agreed with his views, and applauded his eloquence; and when the lecture was over had himself introduced to the speaker. This good man had a great many peculiarities, and was rich enough to be permitted to indulge them. One of these peculiarities was an inclination to find out and encourage 'rising talent.' And he told everybody he had seldom been so much impressed as by the talents of this young man, who was living (innocently) by his wits, and did not know what to do with himself. It is not necessary to describe the steps by which young Haldane ripened from a lecturer upon miscellaneous subjects, literary and philosophical, into a most esteemed preacher. He pursued his studies for a year or two at Mr Baldwin's cost, and at the end of that time was promoted, not of course nominally, but very really, by Mr Baldwin's influence, to the pulpit of the flourishing and wealthy congregation of which that potentate was the head.

This was Stephen Haldane's history; but he was not the sort of man to be produced naturally by such a training. He was full of natural refinement, strangely blended with a contented adherence to all the homely habits of his early life. He had not attempted, had not even thought of, 'bettering' himself. He lived with his mother and sister, two homely Dissenting women, narrow as the little house they lived in, who kept him, his table, and surroundings, on exactly the same model as his father's house had been kept. All the luxuries of the wealthy chapel folks never tempted him to imitation. He did not even claim to himself the luxury of a private study in which to write his sermons, but had his writing-table in the common sitting-room, in order that his womankind might preserve the cold fiction of a 'best room' in which to receive visitors. To be sure, he might have been able to afford a larger house; but then Mrs Haldane and Miss Jane would have been out of place in a larger house. They lived in Victoria Villas, one of those smaller streets which copy and vulgarize the better ones in all London suburbs. It was close to St Mary's Road, in which Drummond's house was situated, and the one set of houses was a copy of the other in little. The arrangement of the rooms, the shape of the garden, the outside aspect was the same, only so many degrees smaller. And this, it must be allowed, was one of the reasons why the Haldanes were unpalatable neighbours to Mrs Drummond; for, as a general rule, the people who lived in St Mary's Road did not know the inferior persons who inhabited Victoria Villas. The smaller copied the greater, and were despised by them in consequence. It was 'a different class,' everybody said. And it may be supposed that it was very hard upon poor Helen to have it known that her husband's closest friend, the man whose opinion he asked about most things, and whom he believed in entirely, was one who combined in himself almost all the objectionable qualities possible. He was a Dissenter—a Dissenting minister—sprung of a poor family, and adhering to all their shabby habits—and lived in Victoria Villas.

The very address of itself was enough to condemn a man; no one who had any respect for his friends would have retained it for an hour. Yet it was this man whom Robert had gone to consult at the greatest crisis of his life.

The other friend upon whom poor Drummond relied was less objectionable in a social point of view. He was a physician, and not in very great practice, being a crotchety man given to inventions and investigations, but emphatically 'a gentleman' according to Helen's own sense of the word. This was so far satisfactory; but if he was less objectionable, he was also much less interesting than Stephen Haldane. He was a shy man, knowing little about women and caring less. He lived all by himself in a great house in one of the streets near Berkeley Square, a house twice as big as the Drummonds', which he inhabited in solitary state, in what seemed to Helen the coldest, dreariest loneliness. She was half sorry for, half contemptuous of him in his big, solemn, doubly-respectable hermitage. He was rich, and had nothing to do with his money. He had few friends and no relations. He was as unlike the painter as could be conceived; and yet in him too Robert believed. Their acquaintance dated back to the same anatomical lectures which had brought Haldane and Drummond together, but Dr Maurice was a lover of art, and had bought Robert's first picture, and thus occupied a different ground with him. Perhaps the irritating influence he had upon Helen was greater than that exercised by Haldane, because it was an irritation produced by his character, not by his circumstances. Haldane paid her a certain shy homage, feeling her to be different from all the women who surrounded himself; but Maurice treated her with formal civility and that kind of conventional deference which old-fashioned people show to the wishes and tastes of an inferior, that he may be set at his ease among them. There were times when she all but hated the doctor, with his courtesy and his silent air of criticism—but the minister she could not hate.

At the same time it must be allowed that to see her husband set out with his new gloves to ask the opinion of these two men, after all the profound thought she had herself given to the subject, and the passionate feeling it had roused within her, was hard upon Helen. To them it would be nothing more than a wise or unwise investment of money, but to her it was a measure affecting life and honour. Perhaps she exaggerated, she was willing to allow—but they would not fail to underrate its importance; they could not—Heaven forbid they ever should!—feel as she did, that Robert, though an R.A., had failed in his profession. They would advise him to hold fast by that profession and leave business alone, which was as much as condemning him to a constant repetition of the despairs and discontents of the past; or they would advise him to accept the new opening held out to him and sever himself from art, which would be as good as a confession of failure. Thus it is evident, whatever his friends might happen to advise, Helen was prepared to resent.

At this moment Mrs Drummond's character was the strangest mixture of two kinds of being. She was, though a mature woman, like a flower bursting out of a rough husk. The old conventional nature, the habits and prejudices of the rich bourgeois existence to which she had been born, had survived all that had as yet happened to her in life. The want of a dining-room, which has been already noted, had been not a trivial accident but a real humiliation to her. She sighed when she thought of the great dinner-parties with mountains of silver on table and sideboard, and many men in black or more gorgeous beings in livery to wait, which she had been accustomed to in her youth; and when she was obliged to furnish a supper for a group of painters who had been smoking half the night in the studio, and who were not in evening dress, she felt almost disgraced. Robert enjoyed that impromptu festivity more than all the dinner-parties; but Helen felt that if any of her old friends or even the higher class of her present acquaintances were to look in and see her, seated at the head of the table, where half a dozen bearded men in morning coats were devouring cold beef and salad, she must have sunk through the floor in shame and dismay. Robert was strangely, sadly without feeling in such matters. It never occurred to him that they could be a criterion of what his wife called 'position;' and he would only laugh in the most hearty way when Helen insisted upon the habits proper to 'people of our class.' But her pride, such as it was, was terribly wounded by all such irregular proceedings. The middle-class custom of dining early and making a meal of 'tea,' a custom in full and undisturbed operation round the corner in Victoria Villas, affected her with a certain horror as if it had been a crime. Had she yielded to it she would have felt that she had 'given in,' and voluntarily descended in the social scale. 'Late dinners' were to her as a bulwark against that social downfall which in her early married life had seemed always imminent. This curious raising up of details into the place of principles had given Helen many an unnecessary prick. It had made her put up with much really inferior society in the shape of people of gentility whose minds were all absorbed in the hard struggle to keep up appearances, and live as people lived with ten times their income, while it cut her off from a great many to whom appearances were less important, and who lived as happened to be most convenient to them, without asking at what hour dukes dined or millionnaires. The dukes probably would have been as indifferent, but not the millionnaires, and it was from the latter class that Helen came. But in the midst of all these all-important details and the trouble they caused her, had risen up, she knew not how, a passionate, obstinately ideal soul. Perhaps at first her thirst for fame had been but another word for social advancement and distinction in the world, but that feeling had changed by means of the silent anguish which had crept on her as bit by bit she understood her husband's real weakness. Love in her opened, it did not blind, her eyes. Her heart cried out for excellence, for power, for genius in the man she loved; and with this longing there came a hundred subtle sentiments which she did not understand, and which worked and fermented in her without any will of hers. Along with the sense that he was no genius, there rose an unspeakable remorse and hatred of herself who had found it out; and along with her discontent came a sense of her own weakness—a growing humility which was a pain to her, and against which her pride fought stoutly, keeping, up to this time, the upper hand—and a regretful, self-reproachful, half-adoration of her husband and his goodness, produced by the very consciousness that he was not so strong nor so great as she had hoped. These mingled elements of the old and the new in Helen's mind made it hard to understand her, hard to realise and follow her motives; yet they explained the irritability which possessed her, her impatience of any suggestion from outside, along with her longing for something new, some change which might bring a new tide into the life which had fallen into such dreary, stagnant, unreal ways.

While she waited at home with all these thoughts whirling about her, Robert went out cheerfully seeking advice. He did it in the spirit which is habitual to men who consult their friends on any important matter. He made up his mind first. As he turned lightly round the corner, swinging his cane, instead of wondering what his friend would say to him, he was making up his mind what he himself would do with all the unusual power and wealth which would come to him through the bank. For instance, at once, there was poor Chance, the sculptor, whose son he could find a place for without more ado. Poor Chance had ten children, and was no genius, but an honest, good fellow, who would have made quite a superior stonemason had he understood his own gifts. Here was one immediate advantage of that bank-directorship. He went in cheerful and confident in this thought to the little house in Victoria Villas. Haldane had been ill; he had spent the previous winter in Italy, and his friends had been in some anxiety about his health; but he had improved again, and Robert went in without any apprehensions into the sitting-room at the back, which looked into the little garden. He had scarcely opened the door before he saw that something had happened. The writing-table was deserted, and a large sofa drawn near the window had become, it was easy to perceive, the centre of the room and of all the interests of its inhabitants. Mrs Haldane, a homely old woman in a black dress and a widow's cap, rose hastily as he came in, with her hand extended, as if to forbid his approach. She was very pale and tremulous; the arm which she raised shook as she held it out, and fell down feebly by her side when she saw who it was. 'Oh, come in, Mr Drummond, he will like to see you,' she said in a whisper. Robert went forward with a pang of alarm. His friend was lying on the sofa with his eyes closed, with an ashy paleness on his face, and the features slightly, very slightly, distorted. He was not moved by the sound of Robert's welcome nor by his mother's movements. His eyes were closed, and yet he did not seem to be asleep. His chest heaved regularly and faintly, or the terrified bystander would have thought he was dead.

Robert clutched at the hand which the old lady stretched out to him again. 'Has he fainted?' he cried in a whisper. 'Have you had the doctor? Let me go for the doctor. Do you know what it is?'

Poor Mrs Haldane looked down silently and cried. Two tears fell out of her old eyes as if they were full and had overflowed. 'I thought he would notice you,' she said. 'He always was so fond of you. Oh, Mr Drummond, my boy's had a stroke!'

'A stroke!' said Drummond under his breath. All his own visions flitted out of his mind like a shadow. His friend lay before him like a fallen tower, motionless, speechless. 'Good God!' he said, as men do unawares, with involuntary appeal to Him who (surely) has to do with those wild contradictions of nature. 'When did it happen? Who has seen him?' he asked, growing almost as pale as was the sufferer, and feeling faint and ill in the sense of his own powerlessness to help.

'It was last night, late,' said the mother. Oh, Mr Drummond, this has been what was working on him. I knew it was never the lungs. Not one of us, either his father's family or mine, was ever touched in the lungs. Dr Mixwell saw him directly. He said not to disturb him, or I would have had him in bed. I know he ought to be in bed.'

'I'll go and fetch Maurice,' cried Robert. 'I shall be back directly,' and he rushed out of the room which he had entered so jauntily. As he flew along the street, and jumped into the first cab he could find, the bank and his directorship went as completely out of his mind as if they had been a hundred years off. He dashed at the great solemn door of Dr Maurice's house when he reached it and rushed in, upsetting the decorous servant. He seized the doctor by the shoulder, who was seated calmly at breakfast. 'Come along with me directly,' he said. 'I have a cab at the door.'

'What is the matter?' said Dr Maurice. He had no idea of being disturbed so unceremoniously. 'Is Mrs Drummond ill? Sit down and tell me what is wrong.'

'I can't sit down. I want you to come with me. There is a cab at the door,' said Robert panting. 'It is poor Haldane. He has had a fit—come at once.'

'A fit! I knew that was what it was,' said Dr Maurice calmly. He waved his hand to the importunate petitioner, and swallowed the rest of his breakfast in great mouthfuls. 'I'm coming; hold your tongue, Drummond. I knew the lungs was all nonsense—of course that is what it was.'

'Come then,' cried Robert. 'Good heavens, come! don't let him lie there and die.'

'He will not die. More's the pity, poor fellow!' said the doctor. 'I said so from the beginning. John, my hat. Lungs, nonsense! He was as sound in the lungs as either you or I.'

'For God's sake, come then,' said the impatient painter, and he rushed to the door and pushed the calm physician into his cab. He had come to consult him about something? Yes, to be sure, about poor Haldane—not to consult him—to carry him off, to compel, to drag that other back from the verge of the grave. If there was anything more in his mind when he started Drummond had clean forgotten it. He did not remember it again till two hours later, when, having helped to carry poor Haldane up-stairs, and rushed here and there for medicines and conveniences, he at last went home, weary with excitement and sympathetic pain. 'I have surely forgotten something,' he said, when he had given an account of all his doings to his wife. 'Good heavens! I forgot altogether that I went to ask somebody's advice.'

CHAPTER V

Mr Burton called next morning to ascertain Drummond's decision, and found that he had been sitting up half the night with Stephen Haldane, and was wholly occupied by his friend's illness. The merchant suffered a little vexation to be visible in his smooth and genial aspect. He was a middle-aged man, with a bland aspect and full development, not fat but ample. He wore his whiskers long, and had an air that was always jovial and comfortable. The cleanness of the man was almost aggressive. He impressed upon you the fact that he not only had his bath every morning, but that his bath was constructed on the newest principles, with water-pipes which wandered through all the house. He wore buff waistcoats and light trousers, and the easiest of overcoats. His watch-chain was worthy of him, and so were the heavy gold buttons at his sleeves. He looked and moved and spoke like wealth, with a roll in his voice, which is only attainable in business, and when business goes very well with you. Consequently the shade of vexation which came over him was very perceptible. He found the Drummonds only at breakfast, though he had breakfasted two hours before, and this mingled in his seriousness a certain tone of virtuous reproof.

'My dear fellow, I don't want to disturb you,' he said; 'but how you can make this sort of thing pay I can't tell. I breakfasted at eight; but then, to be sure, I am only a City man, and can't expect my example to be much thought of at the West-end.'

'Is this the West-end?' said Robert, laughing. 'But if you breakfasted at eight, you must want something more by this time. Sit down and have some coffee. We are late because we have been up half the night.' And he told his new visitor the story of poor Stephen and his sudden illness. Mr Burton was moderately concerned, for he had married Mr Baldwin's only daughter, and was bound to take a certain interest in his father-in-law's protégé. He heard the story to an end with admirable patience, and shook his head, and said, 'Poor fellow! I am very sorry for him,' with due gravity. But he was soon tired of Stephen's story. He took out his watch, and consulted it seriously, muttering something about his appointments.

'My dear good people,' he said, 'it may be all very well for you to spend your time and your emotions on your friends, but a man of business cannot so indulge himself. I thought I should have had a definite answer from you, Drummond, yes or no.'

'Yes,' said Robert with professional calmness. 'I am very sorry. So I intended myself; but this business about poor Haldane put everything else out of my head.'

'Well,' said Mr Burton, rising and walking to the fireplace, according to British habit, though there was no fire, 'you know best what you can do. I, for my part, should not be able to neglect my business if my best friend was on his death-bed. Of course you understand Rivers's is not likely to go begging for partners. Such an offer is not made to every one. I am certain that you should accept it for your own sake; but if you do not think it of importance, there is not another word to say.'

'My dear fellow,' cried Robert, 'of course I think it of importance; and I know I owe it to your consideration. Don't think me ungrateful, pray.'

'As for gratitude, that is neither here nor there,' said the merchant; 'there is nothing to be grateful about. But we have a meeting to-day to arrange the preliminaries, and probably everything will be settled then. I should have liked to place your name at once on the list. To leave such things over, unless you mean simply to abandon them, is a great mistake.'

'I am sure I don't see any particular reason why we should leave it over,' Robert said, faltering a little; and then he looked at his wife. Helen's face was clouded and very pale. She was watching him with a certain furtive eagerness, but she did not meet his eye. There was a tremulous pause, which seemed like an hour to both of them, during the passing of which the air seemed to rustle and beat about Helen's ears. Her husband gazed at her, eagerly questioning her; but she could not raise her eyes—something prevented her, she could not tell what; her eyelids seemed heavy and weighed them down. It was not weakness or fear or a desire to avoid the responsibility of immediate action, but positive physical inability. He looked at her for, perhaps, a full minute by the clock, and then he said slowly, 'I see no reason to delay. I think Helen and I are agreed. This matter put the other out of my head; but it is natural you should be impatient. I think I will accept your kind offer, Burton, without any more delay.'

How easy it is to say such words! The moment they were spoken Robert felt them so simple, so inevitable, and knew that all along he had meant to say them. But still he was somewhat excited; a curious feeling came into his mind, such as a king may feel when he has crossed his neighbour's frontier with an invading army. Half-a-dozen steps were enough to do it; but how to get back again? and what might pass before the going back! The thought caught at his breath, and gave him a tremendous thrill through all his frame.

'Very well,' said Burton, withdrawing his hands from under his coat-tails, and drawing a slightly long breath, which the other in his excitement did not observe. Mr Burton did not show any excitement, except that long breath, which, after all, might have been accidental; no sign or indication of feeling had been visible in him. It was a great, a very great matter to the Drummonds; but it was a small matter to one who had been for years a partner in Rivers's. 'Very well. I will submit your name to the directors to-day. I don't think you need fear that the result will be doubtful. And I am very glad you have come to such a wise decision. Helen, when your husband is rich, as I trust he soon will be, I hope you will fancy a little house at Dura, and be our neighbour. It would be like old times. I should like it more than I can say.'

'I never was fond of Dura,' said Helen, with some abruptness. This reference to his greatness irritated her, as it always did; for whatever new-comer might take a little house at Dura, he was the lord of the place, supreme in the great house, and master of everything. Such an allusion always stirred up what was worst in her, and gave to her natural pride a certain tone of spitefulness and envy, which disgusted and wounded herself. But it did not wound her cousin, it pleased him. He laughed with a suppressed enjoyment and triumph.

'Well,' he said, 'Dura is my home, and a very happy one, therefore, of course, I am fond of it. And it has a great many associations too, some of them, perhaps, not so agreeable. But it is always pleasant to feel, as I do, that everything that has happened to one has been for the best.'

'The conversation has taken a highly edifying tone,' said Robert with some surprise. He saw there was more meant than met the eye, but he did not know what it was. 'We shall all be thanking Providence next, as people do chiefly, I observe, in celebration of the sufferings of others. Well, since you think I am on the fair way to be rich, perhaps I had better thank Providence by anticipation. Must I go with you to-day?'

'Not to-day. You will have full intimation when your presence is wanted. You forget—nothing is settled yet,' said Mr Burton; 'the whole arrangement may come to nothing yet, for what I know. But I must be going; remember me to poor Haldane when he is able to receive good wishes. I hope he'll soon be better. Some of these days I'll call and see him. Good morning, Helen. Good-bye, Drummond. I'm glad you've made up your mind. My conviction is, it will turn out the best day's work you ever did in your life.'

'Is he true, I wonder?' Helen said to herself as the two men left the room, and stood talking in the hall. It was the first time the idea had crossed her mind, and now it took its origin more from the malicious shaft her cousin had shot at herself than from any indication of double-dealing she had seen in him. It was against all the traditions of the Burtons to imagine that he could be anything but true. They had been business people as long as they had been anything, and commercial honour had been their god. It went against her to imagine that 'a relation of mine!' could be other than perfect in this particular; and she sighed, and dismissed the idea from her mind, blaming herself, as she often did now, for ill-temper and suspiciousness. 'It was mean to make that allusion to the past, but it is meaner of me to doubt him on that account,' she said to herself, with a painful sigh. It was so hard in her to overcome nature, and subdue those rebellious feelings that rose in her unawares. 'Why should I care?' she thought, 'it is my vanity. I suppose if the man had never got over my rejection of him I should have been pleased. I should have thought better of him! Such a man as that! After all, we women must be fools indeed.' This was the edifying sentiment in her mind when Robert came back.

'Well, Helen, the die is cast,' he said, half cheerfully, half sadly. 'However we come to shore, the ship has set out. If it were not for poor Stephen I should make to-day a holiday and take you somewhere. This day ought to be distinguished from the rest.'

'I hope he is true. I wonder if he is true?' Helen repeated to herself, half unconsciously, beneath her breath.

'Whom? Your cousin!!' said Robert, with quite two notes of admiration in his tone. 'Why, Helen, what a cynic you are growing. You will suspect me next.'

'Am I a cynic?' she said, looking up at him with a sudden tear in her eye. 'It is because I am beginning to be so wretchedly doubtful about myself.'

This admission burst from her she could not tell how. She had no intention of making it. And she was sorry the moment the words were said. But as for Robert, he gazed at her first in consternation, then laughed, then took her in his kind arms with those laughing accusations of love which are more sweet than any eulogy. 'Yes,' he said, 'you are a very suspicious character altogether, you know so much harm of yourself that it is evident you must think badly of others. What a terrible business for me to have such a wife!'

Thus ended the episode in their lives which was to colour them to their very end, and decide everything else. They had been very solemn about it at the beginning, and had made up their minds to proceed very warily, and ask everybody's advice; but, as so often happens in human affairs, the decision which was intended to be done so seriously had been accomplished in a moment, without consideration, almost without thought. And, being done, it was a weight off the minds of both. They had no longer this disturbing matter between them to be discussed and thought over. Robert dismissed it out of simple light-heartedness, and that delightful economy of sensation which is fortunately so common among the artist class: 'It is done, and all the thinking in the world will not make any difference. Why should I bother myself about it?' If this insouciance sometimes does harm, heaven knows it does a great deal of good sometimes, and gives the artist power to work where a man who felt his anxieties more heavily would fail. Helen had not this happy temper; but she was a woman, more occupied with personal feelings than with any fact, however important. The fact was outside, and never, she thought, could vanquish her—her enemies were within.

Time passed very quietly after this great decision. There was a lull, during which Stephen Haldane grew better, and Mrs Drummond learned to feel a certain friendliness and sympathy for the lonely mother and sister, who were flattered by her inquiries after him. She came even to understand her husband's jokes about Miss Jane, the grim and practical person who ruled the little house in Victoria Villas—whom she sometimes laughed at, but whom little Norah took a violent fancy for, which much mollified her mother. And then, in the matter of Rivers's bank, there began to rise a certain agreeable excitement and importance in their life. 'Drummond among the list of bank directors! Drummond! What does it mean?' This question ran through all the studios, and came back in amusing colours to the two who knew all about it. 'His wife belongs to that sort of people, and has hosts of business connections,' said one. 'The fellow is rich,' said another: 'don't you know what a favourite he is with all the dealers, and has been for ever so long?' 'His wife has money,' was the judgment of a third; 'take my word for it, that is the way to get on in this world. A rich wife keeps you going till you've made a hit—if you are ever going to make a hit—and helps you on.' 'It is all that cousin of hers,' another would say, 'that fellow Burton whom one meets there. He bought my last picture, so I have reason to know, and has a palace in the country, like the rest of those City fellows.' 'What luck some men have!' sighed the oldest of all. 'I am older than Drummond, but none of these good things ever came my way.' And this man was a better painter than Drummond, and knew it, but somehow had never caught the tide. Drummond's importance rose with every new report. When he secured that clerkship for Bob Chance, Chance the sculptor's son, he made one family happy, and roused a certain excitement in many others; for poor artists, like poor clergymen and other needy persons, insist upon having large families. Two or three of the men who were Robert's contemporaries, who had studied with him in the schools, or had guided his early labours, went to see him—while others wrote—describing promising boys who would soon be ready for business, and for whom they would gladly secure something less precarious than the life of art. These applications were from the second class of artists, the men who are never very successful, yet who 'keep on,' as they themselves would say, rambling from exhibition to exhibition, painting as well as a man can be taught to paint who has no natural impulse, or turning out in conscientious marble fair limbs of nymphs that ought, as the only reason for their being, to have sprung ethereal from the stone. And these poor painters and sculptors were often so good, so kindly, and unblamable as men; fond of their families, ready to do anything to push on the sons and daughters who showed 'talent,' or had any means offered of bettering themselves. How gladly Robert would have given away a dozen clerkships! how happy it would have made him to scatter upon them all some share of his prosperity! but he could not do this, and it was the first disagreeable accompaniment of his new position. He had other applications, however, of a different kind. Those in the profession who had some money to invest came and asked for his advice, feeling that they could have confidence in him. 'Rivers's has a name like the Bank of England,' they said; and he had the privilege of some preference shares to allot to them. All this advanced him in his own opinion, in his wife's, in that of all the world. He was no longer a man subject to utter demolition at the hands of an ill-natured critic; but a man endowed with large powers in addition to his genius, whom nobody could demolish or even seriously harm.

Perhaps, however, the greatest height of Drummond's triumph was reached when, the year having crept round from summer to autumn, his friend Dr Maurice came to call one evening after a visit to Haldane. It was that moment between the two lights which is dear to all busy people. The first fire of the year was lit in Helen's drawing-room, which of itself was a little family event. Robert had strayed in from the studio in his painting coat, which he concealed by sitting in the shade by the side of the chimney. The autumn evenings had been growing wistful and eerie for some time back, the days shortening, yet the season still too mild for fires—so that the warm interior, all lit by the kindly, fitful flame, was a novelty and a pleasure. The central figure in the picture was Norah, in a thick white piqué frock, with her brown hair falling on her shoulders, reading by the firelight. The little white figure rose from the warm carpet into the rosy firelight, herself less vividly tinted, a curious little abstract thing, the centre of the life around her, yet taking no note of it. She had shielded her cheek with one of her hands, and was bending her brows over the open book, trying to shade the light which flickered and danced, and made the words dance too before her. The book was too big for her, filling her lap and one crimsoned arm which held its least heavy side. The new-comer saw nothing but Norah against the light as he came in. He stopped, in reality because he was fond of Norah, with a disapproving word.

'At it again!' he said. 'That child will ruin her eyesight and her complexion, and I don't know what besides.'

'Never fear,' said Drummond, with a laugh, out of the corner, revealing himself, and Helen rose from the other side. She had been invisible too in a shady corner. A certain curious sensation came over the man who was older, richer, and felt himself wiser, than the painter. All this Drummond had for his share, though he had not done much to deserve it—whereas in the big library near Berkeley Square there was no fire, no child pushing a round shoulder out of her frock, and roasting her cheeks, no gracious woman rising softly out of the shadows. Of course, Dr Maurice might have been married too, and had not chosen; but nevertheless it was hard to keep from a momentary envy of the painter who could come home to enjoy himself between the lights, and for whom every night a new pose arranged itself of that child reading before the fire. Dr Maurice was a determined old bachelor, and thought more of the child than of the wife.

'Haldane is better to-day,' he said, seating himself behind Norah, who looked up dreamily, with hungry eyes possessed by her tale, to greet him, at her mother's bidding. 'Nearly as well as he will ever be. We must amuse him with hopes of restoration, I suppose; but he will never budge out of that house as long as he lives.'

'But he will live?' said Robert.

'Yes, if you can call it living. Fancy, Drummond! a man about your own age, a year or two younger than I am—a man fond of wandering, fond of movement; and yet shut up in that dreary prison—for life!'

A silence fell upon them all as he spoke. They were too much awed to make any response, the solemnity being beyond words. Norah woke up at the pause. Their voices did not disturb her; but the silence did.

'Who is to be in the dreary prison?' she said, looking round upon them with her big brown wondering eyes.

'Hush! Poor Mr Haldane, dear,' said the mother, under her breath.

Then Norah burst into a great cry. 'Oh, who has done it—who has done it? It is a shame—it is a sin! He is so good.'

'My child,' said the doctor, with something like a sob, 'it is God who has done it. If it had been a man, we would have throttled him before he touched poor Stephen. Now, heaven help us! what can we do? I suppose it is God.'

'Maurice, don't speak so before the child,' said Robert from a corner.

'How can I help it?' he cried. 'If it was a man's doing, what could we say bad enough? Norah, little one, you don't know what I mean. Go back to your book.'

'Norah, go up-stairs and get dressed for dinner,' said Helen. 'But you cannot, you must not be right, doctor. Oh, say you are sometimes deceived. Things happen that you don't reckon on. It is not for his life?'

Dr Maurice shook his head. He looked after Norah regretfully as she went out of the room with the big book clasped in her arms.

'You might have let the child stay,' he said reproachfully. 'There was nothing that could have disturbed her in what I said.'

And then for a moment or two the sound of the fire flickering its light about, making sudden leaps and sudden downfalls like a living thing, was the only sound heard; and it was in this pensive silence, weighted and subdued by the neighbourhood of suffering, that the visitor suddenly introduced a subject so different. He said abruptly—

'I have to congratulate you on becoming a great man, Drummond. I don't know how you have done it. But this bank, I suppose, will make your fortune. I want to venture a little in it on my own account.'

'You, Maurice? My dear fellow!' said Robert, getting up with sudden enthusiasm, and seizing his friend by both his hands, 'you going in for Rivers's! I never was so glad in my life!'

'You need not be violent,' said the doctor. 'Have I said anything very clever, Mrs Drummond? I am going in for Rivers's because it seems such a capital investment. I can't expect, of course, to get put on the board of directors, or to sit at the receipt of custom, like such a great man as you are. Don't shake my hands off, my good fellow. What is there wonderful in this?'

'Nothing wonderful,' said Robert; 'but the best joke I ever heard in my life. Fancy, Helen, I was going to him humbly, hat in hand, to ask his advice, thinking perhaps he would put his veto on it, and prevent me from making my fortune. And now he is a shareholder like the rest. You may not see it, but it is the best joke! You must stay to dinner, old fellow, and we will talk business all the evening. Helen, we cannot let him go to-night.'

And Helen smiled too as she repeated her husband's invitation. Robert had been wiser than his friends, though he had asked nobody's advice but hers. It was a salve to her often-wounded pride. The doctor did not like it half so much. His friend had stolen a march upon him, reversed their usual positions, gone first, and left the other to follow. He stayed to dinner, however, all the same, and pared apples for Norah, and talked over Rivers's afterwards over his wine. But when he left the door to go home, he shrugged his shoulders with a half-satisfied prophecy. 'He will never paint another good picture,' Maurice said, with a certain tone of friendly vengeance. 'When wealth comes in good-bye to art.'

CHAPTER VI

It was on an October day, mellow and bright, when Robert Drummond, with a smile on his face, and a heavy heart in his breast, reached the house in Victoria Villas, to superintend poor Stephen's return to the sitting-room, as he had superintended his removal to his bed. The sitting-room was larger, airier, and less isolated, than the mournful chamber up-stairs, in which he had spent half the summer. It was a heart-rending office, and yet it was one from which his friend could not shrink. Before he went up-stairs the painter paused, and took hold of Miss Jane's hand, and wept, as people say, 'like a child;' but a child's hot thunder-shower of easily-dried tears are little like those few heavy drops that come to the eyes of older people, concentrating in themselves so much that words could not express. Miss Jane, for her part, did not weep. Her gray countenance, which was grayer than ever, was for a moment convulsed, and then she pushed her brother's friend away. 'Don't you see I daren't cry?' she said, almost angrily, with one hard sob. Her brother Stephen was the one object of her life. All the romance of which she was capable, and a devotion deeper than that of twenty lovers, was in her worship of him. And this was what it was coming to! She hurried into the room which she had been preparing for him, which was henceforward to be his dwelling day and night, and shut the door upon the too sympathetic face. As for Robert, he went into his friend's little chamber with cheery salutations: 'Well, old fellow, so you are coming back to the world!' he said. Poor Haldane was seated in his dressing-gown in an easy-chair. To look at him, no chance spectator would have known that he was as incapable of moving out of it as if he had been bound with iron, and everybody about him had been loud in their congratulations on the progress he was making. They thought they deceived him, as people so often think who flatter the incurable with hopes of recovery. He smiled as Robert spoke, and shook his head.

'I am changing my prison,' he said; 'nothing more. I know that as well as the wisest of you, Drummond. You kind, dear souls, do you think those cheery looks you have made such work to keep up, deceive me?'

'What cheery looks? I am as sulky as a bear,' said Robert. 'And as for your prison, Maurice doesn't think so. You heard what he said?'

'Maurice doesn't say so,' said poor Haldane. 'But never mind, it can't last for ever; and we need not be doleful for that.'

The painter groaned within himself as they moved the helpless man down-stairs. 'It will last for ever,' he thought. He was so full of life and consolation himself that he could not realise the end which his friend was thinking of—the 'for ever' which would release him and every prisoner. When they carried the invalid into the room below he gave a wistful look round him. For life—that was what he was thinking.

He looked at the poor walls and commonplace surroundings, and a sigh burst from his lips. But he said immediately, to obliterate the impression of the sigh, 'What a cheerful room it is, and the sun shining! I could not have had a more hopeful day for my first coming down-stairs.'

And then they all looked at each other, heart-struck by what seemed to them the success of their deception. Old Mrs Haldane fell into a sudden outburst of weeping: 'Oh, my poor boy! my poor boy!' she said; and again a quick convulsion passed over Miss Jane's face. Even Dr Maurice, the arch-deceiver, felt his voice choked in his throat. They did not know that their patient was smiling at them and their transparent devices, in the sadness and patience of his heart. The room had been altered in many particulars for his reception, and fitted with contrivances, every one of which contradicted the promises of restoration which were held out to him. He had known it was so, but yet the sight of all the provisions made for his captivity gave him a new pang. He could have cried out, too, to earth and heaven. But what would have been the good? At the end all must submit.

'Now that you are comfortable, Stephen,' said his sister, with a harsh rattle in her voice, which made her appear less amiable than ever, and in reality came out of the deep anguish of her heart, 'there is some one waiting to see you. The chapel people have been very kind. Besides the deputation that came with the purse for you, there are always private members asking how you are, and if they can see you, and how they miss you—till you are able to go back.'

'That will be never, Jane.'

'How do you know? How can any one tell? It is impious to limit God's mercies,' cried Miss Jane harshly; then, suddenly calming down, 'It is Mr Baldwin's son-in-law who has called to-day. They are in the country, and this Mr Burton has come to carry them news of you. May he come in?'

'That is your cousin—your director?' said the invalid with some eagerness. 'I should like to see him. I want you to invest my money for me, Drummond. There is not much; but you must have it, and make something of it in your new bank.'

Mr Burton came in before Drummond could answer. He came in on tiptoe, with an amount of caution which exasperated all the bystanders who loved Stephen. He looked stronger, richer, more prosperous than ever as he sat down, sympathetically, close to Stephen's chair. There he sat and talked, as it were, smoothing the sick man down. 'We must have patience;' he said soothingly. 'After such an illness it will take so long to get up your strength. The sea-side would have been the best thing, but, unfortunately, it is a little late. I am so glad to hear your people are showing you how much they prize such a man as you among them; and I hope, with one thing and another—the pension, and so forth—you will be very comfortable? I would not venture to ask such a question, if it were not for Mr Baldwin. He takes so much interest in all your concerns.'

'I am very glad you have spoken of it,' said Haldane, 'for I want to invest what little money I have in this bank I hear so much of—yours and Drummond's. I feel so much like a dying man—'

'No, no,' said Mr Burton in a deprecating tone, 'nothing half so bad. Providence, you may be sure, has something different in store for you. We must not think of that.'

'At all events, I want to make the best of the money, for my mother and sister,' said Stephen. And then he entered into business, telling them what he had, and how it was invested. His mind had been very full of this subject for some time past. The money was not much, but if he died, it would be all his mother and sister would have to depend upon, and the purse which his congregation had collected for him would increase his little, very little capital. Dr Maurice had gone away, and the two women, though they heard everything, were withdrawn together into a corner. Mrs Haldane had attempted several times to interrupt the conversation. 'What do we care for money!' she had said, with tears in her eyes. 'Let him alone, mother, it will make him happier,' Miss Jane had said in the voice that was so harsh with restrained emotion. And Stephen, with his two visitors beside him, and a flush upon his wan face, expounded all his affairs, and put his fortune into their hands. 'Between you, you will keep my poor little nest-egg warm,' he said, smiling upon them. His illness had refined his face, and gave him a certain pathetic dignity, and there was something that affected both in this appeal.

'I will sit on it myself sooner than let it cool,' Drummond had said with a laugh, yet with the tears in his eyes, with an attempt to lighten the seriousness of the moment. 'Dear old fellow, don't be afraid. Your sacred money will bring a blessing on the rest.'

'That is all very pretty and poetical,' said Mr Burton, with a curious shade passing over his face; 'but if Haldane has the slightest doubt on the subject, he should not make the venture. Of course, we are all prepared in the way of business to win or to lose. If we lose, we must bear it as well as we can. Of course, I think the investment as safe as the Bank of England—but at the same time, Drummond, it would be a very different thing to you or me from what it would be to him.'

'Very different,' said Drummond; but the mere suggestion of loss had made him pale. 'These are uncomfortable words,' he went on with a momentary laugh. 'For my part, I go in to win, without allowing the possibility of loss. Loss! Why I have been doing a great deal in ways less sure than Rivers's, and I have not lost a penny yet, thanks to you.'

'I am not infallible,' said Burton. 'Of course, in everything there is a risk. I cannot make myself responsible. If Haldane has the least doubt or hesitation—'

'If I had, your caution would have reassured me,' said the invalid. 'People who feel their responsibility so much, don't throw away their neighbour's money. It is all my mother has, and all I have. When you are tempted to speculate, think what a helpless set of people are involved—and no doubt there will be many more just as helpless. I think perhaps it would exercise a good influence on mercantile men,' he added, with perhaps a reminiscence of his profession, 'if they knew something personally of the people whose lives are, so to speak, in their hands.'

'Haldane,' said Mr Burton hastily, 'I don't think we ought to take your money. It is too great a risk. Trade has no heart and no bowels. We can't work in this way, you know, it would paralyse any man. Money is money, and has to be dealt with on business principles. God bless me! If I were to reflect about the people whose lives, &c—I could never do anything! We can't afford to take anything but the market into account.'

'I don't see that,' said the painter, who knew as much about business as Mr Burton's umbrella. 'I agree with Haldane. We should be less ready to gamble and run foolish risks, if we remembered always what trusts we have in our hands,—the honour of honest men, and the happiness of families.'

He was still a little pale, and spoke with a certain emotion, having suddenly realised, with a mixture of nervous boldness and terror, the other side of the question. Mr Burton turned away with a shrug of his shoulders.

'It suits you two to talk sentiment instead of business,' he said, 'but that is not in my line. So long as my own credit is concerned, I find that a much greater stimulant than anybody else's. Self-interest is the root of everything—in business; and if you succeed for yourself, which of course is your first motive, you succeed for your neighbours as well. I don't take credit for any fine sentiments. That is my commercial creed. Number one includes all the other numbers, and the best a man can do for his friends is to take care of himself.'

He got up with a slight show of impatience as he spoke. His face was overcast, and he had the half-contemptuous air which a practical man naturally assumes when he listens to anything high-flown. He, for his part, professed to be nothing but a man of business, and had confidence enough in his friends' knowledge of him to be able to express the most truculent sentiments. So, at least, Haldane thought, who smiled at this transparent cynicism. 'I suppose, then, we are justified in thinking anything that is bad of you, and ought not to trust you with a penny?' he said.

'If you trust anything to me personally, of course I shall take care of it,' answered the merchant. 'But what we were talking of was Rivers's—business, not personal friendship. And business cannot afford such risks. You must examine into it, and judge of its claims for yourself. Come, let us dismiss the subject. I will tell Mr Baldwin I found you looking a great deal better than I hoped.'

'But I don't want to dismiss the subject,' said Haldane. 'I am satisfied. I am anxious—'

'Think it over once more, at least,' said the other hastily; and he went away with but scant leave-taking. Mrs Haldane, who was a wise woman, and, without knowing it, a physiognomist, shook her head.

'That man means what he says,' she said with some emphasis. 'He is telling you his real principles. If I were you, Stephen, I would take him at his word.'

'My dear mother, he is one of the men who take pleasure in putting the worst face on human nature, and attributing everything to selfish motives,' said the sick man. 'I very seldom believe those who put such sentiments so boldly forth.'

'But I do,' said his mother, shaking her head with that obstinate conviction which takes up its position at once and defies all reason. Her son made no answer. He leaned back in his chair and closed his eyes. The momentary excitement was over, the friends were gone, and the new and terrible Life settled down upon him. He did not say a word to indicate what was passing through his mind, but he thought of the ship which drifted between the sunset and the mariner, and the nightmare Life-in-Death casting her dies with the less appalling skeleton. It was she who had won.

In the mean time the two directors of Rivers's bank walked out together; one of them recovering all his self-confidence the moment he left the house, the other possessed by a certain tremulous excitement. The idea of risk was new to the painter. He felt a certain half-delightful, half-alarming agitation when he made his first ventures, but that had soon yielded to his absolute confidence in the man who now, with his own lips, had named the fatal word. Robert's imagination, the temperament of the artist, which is so often fantastically moved by trifles, while strong to resist the presence of fact and certainty, had sustained a shock. He did not say anything while they walked up the road under the faded autumnal leaves which kept dropping through the still air upon their heads. In this interval he had gone over within himself all the solid guarantees, all the prestige, all the infallibility (for had it not attained that point?) of Rivers's. Sure as the Bank of England! Such were the words that rose continually to everybody's lips on hearing of it. Robert propped himself up as he went along with one support or another, till he felt ashamed that he could be capable of entertaining a shadow of doubt. But the impression made upon his nerves was not to be overcome by simple self-argument. Time was wanted to calm it down. He felt a certain thrill and jar communicated through all the lines of life. The sensation ran to his very finger-points, and gave a sharp electric shock about the roots of his hair. And it set his heart and his pulse beating, more likely organs to be affected. Loss! That was to say, Helen and the child deprived of the surroundings that made their life so fair; driven back to the poor little lodgings, perhaps, in which his career began, or to something poorer still. Perhaps to want, perhaps to—'What a fool I am!' he said to himself.

'Do you really object to Haldane as one of our shareholders?' he said, with a certain hesitation, at last.

'Object—the idiot!' said Mr Burton. 'I beg your pardon, Drummond, I know he's a great friend of yours; but all that nonsense exasperates me. Why, God bless me, his body is sick, but his mind is as clear as yours or mine. Why can't he judge for himself? I am quite ready to give him, or you, or any one that interests me, the benefit of my experience; but to take you on my shoulders, Drummond, you know, would be simply absurd. I can't foresee what may happen. I am ready to run the risk myself. That's the best guarantee I can give, don't you think? but I won't run any sentimental risks. You may, if you like; they are out of my line.'

'I don't know what you mean by sentimental risks.'

'Oh, as for that, it is easy to explain. The man is very ill: he will never be of any use in life again, and loss would be destruction to him. Therefore I won't take the responsibility. Why, there may be a revolution in England next year for anything I can tell. There may be an invasion. Our funds may be down to zero, and our business paralysed. How can I tell? All these things are within the bounds of possibility, and if they happened, and we went to smash, as we should infallibly, what would Haldane do?'

'If there is nothing to alarm us closer at hand than a revolution or an invasion—' said Drummond with a smile.

'How can we tell? If I were asked to insure England, I should only do it on a very heavy premium, I can tell you. And look here, Drummond, take my advice, always let a man judge for himself, never take the responsibility. If you do, you'll be sorry after. I never knew a good man of business yet who went in, as I said, for sentimental risks.'

'I fear I shall never be a good man of business,' said the painter, with a certain sickness at his heart. 'But tell me now, suppose you were guardian to orphans, what should you do with their money? I suppose that is what you would call a very sentimental risk.'

'Not so bad as Haldane,' said Burton. 'They would be young and able to make their way if the worst came to the worst. If they were entirely in my own hands I should invest the money as I thought best; but if there were other guardians or relations to make a fuss, I should put it in the Three per Cents.'

'I really—don't—quite see what—difference that would make—' Robert commenced, but his companion stopped him almost roughly.

'The question won't bear discussing, Drummond. If I go in with you, will your wife give me some lunch? I have lost my whole morning to please my father-in-law. Don't you bother yourself about Haldane. He is a clear-headed fellow, and perfectly able to judge for himself.'

Then no more was said. If a passing cloud had come over the rich man, it fled at sight of the table spread for luncheon, and the sherry, upon which poor Robert (knowing almost as little about that as he did about business) prided himself vastly. Mr Burton applauded the sherry. He was more conversational even than usual, and very anxious that Drummond should look at a country-house in his neighbourhood. 'If you can't afford it now you very soon will,' he said, and without referring to Rivers's kept up such a continued strain of allusions to the good fortune which was about to pour upon the house, that Robert's nerves were comforted, he could scarcely have told how. But he went and worked all the afternoon in the studio when the City man went off to his business. He laboured hard at Francesca, fixing his whole mind upon her, not even whistling in his profound preoccupation. He had been absent from the studio for some time, and the feel of the old beloved tools was delightful to him. But when the early twilight came and interrupted his work, he went out and took a long walk by himself, endeavouring to shake off the tremor which still lingered about him. It was in his veins and in his nerves, tingling all over him. He reasoned with himself, shook himself up roughly, took himself to task, but yet did not get over it. 'Bah! it is simple sensation!' he said at last, and with a violent effort turned his thoughts in another direction. But the shock had left a tremor about him which was not quite dissipated for days after; for a man who is made of fanciful artist-stuff, is not like a business man with nerves of steel.

CHAPTER VII

Nothing happened, however, to justify Drummond's fears. The success of Rivers's in its new form was as great and as steady to all appearance as that of its ancient phase. People vied with each other in rushing into it, in crowding its coffers and its share lists. Stephen Haldane, 'left to himself,' according to Mr Burton's instructions, had long since deposited all he had in its hands; and almost all of Robert's professional friends who had any money to invest, invested it in the bank which had an R.A. upon the roll of directors. People came to him to ask his advice who in other times would have given him theirs freely, with no such respect for his judgment. But though this was the case, and though ignorant persons in society sometimes wondered how he could make the two occupations compatible, and carry on business and art together, yet the fact was that business and Robert had very little to do with each other. He went to the meetings of the directors now and then. He was blandly present sometimes at an auditing of accounts. He listened at times to the explanations given by Mr Golden, the manager, and found them everything that was reasonable and wise. But beyond that he cannot be said to have taken much part in the management. For this mild part he was abundantly rewarded—so abundantly that he sometimes felt half ashamed, reflecting that the clerks in the offices actually contributed more to the success of the place than he did, though they did not profit half so much. He felt himself justified in taking a nice house in the country, though not at Dura, at the end of the first season, and he gave his wife a pretty little carriage with two ponies on her birthday, in which she drove about with a pleasure perhaps more real than that which any other circumstance of their prosperity gave her. They did not leave their house in St Mary's Road, for it was dear to them in many ways, and still satisfied all their wants; and Robert could not tolerate the idea of another painter using the studio he had built, or another woman enjoying the conservatory which had been made for Helen. 'However rich we may grow—even if we should ever be able to afford that house in Park Lane—we must keep this,' he said; 'no profane foot must come in, no stranger intrude upon our household gods; and Norah must have it after us, the house she was born in.' Thus they planned their gentle romance, though they had been a dozen years married and more, and bought the house they loved with their first disposable money. And Robert still loved his work and kept to it, though he did not need now to trouble about the exhibitions and push on his picture, working from the early morning down to twilight to get it ready. He got a little lazy about finished pictures, to tell the truth. Even Francesca, though he loved her, had been put aside on the spare easel, and never completed. 'I will get up early and set to work in earnest to-morrow,' he always said; but to-morrow generally found him like the day before, making a study of something—sketching in now one subject, now another—tormenting his wife with questions as to which was best. She had a good deal to put up with in this period; but she kept up under it and bore it all smilingly. And Robert, like so many more, made his sketches much better than his pictures, and put ideas upon his canvas which, if he could but have carried them out, might have been great.

Thus two years passed over the pair; and there were times when Helen thought, with a leap of her heart, that ease and leisure had done what care and toil could not do—had roused a spark of divine genius in her husband's breast. Now and then he drew something that went right to her heart, and it was she who had always been his harshest critic. When she said to him one day suddenly, without purpose or meaning, 'I like that, Robert,' he turned round upon her all flushed and glowing, more radiant than when he was made an R.A. It was not that he had supreme confidence in her knowledge of art, but that her backing of him, the support which he had longed for all these years, was more than the highest applause, and invigorated his very soul. But he was so pleased to have pleased her, that he set up his sketch upon a bigger canvas, and worked at it and improved it till he had improved the soul out of it, and Helen applauded no more. He was much mortified and disappointed at this failure; but then in his humility he said to himself, 'What does it matter now? I am an R.A., which is the best I could be in my profession, so far as the world is concerned, and we have something else to stand upon besides the pictures.' Thus he consoled himself, and so did she.

And, in the mean time, Norah kept growing, and became a more distinct feature in the household. She was a feature more than an agent still; though she was nearly twelve, not much was heard of her except the scales, which she still rattled over dutifully every morning, and the snatches of songs she would sing in the lightness of her heart as she went or came. On most ordinary occasions she simply composed such a foreground to the family picture as Maurice had seen that October night. She sat on a stool or on the floor somewhere, with a book clasped in her arms, reading; in summer she and her book together crouched themselves against the window in the room, getting the last gleam of daylight, and in winter she read by the firelight, which crimsoned her all over with a ruddy glow, and scorched her cheeks. Perhaps it was because she was kept conscientiously at work all day that Norah thus devoured all the books she could lay hands on in the evenings. She sat in her corner and read, and heard what was going on all the same, and took no notice. She read everything, from Grimm's Tales and the Arabian Nights to Shakspere, and from Shakspere to Tennyson, with an undiscriminating, all-devouring appetite; and as she sat in a dream, lost in one volume after another, the current of life flowed past, and she was aware of it, and heard a hundred things she was unconscious of hearing, yet remembered years after. She heard discussions between her father and mother which she was supposed to pay no attention to. And she did not pay any attention to them: but only innocently—an unconscious eavesdropper—heard everything, and received it into her mind. This was the child's position in the house; she was the centre of the picture—everything somehow bore a reference to her; she alone was silent in the midst. The other two—who loved her, talked of her, planned for her, contrived that everything that was pretty and pleasant and sweet should surround her waking and sleeping—had yet no immediate need of Norah. They were each other's companions, and she was the third—the one left out. But she was too young to feel any jealousy, or to struggle for a place between them. She had her natural place, always in the foreground, a silent creature, unconsciously observing, laying up provision for her life.

'Are you not afraid to talk of everything before your daughter?' Mr Golden said one day when she had left the room. 'You know the old proverb, "Little pitchers have long ears."'

'Afraid of—Norah?' said Robert. The idea was so extraordinary that he laughed first, though the moment after he felt disposed to be angry. 'My child understands what honour is, though she is so young,' he said with paternal pride, and then laughed, and added, 'That is high-flown of course, but you don't understand her, Golden; how should you? She is a thousand times too deeply occupied to care for what we are saying. Pardon me, but the suggestion, to one who knows her, is so very absurd.'

'Ah, you never know where simplicity ends and sense begins,' said the bank manager. He had become a frequent guest at St Mary's Road. He was a man of Mr Burton's type, but younger, slightly bald, perfectly brushed, clean, and perfumed, and decorous. He was a little too heavy for the rôle of a young man in society: and yet he danced and flirted with the best when an opportunity offered. He never spoke of the City when he could help it: but he spoke a great deal about Lady So-and-so's party, and the fine people he knew. It was difficult to make out how he knew them; but yet he visited, or professed to visit, at a great many of what are called 'good houses.' As manager of the bank he had every man's good opinion—he was at once so enterprising and so prudent, with the most wonderful head for business. There was no one like him for interpreting the 'movements' on the Stock Exchange, or the fluctuations of the Funds. He explained business matters so lucidly that even Drummond understood them, or at least thought he did. But there were a good many people who did not like Mr Golden. Helen for one had a natural antipathy to the man. She allowed that she had no reason for it; that he was very civil, sometimes amusing, and had never done anything she could find fault with. But she disliked him all the same. Norah was more decided in her sentiments, and had a clearer foundation for them. He had insisted on disturbing her from her book one afternoon to shake hands with her; on another he had offered to kiss her, as a child, and she nearly twelve! 'But then you are so little of your age, Miss Norah. I dare say the gentleman took you for nine,' said the maid—an explanation which did not render Norah more favourably inclined towards the manager. And now he was trying to libel her, to traduce her to her father! Even Robert himself was moved by this enormity; it shook his opinion of his counsellor. 'That is all he knows,' Drummond said to himself; and he resumed his conversation more distinctly than ever when Norah came back.

In the mean time the Haldanes had thriven too, in their way. Stephen was as helpless, as far from any hope of moving, as ever; but he was well off, which alleviates much suffering. The walls of his room were hung with Drummond's sketches, half a dozen of them, among which were two pictures of Norah. He lived in an arm-chair elaborately fitted with every possible contrivance, with a reading-desk attached to its arm, and a table close by, which could be raised to any height: and his helpless limbs were covered with a silken quilt of Mrs Haldane's own working. There he passed the day and night without change: but thanks to Miss Jane and her mother, no strange eye had looked upon the helpless man's humiliation; they moved him from his chair to his bed, and did everything for him. The bed was closed up by day, so that no stranger might suspect its existence; and the room was kept airy and bright by the same unwearied watchers. Here he lived, making no complaint. Whatever his feelings might be, whatever the repinings in his mind, he said nothing of them to mortal ear. A shade of weariness the more upon his face, a deeper line than usual between his eyes, were the only tokens that now and then the deep waters overflowed his soul. And as for the mother and sister, who were his slaves and attendants, they had forgotten that there was anything unusual in his condition—they had become accustomed to it. It seemed to them in some sort the course of nature. And God knows whether unconsciously a feeling that it was 'for the best' might not sometimes steal into their minds. He was theirs for ever; no one could step in between them, or draw his heart from their love. Had it been suggested to Miss Jane that such a sentiment was possible, she would have rejected it with horror; and yet in the depths of her heart it was there, out of her own sight.

And he had an occupation in his seclusion which was a blessing to him. He had become the editor of a little magazine, which belonged to his 'denomination,' before he fell ill, and he had been allowed to retain the post. This was the refuge of his mind in his trouble. Poor Stephen, he pleased himself with the idea of still influencing somebody, of preserving his intercourse with the outer world. It had been a very homely little publication when it came into his hands—a record of what the 'denomination' was doing; the new chapels it was building; the prayer-meetings gathered here and there, which might grow into congregations; and the tea-parties, which furnished at once intellectual and social enjoyment for the people. But Stephen had changed that; he had put his mind into it, and worked it into a sort of literary organ. There were reviews in it, and essays, and a great deal of discussion of the questions of the day. These were approached from the standing-ground of the denomination, it is true, but the discussions were often far from being denominational. Up to this time, however, the community gave no signs of disapproval. Mr Baldwin favoured the magazine, and the writer of it was still popular, and not yet forgotten. They gave him some fifty pounds a year for this hard though blessed work which kept his mind alive; and his late congregation gave him fifty pounds; and the money in Rivers's bank had last quarter paid ten per cent. of profit. He was well off, he was indeed rich for his wants, though he was not rolling in wealth like Drummond. Money makes no man happy, but how much good it does! Nothing could make this poor man happy, rooted thus in his immovable calm; but his ten per cent. kept him in comfort, it gave him worship in the eyes of his people, who were not fond of poverty; it procured to him his only consolation. He had no need to be indebted to any one; he could even help the poor people of his former flock, and feel himself independent. He could buy books, and give such quiet comforts and pleasures as they could enjoy to the women who were so good to him. All these were great alleviations of the sick man's lot. But for Rivers's how different would his position have been! He would have been subject to the constant inspection of deacons and brethren; he would have been interfered with in respect to his magazine. All the comfort and freedom which remained to him were the result of the little more which made him independent and put him above criticism. What a poor thing money is, which cannot buy either health or happiness! and yet what a great thing! only the poor know how great.

This time of prosperity had lasted for two years, when Mr Burton withdrew from the direction of the bank. He had enlarged his business greatly in another way, and had no longer time to bestow upon this; and, indeed, he had professed all along his desire to be free. This had been the object of the old company in taking in 'new blood,' and now the new company was able to proceed alone upon its triumphant way.

'It is your turn to get into harness, Drummond,' he said, with a glance in which there was some contempt. Robert did not see the scorn, but he laughed with perhaps a little gentle confidence in his own power to be of use if he should choose to exert himself.

'I must put myself into training first,' he said.

'Golden will do that for you. Golden is the best coach for business I have ever come across,' said Mr Burton. 'He will put you up to everything, good and bad—the dodges as well as the legitimate line. Golden is not a common man of business—he is a great artist in trade.'

There was a certain elation in his air and words. Was he glad to have shaken off the bonds of Rivers's, though they were golden bonds? This was the question which Helen asked herself with a little surprise. The two men were dining at St Mary's Road on the night after Burton's withdrawal, and she was still at table, though they had begun to talk of business. As usual, she who took no part was the one most instructed by the conversation. But she was bewildered, not instructed, by this. She could not make out what it meant. She knew by the best of all proofs that the bank was profitable and flourishing. Why, then, did her cousin show such high spirits? What was his elation about? Long after, she remembered that she had noted this, and then was able to divine the mystery. But now it only surprised her vaguely, like a foreign phrase in the midst of the language she knew.

'The dodges are amusing,' said Mr Golden. 'The legitimate drama is more dignified and imposing, but I rather think there is more fun in the work when you are living on the very edge of ruin. The hairbreadth escapes one has—the sense that it is one's own cleverness that carries one through—the delight of escaping from the destruction that seemed down upon you! There is nothing like that,' he said with a laugh, 'in the steady platitudes of ordinary trade.'

And Mr Burton laughed too, and a glance passed between them, such as might have passed between two old soldiers who had gone many a campaign together. There was a twinkle in their eyes, and the 'Do you remember?' seemed to be on their very lips. But then they stopped short, and went no further. Helen, still vaguely surprised, had to get up and go away to the drawing-room; and what more experiences these two might exchange, or whether her husband would be any the wiser for them, she was no longer able to see. Norah waited her in the other room. She had just come to the end of a book, and, putting it down with a sigh, came and sat by her mother's side. They were alike in general features and complexion, though not in the character of their faces. Norah's hair was brighter, and her expression less stately and graceful than Helen's—she had not so much distinction, but she had more life. Such a woman as her mother she was never likely to be, but her attractions would be great in her own way.

'How nice your velvet gown is, mamma!' said Norah, who was given to long monologues when she spoke at all. 'I like to put my cheek upon it. When I am grown up, I will always wear black velvet in winter, and white muslin in summer. They are the nicest of all. I do not think that you are too old for white. I like you in white, with red-ribbons. When I am a little bigger I should like to dress the same as you, as if we were two sisters. Mayn't we? Everybody says you look so young. But, mamma, ain't you glad to get away from those men, and come in here to me?'

'You vain child!' said Helen. 'I can see you whenever I like, so it is no novelty to me; while papa's friends—'

'Do you think they are papa's friends? I suppose there are no villains now-a-days, like what there are in books?' said Norah. 'The world is rather different from books somehow. There you can always see how everything happens; and there is always somebody clever enough to find out the villains. Villains themselves are not very clever, they always let themselves be found out.'

'But, my dear, we are not talking of villains,' said Helen.

'No, mamma, only of that Mr Golden. I hate him! If you and I were awfully clever, and could see into him, what he means—'

'You silly little girl! You have read too many novels,' said Helen. 'In the world people are often selfish, and think of their own advantage first; but they don't try to ruin others out of pure malice, as they do in stories. Even Norah Drummond sometimes thinks of herself first. I don't know if she is aware of it, but still it happens; and though it is not always a sin to do that, still it is the way that most sins come about.'

This purely maternal and moral turn of the conversation did not amuse Norah. She put her arm round her mother's waist, and laid her cheek against the warm velvet of Helen's gown.

'Mamma, it is not fair to preach when no one is expecting it,' she said in an injured tone; 'and just when I have you all to myself! I don't often have you to myself. Papa thinks you belong to him most. Often and often I want to come and talk, but papa is so greedy: you ought to think you belong to me too.'

'But, my darling, you have always a book,' said Helen, not insensible to the sweet flattery.

'When I can't have you, what else am I to do?' said crafty Norah; and when the gentlemen came into the drawing-room, the two were still sitting together, talking of a hundred things. Mr Golden came up, and tried very hard to be admitted into the conversation, but Norah walked away altogether, and went into her favourite corner, and Mrs Drummond did not encourage his talk. She looked at him with a certain flutter of excited curiosity, wondering if there was anything under that smooth exterior which was dangerous and meant harm; and smiled at herself and said, No, no; enemies and villains exist only in books. The worst of this man would be that he would pursue his own ends, let them suffer who might; and his own ends could not harm Drummond—or so at least Helen thought.

CHAPTER VIII

It was in the summer of the third year of his bank directorship that Robert made his first personal entry into business. The occasion of it was this. One of his early friends who had been at school with him, and with whom he had kept up a precarious and often interrupted intercourse, came to him one morning with an anxious face. He was in business himself, with a little office in one of the dreary lanes in the City, a single clerk, and very limited occupation. He had married young, and had a large family; and Drummond was already aware that while the lines had fallen to himself in pleasant places, poor Markham's lot had been hard and full of thorns. He was now at the very crisis of his troubles. He gave a glance round the painter's handsome studio when he entered, at the pictures on the walls and the costly things about, and the air of evident luxury that pervaded everything, and sighed. His own surroundings were poor and scant enough. And yet he could and did remember that Drummond had started in life a poorer man, with less hopeful prospects than himself. Such a contrast is not lively or inspiriting, and it requires a generous mind to take it kindly, and refrain from a passing grudge at the old companion who has done so much better for himself. Poor Markham had come with a petition, on which, he said, all his future life depended. He had made a speculation which would pay him largely could he only hold out for three months; but without help from his friends this was impossible. It was a large sum that he wanted—more than any private friend would be likely to give him—something between two and three thousand pounds. The welfare of his family, his very existence in a business point of view, and the hopes of his children depended on his ability to tide those three months over. For old friendship's sake, for all the associations of their youth, would Drummond help him? Robert listened with his kindly heart full of sympathy. Long before the story was done, he began to calculate what he had at his disposal, how much he could give; but the sum startled him. He could not produce at a moment's notice a sum of nearly three thousand pounds. With a troubled heart he shook his head and said it was impossible—he had not so much money at his disposal—he could not do it. Then Markham eagerly explained. It was not from his friend's own purse that he had hoped for it; but the bank! On Drummond's introduction, the bank would do it. Rivers's could save him. No such request had ever been made to Robert before. Very few of his friends were business men. Their needs were private needs, and not the spasmodic wants of trade. There were people who had borrowed from himself personally, and some who had been helped by him in other ways; but this was the first appeal made to his influence in the bank. He was startled by it in his innocence of business habits. It seemed to him as if it was like asking a private favour, turning over his own petitioner to a third person. 'He is my friend, give him three thousand pounds.' It seemed to him the strangest way of being serviceable to his neighbour. But poor Markham had all the eloquence of a partially ruined man. He made it clear to Robert, not only that such things were, but they happened continually, and were in the most ordinary course of nature. The end was that they went out together, and had an interview with Mr Golden at the bank. And then Robert found that his acquaintance had not exaggerated, that the matter was even easier than he had represented it, and that there would not be the slightest difficulty in 'accommodating' the man who was Mr Drummond's friend. Markham and he parted at the door of the bank, the one with tears of gratitude in his eyes, blessing God and Robert for saving him, and the other with a bewildered sense of power which he had not realised. He had not known before how much he could do, nor what privileges his directorship put in his hands, and he was confused by the discovery. It bewildered him, as a man might be bewildered to know that he could bestow fertility or barrenness on his fields by a glance: how strange the power was, how sweet in this instance, how—dangerous! Yes, that was the word. He felt afraid of himself as he went home. If such plaints came to him often, it would be so difficult to resist them; and then a kind of horrible dread came over his mind. Would the money ever be paid back that he had got so easily? The thought made his hand shake when he went back to the peaceable work at which no such bewildering risks were run.

When the three months were over, Markham's money was not paid; on the contrary he had fled to Australia, he and all his children, leaving nothing but some wretched old furniture behind him. Poor Drummond was nearly beside himself. He rushed to the bank when he heard the news, and protested that the loss must be his. It was his fault, and of course he must repay it. Mr Golden smiled at him with a genuine admiration of his simplicity. He told him in a fatherly way of a speculation which had been very successful, which had cleared nearly the same sum of money. 'Putting the one to the other, we are none the worse,' he said; 'every commercial concern must make some bad debts.'

Drummond went away with more bewilderment still, with many new thoughts buzzing in his head, thoughts which troubled the composure of his life. He himself being but an artist, and not a merchant, was afraid of money. He touched it warily, trafficked in it with a certain awe. He knew how much labour it required to earn it, and how hard it was to be without it. He could not understand the levity with which Burton and Golden treated that potent thing. To them it was like common merchandise, sugar or salt. A heap of it, as much as would make a poor man's fortune, melted away in a moment, and the bland manager thought nothing of it—it was a bad debt. All this was so strange to him, that he did not know what to make of it. He himself was guilty, he felt, of having thrown away so much which belonged to other people. And every other director on the board had the same power which he had with a painful pleasure discovered himself to have. And they knew better about it than he did; and what check could there be upon them? If every other man among them had been art and part in losing three thousand pounds, what could Robert say? It would not be for him to throw the first stone. He felt like Christian in the story, when, upon the calm hill-side, he suddenly saw a door through which there appeared, open and visible, the mouth of hell. It occurred to Robert to go down to the next meeting of directors, to tell them his own story, and beg that the money lost through his means should be subtracted from his private share of the capital, and to beg all of them to do likewise. He quite made up his mind to this in the first tumult of his thoughts. But before the time for that meeting came, a sense of painful ridicule, that bugbear of the Englishman, had daunted him. They would call him a fool, they would think he was 'canting,' or taking an opportunity to display his own disinterestedness. And accordingly he accepted the misfortune, and was content to permit it to be called a bad debt. But the enlightenment which it threw on the business altogether gave Robert a shock which he did not easily recover. It seemed to show him a possible chasm opening at his very feet, and not at his only, but at the feet of all the ignorant simple people, the poor painters, the poor women, the sick men like Haldane, who had placed their little seed-corn of money in Rivers's bank.

These thoughts were hot in his heart at the time of this misadventure with Markham; and then there came a lull, and he partially forgot them. When no harm is visible, when the tranquil ordinary course of affairs seems to close over a wrong or a blunder, it is so difficult to imagine that everything will not go well. He said as little as possible to Helen on the subject, and she did not take fright fortunately, having many things to occupy her now-a-days. There was her own enlarged and fuller household; the duties of society; her charities, for she was very good to the poor people near Southlees, their house in the country, and kept watch over them even from St Mary's Road. And she had now many friends who came and occupied her time, and carried her off from her husband; so that he had not that resource of talking about it which so often lightens our anxiety, and so often deepens it. In this instance, perhaps, it was as well that he could not awaken her fears to increase and stimulate his own.

And thus everything fell into its usual quietness. Life was so pleasant for them. They had so much real happiness to cushion the angles of the world, and make them believe that all would always be well. Those who have been experienced in pain are apt to tremble and doubt the continuance of happiness when they attain it; but to those who have had no real sorrows it seems eternal. Why should it ever come to an end? This the Drummonds felt with an instinctive confidence. It was easier to believe in any miracle of good than in the least prognostic of evil. The sun was shining upon them; summer was sweet and winter pleasant. They had love, they had ease, they had wealth, as much as they desired, and they believed in it. The passing cloud rolled away from Robert's mind. He reflected that if there was danger there, there was danger in everything; every day, he said to himself, every man may be in some deadly peril without knowing it. We pass beneath the arch that falls next moment; we touch against some one's shoulder unaware, whose touch of infection might be death; we walk over the mined earth, and breathe air which might breed a pestilence, and yet nothing happens to us. Human nature is against everything violent. Somehow she holds a balance, which no one breaks down, though it is possible to be broken down at any moment. The directors might ruin the bank in a week, but they would not, any more than the elements, which are ever ready for mischief, would clash together and produce an earthquake. Such things might be: but never—or so seldom as to be next to never—are.

In the early autumn of that year, however, another shock came upon the ignorant painter. His wife and Norah were at Southlees, where he himself had been. Business had brought him up against his will, business of the gentler kind, concerning art and the Academy, not the bank. He was alone at St Mary's Road, chafing a little over his solitude, and longing for home and the pleasant fields. London, the London he knew and cared for, had gone out of town. August was blazing upon the parks and streets; the grass was the colour of mud, and the trees like untanned leather. The great people were all away in their great houses, and among his own profession those who could afford it had started for Switzerland or some other holiday region, and those who could not had gone for their annual whiff of sea-air. Robert was seated by himself at breakfast, mournfully considering how another day had to be got over, before he could go home, when a hansom dashed up to the door, and Mr Golden, bland and clean as ever, but yet with a certain agitation in his face, came in. He explained eagerly that he had come to Drummond only because the other directors were out of town. 'The fact is,' he said, 'I want you to come with me, not to give you much trouble or detain you long, but to stand by me, if you will, in a crisis. We have had some losses. Those people in Calcutta who chose to stop payment, like fools, and the Sullivans' house at Liverpool.—It is only temporary.—But the Bank of England has made itself disagreeable about an advance, and I want you to come with me and see the governor.'

'An advance! Is Rivers's in difficulties? is there anything wrong? You take away my breath.'

'There is no occasion for taking away your breath,' said Mr Golden; 'it is only for the moment. But it is an awkward time of the year, for everybody is out of town. I should not have troubled you, knowing you were not a business man, but of course the presence of a director gives authority. Don't be alarmed, I beg. I will tell you all about it as we drive along.'

But what Mr Golden told was very inarticulate to Robert, what with the wild confusion produced in his own mind, and the noise and dust of the sultry streets. It was the most temporary difficulty; it was not worth speaking of; it was a simple misunderstanding on the part of the authorities of the Bank of England. 'Why we are worth twenty times the money, and everybody knows it,' said Mr Golden. His words, instead of making Robert confident, made him sick. His sin in that matter of Markham came darkly before him; and, worse even than that, the manager's words recalled Markham's to him. In his case, too, it was to have been merely a temporary difficulty. Drummond's imaginative mind rushed at once to the final catastrophe. He saw ruin staring him in the face—and not only him.

The interview with the authorities of the Bank of England did not make things much clearer to the amateur. They talked of previous advances; of their regret that the sacred name of 'Rivers's' should be falling into mist and darkness; of their desire to have better securities, and a guarantee which would be more satisfactory: to all of which Robert listened with consternation in his soul. But at last the object was attained. Mr Golden wiped the moisture from his forehead as they left the place. 'That has been a tough battle,' he said, 'but thank Heaven! it is done, and we are tided over. I knew they would not be such fools as to refuse.'

'But, good God!' said Robert, 'what have you been doing? What is the meaning of it? Why do you require to go hat in hand to any governor? Is Rivers's losing its position? What has happened? Why don't you call the shareholders together and tell them if anything is wrong?'

'My dear Mr Drummond!' said Mr Golden. He could scarcely do more than smile and say the words.

'Don't smile at me,' said Drummond in the ardour of his heart. 'Do you consider that you have the very lives of hundreds of people in your hands? Call them together, and let them know what remains, for God's sake! I will make good what was lost through me.'

'You are mad,' said Golden, when he saw that his gentle sneer had failed; 'such a step would be ruin. Call together the shareholders! Why, the shareholders—Mr Drummond, for heaven's sake, let people manage it who know what they are about.'

'For heaven's sake! for hell's sake, you mean,' said Robert in his despair. And the words reverberated in his ears, rang out of all the echoes, sounded through the very streets, 'It would be ruin!' Ruin! that was the word. It deafened him, muttering and ringing in his ears.

And yet even after this outburst he was calmed down. Mr Golden explained it to him. It was business; it was the common course of affairs, and only his own entire inexperience made it so terrible to him. To the others it was not in the least terrible, and yet he had no right to conclude that his colleagues were indifferent either to their own danger, or to the danger of the shareholders of whom he thought so much. 'The shareholders of course know the risks of business as well as we do,' Mr Golden said. 'We must act for the best, both for them and for ourselves.' And the painter was silenced if not convinced. This was in the autumn, and during the entire winter which followed the bank went on like a ship in a troubled sea. After a while such a crisis as the one which had so infinitely alarmed him became the commonest of incidents even to Drummond. Now that his eyes had been once enlightened, it was vain to attempt any further concealment. One desperate struggle he did indeed make, when in the very midst of all this anxiety a larger dividend than usual was declared. The innocent man fought wildly against this practical lie, but his resistance was treated as utter folly by the business board, who were, as they said, 'fighting the ship.' 'Do you want to create a panic and a run upon us?' they asked him. He had to be silent, overpowered by the judgment of men who knew better than himself. And then something of the excitement involved in that process of 'fighting the ship' stole into his veins. Somehow by degrees, nobody had been quite aware how, the old partners of Rivers's had gone out of the concern. It was true there had been but three or four to start with; now there was but one left—Lord Rivers, the head of the house, who never took any share in the business, and was as ignorant as the smallest shareholder. The new directors, the fighting directors, were men of a very different class. As the winter went on the ship laboured more and more. Sometimes it seemed to go down altogether, and then rose again with a buoyancy which almost seemed to justify hope. 'Tout peut se rétablir,' they said to each other. 'After all we shall tide it over.' And even Robert began to feel that thrill of delight and relief when a danger was 'tided over,' that admiration, not of his own cleverness, but of the cleverness of others, which Golden had once described. Golden came out now in his true colours; his resources were infinite, his pluck extraordinary. But he enjoyed the struggle in the midst of his excitement and exertion, and Drummond did not enjoy it, which made an immense difference between them.

Things became worse and worse as spring came on. By that time, so far as Drummond was concerned, all hope was over. He felt himself sucked into the terrible whirlpool whence nothing but destruction could come. With a heart unmanned by anxiety, and a hand shaking with suppressed excitement, how could he go into his peaceable studio and work at that calmest work, of art? That phase of his existence seemed to have been over for years. When he went into the room he loved it looked to him like some place he had known in his youth—it was fifty years off or more, though the colour was scarcely dry on the picture which stood idly on the easel. When he was called to Academy meetings, to consultations over an old master, or a new rule, a kind of dull amazement filled his soul. Did people still care for such things—was it still possible that beauty and pleasantness remained in life? There were people in these days who felt even that the painter had fallen into bad ways. They saw his eyes bloodshot and his hand trembling. He was never seen with his wife now when she drove her ponies through the park—even in society Helen went sometimes out alone. And they had been so united, so happy a pair. 'Drummond will have nothing ready in April,' the painters said to each other—'even his diploma picture has never been finished—prosperity has not agreed with him.' When he was visible at all, his vacant air, his tremulous look, the deep lines under his eyes, frightened all his friends. Dr Maurice had spoken to him very seriously, begging that he would be candid and tell his ailments. 'You cannot go on like this,' he said.

'You are killing yourself, Drummond.' 'How much can a man go through without being killed, I wonder?' poor Robert asked, with an unsteady smile, and even his friend stopped short in dismay and perplexity. Was it dissipation? Was it some concealed misery? Could his wife have anything to do with it? These suggestions flitted vaguely through the doctor's mind without bringing any certainty with them. Once he seemed to be getting a clue to the mystery, when Robert rushed in upon him one day, and with a show of levity suggested that Haldane's money should be taken out of the bank. 'I know a better investment, and he should have the very best that is going,' said Drummond. Dr Maurice was somewhat startled, for he had money in Rivers's too.

'Where is there a better investment?' he asked.

'In the Three per Cents.,' said Robert, with a hoarse laugh.

Was he mad? Was he—drunk? The doctor took a day to consider it, to think whether there could be anything in it. But he looked at the dividend papers, showing that Rivers's that year had paid ten per cent. And he called upon Dr Bradcliffe, and asked him to go with him privately, accidentally, one of these days, to see a friend whose brain was going, he feared. The two physicians shook their heads, and said to each other mournfully how common that was becoming. But Fate moved faster than Dr Maurice, and the accidental call was never made.

CHAPTER IX

The life which Helen Drummond lived during this winter would be very hard to describe. Something wrong had happened, she saw, on that rapid visit to town which Robert had made on Academical business in October, leaving her at Southlees. No anxiety about business matters connected with the bank had ever been suggested to her mind. She had long ago accepted, as a matter of course, the fact that wealth was to come from that source, with an ease and regularity very different from the toilsome and slow bread-winning which was done by means of art. She was not surprised by it as Robert was; and enough of the bourgeois breeding was left in her to make her pleased that her husband should see the difference between the possibilities of his profession and of the commerce which she had been wont to hear lauded in her youth. She was almost proud that Trade had done so much for him. Trade came from her side, it was she who had the hereditary connection with it; and the innate idealism of her mind was able to cling to the old-fashioned fanciful conception of beneficent commerce, such as we have all heard of in our educational days. But her pride was not sensitive on this point. What really touched her was the praise or the blame which fell upon him as a painter, and the dread that instantly sprang into her mind was that he had met with something painful to him in this respect—that his opinion had not been received as of weight in the deliberations of the Academy, or his works been spoken of with less respect than they ought to have secured. This was the foolish fancy that took hold of her mind. She questioned him about the Academy meeting till poor Robert—his thoughts occupied about things so very different—grew sick of the subject. Yet he was almost glad of some subject on which to vent a little of his excitement. Yes, they were a set of old fogies, he said, with audacious freedom. They pottered about things they did not understand. They puzzled and hesitated over that Rembrandt, which any one with half an eye could see had been worked at by some inferior hand. They threw cold water upon that loveliest Francia which nobody could see without recognising. They did what they ought not to do, and neglected what was their duty. 'We all do that every day of our lives,' said Helen; 'but what was there that specially vexed you, Robert?' 'Nothing,' he said, looking up at her with eyes full of astonishment;

but there was more than astonishment in them. There was pain, dread, anxiety—a wistful, restless look of suffering. He will not tell me: he will keep it to himself and suffer by himself, not to vex me, Helen said in her own thoughts. And though the autumn was lovely, Robert could not be happy at Southlees that year. He had been very happy the two previous summers. The house was situated on the Thames beyond Teddington. It was rustic and old, with various additions built to it; a red-brick house, grown over with all manner of lichens, irregular in form and harmonious with its position, a house which had grown—which had not been artificially made. The family had lived on the lawn, or on the river, in those halcyon days that were past. There was a fringe of trees at every side except that, shutting in the painter's retirement; but on the river side nothing but a few bright flower-beds, and the green velvet lawn, sloping towards the softly flowing water. One long-leaved willow drooped over the stone steps at which the boat was lying. It was a place where a pair of lovers might have spent their honeymoon, or where the weary and sick might have come to get healing. It was not out of character either with the joy or the grief. Nature was so sweet, so silent, so meditative and calm. The river ran softly, brooding over its own low liquid gurgle. The stately swans sailed up and down. The little fishes darted about in the clear water, and myriads of flying atoms, nameless insect existences, fluttered above. Boating parties going down the stream would pause, with a sigh of gentle envy, to look at the group upon the lawn; the table with books and work on it, with sometimes a small easel beside it or big drawing pad supported on a stand; a low chair with Helen's red shawl thrown over it, and Norah, with her red ribbons, nestled on the sunny turf. They sat there, and worked, and talked, or were silent, with an expansion of their hearts towards everything that breathed and moved; or they spent long days on the river, catching the morning lights upon those nooks which are only known to dwellers on the stream; or pursuing water-lilies through all the golden afternoon in the back-waters which these retired flowers love. The river was their life, and carried them along, day after day. Such a scene could not but be sweet to every lover of nature; but it is doubly sweet when the dumb poetic imagination has by its side that eye of art which sees everything. The painter is a better companion even than the poet—just as seeing is better than saying that you see. Robert was not a genius in art; but he had the artist's animated, all-perceiving eye. Nothing escaped him—he saw a hundred beautiful things which would have been imperceptible to ordinary men—a dew-drop on a blade of grass at his feet charmed him as much as a rainbow—his 'Look, Helen!' was more than volumes of descriptive poetry. They were out and about at all times, 'watching the lights,' as he said in his pleasant professional jargon: in the early mornings, when all was silvery softness and clearness, and the birds were trying over their choicest trills before men woke to hear; in the evening when twilight came gently on, insinuating her filmy impenetrable veil between them and the sunset; and even at full noon, when day is languid at the height of perfection, knowing that perfectness is brother to decadence. The painter and his wife lived in the middle of all these changes, and took them in, every one, to the firmament in their hearts.

Why do we stop in this record of trouble to babble about sunset skies and running waters? Is it not natural? The 'sound as of a hidden brook in the leafy month of June' comes in, by right, among all weird, mysterious harmonies of every tragical fate. 'The oaten pipe and pastoral reed' have their share even in the hurly-burly of cities and noisy discord of modern existence. Robert Drummond had his good things as well as his evil things. For these two summers never man had been more happy—and it is but few who can say so much. His wife was happy with him, her old ghosts exorcised, and a new light suffusing her life. It seemed a new life altogether, a life without discontents, full of happiness, and tranquillity, and hope.

But this autumn Robert was not happy at Southlees. He could not stay there peaceably as he had done before. He had to go to town 'on business,' he said, sometimes twice a week. He took no pleasure in his old delights. Though he could not help seeing still, his 'Look, Helen!' was no longer said in a tone of enthusiasm; and when he had uttered the familiar exclamation he would turn away and sigh. Sometimes she found him with his face hidden in his hands, and pressed against the warm greensward. It was as if he were knocking for admission at the gates of the grave, Helen thought, in that fancifulness which comes of fear as much as of hope. When she questioned him he would deny everything, and work with pretended gaiety. Every time he went to town it seemed to her that five years additional of line and cloud had been added to the lines on his forehead. His hair began to get grey; perhaps that was no wonder, for he was forty, a pilgrim already in the sober paths of middle age, but Helen was nearly ten years younger, and this sign of advancing years seemed unnatural to her. Besides, he was a young man in his heart, a man who would be always young; yet he was growing old before his time. But notwithstanding his want of enjoyment in it he was reluctant that his wife should leave Southlees sooner than usual. He would go into town himself, he declared. He would do well enough—what did it matter for a few weeks? 'For the sake of business it is better that I should go—but the winter is long enough if you come in the end of the month. No, Helen, take the good of it as long as you can—this year.'

'What good shall I get of it alone, and how can I let you live for weeks by yourself?' said Helen. 'You may think it is fine to be independent; but you could not get on without Norah and me.'

'No,' he said, with a shudder. 'God knows life would be a poor thing without Norah and you! but when it is a question of three weeks—I'll go and see my friends; I'll live a jovial bachelor life—'

'Did you see the Haldanes,' she asked, 'when you were in town last?'

It was the most innocent, unmeaning question; but it made him grow pale to the very lips. Did he tremble? Helen was so startled that she did not even realise how it was he looked.

'How cold the wind blows,' he said, with a shiver. 'I must have caught cold, I suppose, last night. The Haldanes? No; I had no time.'

'Robert, something worries you,' she said earnestly. 'Tell me what it is. Whatever it is, it will not be so heavy when you have told me. You have always said so—since ever we have been together.'

'And truly, my darling,' he said. He took her hand and held it tenderly, but he did not look at her. 'I cannot tell you of worries that don't exist, can I?' he added, with an exaggerated cheerfulness. 'I have to pay a little attention to business now the other men are out of town. And business bores me. I don't understand it. I am not clever at it. But it is not worth while to call it a worry. By-and-by they will come back, and I shall be free.'

When he said this he really believed it, not being then fully aware of the tormenting power of the destruction which was about to overwhelm him. He thought the other directors would come back from their holidays, and that he himself would be able to plunge back into that abyss of ignorance which was bliss. But Helen did not believe it: not from any true perception of the state of affairs, but because she could not believe it was business at all that troubled him. Was Robert the kind of man to be disturbed about business? He who cared nothing for it but as a means, who liked money's worth, not money, whose mind was diametrically opposite to all the habits and traditions of trade? She would as soon have believed that her cousin Reginald Burton would be disturbed by a criticism or troubled to get a true balance of light and shade. No, it was not that. It was some real trouble which she did not know of, something that struck deeper than business, and was more important than anything that belonged to bank or market. Such were Helen's thoughts,—they are the thoughts that come most natural to a woman,—that he had been betrayed into some wrong-doing or inadvertent vice—that he had been tempted, and somehow gone astray. This, because it was so much more terrible than anything about business, was the bugbear that haunted her. It was to save her pain, as he thought, that poor Robert kept his secret from her. He did as so many men do, thinking it kindness; and thus left her with a host of horrible surmises to fight against, any one of which was (to her) harder than the truth. There is no way in which men, in their ignorance, inflict more harm upon women than this way. Helen watched in her fear and ignorance with a zealous eagerness that never lost a word, and gave exaggerated importance to many an idle incident. She was doubly roused by her fear of the something coming, against which her defences would not stand, and by her absolute uncertainty what this something was. The three weeks her husband was in town by himself were like three years to her. Not that a shade of jealousy or doubt of his love to herself ever crossed her mind. She was too pure-minded, too proud, to be jealous. But something had come on him, some old trouble out of the past—some sudden horrible temptation; something, in short, which he feared to tell her. That money could be the cause of it, never crossed her thoughts.

And when she went home, things were no better; the house looked bare to her—she could not tell why. It was more than a month before she found out that the Botticelli was gone, which was the light of her husband's eyes; and that little Madonna of the Umbrian school, which he delighted to think Raphael must have had some hand in, in his youth. This discovery startled her much; but worse had come before she made sure of that. The absence of the pictures was bewildering, but still more so was the change in her husband's habits. He would get up early, breakfast hurriedly before she had come down, and go out, leaving a message with the servants. Sometimes he went without breakfast. He avoided her, avoided the long evening talks they had loved, and even avoided her eye, lest she should read more in his face than he meant her to see. All this was terrible to Helen. The fears that overwhelmed her were ridiculous, no doubt; but amid the darkness and tragic gloom which surrounded her, what was she to think? Things she had read in books haunted her; fictitious visions which at this touch of personal alarm began to look real. She thought he might have to bribe some one who knew some early secret in his life, or some secret that was not his—something that belonged to his friends. Oh, if he would but tell her! She could bear anything—she could forgive the past, whatever it might be. She had no bitterness in her feelings towards her husband. She used to sit for hours together in his deserted studio, imagining scenes in which she found out, or he was driven to confide to her, this mystery; scenes of anguish, yet consolation. The studio became her favourite haunt. Was it possible that she had once entered it with languid interest, and been sensible of nothing but disappointment when she saw him working with his heart in his work? She would go all round it now, making her little comment upon every picture. She would have given everything she had in the world to see him back there, painting those pictures with which she had been so dissatisfied—the Francesca, which still stood on its easel unfinished; the sketches of herself which she had once been so impatient of. The Francesca still stood there behind backs; but most of the others had been cleared away, and stood in little stacks against the walls. The place was so orderly that it went to her heart to see it; nothing had been done, nothing disturbed, for weeks, perhaps months; the housemaid was free to go and come as if it had been a common parlour. All this was terribly sad to the painter's wife. The spring was coming on before she found the two sketches which afterwards she held so dearly. They bewildered her still more, and filled her with a thousand fears. One represented a pilgrim on a hilly road, in the twilight of a spring evening. Everything was soft in this picture, clear sky and twinkling stars above; a quiet rural path over the grass; but just in front of the pilgrim, and revealing his uplifted hands and horror-stricken countenance, the opening of a glowing horrible cavern—the mouth of Hell. The other was more mysterious still. It was a face full of anguish and love, with two clasped hands, looking up from the depths of a cave or well, to one blue spot of sky, one star that shone far above. Helen did not know what these sketches meant; but they made her shiver with wonder and apprehension. They were all that he had done this year.

And then something else, of a different kind, came in to bewilder her. Robert, who avoided her, who of evenings no longer talked over his affairs with her, and who probably had forgotten all her wants, let the quarter-day pass without supplying her, as he was in the habit of doing. So great a host of fears and doubts were between the two, that Helen did not remind him of his negligence. It pained her, but in a degree so different. What did that matter? But time went on, and it began to matter. She took her own little dividends, and kept silence; making what use of them she could to fill up the larger wants. She was as timid of speaking to him on this subject as if she had been a young girl. He had never obliged her to do so. She had been the general treasurer of the household in the old days; and even in recent times, he, who was so proud of his wife, had taken care to keep her always supplied with what she wanted. She never had needed to go to him to ask money, and she did not know how to begin. Thus they both went their different way; suffering, perhaps, about equally. His time seemed to himself to be spent in a feverish round of interviews with people who could supply money, or wildly signing his name to papers which he scarcely understood—to bills which he could never dream of paying; they would be paid somehow when the time came, or they could be renewed, or something would be done, he was told. He had carried everything he could make money by away before this time; the title-deeds of his house, his pictures, even, and—this was done with a very heavy heart—his policies of life insurance. Everything was gone. Events went faster as the crisis approached, and Drummond became conscious of little more than his wife's pale face wondering at him, with questioning eyes more pathetic than words, and Golden's face encouraging, or trying to encourage. Between the two was a wild abyss of work, of despair, of tiding over. Every escape more hairbreadth than the last! The wild whirl growing wilder! the awful end, ruin and fell destruction, coming nearer and more near!

It happened at length that Helen one day, in desperation, broke the silence. She came before him when he was on his way out, and asked him to wait, in a hollow voice.

'I don't want to trouble you,' she said, 'since you will not trust me, Robert. I have been trying not to harass you more; but—I have no money left—I am getting into debt—the servants want their wages. Robert—I thought you had forgotten—perhaps—'

He stood and looked at her for a moment, with his hat in his hand, ready to go out. How pale he was! How the lines had contracted in his face! He looked at her, trying to be calm. And then, as he stood, suddenly burst, without warning, into momentary terrible tears, of a passion she could not understand.

'Robert! oh, what is the matter?' she cried, throwing her arms round him. He put his head down on her shoulder, and held her fast, and regained control over himself, holding her to him as if she had been something healing. In her great wonder and pity she raised his head with her hands, and gazed wistfully into his face through her tears. 'Is it money?' she cried, with a great load taken off her heart. 'Oh, Robert, tell me! Is that all?'

'All!' he said: 'my God!' and then kissed her passionately, and put her away from him. 'To-morrow,' he said hoarsely, 'perhaps—I hope—I will tell you everything to-morrow.' He did not venture to look at her again. He went out straight, without turning to the right or left. 'The end must be near now,' he said to himself audibly, as he went out like a blind man. To-morrow! Would to-morrow ever come? 'The end must be near now.'

The end was nearer than he thought. When he reached the bank he found everything in disorder. Mr Golden was not there, nor any one who could give information to the panic-stricken inquirers who were pouring in. It was said the manager had absconded. Rivers's was at an end. For the first ten minutes after Drummond heard the news that awaited him, it was almost a relief to know that the worst had come.

It was a relief for ten minutes, as every catastrophe is; the terrible suspense is cut short—the worst at least is known. But after those ten minutes are over, when the reality suddenly seizes upon the sufferer—when all the vague speechless terrors which he had pushed off from him, with the hope that they might never come, arrive in a flood, and place themselves in one frightful circle round him, like furies, only not merciful enough to have a Medusa among them to freeze him into stone; when every shadowy, gloomy prevision of evil which ever flashed across his mind, to be put away with a shudder, returns with the right of fact, to remain; when not only that thing has happened which has been his dread by day and the horror of his dreams, but a host of other things, circumstances which penetrate to every detail of his life, and affect every creature and every thing he loves, have followed in its train—when all this rushes upon a man after the first tranquillising stupor of despair, who or what is there that can console him? Poor Drummond was helpless in the midst of this great crash of ruin; he was so helpless that the thunder-stricken shareholders and excited clerks who had fallen upon him at first as the only authority to be found, let him slip from among them, hopeless of any help from him. They had driven him wild with questions and appeals—him, a poor fellow who could explain nothing, who had never been of much use except to denude himself of everything he possessed, and pledge his humble name, and be swept into ruin; but they soon saw the uselessness of the appeal. As soon as he could disengage himself he stole away, drawing his hat over his eyes, feeling as if he were a criminal, with the sensation as of a hot fire burning in his heart, and buzzing and crackling in his ears. Was he a criminal? was it his doing? He was stunned by this terrible calamity; and yet, now that it had come, he felt that he had known it was coming, and everything about it, all his life. His whole existence had tended to this point since he was a boy; he knew it, he felt it, he even seemed to remember premonitions of it, which had come to him in his dreams from his earliest days. He went out into the streets in that dumb quiescent state which is so often the first consequence of a great calamity. He offered no remonstrance against his fate. He did not even say to himself that it was hard. He said nothing to himself, indeed, except to croon over, like a chorus, one endless refrain, 'I knew this was how it would be!'

He wandered along, not knowing where he went, till he came to the river, and paused there, looking over the bridge. He did not even know what made him pause, until all at once the fancy jumped into his brain that it would be best to stop there, and cut in one moment the knotted, tangled thread which it was certain no effort of his could ever unravel. He stopped, and the suggestion flashed across him (whether out of his own mind, whether thrown at him by some mocking demon, who could tell?), and then shook his head sadly. No; it was broad day, and there would be a commotion, and he would be rescued—or if not, he, at least his body, would be rescued and carried to Helen, giving her a last association with him which it was insupportable to think of. No, no, he said to himself with a shudder, not now. Just then a hand was laid upon his shoulder; he turned round with the start of a man who feels that nothing is impossible, that everything that is terrible has become likely. Had it been a policeman to arrest him for having murdered somebody he would scarcely have been surprised. But it was not a policeman: it was Mr Burton, fresh and clean and nicely dressed, newly come up from the country, in his light summer clothes, the image of prosperity, and comfort, and cleanliness, and self-satisfaction. A certain golden atmosphere surrounded the man of wealth, like the background on which early painters set a saint; but there was nothing saintly about that apparition. Poor Drummond fell back more than he would have done had it been an arrest for murder. He gave an involuntary glance at himself, feeling in contrast with Mr Burton, as if he must look to the external eye the beggar he was, as if he must be dirty, tattered, miserable, with holes in his shoes and rags at his elbows. Perhaps his woebegone, excited face startled the smooth Philistine at his side as much as if those outward signs of wretchedness had been there.

'Good God, what have you been doing with yourself?' he cried.

'Nothing,' said Drummond vaguely, and then by degrees his senses returned to him. 'If you had been in town yesterday you might have helped us; but it does not matter. Shenken in Liverpool stopped payment yesterday,' he went on, repeating drearily the dreary legend which he had heard at the bank. 'And Rivers's—has stopped payment too.'

'Good God!' said Mr Burton again. It was a shock to him, as every event is when it comes. But he was not surprised. As for Robert, it did not occur to him to consider whether the other was surprised or not, or to be curious how it affected him. He turned his head away and looked at the river again. What attraction there remained for him in this world seemed to lie there.

'Drummond,' said the merchant, looking at him with a certain alarm, 'are you sure you know what you are saying? My God! Rivers's stopped payment! if you had said there had been an earthquake in London it would scarcely be as bad as that.'

Robert did not make any reply. He nodded his head without looking round. What interested him was something black which kept appearing and disappearing in the middle of the turbid muddy stream. It was like a man's head, he thought, and almost felt that he might have taken the plunge without knowing it, and that it might be himself.

'I have felt this was coming,' said Burton. 'I warned Golden you were going on in the wildest way. What could be expected when you fellows who know nothing about money would interfere? Good heavens! to think what a business that was; and all ruined in three years! Drummond! are you mad? Can't you turn round and speak to me? I am one of the shareholders, and I have a right to be answered how it was.'

'Shall you lose much?' said Drummond dreamily, and he turned round without meaning anything and looked in his companion's face. His action was simply fantastical, one of those motiveless movements which the sick soul so often makes; but it was quite unexpected by the other, who fell a step back, and grew red all over, and faltered in his reply.

'Much? I—I—don't know—what you call much. Good heavens, Drummond! are you mad? have you been drinking? Where is Golden?—he at least must know what he is about!'

'Yes,' said the painter fiercely, 'Golden knows what he is about—he has gone off, out of reach of questions—and you—oh—hound!' He gave a sudden cry and made a step forward. A sudden light seemed to burst upon him. He gazed with his dilated bloodshot eyes at the flushed countenance which could not face him. The attitude of the two men was such that the bystanders took note of it; two or three lingered and looked round holding themselves in readiness to interfere. The slight figure of the painter, his ghastly pale face and trembling hand, made him no antagonist for the burly well-to-do merchant; but English sentiment is always on the side of the portly and respectable, and Mr Burton had an unmistakable air of fright upon his face. 'Now, Drummond!—now, Drummond!' he said, with a certain pleading tone. The painter stood still, feeling as if a horrible illumination had suddenly flashed upon the man before him, and the history of their intercourse. He did in that moment of his despair what he could not have done with his ordinary intelligence. He made a rapid summary of the whole and saw how it was. Had he been happy, he would have been too friendly, too charitable, too kind in his thoughts to have drawn such a conclusion. But at this moment he had no time for anything but the terrible truth.

'I see it all,' he said. 'I see it all! It was ruined when you gave it over to us. I see it in every line of your face. Oh, hound! hounds all of you! skulking, dastardly demons, that kill a crowd of honest men to save yourselves—your miserable selves. I see it all!'

'Drummond! I tell you you are mad!'

'Hound!' said Robert again between his clenched teeth. He stood looking at him for a moment with his hands clenched too, and a sombre fire in his eyes. Whether he might have been led into violence had he stood there a moment longer it would be impossible to say. But all the habits of his life were against it, and his very despair restrained him. When he had stood there for a second, he turned round suddenly on his heel without any warning, and almost knocking down a man who was keeping warily behind him ready for any emergency, went away in the opposite direction without saying a word. Burton stood still gazing after him with a mixture of consternation and concern, and something very like hatred. But his face changed when the spectators drew round him to wonder and question. 'Something wrong with that poor gentleman, I fear, sir,' said one. Mr Burton put on a look of regret, sighed deeply, put his hand to his forehead, shook his head, murmured—'Poor fellow!' and—walked away. What could he do? He was not his brother's keeper, much less was he responsible for his cousin's husband—the paltry painter-fellow she had preferred to him. What would Helen think of her bargain now? Mad or drunk, it did not matter which—a pleasant companion for a woman. He preferred to think of this for the moment, rather than of the other question, which was in reality so much more important. Rivers's! Thank heaven he was no money loser, no more than was respectable. He had seen what was coming. Even to himself, this was all that Mr Burton said. He hurried on, however, to learn what people were saying of it, with more anxiety in his mind than seemed necessary. He went to the bank itself with the air of a man going to a funeral. 'The place I have known so long!' he said to another mournful victim who had appeared on the field of the lost battle, but who was not mad like Robert. 'And to think that Golden should have betrayed your confidence! A man I have known since he was that height—a man I could have answered for with my life!'

Meanwhile Drummond strayed on he knew not where. He went back into the City, into the depths of those lanes and narrow streets which he had left so lately, losing himself in a bewildering maze of warehouse walls and echoing traffic. Great waggons jammed him up against the side, loads dangled over his head that would have crushed him in a moment, open cellars yawned for his unsteady feet; but he walked as safe through all those perils as if he had borne a charmed life, though he neither looked nor cared where he was going. His meeting with Burton was forced out of his mind in a few minutes as if it had not been. For the moment it had startled him into mad excitement; but so strong was the stupor of his despair, that in five minutes it was as if it had never been. For hours he kept wandering round and round the scene of his ruin, coming and going in a circle, as if his feet were fast and he could not escape.

It had been morning when he left his house. It was late afternoon when he got back. Oh why was it summer and the days so long? if only that scorching sun would have set and darkness fallen over the place. He stole in under cover of the lilac trees, which had grown so big and leafy, and managed to glide down the side-way to the garden and get to the studio door, which he could open with his key. He had been doing nothing but think—think—all the time; but 'now, at least, I shall have time to think,' he said to himself, as he threw himself down on a chair close to the door—the nearest seat—it no longer mattered where he placed himself or how. He sat huddled up against the wall as sometimes a poor model did, waiting wistfully to know if he was wanted,—some poor wretch to whom a shilling was salvation. This fancy, with a thousand others equally inappropriate, flashed across his mind as he sat there, still with his hat pulled down on his brows in the sunny luxurious warmth of the afternoon. The mere atmosphere, air, and sky, and sunshine would have been paradise to the artist in the poorest time he had ever known before, but they did not affect him now. He sat there in his stupor for perhaps an hour, not even able to rouse himself so far as to shut the door of communication into the conservatory, through which he heard now and then the softened stir of the household. He might have been restored to the sense of life and its necessities, might have been brought back out of the delirium of his ruin at that moment, had any one in the house known he was there. Helen was in the drawing-room, separated from him only by that flowery passage which he had made for her, to tempt her to visit him at his work. She was writing notes, inviting some half-dozen people to dinner, as had been arranged between them, but with a heavy and anxious heart, full of misgiving. She had risen from her writing table three or four times to go to the window and look out for her husband, wondering why he should be so long of coming—while he sat so near her. Mrs Drummond's heart was very heavy. She did not understand what he said to her in the morning—could not imagine how it could be. It must be a temporary cloud, a failure of some speculation, something unconnected with the ordinary course of life, she said to herself. Money!—he was not a business man—it could not be money. If it was only money, why that was nothing. Such was the course of her thoughts. And she paused over her invitations, wondering was it right to give them if Robert had been losing money. But they were old friends whom she was inviting—only half a dozen people—and it was for his birthday. She had just finished the last note, when Norah came dancing into the room, claiming her mother's promise to go out with her; and after another long gaze from her window, Helen made up her mind to go. It was her voice speaking to the maid which roused Robert. 'If Mr Drummond comes in before I return,' he heard her say, 'tell him I shall not be long. I am going with Miss Norah to the gardens for an hour, and then to ask for Mr Haldane; but I shall be back by half-past six.' He heard the message—he for whom it was intended—and rose up softly and went to his studio window, and peeped stealthily out to watch them as they went away. Norah came first, with a skip and gambol, and then Helen. His wife gave a wistful look back at the house as she opened the little gate under the leafy dusty lilacs. Was it with some premonition of what she should find when she came back? He hid himself so that he could not be seen, and gazed at the two, feeling as if that moment was all that life had yet to give him. It was his farewell look. His wife and child disappeared, and he could hear their footsteps outside on the pavement going farther and farther away on their harmless, unimportant walk, while he—He woke up as if it had been out of sleep or out of a trance. She would return by half-past six, and it was now approaching five. For all he had to do there was so little, so very little time.

So he said to himself, and yet when he said it he had no clear idea what he was going to do. He had not only to do it, whatever it was, but to make up his mind, all in an hour and a half; and for the first five minutes of that little interval he was like a man dreaming, stretching out his hands to catch any straw, trying to believe he might yet be saved. Could he leave them—those two who had just left the door—to struggle through the rest of life by themselves? Helen was just over thirty, and her daughter nearly twelve. It was a mature age for a woman; but yet for a woman who has been protected and taken care of all her life, how bitter a moment to be left alone!—the moment when life is at its fullest, demands most, feels most warmly, and has as yet given up nothing. Helen had had no training to teach her that happiness was not her right. She had felt it to be her right, and her whole soul rose up in rebellion against any infringement of that great necessity of being. How was she to live when all was taken from her, even the support of her husband's arm? Robert had never known so much of his wife's character before, but in this awful moment it became clear to him as by an inspiration. How was she to bear it? Credit, honour, money, living—and her husband, too, who could still work for her, shield her. He went to his easel and uncovered the half-finished picture on it, and gazed at it with something that was in reality a dumb appeal to the dumb canvas to help him. But it did not help him. On the contrary, it brought suddenly up before him his work of the past, his imperfect successes, and Helen's kind, veiled, hidden, but unconcealable dissatisfaction. The look of suppressed pain in her face, the subdued tone, the soft languid praise of some detail or accessory, the very look of her figure when she turned away from it, came all before him. Her habit was, when she turned away, to talk to him of other things. How clearly that oft-repeated scene came before him in his despair! She was dutiful, giving him her attention conscientiously as long as was needful; but when he fell back into the fond babble of the maker, and tried to interest her in some bit of drapery, or effect of light, or peculiarity of grouping, she would listen to him sweetly, and—change the subject as soon as possible. It all returned to him—he remembered even the trivial little words she had spoken, the languid air of half fatigue which would come over her. That—along with the meagrest poverty, the hardest homely struggles for daily bread. Could she bear to go back to it? She would lose everything, the house and all that was in it, everything that could be called hers or supposed hers. The only thing that could not be taken from her would be her £100 a year, her little fortune which was settled on her. 'They could live on that,' poor Drummond went on in his dreary miserable thoughts. 'They could exist, it is possible, better without me than with me. Would they be happier to have me in prison, disgraced, and dishonoured, a drag hanging about their neck—or to hear the worst at once, to know that everything was over, that at least their pittance would be theirs, and their peace respected? Everything would be over. Nobody could have any pretext for annoying her about it. They would be sorry for her—even they would be sorry for me. My policies would go to make up something—to clear my name a little. And they would let her alone. She could go to the country. She is so simple in her real tastes. They could live on what she has, if they were only rid of me.' A sigh that was almost a sob interrupted him in his musing. He was so worn out; and was it the grave-chill that was invading him already and making him shiver? He took the canvas on the easel and held it up to the light. 'The drawing is good enough,' he said to himself, 'it is not the drawing. She always owns that. It is—something else. And how can I tell after this that I could even draw? I could not now, if I were to try. My hand shakes like an old man's. I might fall ill like poor Haldane! Ah, my God!' The canvas fell out of his hands upon the floor—a sudden spasm contracted his heart. Haldane! It was the first time that day that he had thought of him. His ruin would be the ruin of his friend too—his friend who was helpless, sick, and yet the support of others. 'Oh, my God, my God!' he wailed with a cry of despair.

And there was no one near to hear him, no one to defend him from himself and from the devil, to lay hands upon him, to bid him live and hope and work, and help them to exist whom he had helped to ruin. He was left all alone in that moment of his agony. God, to whom he had appealed, was beyond the clouds, beyond that which is more unfathomable than any cloud, the serene, immeasurable, impenetrable blue, and held out no hand, sent no voice of comfort. The man fell down where his work had fallen, prone upon the ground, realising in a moment all the misery of the years that were to come. And it was his doing, his doing!—though consciously he would have given himself to be cut to pieces, would have toiled his life out, to make it up now to his friend,—how much more to his wife! What passed in his mind in that awful interval is not to be told. It was the supreme struggle between life and despair, and it was despair that won. When he rose up his face was like the face of an old man, haggard and furrowed with deep lines. He stood still for a moment, looking round him vaguely, and then made a little pilgrimage round the room, looking at everything, with a motive, without a motive, who can tell? his whole faculties absorbed in the exaltation, and bewildering, sombre excitement of such a crisis as can come but once to any man. Then he sat down at his writing-table, and sought out some letter-paper (there were so many scraps of drawing-paper that came first to hand), and slowly wrote a few lines. He had to search for a long time before he could find an envelope to enclose this, and his time was getting short. At last he put it up, and, after another pause, stole through the conservatory, walking stealthily like a thief, and placed the white envelope on a little crimson table, where it shone conspicuous to everybody who should enter. He did more than that; he went and bent over the chair which Helen had pushed away when she rose from it—the chair she always sat on—and kissed it. There was a little bright-coloured handkerchief lying on the sofa, which was Norah's. He took that up and kissed it too, and thrust it into his breast. Did he mean to carry it with him into the dark and silent country where he was going? God knows what was the thought in his mind. The pretty clock on the mantelpiece softly chimed the quarter as he did this, and he started like a thief. Then he took an old great-coat from the wall, an old travelling hat, which hung beside it, and went back to the studio. There was no more time for thought. He went out, leaving the door unlocked, brushing stealthily through the lilacs. The broad daylight played all around him, revealing him to every one, showing to the world how he stole away out of his own house. He had put up the collar of his coat and drawn his hat down over his brows to disguise himself in case he met any one he knew. Any one he knew! It was in case he met his wife, to whom he had just said farewell for ever, and his child, whose little kerchief he was going to take with him into this dismal ruin, into the undiscovered world.

All this might have been changed had he met them; and they were crossing the next street coming home, Helen growing more and more anxious as they approached the door. Had he been going out about some simple everyday business, of course they would have met; but not now, when it might have saved one life from destruction and another from despair. He had watched for a moment to make sure they were not in sight before he went out; and the servants had caught a glimpse of a man whom they did not recognise hiding among the bushes, and were frightened; so, it turned out afterwards, had various other passers-by. But Drummond saw no one—no one. The multitudes in the noisier streets upon which he emerged after a while, were nothing to him. They pushed against him, but he did not see them; the only two figures he could have seen were henceforward to be invisible to him for ever.

For ever! for ever! Was it for ever? Would this crime he was about to commit, this last act of supreme rebellion against the will of that God to whom he seemed to have appealed in vain, would it sever him from them not only in this world, but in the world to come? Should he have to gaze upward, like poor Dives, and see, in the far serene above him, these two walking in glory and splendour, who were no longer his? perhaps surrounded by angels, stately figures of the blessed, without a thought to spare in the midst of that glory for the poor soul who perished for love of them. Could that be true? Was it damnation as well as death he was going to face? Was it farewell for ever, and ever, and ever?

So the awful strain ran on, buzzing in his ears, drowning for him the voices of the crowd—for ever, for ever, for ever. Dives forlorn and far away—and up, up high in the heavens, blazing above him, like a star—

Like that star in the soft sky of the evening which came out first and shone down direct upon him in his wretchedness. How it shone! How she shone!—was it she?—as it grew darker drawing a silver line for him upon the face of the darkening water. Was that to be the spot? But it took years to get dark that night. He lived and grew old while he was waiting thus to die. At last there was gloom enough. He got a boat, and rowed it out to that white glistening line, the line that looked like a silver arrow, shining where the spot was—

The boat drifted ashore that night as the tide fell. In that last act, at least, Nature helped him to be honest, poor soul!

'The studio door is open, mamma,' said little Norah dancing in before her mother, through the lilac bushes. The words seemed to take a weight off Helen's heart.

'Then papa must have come in,' she said, and ran up the steps to the door, which was opened before she could knock by an anxious, half-frightened maid. 'Mr Drummond has come in?' she said, in her anxiety, hasting to pass Jane, who held fast by the door.

'No, ma'am, please, ma'am; but Rebecca and me see a man about not five minutes ago, and I can't find master's topcoat as was a-hanging in the hall—Rebecca says, ma'am, as she thought she see—'

'Papa has not been home after all,' Helen said to her little daughter; 'perhaps Mr Drummond wore his great-coat last night, Jane. Never mind just now; he will tell us when he comes in.'

'But I see the man, and George was out, as he always is when he's wanted. Me and Rebecca—' said Jane.

'Never mind just now,' said Helen languidly. She went into the drawing-room with the load heavier than ever on her heart. What could have kept him so long? What could be making him so miserable? Oh, how cruel, cruel it was not to know! She sat down with a heart like lead on that chair which poor Robert had kissed—not fifteen minutes since, and he was scarcely out of reach now.

'Oh, mamma,' cried Norah, moving about with a child's curiosity; 'here is a letter for you on the little red table. It is so funny, and blurred, and uneven. I can write better than that—look! isn't it from papa?'

Helen had not paid much attention to what the child said, but now she started up and stretched out her hand. The name on the outside was scarcely legible, it was blurred and uneven, as Norah said; and it was very clear to see, could only be a message of woe. But her worst fears, miserable as she felt, had not approached the very skirts of the misery that now awaited her. She tore the envelope open, with her heart beating loud in her ears, and her whole body tingling with agitation. And this was what she read:—

'MY HELEN, MY OWN HELEN,—I have nothing in the world to do now but to bid you good-bye. I have ruined you, and more than you. If I lived I should only be a disgrace and a burden, and your little money that you have will support you by yourself. Oh, my love, to think I should leave you like this! I who have loved you so. But I have never been good enough for you. When you are an angel in heaven, if you see me among the lost, oh, bestow a little pity upon me, my Helen! I shall never see you again, but as Dives saw Lazarus. Oh, my wife, my baby, my own, you will be mine no longer; but have a little pity upon me! Give me one look, Helen, out of heaven.

'I am not mad, dear. I am doing it knowing it will be for the best. God forgive me if I take it upon me to know better than Him. It is not presumption, and perhaps He may know what I mean, though even you don't know. Oh my own, my darlings, my only ones—good-bye, good-bye!'

There was no name signed, no stops to make the sense plain. It was written as wildly as it had been conceived; and Helen, in her terrible excitement, did not make out at first what it could mean. What could it mean? where was he going? The words about Dives and Lazarus threw no light upon it at first. He had gone away. She gave a cry, and dropped her hands upon her lap, with the letter in them, and looked round her—looked at her child, to make sure to herself that she was not dreaming. Gone away! But where, where, and why this parting? 'I don't understand it—he has gone and left us,' she said feebly, when Norah, in her curiosity, came rushing to her to know what it was. 'I don't know what it means. O God, help us!' she said, with an outburst of miserable tears. She was confused to the very centre of her being. Where had he gone?'

'May I read it, mamma?' little Norah asked, with her arms round her mother's neck.

But Helen had the feeling that it was not fit for the child. 'Run and ask who brought it,' she said, glad to be alone; and then read over again, with a mind slowly awakening to its reality, that outburst of love and despair. The letter shook in her hands, salt tears fell upon it as she read. 'If I lived:—I am doing it, knowing.' God, God, what was it he had gone to do? Just then she heard a noise in the studio, and starting to her feet rushed to the conservatory door, crying, 'Robert! Robert!' She was met by Jane and Norah, coming from it; the child was carrying her father's hat in her arms, with a strange look of wonder and dismay on her face.

'Mamma, no one brought the letter,' she said in a subdued, horror-struck tone; 'and here is papa's hat— and the picture is lying dashed down on the floor with its face against the carpet. It is all spoiled, mamma,' sobbed little Norah—'papa's picture! and here is his hat. Oh, mamma, mamma!'

Norah was frightened at her mother's face. She had grown ghastly pale. 'Get me a cab,' she said to the maid, whose curiosity was profoundly excited. Then she sat down and took her child in her arms. 'Norah, my darling,' she said, making a pause between every two words, 'something dreadful has happened. I don't know what. I must go—and see. I must go—and find him—O my God, where am I to go?'

'And me, too,' said the child, clinging to her fast; 'me, too—let us go to the City, mamma!'

'Not you, Norah. It will soon be your bedtime. Oh, my pet, go and kneel down and pray—pray for poor papa.'

'I can pray just as well in the cab,' said Norah; 'God hears all the same. I am nearly twelve—I am almost grown up. You shall not, shall not go without me. I will never move nor say a word. I will run up and get your cloak and mine. We'll easily find him. He never would have the heart to go far away from you and me.'

'He never would have the heart,' Helen murmured the words over after her. Surely not. Surely, surely, he would not have the heart! His resolution would fail. How could he go and leave the two whom he loved best—the two whom alone he loved in this world. 'Run, then, dear, and get your cloak,' she said faintly. The child seemed a kind of anchor to her, holding her to something, to some grasp of solid earth. They drove off in a few minutes, Norah holding fast her mother's hand. They overtook, if they had but known it, and passed in the crowd, the despairing man they sought; and he with his dim eyes saw the cab driving past, and wondered even who was in it—some other sufferer, in the madness of excitement or despair. How was he to know it was his wife and child? They drove to the City, but found no one there. They went to his club, to one friend's house after another, to the picture-dealers, to the railway stations. There, two or three bystanders had seen such a man, and he had gone to Brighton, to Scotland, to Paris, they said. Coming home, they drove over the very bridge where he had been standing waiting for the dark. It was dark by that time, and Helen's eye caught the line of light on the water, with that intuitive wish so common to a painter's wife, that Robert had seen it. Ah, good Lord! he had seen and more than seen. The summer night was quite dark when they got home. Those gleams of starlight were lost in clouds, and all was gloom about the pretty house. Instead of the usual kindly gleam from the windows, nothing was visible as they drew up to the door but the light of a single candle which showed its solitary flame through the bare window of the dining-room. No blind was drawn, or curtain closed, and like the taper of a watcher shone this little miserable light. It chilled Helen in her profound discouragement and fatigue, and yet it gave her a forlorn hope that perhaps he had come. Norah had fallen fast asleep leaning against her. It was all she could do to wake the child as they approached the door; and Jane came out to open the gate with a scared face. 'No, ma'am, master's never been back,' she answered to Helen's eager question; but Dr Maurice, he's here.'

Mrs Drummond put Norah into the woman's arms, and rushed into the house. Dr Maurice met her with a face almost as white as her own, and took her hands compassionately. 'You have heard from him? What have you heard? where is he?' said poor Helen.

'Hush, hush!' he said, 'perhaps it is not so bad as it appears. I don't understand it. Rest a little, and I will show you what he has written to me.'

'I cannot rest,' she said; 'how can I rest when Robert—Let me see it. Let me see it. I am sure to understand what he means. He never had any secrets before. Oh, show it me—show it me!—am not I his wife?'

'Poor wife, poor wife!' said the compassionate doctor, and then he put her into an easy-chair and went and asked for some wine. 'I will show it you only when you have drank this,' he said; 'only when you have heard what I have to say. Drummond is very impulsive you know. He might not do really as he said. A hundred things would come in to stop him when he had time to think. His heart has been broken by this bank business; but when he felt that it was understood he was not to blame—'

'Give me your letter,' she said, holding out her hand to him. She was capable of no more.

'He would soon find that out,' said the doctor. 'Who could possibly blame him? My dear Mrs Drummond, you must take this into account. You must not give him up at once. I have set on foot all sorts of inquiries—'

'The letter, the letter!' she said hoarsely, holding out her hand.

He was obliged to yield to her at last, but not without the consciousness which comforted him that she had heard a great deal of what he had to say. She had not listened voluntarily; but still she had not been able to keep herself from hearing. This was not much comfort to poor Helen, but it was to him. He had made her swallow the wine too; he had done his best for her; and now he could but stand by mournfully while she read her sentence, the words which might be death.

'Maurice, I want you to go to my wife. Before you get this, or at least before you have got to her, I shall be dead. It's a curious thing to say, but it's true. There has been a great crash at the bank, and I am ruined and all I care for. If I lived I could do no good, only harm; but they will be sorry for her if I die. I have written to her, poor darling, to tell her; but I want you to go and stand by her. She'll want some one; and kiss the child for me. If they find me, bury me anywhere. I hope they will never find me, though, for Helen's sake. And poor Haldane. Tell him I knew nothing of it; nothing, nothing! I would have died sooner than let them risk his money. God help us, and God forgive me! Maurice, you are a good fellow; be kind to my poor wife.'

There was a postscript which nobody read or paid any attention to: that is to say, they read it and it died from their minds for the moment as if it meant nothing. It was this, written obliquely like an after-thought—

'The bank was ruined from the first; there was never a chance for us. I found this out only to-day. Burton and Golden have done it all.'

These were the words that Helen read, with Dr Maurice standing mournfully behind watching her every movement. She kept staring at the letter for a long time, and then fell back with a hysterical sob, but without any relief of tears. Dr Maurice stood by her as his friend had asked him. He soothed her, adding every possible reason he could think of (none of which he himself believed in the smallest degree) to show that 'poor Drummond' might change his mind. This was written in the first impulse of despair, but when he came to think—Helen did not listen; but she heard what Dr Maurice said vaguely, and she heard his account of what he had done; he had given information at once to the police; he had engaged people everywhere to search and watch. News would be heard of him to-morrow certainly, if not to-night. Helen rose while he was speaking. She collected herself and restrained herself, exerting all the strength she possessed. 'Will you come with me?' she said.

'Where? where? Mrs Drummond, I entreat you to believe I have done everything—'

'Oh, I am sure of it!' she said faintly; 'but I must go. I cannot—cannot rest. I must go somewhere—anywhere—where he may have gone—'

'But, Mrs Drummond—'

'You are going to say I have been everywhere. So we have, Norah and I—she fell asleep at last, poor child—she does not need me—I must go—'

'It is getting late,' he said; 'it is just ten; if news were to come you would not like to be out of the way. Stay here and rest, and I will go to-morrow; you will want all your strength.'

'I want it all now,' she said, with a strange smile. 'Who thinks of to-morrow? it may never, never come. It may—You are very kind—but I cannot rest.'

She was in the cab again before he could say another word. But fortunately at that moment one of his messengers came in hot haste to say that they thought they had found some trace of 'the gentleman.' He had come off to bring the news, and probably by this time the others were on their way bringing him home. This intelligence furnished Maurice with a weapon against Helen. She allowed herself to be led into the house again, not believing it, feeling in her heart that her husband would never be brought back, yet unable to resist the reasonable conclusion that she must stay to receive him. The short summer darkness passed over her thus; the awful dawn came and looked her in the face. One of the maids sat up, or rather dozed in her chair in the kitchen, keeping a fire alight in case anything might be wanted. And Helen sat and listened to every sound; sat at the window gazing out, hearing carriage wheels and footsteps miles off, as it seemed to her, and now and then almost deceived into hope by the sound of some one returning from a dance or late party. How strange it seemed to her that life should be going on in its ordinary routine, and people enjoying themselves, while she sat thus frozen into desperation, listening for him who would never come again! Her mind was wandering after him through every kind of dreadful scene; and yet it was so difficult, so impossible to associate him with anything terrible. He, always so reasonable, so tender of others, so free from selfish folly. The waking of the new day stole upon the watcher before she was aware; those sounds which are so awful in their power, which show how long it is since last night, how life has gone on, casting aside old burdens, taking on new ones. It was just about ten o'clock, when the morning was at its busiest outside, and Helen, refusing to acknowledge the needs of the new day, still sat at the window watching, with eyes that were dry and hot and bloodshot, with the room all in mournful disorder round her, when Dr Maurice's brougham drew up to the door. He sprang out of it, carrying a coat on his arm; a rough fellow in a blue Jersey and sailor's hat followed him. Maurice came in with that look so different from the look of anxiety, that fatal air, subdued and still and certain, which comes only from knowledge. Whatever might have happened he was in doubt no more.

Helen's long vigil had worn her into that extremity of emotion which can no longer avail itself of ordinary signs. She had not even risen to meet the news. She held out her hand feebly, and gave him a piteous look of inquiry, which her dry lips refused to sound. She looked as if it were possible that she had grown into an idiot as she sat there. He came forward to her, and took her hand in his.

'Dear Mrs Drummond,' he said, 'you will need all your courage; you must not give way; you must think of your child.'

'I know,' she said; her hand dropped out of his as if by its mere weight. She bowed her head as if to let this great salt bitter wave go over her—bowed it down till it sank upon her lap hidden in her clasped hands. There was nothing to be said further, not a word was necessary. She knew.

And yet there was a story to tell. It was told to her very gently, and she had to listen to it, with her face hidden in her hands. She shuddered now and then as she listened. Sometimes a long convulsive sob escaped her, and shook her whole frame; but she was far beyond the ordinary relief of weeping. It was poor Robert's coat which Dr Maurice had brought with him, making all further doubt impossible. The gentleman had thrown it off when he took that boat at Chelsea. It was too warm, he said; 'and sure enough it was mortal warm,' the man added who had come to verify the mournful story. The gentleman had taken a skiff for a row. It was a clear, beautiful night, and he had been warned to keep out of the way of steamers and barges. If any harm came to him, the boatman said, it was not for want of knowing how to manage a boat. The little skiff had drifted in bottom up, and had been found that morning a mile down stream. That was all. Jane, who was the housemaid, went away crying, and drew down all the blinds except that of the room in which her mistress was. 'Surely missis will have the thought to do that,' she said. But poor Helen had not the thought.

And thus it all came to an end—their love, their prosperity, and that mitigated human happiness which they had enjoyed together—happiness not too perfect, and yet how sweet! Norah still slept through the bright morning, neglected by her usual attendant, and tired out by her unusual exertions on the previous night. 'She ought to know,' the maids said to each other, with that eagerness to make evil tidings known which is so strangely common; but the old nurse, who loved the child, would not have her disturbed. It was only when Helen rejected all their entreaties to lie down and rest that Martin consented to rouse the little girl. She came down, with her bright hair all about her shoulders, wrapped in a little white dressing-gown, flying with noiseless bare feet down the staircase, and, without a word of warning, threw herself upon her mother. It was not to console her mother, but to seek her own natural refuge in this uncomprehended calamity. 'Oh, mamma!' said Norah; 'oh, mamma, mamma!' She could find no other words of consolation. Torrents of youthful tears gushed from the child's eyes. She wept for both, while Helen sat tearless. And the blinds were not down nor the shutters closed in that room, as the servants recollected with horror, and the great golden light of morn shone in.

Thus they were left undisturbed in the full day, in the sweet sunshine; scarcely knowing, in the first stupor of misery, how it was that darkness had gathered in the midst of all their world of light.

CHAPTER XII

Helen had not remarked that postscript to her husband's letter, but Dr Maurice had done so, to whom it was addressed; and while she was hiding her head and bearing the first agony of her grief without thought of anything remaining that she might yet have to bear, many things had been going on in the world outside of which Helen knew nothing. Dr Maurice had been Robert's true friend; and after that mournful morning a day and night had passed in which he did not know how to take comfort. He had no way of expressing himself as women have. He could not weep; it even seemed to him that to close out the cheerful light, as he was tempted to do (for the sight of all that brightness made his heart sick), would have been an ostentation of sorrow, a show of sentiment which he had no right to indulge in. He could not weep, but there was something else he could do; and that was to sift poor Robert's accusation, if there was any truth in it; and, if there was, pursue—to he could not tell what end—the murderers of his friend. It is the old savage way; and Dr Maurice set his teeth, and found a certain relief in the thought. He lay down on the sofa in his library, and ordered his servant to close his doors to all the world, and tried to snatch a little sleep after the watch of the previous night. But sleep would not come to him. The library was a large, lofty room, well furnished, and full with books. It was red curtained and carpeted, and the little bit of the wall which was not covered with book-cases was red too, red which looked dark and heavy in the May sunshine, but was very cozy in winter days. The one spot of brightness in the room was a picture of poor Drummond's—a young picture, one of those which he was painting while he courted Helen, the work of youth and love, at a time when the talent in him was called promise, and that which it promised was genius. This little picture caught the doctor's eye as he lay on his sofa, resting the weary frame which had known no rest all night. A tear came as he looked at it—a tear which flowed back again to its fountain, not being permitted to fall, but which did him good all the same. 'Poor fellow! he never did better than that,' Dr Maurice said to himself with a sigh; and then he closed up his eyes tight, and tried to go to sleep. Half an hour after, when he opened them again, the picture was once more the first thing he saw. 'Better!' he said, 'he never did so well. And killed by those infernal curs!' The doctor took himself off his sofa after this failure. It was of no use trying to sleep. He gathered his boots from the corner into which he had hurled them, and drew them on again. He thought he would go and have a walk. And then he remarked for the first time that though he had taken his coat off, the rest of his dress was the same as he had put on last night to go out to dinner. When he went to his room to change this, the sight of himself in the glass was a wonder to him. Was that red-eyed, dishevelled man, with glittering studs in his shirt, and a head heavy with watching and grief—was that the trim and irreproachable Dr Maurice? He gave a grin of horror and fierce mockery at himself, and then sat down in his easy-chair, and hid his face in his hands; and thus, all contorted and doubled up, went to sleep unawares. He was good for nothing that day.

The next morning, before he could go out, Mr Burton called upon him. He was the man whom Dr Maurice most wanted to see. Yet he felt himself jump as he was announced, and knew that in spite of himself his countenance had changed. Mr Burton came in undisturbed in manner or appearance, but with a broad black hatband on his hat—a band which his hatter had assured him was much broader than he had any occasion for—'deep enough for a brother.' This gave him a certain air of solemnity, as it came in in front of him. It was 'a mark of respect' which Dr Maurice had not thought of showing; and Maurice, after poor Haldane, was, as it were, Robert's next friend.

'I have come to speak to you about poor Drummond,' said Mr Burton, taking a chair. 'What a terrible business this has been! I met with him accidentally that morning—the very day it happened. I do not know when I have had such a shock!'

'You met him on the day he took his life?'

'The day he—died, Dr Maurice. I am his relative, his wife's nearest friend. Why should we speak so? Let us not be the people to judge him. He died—God knows how. It is in God's hands.'

'God knows I don't judge him,' said Dr Maurice; and there was a pause.

'I cannot hear that any one saw him later,' said Mr Burton. 'I hear from the servants at St Mary's Road that he was not there. He talked very wildly, poor fellow. I almost thought—God forgive me!—that he had been drinking. It must have been temporary insanity. It is a kind of consolation to reflect upon that now.'

The doctor said nothing. He rustled his papers about, and played impatiently with the pens and paper-cutter on his table. He bore it all until his visitor heaved a demonstrative sigh. That he could not bear.

'If you thought he spoke wildly, you might have looked after him a little,' he said. 'It was enough to make any man look wild; and you, who knew so well all about it—'

'That is the very thing. I did not know about it. I had been out of town, and had heard nothing. A concern I was so much interested in—by which I am myself a loser—'

'Do you lose much?' said Dr Maurice, looking him in the face. It was the same question poor Robert had asked, and it produced the same results. An uneasy flush came on the rich man's countenance.

'We City men do not publish our losses,' he said. 'We prefer to keep the amount of them, when we can, to ourselves. You were in yourself, I believe? Ah! I warned poor Drummond! I told him he knew nothing of business. He should have taken the advice of men who knew. How strange that an ignorant, inexperienced man, quite unaware what he was doing, should be able to ruin such a vast concern!'

'Ruin such a vast concern!' Dr Maurice repeated, stupefied. 'Who?—Drummond? This is a serious moment and a strangely-chosen subject for a jest. I can't suppose that you take me for a fool—'

'We have all been fools, letting him play with edge tools,' said Mr Burton, almost sharply. 'Golden tells me he would never take advice. Golden says—'

'Golden! where is he?' cried Maurice. 'The fellow who absconded? By Jove, tell me but where to lay my hands on him—'

'Softly,' said Mr Burton, putting his hand on Maurice's arm, with an air of soothing him which made the doctor's blood boil. 'Softly, doctor. He is to be found where he always was, at the office, making the best he can of a terribly bad job, looking fifteen years older, poor fellow. Where are you going? Let me have my ten minutes first!'

'I am going to get hold of him, the swindler!' cried Maurice, ringing the bell furiously. 'John, let the brougham be brought round directly. My God! if I was not the most moderate man in existence I should say murderer too. Golden says, forsooth! We shall see what he will say before a jury—'

'My dear Dr Maurice—listen a little—take care what you are doing. Golden is as honourable a man as you or I—'

'Speak for yourself,' said the doctor roughly. 'He has absconded—that's the word. It was in the papers yesterday morning; and it was the answer I myself received at the office. Golden, indeed! If you're a friend of Drummond's, you will come with me and give that fellow into custody. This is no time for courtesy now.'

'How glad I am I came!' said Mr Burton. 'You have not seen, then, what is in the papers to-day? Dr Maurice, you must listen to me; this is simply madness. Golden, poor fellow, has been very nearly made the victim of his own unsuspicious character. Don't be impatient, but listen. When I tell you he was simply absent on Tuesday on his own affairs—gone down to the country, as I might have been myself, if not, alas! as I sometimes think, sent out of the way. The news of Shenken's bankruptcy arrived that morning. Well, I don't mean to say Drummond could have helped that; but he seized the opportunity. Heaven knows how sorry I am to suggest such a thing; it has nearly broken Golden's heart. But these are the facts; what can you make of them? Maurice, listen to me. What did he go and do that for? He was still a young man; he had his profession. If he could have faced the world, why did he do that?'

Dr Maurice replied with an oath. I can make no excuse for him. He stood on his own hearth, with his hand clenched, and blasphemed. There are moments in which a man must either do that, or go down upon his knees and appeal to God, who now-a-days sends no lightning from heaven to kill the slayer of men's souls where he stands. The doctor saw it all as if by a gleam of that same lightning which he invoked in vain. He saw the spider's web they had woven, the way of escape for themselves which they had built over the body of the man who was dead, and could not say a word in reply. But his friend could not find a word to say. Scorn, rage, stupefaction, came upon him. It was so false, so incredible in its falsity. He could no more have defended Robert from such an accusation than he would have defended himself from the charge of having murdered him. But it would be believed: the world did not know any better. He could not say another word—such a horror and disgust came over him, such a sickening sense of the power of falsehood, the feebleness of manifest, unprovable truth.

'This is not a becoming way in which to treat such a subject,' said Mr Burton, rising too. 'No subject could be more painful to me. I feel almost as if, indirectly, I myself was to blame. It was I who introduced him into the concern. I am a busy man, and I have a great deal on my hands, but could I have foreseen what was preparing for Rivers's, my own interest should have gone to the wall. And that he should be my own relation too—my cousin's husband! Ah, poor Helen, what a mistake she made!'

'Have you nearly done, sir?' said the doctor fiercely.

'I shall have done at once, if what I say is received with incivility,' said Mr Burton, with spirit. 'It was to prevent any extension of the scandal that I came here.'

'There are some occasions upon which civility is impossible,' said Maurice. 'I happen to know Robert Drummond; which I hope you don't, for your own sake. And, remember, a great many people know him besides me. I mean no incivility when I say that I don't believe one word of this, Mr Burton; and that is all I have to say about it. Not one word—'

'You mean, I lie!'

'I mean nothing of the sort. I hope you are deceived. I mean that this fellow Golden is an atrocious scoundrel, and he lies, if you will. And having said that, I have not another word to say.'

Then they both stopped short, looking at each other. A momentary doubt was, perhaps, in Burton's mind what to say next—whether to pursue the subject or to let it drop. But no doubt was in Maurice's. He stood rigid, with his back to the vacant fireplace, retired within himself. 'It is very warm,' he said; 'not favourable weather for walking. Can I set you down anywhere? I see my brougham has come round.'

'Thanks,' said the other shortly. And then he added, 'Dr Maurice, you have taken things in a manner very different from what I expected. I thought you would take an interest in saving our poor friend's memory as far as we can—'

'I take no interest in it, sir, whatever.'

'And the feelings of his widow,' said Mr Burton. 'Well, well, very well. Friendship is such a wide word—sometimes meaning so much, sometimes so little. I suppose I must do the best I can for poor Helen by myself, and in my own way.'

The obdurate doctor bowed. He held fast by his formula. He had not another word to say.

'In that case I need not trouble you any longer,' said Mr Burton. But when he was on his way to the door he paused and turned round. 'She is not likely to be reading the papers just now,' he said, 'and I hope I may depend on you not to let these unfortunate particulars, or anything about it, come to the ears of Mrs Drummond. I should like her to be saved that if possible. She will have enough to bear.'

'I shall not tell Mrs Drummond,' said the doctor. And then the door opened and closed, and the visitor was gone.

The brougham stood before Dr Maurice's window for a long time that morning. The old coachman grumbled, broiling on the box; the horses grumbled, pawing with restless feet, and switching the flies off with more and more impatient swingings of their tails. John grumbled indoors, who could not 'set things straight' until his master was out of the way. But the doctor neglected them all. Not one of all the four, horses or men, would have changed places with him could they have seen him poring over the newspaper, which he had not cared to look at that morning, with the wrinkles drawn together on his forehead. There was fury in his soul, that indignation beyond words, beyond self-command, with which a man perceives the rise and growth of a wrong which is beyond his setting right—a lie which he can only ineffectively contradict, struggle, or rage against, but cannot drive out of the minds of men. They had it in their own hands to say what they would. Dr Maurice knew that during all the past winter his friend had been drawn into the work of the bank. He had even cautioned Robert, though in ignorance of the extent of his danger. He had said, 'Don't forget that you are unaccustomed to the excitements of business. They will hurt you, though they don't touch the others. It is not your trade.' These words came back to his mind with the bitterest sense of that absence of foresight which is common to man. 'If I had but known!' he said. And then he remembered, with a bitter smile, his visit to Dr Bradcliffe, his request to him to see poor Drummond 'accidentally,' his dread for his friend's brain. This it was which had affected poor Robert, worse than disease, worse than madness; for in madness or disease there would have been no human agency to blame.

The papers, as Burton had said, were full of this exciting story. Outside in the very streets there were great placards up with headings in immense capitals, 'Great Bankruptcy in the City.—Suicide of a Bank Director.' The absconding of the manager, which had been the news the day before, was thrown into the background by this new fact, which was so much more tragical and important. 'The latest information' was given by some in a Second Edition, so widespread was the commotion produced by the catastrophe; and even those of the public who did not care much for Rivers's, cared for the exciting tale, or for the fate of the unhappy professional man who had rashly involved himself in business, and ruined not only himself, but so many more. The story was so dramatically complete that public opinion decided upon it at once. It did not even want the grieved, indignant letter which Mr Golden, injured man, wrote to the Times, begging that the report against him should be contradicted. This letter was printed in large type, and its tone was admirable. 'I will not prejudge any man, more especially one whose premature end has thrown a cloud of horror over the unfortunate business transactions of the bank with which I have had the honour of being connected for fifteen years,' Mr Golden wrote, 'but I cannot permit my temporary, innocent, and much-regretted absence to be construed into an evidence that I had deserted my post. With the help of Providence, I will never desert it, so long as I can entertain the hope of saving from the wreck a shilling of the shareholders' money.' It was a very good letter, very creditable to Mr Golden; and everybody had read it, and accepted it as gospel, before Dr Maurice got his hand upon it. In the Daily Semaphore, which the doctor did not see, there was already an article on the subject, very eloquent and slightly discursive, insisting strongly upon the wickedness and folly of men who without capital, or even knowledge of business, thus ventured to play with the very existence of thousands of people. 'Could the unfortunate man who has hidden his shame in a watery grave look up this morning from that turbid bed and see the many homes which he has filled with desolation, who can doubt that the worst and deepest hell fabled by the great Italian poet would lose something of its intensity in comparison?—the ineffectual fires would pale; a deeper and a more terrible doom would be that of looking on at all the misery—all the ruined households and broken hearts which cry out to-day over all England for justice on their destroyer.' Fortunately Dr Maurice did not read this article; but he did read the Times and its editorial comments. 'There can be little doubt,' that journal said, 'that the accidental absence of Mr Golden, the manager, whose letter explaining all the circumstances will be found in another column, determined Drummond to his final movement. It left him time to secure the falsified books, and remove all evidence of his guilt. It is not for us to explain by what caprice of despair, after taking all this trouble, the unhappy man should have been driven to self-destruction. The workings of a mind in such an unnatural condition are too mysterious to be discussed here. Perhaps he felt that when all was done, death was the only complete exemption from those penalties which follow the evil-doer on this earth. We can only record the fact; we cannot explain the cause. The manager and the remaining directors, hastily summoned to meet the emergency, have been labouring ever since, we understand, with the help of a well-known accountant, to make up the accounts of the company, as well as that can be done in the absence of the books which there is every reason to suppose were abstracted by Drummond before he left the office. It has been suggested that the river should be dragged for them as well as for the body of the unhappy man, which up to this time has not been recovered. But we doubt much whether, even should such a work be successful, the books would be legible after an immersion even of two or three days. We believe that no one, even the persons most concerned, are yet able to form an estimate of the number of persons to whom this lamentable occurrence will be ruin.'

Dr Maurice put down the paper with a gleam in his face of that awful and heart-rending rage which indignation is apt to rise into when it feels itself most impotent. What could he do to stop such a slander? He could contradict it; he could say, 'I know Robert Drummond; he was utterly incapable of this baseness.' Alas! who was he that the world should take his word for it? He might bring a counter-charge against Golden; he might accuse him of abstracting the books, and being the author of all the mischief; but what proof had he to substantiate his accusation? He had no evidence—not a hair's-breadth. He could not prove, though he believed, that this was all a scheme suggested to the plotters, if there were more than one, or to Golden himself, if he were alone in his villany, by the unlooked-for chance of Drummond's suicide. This was what he believed. All the more for the horrible vraisemblance of the story, could he see the steps by which it had been put together. Golden had absconded, taking with him everything that was damning in the way of books. He had lain hidden somewhere near at hand waiting an opportunity to get away. He had heard of poor Drummond's death, and an opportunity of a different kind, a devilish yet brilliantly successful way of escape, had suddenly appeared for him. All this burst upon Dr Maurice as by a revelation while he sat with those papers before him gnawing his nails and clutching the leading journal as if it had been Golden's throat. He saw it all. It came out before him like a design in phosphorus, twinkling and glowing through the darkness. He was sure of it; but—what to do?

This man had a touch in him of the antique friendship—the bond for which men have encountered all odds and dared death, and been happy in their sacrifice. But even disinterestedness, even devotion, do not give a man the mental power to meet such foes, or to frame a plan by which to bring them to confusion. He grew himself confused with the thought. He could not make out what to do first—how he should begin. He had forgotten how the hours went   what time of the day it was—while he pondered these subjects. The fire in his veins, instead of acting as a simple stimulant, acted upon him like intoxication. His brain reeled under the pressure. 'Will you have lunch, sir, before you go out?' said John, with restrained wrath, but a pretence of stateliness. 'Lunch!—how dare you come into my room, sir, before I ring!' cried his master, waking up and looking at him with what seemed to John murderous eyes. And then he sprang up, tore the papers into little pieces, crammed them into the fireplace, and, seizing his hat, rushed out to the carriage. The coachman was nodding softly on the box. The heat, and the stillness, and the monotony had triumphed even over the propriety of a man who knew all London, he was fond of saying, as well as he knew his own hands. The coachman almost dropped from his box when Maurice, throwing the door of the little carriage open, startled him suddenly from his slumber. The horses, which were half asleep too, woke also with much jarring of harness and prancing of hoof and head.

'To the Times office,' was what the doctor said. He could not go and clutch that villain by the throat, though that might be the best way. It was another kind of lion which he was about to beard in his den.

None of the persons chiefly concerned in this history, except himself, knew as yet whether Reginald Burton was good or bad. But one thing is certain, that there were good intentions in his mind when he startled Dr Maurice with this extraordinary tale. He had a very busy morning, driving from place to place in his hansom, giving up so many hours of his day without much complaint. He had expected Maurice to know what the papers would have told him, had he been less overwhelmed with the event itself of which they gave so strange a version, and he had intended to have a friendly consultation with him about Mrs Drummond's means of living, and what was to be done for her. Something must be done for her, there was no doubt about that. She could not be allowed to starve. She was his own cousin, once Helen Burton; and, no doubt, by this time she had found out her great mistake. It must not be supposed that this thought brought with it any lingering fondness of recollection, any touch of the old love with which he himself had once looked upon her. It would have been highly improper had it done anything of the kind. He had a Mrs Burton of his own, who of course possessed his entire affections, and he was not a man to indulge in any illegitimate emotion. But still he had been thinking much of Helen since this bewildering event occurred. It was an event which had taken him quite by surprise. He did not understand it. He felt that he himself could never be in such despair, could never take 'a step so rash'— the only step a man could take which left no room for repentance. It had been providential, no doubt, for some things. But Helen had been in his mind since ever he had time to think. There was a little glitter in his eye, a little complacent curl about the corners of his mouth, as he thought of her, and her destitute condition, and her helplessness. What a mistake she had made! She had chosen a wretched painter, without a penny, instead of himself. And this was what it had come to. Now at least she must have found out what a fool she had been. But yet he intended to be good to her in his way. He vowed to himself, with perhaps some secret compunction in the depths of his heart, that if she would let him he would be very good to her. Nor was Helen the only person to whom he intended to be good. He went to the Haldanes as well, with kindest sympathy and offers of help. 'Perhaps you may think I was to blame in recommending such an investment of your money?' he said to Stephen, with that blunt honesty which charms so many people. 'But my first thought was of you when I heard of the crash. I wish I had bitten my tongue out sooner than recommended it. The first people who came into my head were my cousin Helen and you.'

Dismay and trouble were in the Haldanes' little house. They had not recovered from the shock. They were like three ghosts—each endeavouring to hide the blackness from each other which had fallen upon their souls.—Miss Jane and her mother, however, had begun to get a little relief in talking over the great misery which had fallen upon them. They had filled the room with newspapers, in which they devoured every scrap of news which bore on that one subject. They sat apart in a corner and read them to each other, while Stephen closed his poor sad eyes and withdrew into himself. It was the only retirement he had, his only way of escape from the monotonous details of their family life, and the constant presence of his nurses and attendants. This man had such attendants—unwearying, uncomplaining, always ready whatever he wanted, giving up their lives to his service—as few men have; and yet there were moments when he would have given the world to be free of them,—now and then, for half an hour, to be able to be alone. He had been sitting thus in his oratory, his place of retirement having shut his doors, and gone into his chamber by that single action of closing his eyes, when Mr Burton came in. The women had been reading those papers to him till he had called to them to stop. They had made his heart sore, as our hearts are being made sore now by tales of wrong and misery which we cannot help, cannot stop, can do nothing but weep for, or listen to with hearts that burn and bleed. Stephen Haldane's heart was so—it was sore, quivering with the stroke it had sustained, feeling as if it would burst out of his breast.

People say that much invoked and described organ is good only for tough physical uses, and knows no sentiment; but surely such people have never had a sore heart.

Poor Stephen's heart was sore: he could feel the great wound in it through which the life-blood stole. Yesterday he had been stupefied. To-day he had begun to wonder why, if a sacrifice was needed, it should not have been him? He who was good for nothing, a burden on the earth; and not Robert, the kindest, truest—God bless him! yes, God bless him down yonder at the bottom of the river, down with Dives in a deeper depth if that might be—anywhere, everywhere, even in hell or purgatory, God bless him! this was what his friend said, not afraid. And the women in the corner, in the mean while, read all the details, every one—about the dragging of the river, about the missing books, about Mr Golden, who had been so wronged. Mrs Haldane believed it every word, having a dread of human nature and a great confidence in the newspapers; but Miss Jane was tormented with an independent opinion, and hesitated and could not believe. It had almost distracted their attention from the fact which there could be no question about, which all knew for certain—their own ruin. Rivers's had stopped payment, whoever was in fault, and everything this family had—their capital, their income, everything was gone. It had stunned them all the first day, but now they were beginning to call together their forces and live again; and when Mr Burton made the little sympathetic speech above recorded it went to their hearts.

'I am sure it is very kind, very kind of you to say so,' said Mrs Haldane. 'We never thought of blaming—you.'

'I don't go so far as that,' said Miss Jane. 'I always speak my mind. I blame everybody, mother; one for one thing, one for another. There is nobody that has taken thought for Stephen, not one. Stephen ought to have been considered, and that he was not able to move about and see to things for himself like other men.'

'It is very true, it is very true!' said Mr Burton, sighing. He shook his head, and he made a little movement of his hand, as if deprecating blame. He held up his hat with the mourning band upon it, and looked as if he might have wept. 'When you consider all that has happened,' he said in a low tone of apology. 'Some who have been in fault have paid for it dearly, at least—'

It was Stephen's voice which broke in upon this apology, in a tone as different as could be imagined—high-pitched, almost harsh. When he was the popular minister of Ormond Street Chapel it was one of the standing remarks made by his people to strangers, 'Has not he a beautiful voice?' But at this moment all the tunefulness and softness had gone out of it. 'Mr Burton,' he said, 'what do you mean to do to vindicate Drummond? It seems to me that that comes first.'

'To vindicate Drummond!' Mr Burton looked up with a sudden start, and then he added hurriedly, with an impetuosity which secured the two women to his side, 'Haldane, you are too good for this world. Don't let us speak of Drummond. I will forgive him—if I can.'

'How much have you to forgive him?' said the preacher. Once more, how much? By this time Mr Burton felt that he had a right to be angry with the question.

'How much?' he said; 'really I don't feel it necessary to go into my own business affairs with everybody who has a curiosity to know. I am willing to allow that my losses are as nothing to yours. Pray don't let us go into this question, for I don't want to lose my temper. I came to offer any assistance that was in my power—to you.'

'Oh, Mr Burton, Stephen is infatuated about that miserable man,' said the mother; 'he cannot see harm in him; and even now, when he has taken his own life and proved himself to be—'

'Stephen has a right to stand up for his friend,' said Miss Jane. 'If I had time I would stand up for him too; but Stephen's comfort has to be thought of first. Mr Burton, the best assistance you could give us would be to get me something to do. I can't be a governess, and needlework does not pay; neither does teaching, for that matter, even if I could do it. I am a good housekeeper, though I say it. I can keep accounts with anybody. I am not a bad cook even. And I'm past forty, and never was pretty in my life, so that I don't see it matters whether I am a woman or a man. I don't care what I do or where I go, so long as I can earn some money. Can you help me to that? Don't groan, Stephen; do you think I mind it? and don't you smile, Mr Burton. I am in earnest for my part.'

Stephen had groaned in his helplessness. Mr Burton smiled in his superiority, in his amused politeness of contempt for the plain woman past forty. 'We can't let you say that,' he answered jocosely, with a look at her which reminded Miss Jane that she was a woman after all, and filled her with suppressed fury. But what did such covert insult matter? It did not harm her; and the man who sneered at her homeliness might help her to work for her brother, which was the actual matter in hand.

'It is very difficult to know of such situations for ladies,' said Mr Burton. 'If anything should turn up, of course—but I fear it would not do to depend upon that.'

'Stephen has his pension from the chapel,' said Miss Jane. She was not delicate about these items, but stated her case loudly and plainly, without even considering what Stephen's feelings might be. 'It was to last for five years, and nearly three of them are gone; and he has fifty pounds a year for the Magazine— that is not much Mr Burton, for all the trouble; they might increase that. And mother and I are trying to let the house furnished, which would always be something. We could remove into lodgings, and if nothing more is to be got, of course we must do upon what we have.'

Here Mr Burton cast a look upon the invalid who was surrounded by so many contrivances of comfort. It was a compassionate glance, but it stung poor Stephen. 'Don't think of me,' he said hoarsely; 'my wants, though I look such a burden upon everybody, are not many after all. Don't think of me.'

'We could do with what we have,' Miss Jane went on—she was so practical, she rode over her brother's susceptibilities and ignored them, which perhaps was the best thing that could have been done—'if you could help us with a tenant for our house, Mr Burton, or get the Magazine committee to give him a little more than fifty pounds. The work it is! what with writing—and I am sure he writes half of it himself— and reading those odious manuscripts which ruin his eyes, and correcting proofs, and all that. It is a shame that he has only fifty pounds—'

'But he need not take so much trouble unless he likes, Jane,' said Mrs Haldane, shaking her head. 'I liked it as it was.'

'Never mind, mother; Stephen knows best, and it is him that we have got to consider. Now, Mr Burton, here is what you can do for us—I should not have asked anything, but since you have offered, I suppose you mean it—something for me to do, or some one to take the house, or a little more money for the Magazine. Then we could do. I don't like anything that is vague. I suppose you prefer that I should tell you plain?'

'To be sure,' said Mr Burton; and he smiled, looking at her with that mixture of contemptuous amusement and dislike with which a plain middle-aged woman so often inspires a vulgar-minded man. That the women who want to work are always old hags, was one of the articles of his creed; and here was an illustration. Miss Jane troubled herself very little about his amusement or his contempt. She did not much believe in his good-will. But if he did mean it, why, it was best to take advantage of his offer. This was her practical view of the subject. Mr Burton turned from her to Stephen, who had taken no part in the talk. Necessity had taught to the sick man its stern philosophy. He had to listen to such discussions twenty times in a day, and he had steeled his heart to hear them, and make no sign.

'What would you say to life in the country?' he said. 'The little help I came to offer in these sad circumstances is not in any of the ways Miss Jane suggests. I don't know anybody that wants to take just this kind of house:' and he glanced round at it with a smile. He to know a possible tenant for such a nutshell! 'And I don't know any situation that would suit your sister, though I am sure she would be invaluable. My father-in-law is the man to speak about the Magazine business. Possibly he could manage that. But what I would offer you if you like, would be a lodging in the country. I have a house down at Dura, which is of no use to me. There is good air and a garden, and all that. You are as welcome as possible if you like to come.'

'A house in the country,' said Mrs Haldane. 'Oh, my boy! Oh, Mr Burton! he might get well there.'

Poor soul! it was her delusion that Stephen was to get well. She took up this new hope with eyes which, old as they were, flashed out with brightness and consolation. 'What will all our losses matter if Stephen gets well?' she went on, beginning to cry. And Miss Jane rose up hastily and went away with a tremulous harshness, shutting her lips up tight, to the other side of the room, to get her work, which she had been neglecting. Miss Jane was like a man in this, that she could not bear tears. She set her face against them, holding herself in, lest she too might have been tempted to join. Of all the subjects of discussion in this world, Stephen's recovery was the only one she could not bear; for she loved her brother like a poet, like a starved and frozen woman who has had but one love in her life.

The old mother was more manageable to Mr Burton's mind than Miss Jane. Her tears and gratitude restored him to what he felt was his proper place,—that of a benefactor and guardian angel. He sat for half an hour longer, and told Mrs Haldane all about the favour he was willing to confer. 'It is close to the gates of my own house, but you must not think that will be an annoyance to us,' he said. 'On the contrary, I don't mean to tell my father-in-law till he sees you there. It will be a pleasant surprise for him. He has always taken so much interest in Haldane. Don't say anything, I beg. I am very glad you should have it, and I hope it will make you feel this dreadful calamity less. Ah yes; it is wretched for us; but what must it be for my poor cousin? I am going to see her now.'

'I don't know her,' said Mrs Haldane. 'She has called at the door to ask for Stephen, very regular. That I suppose was because of the friendship between—but I have only seen her once or twice on a formal call. If all is true that I hear, she will take it hard, being a proud woman. Oh! pride's sinful at the best of times; but in a time like this—'

'Mother!'

'Yes, Stephen, I know; and I am sure I would not for the world say a word against friends of yours; but—'

'I must go now,' said Mr Burton, rising. 'Good-bye, Haldane. I will write to you about the house, and when you can come in. On second thoughts, I will not prevent you from mentioning it to Mr Baldwin, if you please. He is sure to ask what you are going to do, and he will be glad to know.'

He went out from Victoria Villas pleased with himself. He had been very good to these people, who really were nothing to him. He was not even a Dissenter, but a staunch Churchman, and had no sympathy for the sick minister. What was his motive, then? But it was his wife who made it her business to investigate his motives, and we may wait for the result of her examination. All this was easy enough. The kindness he had offered was one which would cost him little, and he had not suffered in this interview as he had done in that which preceded it. But now he had occasion for all his strength; now came the tug of war, the real strain. He was going to see Helen. She had been but three days a widow, and no doubt would be in the depth of that darkness which is the recognized accompaniment of grief. Would she see him? Could she have seen the papers, or heard any echo of their news? On this point he was nervous. Before he went to St Mary's Road, though it was close at hand, he went to the nearest hotel, and had a glass of wine and a biscuit. For such a visit he required all his strength.

But these precautions were unnecessary. The shutters were all closed in St Mary's Road. The lilacs were waving their plumy fragrant branches over a door which no one entered. Mrs Drummond was at home, but saw no one. Even when the maid carried his message to her, the answer was that she could see no one, that she was quite well, and required nothing. 'Not even the clergyman, sir,' said the maid. 'He's been, but she would not see him. She is as white as my apron, and her poor hands you could see the light through 'em. We all think as she'll die too.'

'Does she read the papers?' said Mr Burton anxiously. He was relieved when the woman said 'No.' He gave her half-a-crown, and bade her admit none to the house till he came again. Rebecca promised and curtsied, and went back to the kitchen to finish reading that article in the Daily Semaphore. The fact that it was 'master' who was there called 'this unfortunate man' and 'this unhappy wretch,' gave the strongest zest to it. 'La! to think he could have had all that on his mind,' they said to each other. George was the only one who considered it might be 'a made-up story,' and he was believed to say so more from 'contrariness,' and a desire to set up for superior wisdom, than because he had any real doubt on the subject. 'A person may say a thing, but I never heard of one yet as would go for to put it in print, if it wasn't true,' was Rebecca's comment. 'I'm sorry for poor master, all the same,' said Jane the housemaid, who was tender-hearted, and who had put on an old black gown of her own accord. The servants were not to get mourning, which was something unheard of; and they had all received notice, and, as soon as Mrs Drummond was able to move, were to go away.

For that matter, Helen was able to move then—able to go to the end of the earth, as she felt with a certain horror of herself. It is so natural to suppose that physical weakness should come in the train of grief; but often it does not, and the elastic delicate strength of Helen's frame resisted all the influences of her sorrow. She scarcely ate at all; she slept little; the world had grown to her one great sea of darkness and pain and desolation: and yet she could not lie down and die as she had thought she would, but felt such a current of feverish energy in all her veins as she had never felt before. She could have done anything—laboured, travelled, worked with her hands, fought even, not like a man, but like twenty men. She was conscious of this, and it grieved and horrified her. She felt as a woman brought up in conventional proprieties would naturally feel, that her health ought to have been affected, that her strength should have failed her. But it had not done so. Her grief inflamed her rather, and set her heart on fire. Even now, in these early days, when custom decreed that she ought to be incapable of exertion, 'keeping her bed,' she felt herself in possession of a very flood of energy and excited strength. She was miserable, but she was not weak. She shut herself up in the darkened house all day, but half the night would walk about in her garden, in her despair, trying to tame down the wild life which had come with calamity. Poor little Norah crept about everywhere after her, and lay watching with great wide-open eyes, through the silvery half-darkness of the summer night, till she should come to bed. But Norah was not old enough to understand her mother, and was herself half frightened by this extraordinary change in her, which affected the child's imagination more than the simple disappearance of her father did, though she wept and longed for him with a dreary sense that unless he came back life never could be as of old, and that he would never, never come back. But all the day long Mrs Drummond sat in her darkened room, and 'was not able to see any one.' She endured the vigil, and would have done so, if she had died of it. That was what was called 'proper respect:' it was called the conventional necessity of the moment. Mr Burton called again and again, but it was more than a fortnight before he was admitted. And in the mean time he too had certain preparations to go through.

CHAPTER XIV

Mr Burton was a man who was accustomed in his own house to have, in a great degree, his own way; but this was not because his wife was disinclined to hold, or incapable of forming, an opinion of her own. On the contrary, it was because he was rather afraid of her than otherwise, and thought twice before he promulgated any sentiments or started any plan which was likely to be in opposition to hers. But he had neither consulted her, nor, indeed, thought much of what she would say, in the sudden proposal he had made to the Haldanes. He was not a hasty man; but Dr Maurice's indignation had made an impression upon him, and he had felt all at once that in going to the Haldanes and to Helen, he must not, if he would preserve his own character, go with merely empty sympathy, but must show practically his pity for them. It was perhaps the only time in his life that he had acted upon a hasty idea without taking time to consider; and a chill doubt, as to what Clara would say, was in his mind as he turned his face homewards. Dura was about twenty miles from town, in the heart of one of the leafiest of English counties; the station was a mile and a half from the great house, half of which distance, however, was avenue; and Mr Burton's phaeton, with the two greys—horses which matched to a hair, and were not equalled in the stables of any potentate in the county—was waiting for him when the train arrived. He liked to drive home in this glorious way, rousing the village folks and acting as a timepiece for them, just as he liked the great dinner-bell, which the old Harcourts sounded only on great occasions, to be rung every day, letting the whole neighbourhood know that their local lord, their superior, the master of the great house, was going to dinner. He liked the thought that his return was an event in the place almost justifying the erection of a standard, as it was erected in a royal castle not very far off, when the sovereign went and came. Our rich man had not gone so far as yet, but he would have liked it, and felt it natural. The village of Dura was like a collection of beads threaded on the long white thread of road which ran from the station to the house—and occupied the greater part of the space, with single houses straggling at either end, and a cluster in the middle. The straggling houses at the end next the station were white villas, built for people whose business was in town, and who came home to dinner by the same train which brought Mr Burton, though their arrival was less imposing; but where the clump of dwelling-places thickened, the houses toned down into old-fashioned, deeply-lichened brick, with here and there a thatched roof to deepen, or a white-washed gable to relieve, the composition. At the end nearest the great house the village made a respectful pause, and turned off along a slanting path, which showed the tower of the church behind over the trees. The rectory, however, a pretty house buried in shrubberies, fronted the high road with modest confidence; and opposite it was another dwelling-place, in front of which Mr Burton drew up his horses for a moment, inspecting it with a careful and anxious eye. His heart beat a little quicker as he looked. His own gate was in sight, and these were the very grounds of Dura House, into which the large walled garden of this one intruded like a square wedge. In front there were no shrubberies, no garden, nothing to divide it from the road. A double row of pollard limes—one on the edge of the foot-path, one close to the house—indicated and shaded, but did not separate it from the common way. The second row of limes was level with the fence of the Dura grounds, and one row of white flagstones lay between them and the two white steps, the green door, and shining brass knocker of the Gatehouse. It was a house which had been built in the reign of the first George, of red brick, with a great many windows, three-storied, and crowned by a pediment, with that curious mixture of the useful and (supposed) ornamental, which by this time has come to look almost picturesque by reason of age. It had been built for the mother of one of the old Harcourts, a good woman who had been born the Rector's daughter of the place, and loved it and its vicinity, and the sight of its comings and goings. This was the origin of the Gatehouse; but since the days of Mrs Dunstable Harcourt it had rarely been inhabited by any of the family, and had been a trouble more than an advantage to them. It was too near the hall to be inhabited by strangers, and people do not always like to establish their own poor relations and dependents at their very gates. As the Harcourts dwindled and money became important to them, they let it at a small rate to a maiden household, two or three old ladies of limited means, and blood as blue as their own. And when Dura ceased, except on county maps, to be Harcourt-Dura, and passed into the hands of the rich merchant, he, too, found the Gatehouse a nuisance. There had been talk of pulling it down, but that would have been waste; and there had been attempts made to let it to 'a suitable tenant,' but no suitable tenant had been found. Genteel old ladies of blue blood had not found the vicinity of the Burtons a comfort to them as they did that of the Harcourts. And there it stood empty, echoing, void, a place where the homeless might be sheltered. Did Mr Burton's heart glow with benevolent warmth as he paused, drawing up his greys, and looked at it, with all its windows twinkling in the sun? To one of these windows a woman came forward at the sound of his pause, and, putting her face close to the small pane, looked out at him wondering. He gave her a nod, and sighed; and then flourished his whip, and the greys flew on. In another moment they had turned into the avenue and went dashing up the gentle ascent. It was a pretty avenue, though the trees were not so old as most of the Dura trees. The sunset gleamed through it, slanting down under the lowest branches, scattering the brown mossy undergrowth with lumps of gold. A little pleasant tricksy wind shook the branches and dashed little mimic showers of rain in the master's face: for it had been raining in the afternoon, and the air was fresh and full of a hundred nameless odours; but Mr Burton gave forth another big sigh before he reached the house. He was a little afraid of what his wife would say, and he was afraid of what he had done.

He did not say anything about it, however, till dinner was over. The most propitious moment seemed that gentle hour of dessert, when the inner man is strengthened and comforted, and there is time to dally over the poetic part of the meal—not that either of the Burtons were poetical. They were alone, not even the children being with them, for Mrs Burton disapproved of children coming to dessert; but all the same, she was beautifully dressed; he liked it, and so did she. She made very little difference in this particular between her most imposing dinner parties and those evenings which she spent tête-à-tête with her husband. When her aunts, who had old-fashioned ideas about extravagance, remonstrated with her, she defended herself, saying she could afford it, and he liked to see her well dressed. Mr Burton hated to have any scrap of capital unemployed; and the only interest you could get from your jewels was the pleasure of wearing them, and seeing them worn, he said. So Mrs Burton dined with her husband in a costume which a French lady of fashion would have considered appropriate to a ball or royal reception, with naked shoulders and arms, and lace and ornaments. Madame la Duchesse might have thought it much too fine, but Mrs Burton did not. She was a pale little woman, small and thin, but not without beauty. Her hair was not very abundant, but it was exquisitely smooth and neat. Her uncovered shoulders were white, and her arms round and well-formed; and she had clear blue eyes, so much brighter than anybody expected, that they took the world by surprise: they were cold in their expression, but they were full of intelligence, and a hundred times more vivid and striking than anything else about her, so that everybody observed and admired Mrs Burton's eyes.

'What has been going on to-day? What have you been doing?' she asked, when the servants went away. The question sounded affectionate, and showed at least that there was confidence between the husband and wife.

'Very much as usual,' Mr Burton said, with colloquial ease; and then he stopped and cleared his throat. 'But for my own part I have done something rather foolish,' he said, with an almost imperceptible tremor in his voice.

'Indeed?' She gave a quick glance up at him; but she was not excited, and went on calmly eating her strawberries. He was not the kind of man of whose foolish actions a wife is afraid.

'I have been to see the Haldanes to-day,' he said, once more clearing his throat; 'and I have been to Helen Drummond's, but did not see her. The one, of course, I did out of regard for your father; the other—I was so distressed by the sight of that poor fellow in his helplessness, that I acted on impulse, Clara. I know it's a foolish thing to do. I said to myself, here are two families cast out of house and home, and there is the Gatehouse—'

'The Gatehouse!'

'Yes, I was afraid you would be startled; but reflect a moment: it is of no use to us. We have got nobody to occupy it. You know, indeed, how alarmed you were when your aunt Louisa took a fancy to it; and I have tried for a tenant in vain. Then, on the other hand, one cannot but be sorry for these poor people. Helen is my cousin; she has no nearer friend than I am. And your father is so much interested in the Haldanes—'

'I don't quite understand,' said Mrs Burton, with undisturbed composure; 'my father's interest in the Haldanes has nothing to do with the Gatehouse. Are they to live there?'

'That was what I thought,' said her husband, 'but not, of course, if you have any serious dislike to it—not if you decidedly object—'

'Why should I decidedly object?' she said. 'I should if you were bringing them to live with me; but otherwise—It is not at all suitable—they will not be happy there. It will be a great nuisance to us. As it is, strangers rather admire it—it looks old-fashioned and pleasant; but if they made a squalid place of it, dirty windows, and cooking all over the house—'

'So far as my cousin is concerned, you could have nothing of that kind to fear,' said Mr Burton, ceasing to be apologetic. He put a slight emphasis on the word my; perhaps upon this point he would not have been sorry to provoke his wife, but Clara Burton would not gratify her husband by any show of jealousy. She was not jealous, she was thinking solely of appearances, and of the possible decadence of the Gatehouse.

'Besides, Susan must stay,' he continued, after a pause; 'she must remain in charge; the house must be kept as it ought to be. If that is your only objection, Clara—'

'I have made no objection at all,' said Mrs Burton; and then she broke into a dry little laugh. 'What a curious establishment it will be—an old broken-down nurserymaid, a Dissenting minister, and your cousin! Mr Burton, will she like it? I cannot say that I should feel proud if it were offered to me.'

His face flushed a little. He was not anxious himself to spare Helen's feelings. If he had found an opportunity, it would have been agreeable to him to remind her that she had made a mistake; but she was his own relation, and instinct prompted him to protect her from his wife.

'Helen is too poor to allow herself to think whether she likes it or not,' he said.

His wife gave a sharp glance at him across the table. What did he mean? Did he intend to be kind, or to insult the desolate woman? Clara asked herself the question as a philosophical question, not because she cared.

'And is your cousin willing to accept it from you, after—that story?' she said.

'What story? You mean about her husband. It is not my story. I have nothing to do with it; and even if I had, surely it is the man who does wrong, not the man who tells it, that should have the blame; besides, she does not know.'

'Ah, that is the safest,' said Clara. 'I think it is a very strange story, Mr Burton. It may be true, but it is not like the truth.'

'I have nothing to do with it,' he exclaimed. He spoke hotly, with a swelling of the veins on his temples. 'There are points of view in which his death was very providential,' he said.

And once more Clara gave him a sharp glance.

'It was the angel who watches over Mr Golden that provided the boat, no doubt,' she answered, with a contraction of her lips; then fell back into the former topic with perfect calm. 'I should insist upon the house being kept clean and nice,' she said, as she rose to go away.

'Surely—surely; and you may tell your father when you write, that poor Haldane is so far provided for.' He got up to open the door for her, and, detaining her for a moment, stooped down and kissed her forehead. 'I am so much obliged to you, Clara, for consenting so kindly,' he said.

A faint little cold smile came upon her face. She had been his wife for a dozen years; but in her heart she was contemptuous of the kiss which he gave her, as if she had been a child, as a reward for her acquiescence. It is to be supposed that she loved him after her fashion. She had married him of her free will, and had never quarrelled with him once in all their married life. But yet had he known how his kiss was received, the sting would have penetrated even through the tough covering which protected Reginald Burton's amour propre, if not his heart. Mrs Burton went away into the great drawing-room, where her children, dressed like little princes in a comedy, were waiting for her. The Harcourts in the old days, had made a much smaller room their family centre; but the Burtons always used the great drawing-room, and lived, as it were, in state from one year's end to another. Here Clara Burton dwelt—a little anonymous spirit, known to none even of her nearest friends. They were all puzzled by her 'ways,' and by the blank many-sided surface like a prism which she presented to them, refusing to be influenced by any. She did not know any more about herself than the others did. Outside she was all glitter and splendour; nobody dressed so well, nobody had such jewels, or such carriages, or such horses in all the county. She used every day, and in her homeliest moments, things which even princes reserve for their best. Mrs Burton made it a boast that she had no best things; she was the same always, herself—and not her guests or anything apart from herself—being the centre of life in her house and in all her arrangements. The dinner which the husband and wife had just eaten had been as varied and as dainty, as if twenty people had sat down to it. It was her principle throughout her life. And yet within herself the woman cared for none of these things. Another woman's dress or jewels was nothing to her. She was totally indifferent to the external advantages which everybody else believed her to be absorbed in. Clara was very worldly, her aunts said, holding up their hands aghast at her extravagance and costly habits; but the fact was, that Clara made all her splendours common, not out of love for them, but contempt for them: a thing which nobody suspected. It is only a cynical soul that could feel thus, and Mrs Burton's cynicism went very deep. She thought meanly of human nature, and did not believe much in goodness; but she seldom disapproved, and never condemned. She would smile and cast about in her mind (unawares) for the motive of any doubtful action, and generally ended by finding out that it was 'very natural,' a sentence which procured her credit for large toleration and a most amiable disposition, but which sprang really from the cynical character of her mind. It did not seem to her worth while to censure or to sermonize. She did not believe in reformation; and incredulity was in her the twin-brother of despair; but not a tragical despair. She took it all very calmly, not feeling that it was worth while to be disturbed by it; and went on unconsciously tracking out the mean motives, the poor pretensions, the veiled selfishness of all around her. And she was not aware that she herself was any better, nor did she claim superiority—nay, she would even track her own impulses back to their root, and smile at them, though with a certain bitterness. But all this was so properly cloaked over that nobody suspected it. People gave her credit for wisdom because she generally believed the worst, and was so very often right; and they thought her tolerant because she would take pains to show how it was nature that was in fault, and not the culprit. No one suspected the terrible little cynic, pitiless and hopeless that she was in her heart.

And yet this woman was the mother of children, and had taught them their prayers, and was capable at that or any other moment of giving herself to be torn in pieces for them, as a matter of course, a thing which would not admit a possibility of doubt. She had thought of that in her many thinkings, had attempted to analyze her own love, and to fathom how much it was capable of. 'As much as a tiger or a bear would do for her cubs,' she had said to herself, with her usual smile. The strangest woman to sit veiled by Reginald Burton's fireside, and take the head of his table, and go to church with him in the richest, daintiest garments which money and skill could get for her! She was herself to some degree behind the scenes of her own nature; but even she could not always discriminate, down among the foundations of her being, which was false and which was true.

She went into the drawing-room, where her little Clara and Ned were waiting. Ned was thirteen, a year older than Norah Drummond. Mr Burton had determined that he would not be behind the cousin who refused him, nor allow her to suppose that he was pining for her love, so that his marriage had taken place earlier than Helen's. Ned was a big boy, very active, and not given to book-learning; but Clara, who was a year younger, was a meditative creature like her mother. The boy was standing outside the open window, throwing stones at the birds in the distant trees. Little Clara stood within watching him, and making her comments on the sport.

'Suppose you were to kill a poor little bird. Suppose one of the young ones—one of the baby ones—were to try and fly a little bit, and you were to hit it. Suppose the poor papa when he comes home—'

'Oh, that's enough of your supposes,' said the big boy. 'Suppose I were to eat you? But I don't want to. I don't think you would be nice.'

'Ned!' said a voice from behind Clara, which thrilled him through and through, and made the stones fall from his hands as if they had been suddenly paralyzed, and were unable to grasp anything. 'I know it is natural to boys to be cruel, but I had rather not have it under my own eyes.'

'Cruel!' cried Ned, with some discontent. 'A parcel of wretched sparrows and things that can't sing a note. They have no business in our trees. They ought to know what they would get.'

'Are boys always cruel, mamma?' said little Clara, laying hold upon her mother's dress. She was like a little princess herself, all lace and embroidery and blue ribbons and beautifulness. Mrs Burton made no answer. She did not even wait to see that her boy took no more shots at the birds. She drew a chair close to the window, and sat down; and as she took her seat she gave vent to a little fretful sigh. She was thinking of Helen, and was annoyed that she had actually no means of judging what were the motives that would move her should she come to Dura. It was difficult for her to understand simple ignorance and unsuspiciousness, or to give them their proper place among the springs of human action. Her worst fault philosophically was that of ignoring these commonest influences of all.

'Mamma, you are thinking of something,' said little Clara. 'Why do you sigh, and why do you shake your head?'

'I have been trying to put together a puzzle,' said her mother, 'as you do sometimes; and I can't make it out.'

'Ah, a puzzle,' said Ned, coming in; 'they are not at all fun, mamma. That beastly dissected map Aunt Louisa gave me—by Jove! I should like to take the little pieces and shy them at the birds.'

'But, mamma,' said Clara, 'are you sure it is only that? I never saw you playing with toys.'

'I wonder if I ever did?' said Mrs Burton, with a little gleam of surprise. 'Do you remember going to London once, Clara, and seeing your cousin, Norah Drummond? Should you like to have her here?'

'She was littler than me,' said Clara, promptly, 'though she was older. Papa told me. They lived in a funny little poky house. They had no carriages nor anything. She had never even tried to ride; fancy, mamma! When I told her I had a pony all to myself, she only stared. How different she would think it if she came here!'

Her mother looked at the child with a curious light in her cold blue eyes. She gave a little harsh laugh.

'If it were not that it is natural, and you cannot help it,' she said, 'I should like to whip you, my dear!'

CHAPTER XV

Next morning the family at Dura paid a visit to the Gatehouse, to see all its capabilities, and arrange the changes which might be necessary. It was a bright morning after the rain, and they walked together down the dewy avenue, where the sunshine played through the network of leaves, and the refreshed earth sent up sweet odours. All was pleasant to sight and sound, and made a lightsome beginning to the working day. Mr Burton was pleased with himself and everything surrounding him. His children (he was very proud of his children) strolled along with their father and mother, and there was in Ned a precocious imitation of his own walk and way of holding himself which at once amused and flattered the genial papa. He was pleased by his boy's appreciation of his own charms of manner and appearance; and little Clara was like him, outwardly, at least, being of a larger mould than her mother. His influence was physically predominant in the family, and as for profounder influences these were not much visible as yet. Mrs Burton had a toilette fraîche of the costliest simplicity. Two or three dogs attended them on their walk—a handsome pointer and a wonderful hairy Skye, and the tiniest of little Maltese terriers, with a blue ribbon round its neck such as Clara had, of whose colours her dog was a repetition. When she made a rush now and then along the road, herself like a great white and blue butterfly, the dogs ran too, throwing up their noses in the air, till Ned, marching along in his knickerbockers, with his chest set out, and his head held up like his father's, whistled the bigger ones to his masculine side. It was quite a pretty picture this family procession; they were so well off, so perfectly supplied with everything that was pleasant and suitable, so happily above the world and its necessities. There was a look of wealth about them that might almost have seemed insolent to a poor man. The spectator felt sure that if fricasseed bank-notes had been good to eat, they must have had a little dish of that for breakfast. And the crown of all was that they were going to do a good action—to give shelter and help to the homeless. Many simple persons would have wept over the spectacle, had they known it, out of pure delight in so much goodness—if Mrs Burton, looking on with those clear cold blue eyes of hers, had not thrown upon the matter something of a clearer light.

The inspection was satisfactory enough, revealing space sufficient to have accommodated twice as many people. And Mr Burton found it amusing too; for Susan, who was in charge, was very suspicious of their motives, and anxious to secure that she should not be put upon in any arrangement that might be made. There was a large, quaint old drawing-room, with five glimmering windows—three fronting to the road and two to the garden—not French sashes, cut down to the ground, but old-fashioned English windows with a sill to them, and a solid piece of wall underneath. The chimney had a high wooden mantelpiece with a little square of mirror let in, too high up for any purpose but that of giving a glimmer of reflection. The carpet, which was very much worn, was partially covered by a tightly strained white cloth, as if the room had been prepared for dancing. The furniture was very thin in the legs and angular in its proportions; some of the chairs were ebony, with bands of faded gilding and covers of minute old embroidery, into which whole lives had been worked. The curtains were of old-fashioned, big-patterned chintz—like that we call Cretonne now-a-days—with brown linings. Everything was very old and worn, but clean and carefully mended. The looker-on felt it possible that the entrance of a stranger might so break the spell that all might crumble into dust at a touch. But yet there was a quaint, old-fashioned elegance—not old enough to be antique, but yet getting venerable—about the silent old house. Mr Burton was of opinion that it would be better with new red curtains and some plain, solid mahogany; but, if the things would do, considered that it was unnecessary to incur further expense. When all the necessary arrangements had been settled upon, the family party went on to the railway station. This was a very frequent custom with them. Mr Burton liked to come home in state—to notify his arrival by means of the high-stepping greys and the commotion they made, to his subjects; but he was quite willing to leave in the morning with graceful humility and that exhibition of family affection which brings even the highest potentates to a level with common men. When he arrived with his wife and his children and his dogs at the station, it was touching to see the devotion with which the station-master and the porters and everybody about received the great man. The train seemed to have been made on purpose for him—to have come on purpose all the way out of the Midland Counties; the railway people ran all along its length as soon as it arrived to find a vacant carriage for their demigod. 'Here you are, sir!' cried a smiling porter. 'Here you are, sir!' echoed the station-master, rushing forward to open the door. The other porter, who was compelled by duty to stand at the little gate of exit and take the tickets, looked gloomily upon the active service of his brethren, but identified himself with their devotion by words at least, since nothing else was left him. 'What d'ye mean by being late?' he cried to the guard. 'A train didn't ought to be late as takes gentlemen to town for business. You're as slow, you are, as if you was the ladies' express.'

Mr Burton laughed as he passed, and gladness stole into the porter's soul. Oh, magical power of wealth! when it laughs, the world grows glad. To go into the grimy world of business, and be rubbed against in the streets by men who did him no homage, must be hard upon such a man, after the royal calm of the morning and all its pleasant circumstances. It was after just such another morning that he went again to St Mary's Road, and was admitted to see his cousin. She had shut herself up for a fortnight obstinately. She would have done so for a year, in defiance of herself and of nature, had it been possible, that all the world might know that Robert had 'the respect' due to him. She would not have deprived him of one day, one fold of crape, one imbecility of grief, of her own will. She would have been ill, if she could, to do him honour. All this was quite independent of that misery of which the world could know nothing, which was deep as the sea in her own heart. That must last let her do what she would. But she would fain have given to her husband the outside too. The fortnight, however, was all that poor Helen could give. Already stern need was coming in, and the creditors, to whom everything she had belonged. When Mr Burton was admitted, the man had begun to make an inventory of the furniture. The pretty drawing-room was already dismantled, the plants all removed from the conservatory; the canvases were stacked against the wall in poor Robert's studio, and a picture-dealer was there valuing them. They were of considerable value now—more than they would have been had it still been possible that they should be finished. People who were making collections of modern pictures would buy them readily as the only 'Drummond' now to be had. Mr Burton went and looked at the pictures, and pointed out one that he would like to buy. His feelings were not very delicate, but yet it struck a certain chill upon him to go into that room. Poor Drummond himself was lying at the bottom of the river—he could not reproach any one, even allowing that it was not all his own fault. And yet—the studio was unpleasant to Mr Burton. It affected his nerves; and in anticipation of his interview with Helen he wanted all his strength.

But Helen received him very gently, more so than he could have hoped. She had not seen the papers. The world and its interests had gone away from her. She had read nothing but the good books which she felt it was right to read during her seclusion. She was unaware of all that had happened, unsuspicious, did not even care. It had never occurred to her to think of dishonour as possible. All calamity was for her concentrated in the one which had happened, which had left her nothing more to fear. She was seated in a very small room opening on the garden, which had once been appropriated to Norah and her playthings. She was very pale, with the white rim of her cap close round her face, and her hair concealed. Norah was there too, seated close to her mother, giving her what support she could with instinctive faithfulness. Mr Burton was more overcome by the sight of them than he could have thought it possible to be. They were worse even than the studio. He faltered, he cleared his throat, he took Helen's hand and held it—then let it drop in a confused way. He was overcome, she thought, with natural emotion, with grief and pity. And it made her heart soft even to a man she loved so little. 'Thanks,' she murmured, as she sank down upon her chair. That tremor in his voice covered a multitude of sins.

'I have been here before,' he said.

'Yes, so I heard; it was very kind. Don't speak of that, please. I am not able to bear it, though it is kind, very kind of you.'

'Everybody is sorry for you, Helen,' he said, 'but I don't want to recall your grief to your mind—'

'Recall!' she said, with a kind of miserable smile. 'That was not what I meant; but—Reginald—my heart is too sore to bear talking. I—cannot speak, and—I would rather not cry—not just now.'

She had not called him Reginald before since they were boy and girl together; and that, and the piteous look she gave him, and her tremulous protest that she would rather not cry, gave the man such a twinge through his very soul as he had never felt before. He would have changed places at the moment with one of his own porters to get out of it—to escape from a position which he alone was aware of. Norah was crying without restraint. It was such a scene as a man in the very height of prosperity and comfort would hesitate to plunge into, even if there had not risen before him those ghosts in the newspapers which one day or other, if not now, Helen must find out.

'What I wanted to speak of was your own plans,' he said hastily, 'what you think of doing, and—if you will not think me impertinent—what you have to depend upon? I am your nearest relation, Helen, and it is right I should know.'

'If everything has to be given up, I suppose I shall have nothing,' she said faintly. 'There was my hundred a year settled upon me. The papers came the other day. Who must I give them to? I have nothing, I suppose.'

'If your hundred a year was settled on you, of course you have that, heaven be praised,' said Mr Burton, 'nobody can touch that. And, Helen, if you like to come back to the old neighbourhood, I have part of a house I could offer you. It is of no use to me. I can't let it; so you might be quite easy in your mind about that. And it is furnished after a sort; and it would be rent free.'

The tears which she had been restraining rushed to her eyes. 'How kind you are!' she said. 'Oh, I can't say anything, but you are very, very kind.'

'Never mind about that. You used to speak as if you did not like the old neighbourhood—'

'Ah!' she said, 'that was when I cared. All neighbourhoods are the same to me now.'

'But you will get to care after a while,' he said. 'You will not always be as you are now.'

She shook her head with that faint little gleam of the painfullest smile. To such a suggestion she could make no answer. She did not believe her grief would ever lighten. She did not wish to feel differently. She had not even that terrible experience which teaches some that the broken heart must heal one way or other—mend of its wound, or at least have its wound skinned over; for she had never been quite stricken down to the ground before.

'Anyhow, you will think of it,' Mr Burton said in a soothing tone. 'Norah, you would like to come and live in the country, where there was a nice large garden and plenty of room to run about. You must persuade your mother to come. I won't stay now to worry you, Helen, and besides, my time is precious; but you will let me do this much for you, I hope.'

She stood up in her black gown, which was so dismal and heavy, without any reflection of light in its dull blackness, and held out to him a hand which was doubly white by the contrast, and thin with fasting and watching. 'You are very kind,' she said again. 'If I ever was unjust to you, forgive me. I must have a home—for Norah; and I have nowhere—nowhere to go!'

'Then that is settled,' he said with eagerness. It was an infinite relief to him. Never in his life had he been so anxious to serve another. Was it because he had loved her once? because he was fond of her still? because she was his relation? His wife at that very moment was pondering on the matter, touching it as it were with a little sharp spear, which was not celestial like Ithuriel's. Being his wife, it would have been natural enough if some little impulse of jealousy had come across her, and moved her towards the theory that her husband did this out of love for his cousin. But Mrs Burton had not blood enough in her veins, and she had too clear an intelligence in her head, to be jealous. She came to such a very different conclusion, that I hesitate to repeat it; and she, too, half scared by the long journey she had taken, and her very imperfect knowledge of the way by which she had travelled, did not venture to put it into words. But the whisper at the bottom of her heart was, 'Remorse! Remorse!' Mrs Burton herself did not know for what, nor how far her husband was guilty towards his cousin.

But it was a relief to all parties when this interview was over. Mr Burton went away drawing a long breath. And Helen applied herself courageously to the work which was before her. She did not make any hardship to herself about those men who were taking the inventory. It had to be, and what was that— what was the loss of everything in comparison—The larger loss deadened her to the smaller ones, which is not always the case. She had her own and Norah's clothes to pack, some books, a few insignificant trifles which she was allowed to retain, and the three unfinished pictures, which indeed, had they not been given to her, she felt she could have stolen. The little blurred sketch from the easel, a trifling subject, meaning little, but bearing in its smeared colours the last handwriting of poor Robert's despair; and that wistful face looking up from the depths, up to the bit of blue sky far above and the one star. Was that the Dives he had thought of, the soul in pain so wistful, so sad, yet scarcely able to despair? It was like his letter, a sacred appeal to her not on this earth only, but beyond—an appeal which would outlast death and the grave. 'The door into hell,' she did not understand, but she knew it had something to do with her husband's last agony. These mournful relics were all she had to take with her into the changed world.

A woman cannot weep violently when she is at work. Tears may come into her eyes, tears may drop among the garments in which her past is still existing, but her movements to and fro, her occupations, stem the full tide and arrest it. Helen was quite calm. While Norah brought the things for her out of the drawers she talked to the child as ordinary people talk whose hearts are not broken. She had fallen into a certain stillness—a hush of feeling. It did her good to be astir. When the boxes were full and fastened she turned to her pictures, enveloping them carefully, protecting the edges with cushions of folded paper. Norah was still very busy in finding the cord for her, and holding the canvases in their place. The child had rummaged out a heap of old newspapers, with which the packing was being done. Suddenly she began to cry as she stood holding one in her hand.

'Oh, mamma!' she said, looking up with big eyes in Helen's face. Crying was not so rare in the house as to surprise her mother. She said—

'Hush, my darling!' and went on. But when she felt the paper thrust into her hand, Helen stopped short in her task and looked, not at it but at Norah. The tears were hanging on the child's cheeks, but she had stopped crying. She pointed to one column in the paper and watched her mother with eyes like those of Dives in the picture. Helen gave a cry when she looked at it, 'Ah!' as if some sharp blow had been given to her. It was the name, nothing but her husband's name, that had pierced her like a sudden dagger. But she read on, without doubting, without thinking. It was the article written two days before on the history of the painter Drummond, 'the wretched man,' who had furnished a text for a sermon to the Daily Semaphore.

Norah had read only a sentence at the beginning which she but partially understood. It was something unkind, something untrue about 'poor papa.' But she read her mother now instead, comprehending it by her looks. Helen went over the whole without drawing breath. It brought back the blood to her pale cheeks; it ran like a wild new life into every vein, into every nerve. She turned round in the twinkling of an eye, without a pause for thought, and put on the black bonnet with its overwhelming crape veil which had been brought to her that morning. She had not wanted it before. It was the first time in her life that she had required to look at the world through those folds of crape.

'May I come too, mamma?' said Norah softly. She did not know where they were going; but henceforward where her mother was there was the place for Norah, at home or abroad, sleeping or waking. The child clung to Helen's hand as they opened the familiar door, and went out once again— after a lifetime—into the once familiar, the changed and awful world. A summer evening, early June, the bloom newly off the lilacs, the first roses coming on the trees; the strange daylight dazzled them, the sound of passing voices buzzed and echoed as if they had been the centre of a crowd. Or rather, this was their effect upon Helen. Norah clinging to her hand, pressed close to her side, watched her, and thought of nothing more.

Dr Maurice was going to his solitary dinner. He had washed his hands and made himself daintily nice and tidy, as he always was; but he had not changed his morning coat. He was standing with his back against the writing-table in his library, looking up dreamily at poor Drummond's picture, and waiting for the sound of the bell which should summon him into the next room to his meal. When the door bell sounded instead impatience seized him.

'What fool can be coming now?' he said to himself, and turned round in time to see John's scared face peeping into the room before he introduced those two figures, those two with their dark black dresses, the one treading in the very steps of the other, moving with her movement. He gave a cry of surprise. He had not seen them since the day after Drummond's death. He had gone to inquire, and had left anxious kind messages, but he, too, had conventional ideas in his mind and had thought the widow 'would not be able' to see any one. Yet now she had come to him—

'Dr Maurice,' she said, with no other preliminary, coming forward to the table with her newspaper, holding out no hand, giving him no salutation, while Norah moved with her step for step, like a shadow. 'Dr Maurice, what does this mean?'

I would not like to say what despairing thought Dr Maurice might have had about his dinner in the first moment when he turned round and saw Helen Drummond's pale face under her crape veil, but there were many thoughts on the subject in his household, and much searchings of heart. John had been aghast at the arrival of visitors, and especially of such visitors, at such a moment; but his feelings would not permit him to carry up dinner immediately, or to sound the bell, the note of warning.

'I canna do it, I canna do it—don't ask me,' he said, for John was a north-country-man, and when his heart was moved fell back upon his old idiom.

'Maybe the lady would eat a bit herself, poor soul,' the cook said in insinuating tones. 'I've known folks eat in a strange house, for the strangeness of it like, when they couldn't swallow a morsel in their own.'

'Don't ask me!' said John, and he seized a stray teapot and began to polish it in the trouble of his heart. There was silence in the kitchen for ten minutes at least, for the cook was a mild woman till driven to extremities; but to see fish growing into wool and potatoes to lead was more than any one could be expected to bear.

'Do you see that?' she said in despair, carrying the dish up to him, and thrusting it under his eyes. John threw down his teapot and fled. He went and sat on the stairs to be out of reach of her remonstrances. But the spectre of that fish went with him, and would not leave his sight; the half-hour chimed, the three-quarters—

'I canna stand this no longer!' John said in desperation, and rushing up to the dining-room, sounded the dinner-bell.

Its clang disturbed the little party in the next room who were so differently occupied. Helen was seated by the table with a pile of papers before her; her hands trembled as she turned from one to another, but her attention did not swerve. She was following through them every scrap that bore upon that one subject. Dr Maurice had procured them all for her. He had felt that one time or other she must know all, and that then her information must be complete. He himself was walking about the room with his hands in his pocket, now stopping to point out or explain something, now taking up a book, unsettled and unhappy, as a man generally looks when he has to wait, and has nothing to do. He had sought out a book for Norah, to the attractions of which the poor child had gradually yielded. At first she had stood close by her mother. But the contents of those papers were not for Norah's eye, and Helen herself had sent her away. She had put herself in the window, her natural place; the ruddy evening light streamed in upon her, and found out between the black of her dress and that of her hat, a gleam of brown hair, to which it gave double brightness by the contrast; and gradually she fell into her old attitude, her old absorption. Dr Maurice walked about the room, and pondered a hundred things. He would have given half he possessed for that fatherless child who sat reading in the light, and forgetting her childish share of sorrow. The mother in her mature beauty was little to him—but the child—a child like that! And she was not his. She was Robert Drummond's, who lay drowned at the bottom of the river, and whose very name was drowned too in those bitter waters of calumny and shame. Strange Providence that metes so unequally to one and to another. The man did not think that he too might have had a wife and children had he so chosen; but his heart hankered for this that was his neighbour's, and which no magic, not even any subtle spell of love or protecting tenderness, could ever make his own.

And Helen, almost unconscious of the presence of either, read through those papers which had been preserved for her. She read Golden's letter, and the comment upon it. She read the letter which Dr Maurice had written, contradicting those cruel assertions. She read the further comments upon that. How natural it was; how praiseworthy was the vehemence of friends in defence of the dead—and how entirely without proof! The newspaper pointed out with a cold distinctness, which looked like hatred to Helen, that the fact of the disappearance of the books told fatally against 'the unhappy man.' Why did he destroy those evidences which would no doubt have cleared him had he acted fairly and honestly? Day by day she traced the course of this controversy which had been going on while she had shut herself up in the darkness. It gleamed across her as she turned from one to another that this was why her energy had been preserved and her strength sustained. She had not broken down like other women, for this cause. God had kept her up for this. The discussion had gone on down to that very morning, when a little editorial note, appended to a short letter—one of the many which had come from all sorts of people in defence of the painter—had announced that such a controversy could no longer be carried on 'in these pages.' 'No doubt the friends of Mr Drummond will take further steps to prove the innocence of which they are so fully convinced,' it said, 'and it must be evident to all parties that the columns of a newspaper is not the place for a prolonged discussion on a personal subject.' Helen scarcely spoke while she read all these. She did not hear the dinner-bell. The noise of the door when Dr Maurice rushed to it with threatening word and look, to John's confusion, scarcely moved her. 'Be quiet, dear,' she said unconsciously, when the doctor's voice in the hall, where he had fallen upon his servant, came faintly into her abstraction. 'You rascal! how dare you take such a liberty when you knew who was with me?' was what Dr Maurice was saying, with rage in his voice. But to Helen it seemed as if little Norah, forgetting the cloud of misery about her, had begun to talk more lightly than she ought. 'Oh, my child, be quiet,' she repeated; 'be quiet!' all her soul was absorbed in this. She had no room for any other thought.

Dr Maurice came back with a flush of anger on his face. 'These people would think it necessary to consider their miserable dishes if the last judgment were coming on,' he said. He was a kind man, and very sorry for his friend's widow. He would have given up much to help her; but perhaps he too was hungry, and the thought of the spoilt dishes increased his vehemence. She looked at him, putting back her veil with a blank look of absolute incomprehension. She had heard nothing, knew nothing. Comfort, and dinners, and servants, and all the paraphernalia of ordinary life, were a hundred miles away from her thoughts.

'I have read them all,' she said in a tone so low that he had to stoop to hear her. 'Oh, that I should have lost so much time in selfish grieving! I thought nothing more could happen after. Dr Maurice, do you know what I ought to do?'

'You!' he said. There was something piteous in her look of appeal. The pale face and the gleaming eyes, the helplessness and the energy, all struck him at a glance—a combination which he did not understand.

'Yes—me! You will say what can I do? I cannot tell the world what he was, as you have done. Thanks for that,' she said, holding out her hand to him. 'The wife cannot speak for her husband, and I cannot write to the papers. I am quite ignorant. Dr Maurice, tell me if you know. What can I do?'

Her gleam of wild indignation was gone. It had sunk before the controversy, the discussion which the newspapers would no longer continue. If poor Robert had met with no defenders, she would have felt herself inspired. But his friends had spoken, friends who could speak. And deep depression fell over her. 'Oh!' she said, clasping her hands, 'must we bear it? Is there nothing—nothing I can do?'

Again and again had he asked himself the same question. 'Mrs Drummond,' he said, 'you can do nothing; try and make up your mind to it. I hoped you might never know. A lady can do nothing in a matter of business. You feel yourself that you cannot write or speak. And what good would it do even if you could? I say that a more honourable man never existed. You could say, I know, a great deal more than that; but what does it matter without proof? If we could find out about those books—'

'He did not know anything about books,' said Helen; 'he could not even keep his own accounts—at least it was a trouble to him. Oh, you know that; how often have we—laughed—Oh, my God, my God!'

Laughed! The words brought the tears even to Dr Maurice's eyes. He put his hand on her arm and patted it softly, as if she had been a child. 'Poor soul! poor soul!' he said: the tears had got into his voice too, and all his own thoughts went out of his mind in the warmth of his sympathy. He was a cautious man, not disposed to commit himself; but the touch of such emotion overpowered all his defences. 'Look here, Mrs Drummond,' he said; 'I don't know what we may be able to do, but I promise you something shall be done—I give you my word. The shareholders are making a movement already, but so many of them are ruined, so many hesitate, as people say, to throw good money after the bad. I don't know why I should hesitate, I am sure. I have neither chick nor child.' He glanced at Norah as he spoke— at Norah lost in her book, with the light in her hair, and her outline clear against the window. But Helen did not notice, did not think what he could mean, being absorbed in her own thoughts. She watched him, notwithstanding, with dilating eyes. She saw all that at that moment she was capable of seeing in his face—the rising resolution that came with it, the flash of purpose. 'It ought to be done,' he said, 'even for justice. I will do it—for that—and for Robert's sake.'

She held out both her hands to him in the enthusiasm of her ignorance. 'Oh, God bless you! God reward you!' she said. It seemed to her as if she had accomplished all she had come for, and had cleared her husband's name. At least his friend had pledged himself to do it, and it seemed to Helen so easy. He had only to refute the lies which had been told; to prove how true, how honest, how tender, how good, incapable of hurting a fly; even how simple and ignorant of business, more ignorant almost than she was, he had been; a man who never had kept any books, not even his own accounts; who had a profession of his own, quite different, at which he worked; who had not been five times in the City in his life before he came connected with the Rivers's. After she had bestowed that blessing, it seemed to her almost as if she were making too much of it, as if she had but to go herself and tell it all, and prove his whitest innocence. To go herself—but she did not know where.

Dr Maurice came down with a little tremulousness of excitement about him from the pinnacle of that resolution. He knew better what it was. Her simple notion of 'going and telling' resolved itself, in his mind, to an action before the law-courts, to briefs, and witnesses, and expenditure. But he was a man without chick or child; he was not ruined by Rivers's. The sum he had lost had been enough to give him an interest in the question, not enough to injure his powers of operation. And it was a question of justice, a matter which some man ought to take up. Nevertheless it was a great resolution to take. It would revolutionize his quiet life, and waste the substance which he applied, he knew, to many good uses. He felt a little shaken when he came down. And then—his dinner, the poor friendly unfortunate man!

'Let Norah come and eat something with me,' he said, 'the child must be tired. Come too and you shall have a chair to rest in, and we will not trouble you; and then I will see you home.'

'Ah!' Helen gave an unconscious cry at the word. But already, even in this one hour, she had learned the first hard lesson of grief, which is that it must not fatigue others with its eternal presence—that they who suffer most must be content often to suffer silently, and put on such smiles as are possible—the ghost must not appear at life's commonest board any more than at the banquet. It seemed like a dream when five minutes later she found herself seated in an easy-chair in Dr Maurice's dining-room, painfully swallowing some wine, while Norah sat at the table by him and shared his dinner. It was like a dream; twilight had begun to fall by this time, and the lamp was lighted on the table—a lamp which left whole acres of darkness all round in the long dim room. Helen sat and looked at the bright table and Norah's face, which turning to her companion began to grow bright too, unawares. A fortnight is a long age of trouble to a child. Norah's tears were still ready to come, but the bitterness was out of them. She was sad for sympathy now. And this change, the gleam of light, the smile of her old friend—his fond, half-mocking talk, felt like happiness come back. Her mother looked on from the shady corner where she was sitting, and understood it all. Robert's friend loved him; but was glad now to pass to other matters, to common life. And Robert's child loved him; but she was a child, and she was ready to reply to the first touch of that same dear life. Helen was growing wiser in her trouble. A little while ago she would have denounced this changeableness, and struggled against it. But now she understood and accepted what was out of her power to change.

And then in the pauses of his talk with Norah, which was sweet to him, Dr Maurice heard all their story—how the house was already in the creditors' hands, how they had prepared all their scanty possessions to go away, and how Mr Burton had been very kind. Helen had not associated him in any way with the assault on her husband's memory. She spoke of him with a half gratitude which filled the doctor with suppressed fury. He had been very kind—he had offered her a house.

'I thought you disliked Dura,' he said with an impatience which he could not restrain.

'And so I did,' she answered drearily, 'as long as I could. It does not matter now.'

'Then you will still go?'

'Still? Oh, yes; where should we go else? The whole world is the same to us now,' said Helen. 'And Norah will be happier in the country; it is good air.'

'Good air!' said Dr Maurice. 'Good heavens, what can you be thinking of? And the child will grow up without any one to teach her, without a—friend. What is to be done for her education? What is to be done—Mrs Drummond, I beg your pardon. I hope you will forgive me. I have got into a way of interfering and making myself ridiculous, but I did not mean—'

'Nay,' said Helen gently, half because she felt so weary, half because there was a certain comfort in thinking that any one cared, 'I am not angry. I knew you would think of what is best for Norah. But, Dr Maurice, we shall be very poor.'

He did not make any reply; he was half ashamed of his vehemence, and yet withal he was unhappy at this new change. Was it not enough that he had lost Drummond, his oldest friend, but he must lose the child too, whom he had watched ever since she was born? He cast a glance round upon the great room, which might have held a dozen people, and in his mind surveyed the echoing chambers above, of which but one was occupied. And then he glanced at Norah's face, still bright, but slightly clouded over, beside him, and thought of the pretty picture she had made in the library seated against the window. Burton, who was their enemy, who had been the chief agent in bringing them to poverty, could give them a home to shelter their houseless heads. And why could not he, who had neither chick nor child, who had a house so much too big for him, why could not he take them in? Just to have the child in the house, to see her now and then, to hear her voice on the stairs, or watch her running from room to room, would be all he should want. They could live there and harm nobody, and save their little pittance. This thought ran through his mind, and then he stopped and confounded Burton. But Burton had nothing to do with it. He had better have confounded the world, which would not permit him to offer shelter to his friend's widow. He gave a furtive glance at Helen in the shadow. He did not want Helen in his house. His friend's wife had never attracted him; and though he would have been the kindest of guardians to his friend's widow, still there was nothing in her that touched his heart. But he could not open his doors to her and say, 'Come.' He knew if he did so how the men would grin and the women whisper; how impertinent prophecies would flit about, or slanders much worse than impertinent. No, he could not do it; he could not have Norah by, to help on her education, to have a hand in her training, to make her a child of his own. He had no child. It was his lot to live alone and have no soft hand ever in his. All this was very ridiculous, for, as I have said before, Dr Maurice was very well off; he was not old nor bad-looking, and he might have married like other men. But then he did not want to marry. He wanted little Norah Drummond to be his child, and he wanted nothing more.

Helen leaned back in her chair without any thought of what was passing through his heart. That her child should have inspired a grande passion at twelve had never entered her mind, and she took his words in their simplicity and pondered over them. 'I can teach her myself,' she said with a tremor in her voice. This man was not her friend, she knew. He had no partial good opinion of her, such as one likes one's friends to have, but judged her on her merits, which few people are vain enough to put much trust in; and she thought that very likely he would not think her worthy of such a charge. 'I have taught her most of what she knows,' she added with a little more confidence. 'And then the great thing is, we shall be very poor.'

'Forgive me!' he said; 'don't say any more. I was unpardonably rash—impertinent—don't think of what I said.'

And then he ordered his carriage for them and sent them home. I do not know whether perhaps it did not occur to Helen as she drove back through the summer dusk to her dismantled house what a difference there was between their destitution and poverty and all the warm glow of comfort and ease which surrounded this lonely man. But there can be no doubt that Norah thought of it, who had taken in everything with her brown eyes, though she said little. While they were driving along in the luxurious smoothly-rolling brougham, the child crept close to her mother, clasping Helen's arm with both her hands. 'Oh, mamma,' she said, 'how strange it is that we should have lost everything and Dr Maurice nothing, that he should have that great house and this nice carriage, and us be driven away from St Mary's Road! What can God be thinking of, mamma?'

'Oh, Norah, my dear child, we have each other, and he has nobody,' said Helen; and in her heart there was a frenzy of triumph over this man who was so much better off than she was. The poor so often have that consolation; and sometimes it is not much of a consolation after all. But Helen felt it to the bottom of her heart as she drew her child to her, and felt the warm, soft clasp of hands, the round cheek against her own. Two desolate, lonely creatures in their black dresses—but two, and together; whereas Dr Maurice, in his wealth, in his strength, in what the world would have called his happiness, was but one.

The pretty house in St Mary's Road—what a change had come upon it! There was a great painted board in front describing the desirable residence, with studio attached, which was to be let. The carpets were half taken up and laid in rolls along the floor, the chairs piled together, the costly, pretty furniture, so carefully chosen, the things which belonged to the painter's early life, and those which were the product of poor Drummond's wealth, all removed and jumbled together, and ticketed 'Lot 16,' 'Lot 20.' 'Lot 20' was the chair which had been Helen's chair for years—the one poor Robert had kissed. If she had known that, she would have spent her last shilling to buy it back out of the rude hands that turned it over. But even Helen only knew half of the tragedy which had suddenly enveloped her life. They threaded their way up-stairs to their bed-room through all those ghosts. It was still early; but what could they do down-stairs in the house which no longer retained a single feature of home? Helen put her child to bed, and then sat down by her, shading the poor little candle. It was scarcely quite dark even now. It is never dark in June. Through the open window there came the sound of voices, people walking about the streets after their work was over. There are so many who have only the streets to walk in, so many to whom St Mary's Road, with its lilacs and laburnums and pretty houses, was pleasant and fresh as if it had been in the depths of the country. Helen saw them from the window, coming and going, so often two, arm in arm, two who loitered and looked up at the lighted house, and spoke softly to each other, making their cheerful comments. The voices sounded mellow, the distant rattle of carriages was softened by the night, and a soft wind blew through the lilacs, and some stars looked wistfully out of the pale sky. Why are they so sad in summer, those lustrous stars? Helen looked out at them, and big tears fell softly out of her eyes. Oh, face of Dives looking up! Oh, true and kind and just and gentle soul! Must she not even think of him as in heaven, as hidden in God with the dead who depart in faith and peace, but gone elsewhere, banished for ever? The thought crossed her like an awful shadow, but did not sting. There are some depths of misery to which healthy nature refuses to descend, and this was one. Had she felt as many good people feel on this subject, and as she herself believed theoretically that she felt, I know what Helen would have done. She would have gone down to that river and joined him in his own way, wherever he was, choosing it so. No doubt, she would have been wrong. But she did not descend into that abyss. She kept by her faith in God instinctively, not by any doctrine. Did not God know? But even the edge of it, the shadow of the thought, was enough to chill her from head to foot. She stole in from the window, and sat down at the foot of the bed where Norah lay, and tried to think. She had thought there could be no future change, no difference one way or other; but since this very morning what changes there were!—her last confidence shattered, her last comfort thrust from her. Robert's good name! She sat quite silent for hours thinking it over while Norah slept. Sometimes for a moment it went nigh to make her mad. Of all frantic things in the world, there is nothing like that sense of impotence—to feel the wrong and to be unable to move against it. It woke a feverish irritation in her, a sourd resentment, a rage which she could not overcome, nor satisfy by any exertion. What could she do, a feeble woman, against the men who had cast this stigma on her husband? She did not even know who they were, except Golden. It was he who was the origin of it all, and whose profit it was to prove himself innocent by the fable of Robert's guilt! It was the most horrible farce, a farce which was a tragedy, which every one who knew him must laugh at wildly among their tears. But then the world did not know him; and the world likes to think the worst, to believe in guilt as the one thing always possible. That there were people who knew better had been proved to her—people who had ventured to call out indignantly, and say, 'This is not true,' without waiting to be asked. Oh, God bless them! God bless them! But they were not the world.

When the night was deeper, when the walkers outside had gone, when all was quiet, except now and then the hurried step of a late passer-by, Helen went to the window once more, and looked out upon that world. What a little bit of a world it is that a woman can see from her window!—a few silent roofs and closed windows, one or two figures going and coming, not a soul whom she knew or could influence; but all those unknown people, when they heard her husband's name, if it were years and years hence, would remember the slander that had stained it, and would never know his innocence, his incapacity even for such guilt. This is what gives force to a lie, this is what gives bitterness, beyond telling, to the hearts of those who are impotent, whose contradiction counts for nothing, who have no proof, but only certainty. What a night it was!—like Paradise even in London. The angels might have been straying through those blue depths of air, through the celestial warmth and coolness, without any derogation from their high estate. It was not moonlight, nor starlight, nor dawn, but some heavenly combination of all three which breathed over the blue arch above, so serene, so deep, so unfathomable; and down below the peopled earth lay like a child, defenceless and trustful in the arms of its Maker. 'Dear God, the very city seems asleep!' But here was one pair of eyes that no sleep visited, which dared not look up to heaven too closely lest her dead should not be there; which dared not take any comfort in the pity of earth, knowing that it condemned while it pitied. God help the solitary, the helpless, the wronged, those who can see no compensation for their sufferings, no possible alchemy that can bring good out of them! Helen crept to bed at last, and slept. It was the only thing in which there remained any consolation; to be unconscious, to shut out life and light and all that accompanies them; to be for an hour, for a moment, as good as dead. There are many people always, to whom this is the best blessing remaining in the world.

The morning brought a letter from Mr Burton, announcing that the house at Dura was ready to receive his cousin. Helen would have been thankful to go but for the discovery she had made on the previous day. After that it seemed to her that to be on the spot, to be where she could maintain poor Robert's cause, or hear of others maintaining it, was all she wanted now in the world. But this was a mere fancy, such as the poor cannot indulge in. She arranged everything to go to her new home on the next day. It was time at least that she should leave this place in which her own room was with difficulty preserved to her for another night. All the morning the mother and daughter shut themselves up there, hearing the sounds of the commotion below—the furniture rolled about here and there, the heavy feet moving about the uncarpeted stairs and rooms that already sounded hollow and vacant. Bills of the sale were in all the windows; the very studio, the place which now would have been sacred if they had been rich enough to indulge in fancies. But why linger upon such a scene? The homeliest imagination can form some idea of circumstances which in themselves are common enough.

In the afternoon the two went out—to escape from the house more than anything else. 'We will go and see the Haldanes,' Helen said to her child; and Norah wondered, but acquiesced gladly. Mrs Drummond had never taken kindly to the fact that her husband's chief friend lived in Victoria Villas, and was a Dissenting minister with a mother and sister who could not be called gentlewomen. But all that belonged to the day of her prosperity, and now her heart yearned for some one who loved Robert— some one who would believe in him—to whom no vindication, even in thought, would be necessary. And the Haldanes had been ruined by Rivers's. This was another bond of union. She had called but once upon them before, and then under protest; but now she went nimbly, almost eagerly, down the road, past the line of white houses with their railings. There had been much thought and many discussions over Mr Burton's proposal within those walls. They had heard of it nearly a fortnight since, but they had not yet made any formal decision; that is to say, Mrs Haldane was eager to go; Miss Jane had made a great many calculations, and decided that the offer ought to be accepted as a matter of duty; but Stephen's extreme reluctance still kept them from settling. Something, however, had occurred that morning which had added a sting to Stephen's discouragement, and taken away the little strength with which he had faintly maintained his own way. In the warmth and fervour of his heart, he had used his little magazine to vindicate his friend. A number of it had been just going to the press when the papers had published Drummond's condemnation, and Haldane, who knew him so well—all his weakness and his strength—had dashed into the field and proclaimed, in the only way that was possible to him, the innocence and excellence of his friend. All his heart had been in it; he had made such a sketch of the painter, of his genius (poor Stephen thought he had genius), of his simplicity and goodness and unimpeachable honour, as would have filled the whole denomination with delight, had the subject of the sketch been one of its potentates or even a member of Mr Haldane's chapel. But Robert was not even a Dissenter at all, he had nothing to do with the denomination; and, to tell the truth, his éloge was out of place. Perhaps Stephen himself felt it was so after he had obeyed the first impulse which prompted it. But at least he was not left long in doubt. A letter had reached him from the magazine committee that morning. They had told him that they could not permit their organ to be made the vehicle of private feeling; they had suggested an apology in the next number; and they had threatened to take it altogether out of his hands. Remonstrances had already reached them, they said, from every quarter as to the too secular character of the contents; and they ventured to remind Mr Haldane that this was not a mere literary journal, but the organ of the body, and intended to promote its highest, its spiritual interests. Poor Stephen! he was grieved, and he writhed under the pinch of this interference. And then the magazine not only brought him in the half of his income, but was the work of his life—he had hoped to 'do some good' that way. He had aimed at improving it, cutting short the gossip and scraps of local news, and putting in something of a higher character. In this way he had been able to persuade himself, through all his helplessness, that he still possessed some power of influence over the world. He had been so completely subdued by the attack, that he had given in about Mr Burton's house, and that very day the proposal had been accepted; but he had not yet got the assault itself out of his head. All the morning he had been sitting with the manuscripts and proofs before him which were to make up his new number, commenting upon them in the bitterness of his heart.

'I suppose I must put this in now, whether I like it or not,' he said. 'I never suspected before how many pangs ruin brings with it, mother; not one, but a legion. They never dreamt of interfering with me before. Now look at this rabid, wretched thing. I would put it in the fire if I dared, and free the world of so much ill-tempered folly; but Bateman wrote it, and I dare not. Fancy, I dare not! If I had been independent, I should have made a stand. And my magazine—all the little comfort I had   '

'Oh, Stephen, my dear! but what does it matter what you put in if they like it? You are always writing, writing, wearing yourself out. Why shouldn't they have some of the trouble. You oughtn't to mind—'

'But I do mind,' he said, with a feeble smile. 'It is all I have to do, mother. It is to me what I am to you; you would not like to see me neglected, fed upon husks, like the prodigal.'

'Oh, Stephen dear, how can you talk so?—you neglected!' said his mother with tears in her eyes.

'Well, that is what I feel, mother. I shall have to feed my child with husks—tea-meetings and reports of this and that chapel, and how much they give. They were afraid of me once; they dared not grumble when I rejected and cut out; but—it is I who dare not now.'

Mrs Haldane wisely made no reply. In her heart she had liked the magazine better when it was all about the tea-meetings and the progress of the good cause. She liked the bits of sectarian gossip, and to know how much the different chapels subscribed, which congregation had given its minister a silver teapot, and which had given him his dismissal. All this was more interesting to her than all Stephen's new-fangled discussions of public matters, his eagerness about education and thought, and a great many other things that did not concern his mother. But she held this opinion within herself, and was as indignant with the magazine committee as heart could desire. The two fell silent for some time, he going on with his literature, and she with her sewing, till the only servant they had left, a maiden, called par excellence 'the girl,' came in with a tray laden with knives and forks to lay the cloth for dinner. The girl's eyes were red, and a dirty streak across one cheek showed where her tears had been wiped away with her apron.

'What is the matter?' said Mrs Haldane.

'Oh, please, it's Miss Jane,' cried the handmaid. 'She didn't ought to speak so; oh, she didn't ought to. My mother's a seat-holder in our chapel, and I'm a member. I'm not a-going to bear it! We ain't folks to be pushed about.'

'Lay the cloth, and do it quietly,' said the old lady. And with a silent exasperation, such as only a woman can feel, she watched the unhandy creature. 'Thank heaven, we shall want no girl in the country,' she said to herself. But when her eye fell on Stephen, he was actually smiling—smiling at the plea for exception, with that mingled sadness and bitterness which it pained his mother to see. The girl went on sniffing and sobbing all the same. She had already driven her other mistress almost frantic in the kitchen. Miss Jane had left a little stew, a savoury dish such as Stephen's fanciful appetite required to tempt it, by the fire, slowly coming to perfection. 'The girl' had removed it to the fender, where it was standing, growing cold, just at the critical moment when all its juices should have been blending under the gentle, genial influence of the fire. Common cooks cannot stew. They can boil, or they can burn; but they never catch the delicious medium between. Only such persons as cook for love, or such as possess genius, can hit this more than golden mean. Miss Jane combined both characters. She did it con amore and per amore; and when she found her fragrant dish set aside for the sake of 'the girl's' kettle, her feelings can be but faintly imagined by the uninitiated. 'I wish I could beat you,' she said, with natural exasperation. And this to 'a joined member,' a seat-holder's daughter! Stephen laughed when the tale was repeated to him, with a laugh which was full of bitterness. He tried to swallow his portion of the stew, but it went against him. 'It is the same everywhere,' he said; 'the same subjection of the wise to the foolish, postponing of the best to the worst. Rubbish to please the joined members—silence and uselessness to us.'

'Oh, Stephen!' said Mrs Haldane, 'you know I am not always of your way of thinking. After all there is something in it; for when a girl is a church member, she can't be quite without thought; and when she neglects her work, it is possible, you know, that she might be occupied with better things. I don't mean to say that it is an excuse.'

'I should think not, indeed,' said Miss Jane. 'I'd rather have some one that knew her work, and did it, than a dozen church members. A heathen to-day would have been as much use to me.'

'That may be very true,' said her mother; 'but I think, considering Stephen's position, that such a thing should not be said by you or me. In my days a person stood up for chapel, through thick and thin, especially when he had a relation who was a minister. You think you are wiser, you young ones, and want to set up for being liberal, and think church as good as chapel, and the world, so far as I can make out, as good as either. But that way of thinking would never answer me.'

'Well, thank heaven,' said Miss Jane in a tone of relief, 'in the country we shall not want any "girl."'

'That is what I have been thinking,' said Mrs Haldane with alacrity; and in the painful moment which intervened while the table was being cleared and the room put in order, she painted to herself a fancy picture of 'the country.' She was a Londoner born, and had but an imperfect idea what the word meant. It was to her a vague vision of greenness, parks and trees and great banks of flowers. The village street was a thing she had no conception of. A pleasant dream of some pleasant room opening on a garden, and level with it, crossed her mind. It was a cottage of romance, one of those cottages which make their appearance in the stories which she half disapproved of, yet felt a guilty pleasure in reading. There had been one, an innocent short one, with the gentlest of good meanings, in the last number of Stephen's magazine, with just such a cottage in it, where a sick heroine recovered. She thought she could see the room, and the invalid chair outside the door, in which he could be wheeled into the garden to the seat under the apple-tree. Her heart overflowed with that pleasant thought. And Stephen might get well! Such a joy was at the end of every vista to Mrs Haldane. She sat and dreamed over this with a smile on her face while the room was being cleared; and her vision was only stayed by the unusual sound of Helen's knock at the door.

'It will be some one to see the house,' said Miss Jane, and she went away hurriedly, with loud-whispered instructions to the girl, into 'the front drawing-room,' to be ready to receive any applicant; so that Miss Jane was not in the room when Helen with her heart beating, and Norah clinging close to her as her shadow, was shown abruptly into the invalid's room. 'The girl' thrust her in without a word of introduction or explanation. Norah was familiar in the place, though her mother was a stranger. Mrs Haldane rose hastily to meet them, and an agitated speech was on Helen's lips that she had come to say good-bye, that she was going away, that they might never meet again in this world,—when her eye caught the helpless figure seated by the window, turning a half-surprised, half-sympathetic look upon her. She had never seen poor Stephen since his illness, and she was not prepared for this complete and lamentable overthrow. It drove her own thoughts, even her own sorrows, out of her mind for the moment. She gave a cry of mingled wonder and horror. She had heard all about it, but seeing is so very different from hearing.

'Oh, Mr Haldane!' she said, going up to him, forgetting herself—with such pity in her voice as he had not heard for years. It drove out of his mind, too, the more recent and still more awful occasion he had to pity her. He looked at her with sudden gratitude in his eyes.

'Yes, it is a change, is it not?' he said with a faint smile. He had been an Alp-climber, a mighty walker, when she saw him last.

Some moments passed before she recovered the shock. She sat down by him trembling, and then she burst into sudden tears—not that she was a woman who cried much in her sorrow, but that her nerves were affected beyond her power of control.

'Mr Haldane, forgive me,' she faltered. 'I have never seen you since—and so much has happened—oh, so much!'

'Ah, yes,' he said. 'I could cry too—not for myself, for that is an old story. I would have gone to you, had I been able—you know that; and it is very, very kind of you to come to me.'

'It is to say good-bye. We are going away to the country, Norah and I,' said Helen; 'there is no longer any place for us here. But I wanted to see you, to tell you—you seem—to belong—so much—to the old time.'

Ah, that old time! the time which softens all hearts. It had not been perfect while it existed, but now how fair it was! Perhaps Stephen Haldane remembered it better than she did; perhaps it might even cross his mind that in that old time she had not cared much to see him, had not welcomed him to her house with any pleasure. But he was too generous to allow himself even to think such a thought, in her moment of downfall. The depths were more bitter to her even than to him. He would not let the least shadow even in his mind fret her in her great trouble. He put out his hand, and grasped hers with a sympathy which was more telling than words.

'And I hope your mother will forgive me too,' she said with some timidity. 'I thought I had more command of myself. We could not go without coming to say good-bye.'

'It is very kind—it is more than I had any right to expect,' said Mrs Haldane. 'And we are going to the country too. We are going to Dura, to a house Mr Burton has kindly offered to us. Oh, Mrs Drummond, now I think of it, probably we owe it to you.'

'No,' said Helen, startled and mystified; and then she added slowly, 'I am going to Dura too.'

'Oh, how very lucky that is! Oh, how glad I am!' said the old lady. 'Stephen, do you hear? Of course, Mr Burton is your cousin; it is natural you should be near him. Stephen, this is good news for you. You will have Miss Norah, whom you were always so fond of, to come about you as she used to do—that is, if her mamma will allow her. Oh, my dear, I am so glad! I must go and tell Jane. Jane, here is something that will make you quite happy. Mrs Drummond is coming too.'

She went to the door to summon her daughter, and Helen was left alone with the sick man. She had not loved him in the old time, but yet he looked a part of Robert now, and her heart melted towards him. She was glad to have him to herself, as glad as if he had been a brother. She put her hand on the arm of his chair, laying a kind of doubtful claim to him. 'You have seen what they say?' she asked, looking in his face.

'Yes, all; with fury,' he said, 'with indignation! Oh my God, that I should be chained here, and good for nothing! They might as well have said it of that child.'

'Oh, is it not cruel, cruel!' she said.

These half-dozen words were all that passed between them, and yet they comforted her more than all Dr Maurice had said. He had been indignant too, it is true; but not with this fiery, visionary wrath—the rage of the helpless, who can do nothing.

When Miss Jane came in with her mother, they did the most of the talking, and Helen shrunk into herself; but when she had risen to go away, Stephen thrust a little packet into her hand. 'Read it when you go home,' he said. It was his little dissenting magazine, the insignificant brochure which she would have scorned so in the old days. With what tears, with what swelling of her heart, with what an agony of pride and love and sorrow she read it that night!

And so the old house was closed, and the old life ended. Henceforward, everything that awaited her was cold and sad and new.

CHAPTER I

Helen had still another incident before her, however, ere she left St Mary's Road. It was late in the afternoon when she went back. To go back at all, to enter the dismantled place, and have that new dreary picture thrust into her mind instead of the old image of home, was painful enough, and Norah's cheeks were pale, and even to Helen the air and the movement conveyed a certain relief. They went into the quieter part of the park and walked for an hour or two saying little. Now and then poor Norah would be beguiled into a little monologue, to which her mother lent a half attention—but that was all. It was easier to be in motion than to keep still, and it was less miserable to look at the trees, the turf, the blue sky, than at the walls of a room which was full of associations of happiness. They did not get home until the carriages were beginning to roll into the park for the final round before dinner. And when they reached their own house, there stood a smart cabriolet before it, the horse held by a little tiger. Within the gate two gentlemen met them coming down the steps. One of them was a youth of eighteen or nineteen, who looked at Helen with a wondering awe-stricken glance. The other was—Mr Golden. Norah had closed the garden door heedlessly after her. They were thus shut in, the four together confronting each other, unable to escape. Helen could not believe her eyes. Her heart began to beat, her pale cheeks to flush, a kind of mist of excitement came before her vision. Mr Golden, too, was not without a certain perturbation. He had not expected to see any one. He took off his hat, and cleared his voice, and made an effort to seem at his ease.

'I had just called,' he said, 'to express—to inquire—I did not know things had been so far advanced. I would not intrude—for the world.'

'Oh!' cried Helen, facing him, standing between him and the door, 'how dare you come here?'

'Dare, Mrs Drummond? I—I don't understand—'

'You do understand,' she said, 'better—far better than any one else does. And how dare you come to look at your handiwork? A man may be what you are, and yet have a little shame. Oh, you robber of the dead! if I had been anything but a woman, you would not have ventured to look me in the face.'

He did not venture to look her in the face then; he looked at his companion instead, opening his eyes, and nodding his head slightly, as if to imply that she was crazed. 'It is only a woman who can insult a man with impunity,' he said, 'but I hope I am able to make allowance for your excited feelings. It is natural for a lady to blame some one, I suppose. Rivers, let us go.'

'Not till I have spoken,' she cried in her excitement. 'This is but a boy, and he ought to know whom he is with. Oh, how is it that I cannot strike you down and trample upon you? If I were to call that policeman he would not take you, I suppose. You liar and thief! don't dare to answer me. What, at my own door; at the door of the man whose good name you have stolen, whom you have slandered in his grave—oh my

God! who has not even a grave because you drove him mad!—' she cried, her eyes blazing, her cheeks glowing, all the silent beauty of her face growing splendid in her passion.

The young man gazed at her as at an apparition, his lips falling apart, his face paling. He had never heard such a voice, never seen such an outburst of outraged human feeling before.

'Mrs Drummond, this is madness. I—I can make allowance for—for excitement—'

'Be silent, sir,' cried Helen, in her fury. 'Who do you suppose cares what you think? And how dare you open your mouth before me? It is I who have a right to speak. And I wish there were a hundred to hear instead of one. This man had absconded till he heard my husband was dead. Then he came back and assumed innocence, and laid the blame on him who—could not reply. I don't know who you are; but you are young, and you should have a heart. There is not a liar in England—not a thing so vile as this man. He has plundered the dead of his good name. Now go, sir. I have said what I had to say.'

'Mrs Drummond, sometime you will have to answer—sometime you will repent of this,' cried Golden, losing his presence of mind.

'I shall never repent it, not if you could kill me for it,' cried Helen. 'Go; you make the place you stand on vile. Take him away from my sight. I have said what I had to say.'

Mr Golden made an effort to recover himself. He struck his young companion on the shoulder with an attempt at jocularity.

'Come, Rivers,' he said, 'come along, we are dismissed. Don't you see we are no longer wanted here?'

But the lad did not answer the appeal. He stayed behind with his eyes still fixed upon Helen.

'Please, don't blame me,' he said. 'Tell me if I can do anything. I—did not know—'

'Thank you,' she said faintly. Her excitement had failed her all at once. She had put her arms round Norah, and was leaning upon her, haggard and pale as if she were dying. 'Thank you,' she repeated, with a motion of her hand towards the door.

The youth stole out with a sore heart. He stood for a moment irresolute on the pavement. The cab was his and not Golden's; but that personage had got into it, and was calling to him to follow.

'Thanks,' said young Rivers, with the impetuosity of his years. 'I shall not trouble you. Go on pray. I prefer to walk.'

And he turned upon his heel, and went rapidly away. He was gone before the other could realise it; and it was with feelings that it would be impossible to describe, with a consciousness that seemed both bodily and mental of having been beaten and wounded all over, with a singing in his ears, and a bewildered sense of punishment, that Golden picked up the reins and drove away. It was only a few sharp words from a woman's tongue, a thing which a man must steel himself to bear when his operations are of a kind which involve the ruin of families. But Helen had given her blow far more skilfully, far more effectively, than she was aware of. She had clutched at her first chance of striking, without any calculation of results; and the youth she had appealed to in her excitement might have been any nameless lad for what she knew. It was Mr Golden's hard fate that he was not a nameless lad. He was Cyril Rivers, Lord Rivers's eldest son. The manager drove on a little way, slowly, and in great perturbation. And then he drew up the horse, and sprang to the ground.

'You had better go home,' he said to the little groom.

And then, still with that sense of bodily suffering as well as mental, he made his way through Kensington Gardens to the drive. He was a man of fashion, too, as well as a man of business—if he ever could hold up his head again.

Of course he did hold up his head, and in an hour after was ready to have made very good fun of the 'scolding' he had received, and the impression it had made on his young companion.

'I don't wonder,' he said; 'though her rage was all against me, I could not help admiring her. You never can tell what a woman is till you see her in a passion. She was splendid. Her friends ought to advise her to go on the stage.'

'Why should she go on the stage?' said some one standing by.

'Because she is left a beggar. She has not a penny, I suppose.'

'It is lucky that you have suffered so little when so many people are beggared, Golden,' said one of his fine friends.

This little winged shaft went right into the wound made by Helen's fiery lance, and so far as sensation went (which was nothing) Mr Golden had not a happy time that night.

As for Helen, she went in, prostrated by her own vehemence, and threw herself down on her bed, and hid her face from the light. After the first excitement was over shame seized upon her. She had descended from her proper place. She had flown into this outburst of passion and rage before her child. She had lowered herself in Norah's eyes, as she thought—though the child would not take her arm from her neck, nor her lips from her cheek, but clung to her sobbing, 'Oh, poor mamma! poor mamma!' with sympathetic passion. All this fiery storm through which she had passed had developed Norah. She had gained three or four years in a day. At one bound, from the child who was a piece of still life in the family, deeply beloved, but not needed, by the two who were each other's companions, she had become, all at once, her mother's only stay, her partizan, her supporter, her comrade-in-arms. It is impossible to over-estimate the difference this makes in a child's, and especially in a girl's, life. It made of her an independent, thinking, acting creature, all in a moment. For years everything had been said before her, under the supposition that Norah, absorbed in her book, heard nothing. But she had heard a thousand things. She knew all now without any need of explanation, as well as so young a mind could understand. And she began to grope in her mind towards further knowledge, to put things together which even her mother had not thought of.

'Do you know who the boy was, mamma?' she whispered, after she had sat a long time on the bed, silently consoling the sufferer. 'Oh, I am so glad you spoke, he will never forget it. Now one more knows it besides you and me.'

'There are others who know, dear,' said Helen, who had still poor Stephen's magazine in her hand.

'Yes,' said Norah, 'Dr Maurice and the people who wrote to the papers; but, mamma, nobody like you and me. Whatever they say we know. I am little, and I suppose I shall always be little; but that does not matter. I shall soon be grown up, and able to help. And, mamma, this shall be my work as well as yours—I shall never stop till it is done—never, all my life!'

'Oh, my darling!' cried Helen, clasping her child in her arms. It was not that she received the vow as the child meant it, or even desired that in Norah's opening life there should be nothing of more importance than this early self-devotion; but the sympathy was sweet to her beyond describing, the more that the little creature, who had played and chattered by her side, had suddenly become her friend. In the midst of her sorrow and pain, and even of the prostration and sensitive visionary shame with which this encounter had filled her, she had one sudden throb of pleasure. She was not alone any more.

It was Helen who fell asleep that evening worn out with emotion, and weariness, and suffering. And then Norah rose up softly, and made a pilgrimage by herself all over the deserted house. She went through the conservatory, where, of all the beautiful things poor Robert had loved to see, there remained nothing but the moonlight which filled its emptiness; and into the studio, where she sat down on the floor beside the easel, and clasped her arms round it and cried. She was beginning to weary of the atmosphere of grief, beginning to long for life and sunshine, but yet she clung to the easel and indulged in one childish passion of sobs and tears. 'Oh, papa!' That was all Norah said to herself. But the recollection of all he had been, and of all that had been done to him, surged over the child, and filled her with that sense of the intolerable which afflicts the weak. She could not bear it, yet she had to bear it; just as her mother, just as poor Haldane had to bear—struggling vainly against a power greater than theirs, acquiescing when life and strength ran low, sometimes for a moment divinely consenting, accepting the will of God. But it is seldom that even the experienced soul gets so far as that.

Next morning Mrs Drummond and her daughter went to Dura. Their arrival at the station was very different from that of Mr Burton. No eager porters rushed at them as they stepped out of the railway carriage; the station-master moved to the other side; they landed, and were left on the platform by themselves to count their boxes while the train swept on. It was the first time it had ever happened so to Helen. Her husband had always either been with her, or waiting for her, wherever she travelled. And she was weary with yesterday's agitation, and with all that had so lately happened. Norah came forward and took everything in hand. It was she who spoke to the porter, and set the procession in order.

'Cab? Bless you, miss! there ain't but one in the place, and it's gone on a 'xcursion,' he said, 'but I'll get a wheelbarrow and take 'em down. It ain't more than ten minutes' walk.'

'I know the way,' said Helen; and she took her child's hand and walked on into the familiar place. She had not been there since her marriage; but oh! how well she knew it! She put her crape veil over her face to hide her from curious eyes; and it threw a black mist at the same time over the cheerful village. It seemed to Helen as if she was walking in a dream. She knew everything, every stone on the road, the names above the shops, the forms of the trees. There was one great elm, lopsided, which had lost a huge branch (how well she remembered!) by a thunderstorm when she was a child; was it all a dream? Everything looked like a dream except Norah; but Norah was real. As for the child, there was in her heart a lively thrill of pleasure at sight of all this novelty which she could not quite subdue. She had no veil of crape over her eyes, and the red houses all lichened over, the glimpses of fields and trees, the rural aspect of the road, the vision of the common in the distance, all filled her with a suppressed delight. It was wrong, Norah knew; she called herself back now and then and sighed, and asked herself how she could be so devoid of feeling; but yet the reaction would come. She began to talk in spite of herself.

'I think some one might have come to meet us at the station,' she said. 'Ned might have come. He is a boy, and can go anywhere. I am sure, mamma, we would have gone to make them feel a little at home. Where is the Gatehouse? What is that place over there? Why there are shops—a draper's and a confectioner's—and a library! I am very glad there is a library. Mamma, I think I shall like it; is that the common far away yonder? Do you remember any of the people? I should like to know some girls if you will let me. There is little Clara, of course, who is my cousin. Do you think we shall live here always, mamma?'

Norah did not ask nor, indeed, look for any answer to this string of questions. She made a momentary pause of courtesy to leave room for a reply, should any come; but Helen's thoughts were full of the past, and as she made no answer Norah resumed the strain.

'It looks very cheerful here, mamma; though it is a village, it does not look dull. I like the red tiles on the cottages and all this red-brick; perhaps it is a little hot-looking now, but in winter it will be so comfortable. Shall we be able to get our things here without going to town? That seems quite a good shop. I wonder what Mrs Burton and Clara do? But then they are so rich, and we are—poor. Shall I be able to have any lessons, mamma? Can I go on with my music? I wonder if Clara has a governess. She will think it very strange that you should teach me. But I am very glad; I like you better than twenty governesses. Mamma, will it make any difference between Clara and me, them being so rich and us so poor?'

'Oh, Norah, I cannot tell you. Don't ask so many questions,' said Helen.

Norah was wounded; she did not give up her mother's hand, but she loosed her hold of it to show her feelings. She had been very sympathetic, very quiet, and respectful of the grief which in its intensity was beyond her; and now she seemed to herself to have a right to a little sympathy in return. She could understand but dimly what was in her mother's mind; she did not know the associations of which Dura was full; and it was hard to be thus stopped short in that spring of renovating life. As she resigned herself to silence, a feeling of injury came over her; and here, just before her eyes, suddenly appeared a picture of life so different from hers. She saw a band of children gathered about the gate of a house, which stood at a short distance from the road, surrounded by shrubberies and distinguished by one great splendid cedar which stretched its glorious branches over the high garden wall behind, and made a point in the landscape. A lady was driving a little pony-carriage through the open gate, while the children stood watching and waving their hands to her. 'Good-bye, mamma,' 'Don't be long,' 'And mind you bring back Clara with you,' they were calling to her. With a wistful sense of envy Norah gazed and wondered who they were, and if she should ever know them. 'Why are people so different?' she asked herself. She had nobody in the world but her mother, lost behind that crape veil, lost in her own thoughts, who told her not to ask questions, while those other little girls had a smiling mamma in a pretty pony-carriage, who was taking one to drive with her, and was to bring Clara back to see them. Which Clara? Was it the Clara who belonged to Norah, her own cousin, to whom she had a better right than any one? Norah's heart sank as she realized this. No doubt Clara must have many friends; she could not stand in need of Norah as Norah did of her. She would be a stranger, an interloper, a new little girl whom nobody knew, whom nobody perhaps would care to know. Tears came to the child's eyes. She had been a woman last night rising to the height of the tragedy in which her little life was involved; but now Nature had regained its sway, and she was only twelve years old. It was while her mind was occupied with these thoughts that her mother interrupted them, suddenly pressing her hand.

'Norah, this is our house, where we are to live,' said Helen. Her voice faltered, she held the child's hand as if for support. And now they were at their own door.

Norah gazed at it with a certain dismay. She, too, like Mr Haldane, had her theory about a house in the country. It must be like Southlees, she thought, though without the river; or perhaps, as they had grown poor, it might be something a little better than the lodge at Southlees, a little cottage; but she had never dreamed of anything like this tall red-brick house which twinkled at her with all its windows. She was awed and chilled, and a little frightened, as she crossed the road. Susan was standing at the open door parleying with the porter about their boxes, which she declined to admit till 'the family' came. The one fear which possessed Susan's life, the fear of being 'put upon,' was strong in her at this moment. But she set the balance straight for Norah, by making a sudden curtsey, which tempted the child so sorely to laughter, that her eyes began to shine and her heart to rise once more. She ran up the white steps eagerly before her mother. 'Oh, mamma, I am first. I can say welcome to you,' she said.

But the sight of the drawing-room, into which Susan ushered them, solemnly closing the door after them, struck a moment's chill to Norah's heart. It seemed so strange to be thus shut in, as if it was not their own house but a prison. It was afternoon, and the sunshine had all gone from that side of the road, and the graceful, old-fashioned room looked dim and ghostly to eyes which had just come out of the light. The windows all draped with brown and grey, the old-fashioned slim grand piano in the corner ('I shall have my music,' said Norah), the black japanned screen with its funny little pictures, the high carved mantelpiece with that square mirror which nobody could see into, puzzled the child, at once attracting and repelling her. There was another round, convex mirror like a shield, on the side wall, but even that did not enable Norah to see herself, it only made a little twinkling picture of her in a vast perspective of drawing-room. Helen had seated herself as soon as the door was shut, and there was she, too, in the picture like a lady come to call. What a strange, dim, ghostly place it was! The bumping of the boxes as they went up-stairs was a comfort to Norah. It was a sound of life breaking the terrible silence. She asked herself what would happen when it was over. Should they fall under some charm and sleep there, like the enchanted princess, for a hundred years? And to think that all this was within reach of that lady in the pony-carriage, and of her children who waved their hands to her!—so near, yet in a different world.

'Mayn't we go and see the house, mamma?' Norah whispered, standing close to her mother's side. 'Shouldn't you like to see where we are to sleep? Shouldn't you like to get out of this room? It frightens me so; it feels like a prison. Oh, mamma! perhaps it would not look so strange—and so—dull—and so—funny,' cried Norah, feeling disposed to cry, 'if you would take your bonnet off.'

Just at this moment there was a sound in the road which stirred the whole village into life, and roused Norah. She ran to the window to see what it was. It was an event which happened every evening, which all the children in Dura ran to see, though they were so familiar with it. It was Mr Burton driving his high-stepping bays home from the station. He had come by the express made on purpose for him and such as him, which arrived half-an-hour later than the train by which the Drummonds had come. Norah climbed up on her knees on a chair to see over the little old-fashioned blinds. There was some one seated by Mr Burton in the dog-cart, some one who looked at the Gatehouse, as Mr Burton did, while they dashed past. At the sight of him Norah started, and from a little fantastical child became a woman all at once again. It was the young man who the day before had been with Mr Golden at St Mary's Road, he who had heard her father's vindication, and had believed it, and 'was on our side,' Norah felt, against all the world.

There is always a little excitement in a village over a new inhabitant, and the Drummonds were not common strangers to be speculated vaguely about. There were many people in Dura who remembered Helen in her beauty and youth. And next morning, when it became known that she had arrived at the Gatehouse, the whole place burst into gossip on the subject. Even the new people, the City people who lived in the white villas near the station, were moved by it. For poor Drummond's story was known everywhere, and his miserable fate, and the discussion in the newspapers. Even here, in the quietness of the country, people took sides, and public opinion was by no means so unanimous as poor Helen had supposed. The papers had accepted her husband's guilt as certain, but opinion was very much divided on the subject among people who had means of knowing. 'Burton ought to have warned that poor fellow,' one of the City gentlemen said to another at the station, going up by the early train. 'I would not trust a simpleton in the hands of a smart man like Golden.'

'Do you think he was a simpleton?' said the other.

'In business, yes—' said the first speaker.

'How could he be otherwise? But, by Jove, sir, what a splendid painter! I never saw anything I liked better than that picture of his in the last Exhibition. Poor fellow! And to put him in Golden's hands, a man well known to be up to every dodge. I wonder what Burton could be thinking of. I wonder he can look that poor lady in the face.'

'I should just like to find out how much Burton himself knew about it,' said the other, nodding his head.

'And so should I,' the first speaker said significantly, as they took their place in the train.

Thus it will be seen that the world, which Helen thought of so bitterly as all against her, was by no means so clear on the subject. At the breakfast-table in the Rectory the conversation took a still more friendly tone.

'I hear that poor Mrs Drummond has come to the Gatehouse,' said Mrs Dalton. 'I almost think I saw her yesterday—a tall woman, in a crape veil, with a little girl about Mary's size. I shall make a point of calling the first time I go out. Oh, George, what a sad, sad story! I hope she will let me be of some use to her.'

'I don't see that you can be of much use,' said her husband. 'She has the Burtons, of course, to fall back upon. How strange to think of Helen Burton coming back here! I could not have supposed it possible. So proud a girl! And how that man at Dura could ask her! I suppose he feels the sweetness of revenge in it. Everybody knew she refused him.'

'Oh George, hush! the children,' cried Mrs Dalton under her breath.

'Psha! everybody knows. What a difference it would have made to her, though! It is strange she should have chosen to come and live in sight of his splendour.'

'Oh, do you think she cares about his splendour? Poor soul!' said kind Mrs Dalton, with tears in her eyes. 'She must have very different thoughts in her mind. Most likely she was glad of any shelter where she could hide her head, after all the newspapers and the publicity. Oh, George! it must be doubly hard upon her if she was proud.'

'Probably it was her pride that made her husband such a fool,' said the rector. 'You women have a great deal to answer for. If she drove him into that thirst for money-making—a thing he could know nothing about—You are all fond of money—'

'For money's worth, George,' said Mrs Dalton humbly. She could not deny the accusation. For her own part she would have done anything for money—she with her eight children, and Charlie's education so dreadfully on her mind.

'Oh, I don't say you are miserly,' said the rector, who was a literary man of superior mind, and hated to be bothered by family cares, which incapacitated him for thought; 'but when a woman wants more than her husband can give her, what is the unhappy man to do? Ne sutor ultra crepidam. Which means, Mary—'

'I have heard it before,' said his wife meekly. 'I think I know what it means.'

'Then you see what comes of it,' said Mr Dalton. 'I don't believe a word that is in the papers. I seldom do. He went and got himself involved and bamboozled. How was he to know what he was doing? I don't blame poor Drummond, but I am not so sure it was not her fault.'

At the great house the talk was different; there was no discussion of the rights or wrongs of the question. Mr Burton, indeed, preferred not to speak of Mr Drummond; and young Mr Rivers, who had come down with him on the previous night, had got no opening to report the scene of which he had been a spectator. They were early people, and though they had entertained a large party the night before, their breakfast was earlier than that at the Rectory. They were all out on the lawn, visitors, children, dogs, and all, while Mr Dalton drank his coffee. Ned was busily employed training the Skye to jump over a stick, an exercise which was not much to Shaggy's taste; while the big pointer (who was only in his babyhood, though he was so big, and was imbecile, as puppies are) looked on, and made foolish springs and vaults about his clever brother. Malta, in his blue ribbon, kept close by Mrs Burton's side, and looked on at the performance with the contemptuous toleration of a superior being; and Clara, also decked with blue ribbons, hung by her mother too.

'You had better come with me and see Helen, said the head of the house. 'I told you she arrived last night.'

'Now!' said Mrs Burton, with some surprise. She had her gardening gloves on and a basket in her hand for flowers. These she would have laid down at once, had it been only a walk to the station which was in question; but this was a different affair.

'Yes; why not now?' said her husband with that roll of wealth and comfort in his voice. 'We are relations, we need not stand upon ceremony. You mean to call on her some time, I suppose.'

'Oh, certainly, I shall call; but not at this hour, Mr Burton. I have only seen her once. Familiarity would be impertinence in me.'

'Pshaw, nonsense! one of your fantastic notions,' he said. 'I have seen her more than once, and I can't afford to stand on ceremony. Come along. I am going there now.'

'Then I think you should go immediately,' said Mrs Burton, looking at her watch, 'or you will be too late for the train. Clara, papa will not want us this morning; we can go for some flowers. You will be back by the usual train? I will pick you up at the station, if you like, for I have some calls to make to-day.'

'As you please,' said her husband; 'but I can't understand why you should cross me, Clara, about my cousin. You don't mean to say,' he added with a laugh, 'that you have any—feeling on the subject? That you are—ever so little—piqued about poor Helen? I shouldn't like to use the other word.'

Clara Burton looked at her husband very calmly. She was not offended. It was human nature; men were known to possess this kind of vanity, though it was so strange. 'I am not at all piqued,' she said; 'but I like to be civil. I don't suppose Mrs Drummond and I will be moved to rush into each other's arms all at once, and I don't wish to look as if I paid her less respect because she is poor. If you are going there, you ought to go immediately. You will be late for the train.'

'Confound your composure!' Mr Burton said to himself, as he went down the avenue.

It would have pleased him had his wife been a little discomposed. But, after a while, he took comfort, saying to himself that Clara was a consummate little actress, but that she could not take him in. Of course, she was nettled by the presence of his old love, and by his haste to visit her; but she was proud, and would not show it. He felt a double triumph in the sense that these two women were both affected, and endured, for his sweet sake, a certain amount of pain. He set out his chest more than ever, and held up his head. Now was his moment of triumph over the woman who had once rejected him. Had he been able to induce her to come to Dura while she was still prosperous, the triumph would have been sweeter, for it would have been unmingled with any tinge of regretful or remorseful feeling; but as it was it was sweet. For the first time she would see him in his full importance, in all his state and splendour, she would see him from the depths of her own humiliation, and the force of a contrast greater than he had desired, more complete even than he had dreamed, must already have flashed upon her. Yes, now she would see what she had lost—what a mistake she had made. He meant to be very kind; he would have given her anything she chose to ask for, if she but showed the least sign of penitence, of clearer perception, of being aware of what she had lost. There was nothing which her cousin would not have done for Helen; but he could not resign his own delightful consciousness of triumph. Under this genial influence, he was overflowing with good-nature and kindness.

'What! come out for a little sunshine, old John,' he said to the old man at the lodge, who was seated basking in the warmth on the bench at his door. 'Good for the rheumatics, ain't it, a day like this? I envy you, old fellow, with nothing to do but sit by your door in the sun and sniff your flowers; you are better off than I am, I can tell you.'

'Ay, ay! master, it's fine for me; but you wouldn't think much on't yourself, if you had it,' said old John.

Mr Burton went on laughing and waving his hand, amused with the old man's impudence.

'If I had it myself,' he said, with a smile, 'I!—' The thought tickled him. It was hard to believe that he himself, a man in the prime of life, growing richer every day, was made of the same clay as old John; and yet of course it was so, he admitted good humouredly. His mind was full of his own benevolence and kind-heartedness as he pursued his way to visit his cousin. What quantities of people were dependent upon his will and pleasure—upon his succour and help! his servants, so many that he could scarcely count them; the clerks in his office; the governess who taught Clara, and who in her turn supported her mother and sisters; and then there was old Stephenson in the village, in his decay, who had once been in Mr Burton's office; and his old nurse; and the poor Joneses and Robinsons, whose boys he had taken in as errand boys. He ran over this list with such a pleasant sense of his goodness, that his face shone in the morning sunshine. And at the head of all, first of his pensioners, chief of his dependents—Helen! Mr Burton laughed half aloud, and furtively rubbed his hands. Yes, yes, by this time there could be no doubt she must have found out her mistake.

Helen had got up that morning with the determination to put grief away from the foreground of her life, and resume such occupations as remained to her. Norah's books had been got out, and her music, and some work—small matters which made a difference in the ghostly drawing-room already, and brought it back to life. Helen was standing by the table arranging some flowers when Mr Burton came in. Norah had gathered them almost before the dew was off them, and stood by her mother watching her as she grouped them together.

'I wish I could arrange flowers as you do, mamma,' Norah was saying admiringly. 'How nice it must be to be able to do everything one tries! They will not come right when I do it. You are like the fairy that touched the feathers with her wand, and they all came together as they ought. I wonder how you do it. And you never break anything or spoil anything; but if I only look at a vase it breaks.'

Norah was saying this with a rueful look when Mr Burton's smart summons came to the door; and the next minute he had come in, bringing so much air with him into the room, and motion, and sense of importance. Helen put the flowers aside hastily and gave him her hand.

'So you are making use of the garden,' he said, taking note of everything with an eye of proprietorship; 'quite right, quite right. I hope you will make yourselves quite at home. It is a funny old house, but it is a good style of a place. You need not be ashamed to receive any one here. And I have no doubt you will find everybody very civil, Helen. I have let the people in Dura know you are my cousin. That, though I say it that shouldn't, is a very good passport here.'

'I hope you will not take any trouble about us,' said Helen hastily. 'All I want is to be quiet. I do not care for civilities.'

'But you prefer them to incivilities, I hope,' said Mr Burton. 'My wife thinks I am wrong to come in this unceremonious way to call. I wanted her to come with me, but she would not. You ladies have your own ways of acting. But I felt that you would be mortified if you saw me pass the door.'

'Oh no. I should not have been mortified.'

'I will take care you sha'n't,' he said, the roll in his voice sounding more full of protection and benevolence than ever. 'I have not much time now. But, my dear Helen, remember that I am always at your service—always. I have mentioned you to all the nicest people. And we hope very soon to see you at the House. I should not have brought you here, I assure you, without intending to be a friend to you in every way. You may rely upon me.'

'You are very kind,' was all Helen could say.

'I want to be kind. You cannot please me better than by asking me for what you want. Tell me always when your mother wants anything, Norah. There now, I won't say any more; you understand me, Helen. I have a few things in my power, and one of them is to make you comfortable. When you have time to see about you you will perceive that things have gone very well with me: not that I intend to boast; but Providence, no doubt, has been very kind. My wife will call this afternoon, and should you like a drive or anything, I am sure Clara—'

'Please don't trouble. I would rather be quiet. You forget,' said Helen, with a momentary sharpness in her voice, 'that Providence, which has been so kind to you, has been hard upon us.'

'My dear Helen! you are too good and pious, I am sure, not to know that we ought not to repine.'

'I don't think I repine, and I am sure you mean to be kind; but oh! if you would take pity on me, and let me alone—'

It was all she could do to keep from tears. But she would not weep before him. Her jealousy of him and distrust were all coming back. Instinctively she felt the triumph in his voice.

'Poor Helen!' said Mr Burton, 'poor girl! I will not trouble you longer just now. You shall not be bothered. Good-bye; trust to me, and I will take care of you, my poor dear!'

It was ludicrous, it was pitiable; she scorned herself for the impression it made upon her; but how could she help it? She felt that she hated Reginald Burton, as he stood before her in all his wealth and comfort, patronising and soothing her. When he was gone, she rushed up to her room, that Norah might not see her weakness, to weep a few hot, burning tears, and to overcome the wild, unreasonable anger that swelled in her heart. It was his moment of triumph. Perhaps Helen felt it all the more because, deep down in her heart, she had a consciousness that she too had once triumphed over him, and rejoiced to feel that she could humble him. This was a hard punishment for such an old girlish offence; but still it felt like a punishment, and added a sting to everything he did and said. And whether it was at that moment or at a later period, she herself could not have told, but a sudden gleam came across her of some words which she had once read somewhere—'Burton and Golden have done it.' Whence came these words? had she dreamt them? had she read them somewhere? They came before her as if they had been written upon the wall. Burton and Golden! Was it true? What could it mean?

Mrs Burton called in the afternoon. She had Clara with her, and what was still more remarkable, young Mr Rivers, who was staying in the house, but who up to this time had made no mention of the scene he had witnessed. Perhaps it was for lack of an opportunity, perhaps because he did not know how far it would be safe to mention Helen—whom he heard spoken of as a relative, yet not with the feeling which moved his own mind when he thought of her. Cyril Rivers was but a big boy, though he began to think himself a man, and Helen had moved him to that sudden fantastic violence of admiration with which an older woman often momentarily inspires a boy. He was eager to go with Mrs Burton to call. He would walk down with her, he said, and continue his walk after the carriage had picked her up; and in his heart he said to himself that he must see that woman again. He was full of awe and enthusiasm at the thought of her. She was to him like the heroine of a tragedy, of a story more striking, more affecting than any tragedy he had ever heard of; for this was real, and she was a true woman expressing her natural sentiments, forgiving nothing. It seemed to bring the youth, who was all thrilling with natural romance, within that charmed inner circle of emotion and passion which is, though it is seldom visible, the centre and heart of life.

But Helen bore a very different aspect when she waited to receive Mrs Burton's call from that which she bore at the door of St Mary's Road, confronting Golden. Her flush of colour and glow of energy and vehemence were gone. She was seated, pale and silent, by the table near the window, with her dead white cap encircling her face, and some needlework in her hand. It was not the same Mrs Drummond, was young Rivers' first disappointed thought. And when she invited the party to sit down, and began to talk about the weather and the country round, he was so bewildered that he longed to steal away. The two ladies sat opposite to each other, and said the sort of things which all ladies say when they call or are called upon. Helen's tone was low, and her voice fell; but these and her black dress were the only things that made it apparent that anything had happened to her. It was only when this little artificial conversation flagged and a pause occurred that the real state of affairs became even slightly visible. The momentary silence fell heavy upon people who had so much on their minds; and while they all sat motionless, the little mirror on the wall made a picture of them in little, which looked like a caricature, full of humourous perception and significance. Mrs Burton had been hesitating as to what she should say. Helen was a study to her, of which she had as yet made nothing; and perhaps it was as much from curiosity as any other feeling that she at last introduced a subject more interesting than the weather or the landscape. It was after a second pause still more serious than the first.

'It must be very strange to you coming back to Dura after all that has happened. It must be—hard upon you,' she said.

'Yes; it is hard,' Helen could not trust herself to many words.

'If there is anything in which I can be of use,' Mrs Burton began, 'will you let me know? If there is anything that can make it less painful for you. I should be very glad to be of any use.'

Mrs Drummond made no reply; she gave a little bow, and went on with the needlework she held in her hands, but not as if she cared for that. She was not like what he had thought, but yet young Rivers got up with a certain tremulous awe and approached her. She had not recognised him. She turned her eyes upon him wondering what he could have to do with her. Her heart was steeled to encounter all those words of routine which she knew would have to be said—but who was this boy?

'I think I will go now,' he said hastily to Mrs Burton; and then he lowered his voice. 'May I say just one word? If I can ever do anything to set things right, will you let me know? I shall never forget what you said—on Tuesday.'

'On Tuesday?' Helen repeated, in her great surprise looking at him. She ran over Tuesday's proceedings in her mind; at first in vain, and then a little flush came over her face. 'Ah,' she said, 'it was you who came with—Mr Golden. I remember now.'

'But I shall never be with him again,' said the youth with energy, which brought the responsive blood to his cheeks. 'Of that you may be sure. I am Cyril Rivers. I am not much good now, but I might be—afterwards. Will you remember me? Will you let me serve you if ever I can?'

'Thanks,' said Helen, putting out her hand, with a sudden softness in her voice.

The lad was young, romantic, chivalrous. She was to him like some majestic dethroned queen in her sorrow and wronged estate. He stooped down, and touched her white fingers with his lips, and then, without looking round, turned, and went away. His impulsive generous words, his fanciful pledge of eagerness to help her, went to Helen's heart. She had not expected this, and it surprised and touched her. She was not conscious for a moment of her visitor's steady, investigating glance.

'What a romantic boy!' said Mrs Burton, with a smile.

'Yes,' said Helen, and she called herself back with an effort. 'But romance sometimes does one good. It is a surprise at least.'

'At that age it does not matter much. I did not know you knew the Riverses,' said Mrs Burton. 'This is the eldest son, to be sure; but since the late misfortune they are quite poor. They have not much in their power.'

She said this with a charitable motive. It seemed to her as if Helen must mean something by it. Everybody appeared to mean something in the eyes of this philosopher. And she was a little moved by the misfortunes of the woman beside her. She thought it was kind to warn her not to waste her efforts. Helen, on her side, did not know in the least what Mrs Burton meant; did not suppose she meant anything indeed, and sat patient, accepting this speech with the others as an effort to make conversation, not ungrateful to Mrs Burton, but wondering when she would go away.

Meanwhile Cyril Rivers hastened out full of emotion. He took the wrong turn in going out, and before he knew, found himself in the garden, where the two girls were 'making acquaintance,' as Mrs Burton had bidden them do. Clara was big and fair, with her father's full form, and a beautiful complexion, the greatest possible contrast to little Norah, with her light figure, and faint rose tints. But Norah at this moment was flushed and angry, looking as her mother had done that memorable evening at St Mary's Road.

'Oh, do come here, Mr Rivers,' said Clara, 'Norah is so cross. I only said what papa says so often—that it would be wretched to live in the country without a carriage or a pony or anything. Don't you think so too?'

Norah flushed more deeply than ever. 'I am not cross. We did not come to live in the country for pleasure, and what does it matter to us about carriages and ponies? We are poor.'

'And so am I,' said the boy, with that instinctive adoption of 'our side' which Norah had attributed to him. He thought how pretty she was as she lifted her brown eyes. What a pretty child! and he was approaching twenty, a man, and his heart yearned over the helpless and sorrowful. 'I shall have to sell my horses and go afoot; but I don't think I shall be wretched. Everybody cannot be rich like Mr Burton, you know.'

'But you are always Lord Rivers's son,' said Clara. 'You can have what you like everywhere. I think it is very cross of Norah not to care.'

And Mr Burton's daughter, foiled in her first attempt to secure her own cousin's envy and admiration, looked as if she would like to cry. Young Rivers laughed as he went away at her discomfiture. As he turned to find the right way of exit, he looked back upon them with an unconscious comparison. He did not know or think what was Norah Drummond's descent. He took her unconsciously as the type of a higher class impoverished but not fallen, beside that small representative of the nouveaux riches. And all his sympathies were on the side of the former. He pulled a little white rosebud from a tree as he passed, and put it in his coat with a meaning which was partly real and partly fantastic. They were poor, they were injured, and wronged, and in trouble. He put their colours, as it were, in his helmet. Foolish boy, full of romance and nonsense! one day or other in their cause he felt he might couch his lance.

CHAPTER III

The next day after Mrs Burton's carriage had been seen at Helen's door a great many people called on Mrs Drummond—all 'the nicest people'—some who had known her or known about her in the old days, some who came because she was Mr Burton's cousin, and some who took that means of showing their sympathy. The door was besieged; and Susan, half-flattered by the importance of her position, half-alarmed lest this might be a commencement of the system of putting upon which she dreaded, brought in the cards, gingerly holding them in a hand which she had wrapped up in her apron, and giving a little sketch of the persons represented. There was the doctor's wife, and the major's lady, and Mrs Ashurst from the Row, and 'them London folks,' all of whom were sensible enough to make their advances solely in this way. Mrs Dalton was the only person admitted. Helen was too well brought up, she had too much sense of the proprieties of her position, to shut her door against the clergyman's wife—who brought her husband's card, and explained that he would have come too but for the fear of intruding too early.

'But I hope you will let us see you,' the kind woman added. 'We are such near neighbours. My eldest little girl is the same age as yours. I think we should understand each other. And I have such a busy life—to be able to run across and talk things over now and then would be such a comfort to me.'

'You mean it would be a comfort to me,' said Helen, 'the sight of a kind face.'

'And Norah will come and see my Mary. They can take their walks together, and amuse each other. It is such a pleasure to me,' said Mrs Dalton, 'to look across at these windows, and think that you are here.' She had said so much with the amiable power of make-believe, not exactly deception, which an affectionate temper and her position as clergy-woman made natural to her—when she caught Helen's eye, and nature suddenly had the mastery. 'Oh, Mrs Drummond, how I babble! I am so sorry, so sorry!' she said, and her eyes ran over with tears, though Helen did not weep. It is not easy to repel such a visitor. They grew friends at that first interview, while Norah stood by and made her observations too.

'May I go and see Mary?' she asked, when Mrs Dalton had gone. 'I think I shall like her better than Clara Burton. How funny it must be to have so many brothers and sisters, mamma; and I who never had either a brother or a sister! I should like to have had just one—a little sister with blue eyes. But, then, if you had been very fond of her, fonder than of me, I should not have liked that. Perhaps, on the whole, a brother would have been the best. A boy is a change—they are useless, and yet they are nice—for a long walk, for instance. I wish I had had a big brother, older than me—quite old—almost grown up. How funny it would have been! I wonder what we should have called him. If he had been as big as—Mr Rivers, for instance—that would have been nice for you too.'

Helen smiled, and let the child run on. It was the music to which her life was set. Norah's monologue accompanied everything. Sometimes, indeed, an answer was necessary, which interrupted the strain, but generally a word, a smile, or a monosyllable was enough. She went on weaving her big brother out of her imagination; it was more delightful than speculating about Mary Dalton.

'I am sure it would have been nice for you too,' she said. 'He would have given you his arm when you were tired, and looked after the luggage, and locked all the doors at nights. The only thing is, it would have been a great expense. When people are poor, I suppose they can't afford to have boys. They want so many things. But yet he would have been nice all the same. I hope he would have had a pretty name; not so short as Ned, and not so common as Charlie. Charlie is the eldest of the Daltons—such a big boy. Oh, I wonder what our boy's name would have been? Do you like Oswald, mamma, or Eustace? Eustace sounds like a priest or something dreadfully wise. I don't like solemn boys. So long as he was big and strong, and not too clever. But oh, dear, dear, what is the use of talking? We never can have a big boy, I suppose? I must be content with other girls' brothers. I shall never have one of my very own.'

'The less you have to do with other girls' brothers the better, Norah,' said Helen, beguiled into a smile.

'I do not care for them, I am sure,' said Norah, with dignity; 'though I don't dislike gentlemen, mamma—quite old gentlemen, like Dr Maurice and Mr Haldane, are very nice. And I should like to have had—Mr Rivers, for instance—for a big brother. I rather think, too, I like Ned Burton better than Clara. It is more natural to hear a boy talk of ponies and things. She never thinks of anything else—dogs, and horses, and carriages, and the fine things she has. It is not polite to talk of such things to people who have not got them. I told her I did not care for ponies, nor grapes, nor hot-house flowers; and that I would rather live in London than at the House. And, oh, so many—stories, mamma! Is it wrong to tell a little fib when you don't mean any harm? Just a little one, when people boast and make themselves disagreeable—and when you don't mean any harm?'

'It is always wrong to tell fibs; and I don't know the difference between big ones and little ones,' said Helen.

'Oh, mamma, but I do! A big story is—for instance. If I were to say Susan had stolen your watch, that would be a wicked lie. But when I say I don't care for grapes, and would not like to have a pony, it isn't quite true, but then it makes Clara be quiet, and does nobody any harm. I am sure there is a great difference. It would be very nice to have a pony, you know. Only think, mamma, to go cantering away across the common and on the turf! But I would not give in to say that I should like to be Clara, or that she was better off than me!'

Norah's casuistry silenced her mother. She shook her head, but she did not say anything. Something of the same feeling was, indeed, in her own mind. She, too, would have liked to be contemptuous of the luxuries which her neighbours dangled before her eyes. And Norah resumed her monologue. The mother only partially heard it, waking up now and then to give the necessary response, but carrying on all the time her own separate thread of cogitation, which would not shape itself into words. The old parlour, with its brown-grey curtains and all its spindle-legged furniture, enclosed and seemed to watch the human creatures who disturbed the silence. A room which has been long unoccupied, and which is too large for its new inhabitants, has often this spectator look. The pictures looked down from the walls and watched; up in the little round mirror two people in a miniature interior, who were in reality reflections of the two below, but looked quite different, glanced down upon them, and watched also.

The sky looked in through the five windows, and the lime-trees in front kept tapping with their branches against the panes to show that they were looking on. All the rest were clandestine, but the lime-trees were honest in their scrutiny. And in the midst of it the mother and daughter led their subdued lives. Norah's voice ran through all like a brook or a bird. Helen was mostly silent, saying little. They had a roof to shelter them, enough of daily bread, the kindness of strangers outside, the rude but sympathetic kindness of Susan within. This was more, a great deal more, than often falls to the lot of human wrecks after a great shipwreck. Norah after a little while accepted it as the natural rule of life, and forgot every other; and Helen was silent, though she did not forget. The silence of the house, however, by times oppressed the child. She lay awake in the great bed-room up-stairs, afraid to go to sleep till her mother should come; and even in the daylight there were moments when Norah was afraid of the ghostly drawing-room, and could not but feel that weird aged women, the Miss Pagets, whom her mother had known, or some of the old Harcourts, were watching her from behind the doors, or from the shade of the curtains. There was a deep china closet beside the fireplace with one particular knot in the wood-work which fascinated Norah, and made her feel that some mysterious eye was gazing at her from within. But all these fancies dispersed the moment Mrs Drummond appeared. There was protection in the soft rustle of her gown, the distant sound of her voice. And so the routine of life—a new routine, but soon firmly established, supporting them as upon props of use and wont, began again. There were the lessons in the morning, and Norah's music, and a long walk in the afternoon; and they went to bed early, glad to be done with life and another day. Or at least Helen was glad to be done with it—not Norah, to whom it was the opening of the story, and to whom once more the sunshine began to look as sweet as ever, and each new morning was a delight.

A few weeks after their arrival the Haldanes followed them. Miss Jane had written beforehand begging for information about the house and the journey; and it was only then that Helen learned, with a mortification she could scarcely overcome, that the Gatehouse was to be their refuge too. This fact so changed the character of her cousin's kindness to her, that her pride was with difficulty subdued to silence; but she had sufficient self-control to say nothing—pride itself coming to her aid.

'Perhaps you would be so good as to send me a line with a few particulars,' Miss Jane wrote. 'I should like to know for myself and mother if there is a good minister of our denomination, and if you would mention the price of meat, and how much you are giving for the best butter, I should be very much obliged. I should like to know if there is a good room on the ground-floor that would do for Stephen, and if we could have a Bath-chair to bring him down from the station, for I am very distrustful of cabs. Also about a charwoman, which is very important. I am active myself and always look after the washing, so that one strong handy woman to come from six in the morning till two would do all I should require.'

Mrs Drummond made an effort and answered all these questions, and even walked to the station to see them arrive. It was a mournful sight enough. She stood and looked on with her heart aching, and saw the man whom she had known so different lifted out of the carriage and put into the invalid chair. She saw the look of dumb anguish and humiliation in his eyes which showed how he felt this public exposure of his weakness. He was very patient; he smiled and thanked the people who moved him: yet Helen, with her perceptions quickened by her own suffering, felt the intolerable pain in the other's soul, and went away hurriedly, not to afflict him further by her presence. What had he done? How had this man sinned more than others? All the idlers that lounged about and watched him, were they better or dearer to God than he was? Mrs Drummond was half a Pagan, though she did not know it. She hurried away with a miserable sense that it was past bearing. But Stephen set his lips tight and bore it. He bore the looks of the village people who came out to their doors to look at him as he passed. As for his mother and sister, they scarcely remarked his silence. They were so happy that everything had gone off so well, that he had borne it so easily.

'I don't think he looks a bit the worse,' said Miss Jane.

They were the tenderest, the most patient of nurses, but they had accepted his illness long ago as a matter of course. From the moment he was placed in the chair, and so off their mind, as it were, the luggage came into the ascendant and took his place. They had a wonderful amount of parcels, mostly done up in brown paper. Mrs Haldane herself carried her pet canary in its cage, tied up in a blue-and-white handkerchief. She was more anxious about this for the moment than about her son. The procession was one which caught everybody's eye. First two wheelbarrows with the luggage, the first of which was occupied by Stephen's bed and chair, the other piled up with boxes, among the rest two portmanteaus of his own, on which he could still read, on old labels which he had preserved with pride, the names of Naples, Florence, and Rome. Had he been actually there, he who was now little more than a piece of luggage himself? Miss Jane divided her attentions between her brother and the second wheelbarrow, on which the brown-paper parcels were tumbling and nodding, ready to fall. His mother walked on the other side, holding fast by the parcel in the blue-and-white handkerchief. Mrs Burton, who was passing in her carriage, stopped to look after them. She, too, had known Stephen in better days. She did not ask passionate questions as Helen was doing; but she felt the shock in her way, and only comforted herself by thinking that the feelings get blunted in such unfortunate cases, and that no doubt other people felt more for him than he felt for himself.

But notwithstanding the callousness which use had brought, there was no indifference to Stephen's comfort in the minds of his attendants. Everything was arranged for him that evening as if he had been surrounded by a crowd of servants. When Helen went to see him he was seated by the window with flowers upon his table and all his papers arranged upon it. The flowers were not very choice; they were of Miss Jane's selection, and marigolds and plumy variegated grass looked beautiful in her eyes. Yet nothing but love could have put everything in its place so soon, and metamorphosed all at once the dining-room of the Gatehouse into Stephen's room, where everything bore a reference to him and was arranged for his special comfort. Perhaps they did not always feel for him, or even see what room there was for feeling. But this they could do—and in it they never failed.

'Does not he look comfortable?' Miss Jane said with triumph. 'You would think to see him he had never budged from his chair. And he got through the journey very well. If you but knew how frightened I was when we set out!'

Stephen looked at Mrs Drummond with a smile. There were some lines about his mouth and a quiver in his upper lip which spoke to her more clearly than to his sister. Helen had not been in the way of going out of herself to sympathise with others; and it seemed to her as if she had suddenly got a new pair of eyes, an additional sense. While they were all talking she saw what the journey had really cost him in his smile.

'It is strange to see the world again after so long,' he said, 'and to realise that once one walked about it quite carelessly like other people, without thinking what a thing it was.'

'But, Stephen, I am sure you don't repine,' said his mother, 'you know whose will it is, and you would not have it different? That is such a comfort whatever we may have to suffer.'

'You would not have it different!'

Helen looked at him almost with tears in her eyes.

'That is a great deal to say, mother,' he answered with a suppressed sigh; while she still went on asking herself passionately what had he done? what had he done?

'I think the charwoman will suit very well,' said Miss Jane. 'She seems clean, and that is the great thing. I am very well satisfied with everything I have seen as yet. The kitchen garden is beautiful. I suppose as there is no division, we are to have it between us—that and the fruit? I have been thinking a few fowls would be very nice if you have no objection. They cost little to keep, and to have your own eggs is a great luxury. And meat seems reasonable. I am very well satisfied with all I have seen.'

'If we only knew about the chapel,' said Mrs Haldane. 'So much of your comfort depends on your minister. If he is a nice man he will be company for Stephen. That is what I am most afraid of—that he will be dull in the country. There was always some one coming in about the magazine or some society or other when we were in town. I am afraid, Stephen, you will feel quite lost here.'

'Not for want of the visitors, mother,' he said; 'especially if Mrs Drummond will spare me Norah. She is better than any minister—not meaning any slight to my brethren,' he added, in a half-apologetic, half-laughing tone. He could laugh still, which was a thing Helen found it very difficult to understand.

'Norah is very nice, and I like dearly to see her,' said his mother; 'but, Stephen, I don't like to hear you talk like that. Mrs Drummond is not to know that it is all your nonsense. You were always such a one for a joke.'

'My jokes have not been very brilliant lately,' he said, with a smile. Mrs Haldane rose at that moment to help her daughter with something she was moving to the other end of the room, and Stephen, seizing the opportunity, turned quickly round upon Helen, who was sitting by him. 'You are very sorry for me,' he said, with a mixture of gratitude and impatience. 'Don't! it is better not!'

'How can I help it?' cried Helen. 'And why is it better not?'

'Because I cannot bear it,' he said, almost sternly.

This passed in a moment, while the unconscious women at the other end had altered the position of a table. Never man had more tender nurses than these two; but they had ceased to be sorry for him in look or word. They had accepted their own fate and his; his helplessness was to them like the daylight or the dark, a thing inevitable, the course of nature; and the matter-of-fact way in which they had learned to treat it made his life supportable. But it was difficult for a stranger to realise such a fact.

'I never told you that we were disappointed about letting the house,' said Miss Jane. 'A great many people came, but no one who was satisfactory. It is a great loss. I have left a person in it to try for a few months longer. People are very unprincipled, coming out of mere curiosity, and turning over your blankets and counterpanes without a thought.'

Here the conversation came to a pause, and Helen rose. She was standing saying her farewells and making such offers of assistance as she could, when the daily event with which she had grown familiar took place.

'There is some one coming,' said Stephen, from the window. 'It ought to be the queen by the commotion it makes: but it is only Burton.'

And Mrs Haldane and Miss Jane both rushed forward to see. Helen withdrew out of sight with a secret bitterness which she could not have put into words. Mr Burton was driving home from the station in all his usual importance. His horses were groomed to perfection, the mountings of his harness sparkled in the sun. He half drew up as he passed, making his bays prance and express their disapprobation, while he took off his hat to the new arrivals. It was such a salutation as a jocund monarch might have tossed at a humble worshipper, mock ceremony and conscious condescension. The women looking out never thought of that. They ran from one window to another to watch him entering the avenue, they talked to each other of his fine horses, the neat groom beside him, and how polite he was. Stephen had been looking on, too, with keen interest. A smile was on his face, but the lines above his eyes were contracted, and the eyes themselves gleamed with a sudden fire which startled Helen.

'I wonder what he thinks of it all,' he said to her under his breath, 'if he thinks at all. I wonder if he is comfortable when he reflects who are living at his gates?'

The words were said so low that she had to stoop to hear; and with a wondering thrill of half-comprehension she looked at him. What did he mean? From whence came that tone which was almost fierce in its self-restraint? It seemed to kindle a smouldering fire in her, of the nature of which she was not quite aware. 'Burton and Golden' suddenly flashed across her thoughts again. Where was it she had seen the names linked together? What did it mean? and what did Stephen mean? She felt as if she had almost found out something, which quickened her pulse and made her heart beat—almost. But the last point of enlightenment was yet to come.

'Now he has turned in at the gate,' said Miss Jane. 'Well, for my part, I am glad to have seen him; and to think that a man could do all that by his own exertions! If he had been a nobleman I should not have thought half so much of it. I suppose, now, that could not be seen anywhere but in England? You may smile, Stephen, and think me very vulgar-minded; but I do think it is a very wonderful sight.'

And thus the second household settled down, and became a part of the landscape which the family at Dura surveyed with complaisant proprietorship, and through which Mr Burton drove every afternoon, calling admiring spectators to all the windows. The rich man had never enjoyed the commotion he made so much as he did now when he could see at the Gatehouse those faces looking out. There was scarcely an evening but Miss Jane or her mother would stand up to see him, gazing with unconscious worship at this representative of wealth and strength, and that practical power which sways the world; while Norah would clamber up on a chair behind the blinds at the other end, and look out with her big brown eyes full of serious observation. He thought Norah wondered and worshipped too, not being able to understand the language of her eyes. And sometimes he would see, or think he saw, her mother behind her. When he did so he went home in high good-humour, and was more jocular than usual; for nothing gave him such a sense of his own greatness, his prosperity, and superiority to common flesh and blood, as the homage, or supposed homage, paid to him by those lookers-on at the windows of the Gatehouse.

Mr Burton's satisfaction came to a climax when his father-in-law came to pay his next visit, which happened not very long after the arrival of the Haldanes. Mr Baldwin, as we have said, was a Dissenter, and something like a lay bishop in his denomination. He was very rich, and lived very plainly at Clapham with his two sisters, Mrs Everett and Miss Louisa. They were all very good people in their way. There was not a man in England who subscribed to more societies or presided at a greater number of meetings. He spent half his income in this way; he 'promoted' charities as his son-in-law promoted joint-stock companies; and prided himself on the simplicity of his living and his tastes, notwithstanding his wealth. When he and his sisters came to pay a visit at Dura they walked from the station, leaving their servants and their boxes to follow in a fly. 'We have the use of our limbs, I am thankful to Providence,' one of the sisters would say; 'why should we have a carriage for a little bit of road like that?' They walked in a little procession, the gentleman in advance, like a triumphant cock in front of his harem, the two ladies a little behind. Mr Baldwin wore his hat on the back of his head, and a white tie, like one of his favourite ministers; he had a round, chubby face, without any whiskers, and a complexion almost as clear as little Clara's. The two ladies were like him, except that Mrs Everett, who was a widow, was large and stout, and Miss Louisa pale and thin. They walked along with a natural feeling of benevolent supremacy, making their remarks on everybody and everything with distinct voices. When they got to the Gatehouse they paused and inspected it, though the windows were all open.

'I think Reginald was wrong to give such a house as this to those poor people,' said the married sister in front of the door. 'It is a handsome house. He might have found some little cottage for them, and let this to a family.'

'But, Martha, he gave what he had, and it is that that is always accepted,' said Miss Louisa.

The brother drowned her plaintive little voice with a more decided reply—

'I am very glad Haldane has such good quarters. As for the lady, I suppose she was not to blame; but when a man flies in the face of Providence I would not reward him by providing for his wife and family. I agree with Martha. It is a waste of the gifts of God to give this house to poor people who cannot enjoy it; but still Burton is right on the whole. If you cannot do better with your property, why should not you use it to make friends of the mammon of unrighteousness? I approve of his charity on the whole.'

Inside the recipients of the charity sat and heard all through the open windows. But what then? Mr Baldwin and his sisters were not responsible for that. They went on to the avenue making the same candid and audible remarks all along the road. It was not necessary that they should exercise self-restraint. They were in the dominions of their relation. They were absolute over all foolish sentiment and false pride. They said it loud out, frankly, whatever they might have to say. The arrival of these visitors always made a certain commotion at Dura. It moved Mr Burton a great deal more than it did his wife. Indeed, if there was anything which vexed him in her exemplary behaviour, it was that she would not make temporarily the changes which he thought were 'only respectful' to suit the tastes of her father and aunts. 'You know your father likes only plain roast and boiled,' he would say to her, half-indignantly, adding, with a laugh, 'and minister sauce.' This last was one of his favourite jokes, though it did not strike his wife as particularly brilliant. But the minister sauce was the only thing which Mrs Burton provided for her father. She held fast by her menu, though he disapproved of it. She dressed herself tranquilly for dinner, though her aunts held up their hands, and asked her solemnly if she knew what all this extravagance must come to? In these matters Clara would not give way; but she asked the minister of the chapel in the village to dinner, and it was in the presence of this functionary that Mr Baldwin filled up the measure of his son-in-law's content.

'I see you have been very generous to poor Haldane,' he said. 'I am very much obliged to you, Burton. He is my own man; I should have been compelled to do something for him if you had not taken him up; and my hands are always so full! You will find I do not forget it. But it was a great waste to put him into such a handsome house.'

'I am delighted to have pleased you,' said Mr Burton. 'It was an empty house; and I have put my cousin, Mrs Drummond, in the other end, whom I was obliged to take care of. It was the cheapest way of doing it. I am most happy to think I have relieved you, even of so little as that.'

'Oh yes, you have relieved me,' said Mr Baldwin. 'I sha'n't forget it. It will be an encouragement to Mr Truston and to many of the brethren to see that a sick friend is never abandoned. I don't mean to say that you want any inducement—but, still, when you can see that even in the case of failing strength—'

'Oh yes. I am sure it is most encouraging,' the poor minister faltered.

Encouraging to think of Stephen Haldane, who was thus provided for! The two rich men went on with their talk over their wine, while some confused speculation as to the ways of Providence went through the head of their companion. He was young, and he felt ill at ease, and he did not like to interfere much. Had it been Mr Dalton he would have been less easily silenced. Thus Mr Burton found his benevolence in one particular at least attended with the most perfect success.

CHAPTER IV

And everything settled down, and Nature resumed her common round. This is what Nature does in all circumstances. There never was so bad a storm but next morning the thrifty mother took heart and set to work again as best she could to make amends for it. It is only when the storm affects human hearts and lives that this cheerful, pathetic effort to get the better of it becomes terrible; for the mending in such cases is so often but superficial, the cure impossible. Other trees grow up to fill the gap made by the one blown down; but not other loves or other hopes. Yet gradually the tempest calms, the wreck is swept away, and some things that are new are always better than some things that were old, even though the old can never be replaced while life goes on.

Of all the dwellers in the Gatehouse, it was poor Haldane who felt this the most. The reality of this life in the country was very different from the anticipation. The fresh air which his mother had hoped to have for Stephen—the cottage garden which they had all dreamt of (even he himself by moments), where he could be wheeled in his chair to sit under the apple-tree and smell the flowers—had vanished from their list of possibilities. All the fresh air he could have was from the open window by which his chair was placed. But not even the garden and the apple-tree would have done so much for him as the varieties of the country road. Instead of the garden walls at Victoria Villas, the strip of dusty grass, the chance sight of a neighbour's child at play, or (more likely) of a neighbour's clothes hung out to dry, he had a genuine rural highroad, with all its sights. He saw the carts passing with rural produce, full of big baskets of vegetables for the London market; he saw the great waggons of odorous hay, with a man asleep on the top, half-buried in the warm and fragrant mass, or cracking his whip on the path, and shouting drowsy, inarticulate calls to the horses, who took their own way, and did not mind him; he saw the carriages gleam past with the great people, whom by degrees he got to know; and then the Rectory children were always about, and Mrs Dalton in her pony-chaise, and the people coming and going from the village. There were two of the village folk in particular who brought a positive pleasure into his life—not a pair of lovers, or any pretty group, but only Clippings, the tailor, and Brown, the shoemaker, who strolled down the road in the evening to smoke their pipes and talk politics as far as the Rectory gate. Clippings, who lived 'up town,' was always decorous in his shabby coat; but Brown, whose shop was 'at the corner,' came in his shirt-sleeves, with his apron turned up obliquely to one side. They would stop just opposite his window when they got hot in their discussion. Sometimes it was the parish they talked of, sometimes the affairs of the state, and it was in Stephen's mind sometimes to invite them to cross the road, and to have his say in the matter. They were not men of education or intelligence perhaps; but they were men, living the natural human life from which he had been torn, and it did him good to watch them. After a while they began to look over at him and take off their hats, half with village obsequiousness to a possible customer, half with natural feeling for a soul in prison; and he gave them a nod in return.

But this vulgar fancy of his was not quite approved of within. 'If you are so friendly with these men, Stephen, you will have them coming over, and poisoning the whole house with tobacco,' Mrs Haldane said, with an expressive sniff. 'I think I smell it even now.' But his mother was not aware that the scent of the tobacco was like an air of paradise to poor Stephen, who had loved it well enough when he was his own master, though it had become impossible now.

Mrs Haldane, however, did not say a word against Mr Dalton's cigar, which he very often smoked under Stephen's window in those summer mornings, lounging across in his study coat. It must be remembered that Stephen was not a Dissenting minister pur et simple, but a man whose name had been heard in the literary world, especially in that literary world which Mr Dalton, as a 'thoughtful' and 'liberal' clergyman, chiefly affected. The rector felt that it was kind to go and talk to poor Haldane, but he was not so overwhelmingly superior as he might have been under other circumstances. He did not set him down at once at a distance of a hundred miles, as he did Mr Truston, the minister of the chapel at Dura, by the mere suavity of his 'good morning.' On the contrary, they had a great deal of talk. Mr Dalton was a man who piqued himself on his Radicalism, except when he happened to come in contact with Radicals, and he was very great in education, though he left the parish schools chiefly to his wife. When anything had happened which was more than ordinarily interesting in public affairs, he would stride across with gaiety to the encounter: 'I told you your friend Bright was not liberal-minded enough to see that distinction,' he would say; or, 'Gladstone has gone off on another search after truth;' and then the battle would go on, while Stephen sat inside and his interlocutor paced the white flags in front of the Gatehouse up and down under the windows with that fragrant cigar. Sometimes Mary would come flying over from the Rectory: 'Papa, papa, you are wanted. There are some papers to sign, and mamma can't do it, she says.' 'Pazienza!' the rector would answer, for he had travelled too.

And then on the Saturday there were other diversions for Stephen. Old Ann from the farm of Dura Den would whip up her old white pony and stop her cart under his window. She had her grandson with her, a chubby lad of twelve, in a smock-frock, beautifully worked about the shoulders, with cheeks as red as the big poppies in the nosegay which his grandmother made a point of bringing every Saturday to the poor sick gentleman.

'And how do you do, sir, this fine fresh morning?' she would shout to him. 'I hope as I sees you better. Sammy, give me the flowers. It's old-fashioned, master, but its sweet; and I just wish I see you able to come and fetch 'em for yourself.'

'Thank you, Ann; but I fear that's past hoping for,' Stephen would say with a smile.

The same colloquy passed between them every week, but they did not tire of it, and the little cart with its mixture of colours, the red carrots, and white cauliflowers, and many-tinted greens, was a pleasant sight to him. He did not object even to the pungent odour of the celery, which often communicated itself to his bouquet. The white pony, and the red and white and green of the vegetables, and Old Ann with a small face, like a russet winter apple, under her deep bonnet, and her little red shawl, trimly tied in round her waist by the great, many-pocketed apron; and Sammy trudging behind, with boots like buckets, with a basket of crimson cabbage for pickles on his arm, and his puffy, peony cheeks, made up a homely picture which delighted the recluse. It was an event for him when the Saturday came round, and he began (he said) to be fond of the smell of celery, and to think double poppies very handsome, showy flowers to put into a nosegay. Miss Jane took an interest in Ann too, but it was of a different kind. She would go out to the door, and have long discussions with her on various subjects quite as interesting as the rector's battles with Stephen—whether the butter was rising, and what was the cheapest for her poultry; for Ann's butter and her poultry were the best in Dura, and when she knew you, and felt that you were to be depended upon, she was not dear, Miss Jane always said.

There was also another visitor, who came once a week, not to Stephen's window, but to make a call in all proper state. This was Mr Truston, the minister of the chapel, who was, like Stephen, a protégé of Mr Baldwin, but had not either done so much credit or given so much trouble to the denomination as Haldane had. Mr Truston was aware how his new acquaintance was spoken of by the community, and his mind was much divided between veneration for Stephen's powers and a desire to be faithful with his brother. If he could be the humble instrument of setting him quite right with the denomination and preserving the efficiency of the magazine, he felt that he would not have lived in vain. But it was a dreadful trial to his modesty to assume an admonitory position to one whom he respected so much. He confided his difficulties to Mrs Wigginton, the wife of the draper at Dura, who was a leading member of the congregation, and a very thoughtful woman; and she had given him a great deal of encouragement, and put his duty before him in the clearest light.

'The thing is to keep him to fundamental principles,' Mrs Wigginton said. 'I would excuse a great deal if he preserved these. We may be superior to distinctions, and know that there is good both in church and chapel. But that will not do for the common mass. And we must support the denomination, Mr Truston. It has its faults—but, whatever its faults may be, we must stand by our flag.'

'Ah, I wish you would take him in hand,' said the minister with a sigh; but, all the same, such inspiration as this did not go for nothing. He began to call on the Haldanes every week; and when he had screwed up his courage he meant to be very faithful with Stephen; but a man cannot begin that process all at once.

Thus the Haldanes settled down in the Gatehouse; and their settling down affected Helen with that unintentional example and encouragement, which people convey to each other without meaning it. They were all very poor, but Miss Jane, who had never been very rich, and who had been trained to live on the smallest sum imaginable, made no hardship of her poverty, and communicated a certain cheerfulness about it even to her neighbour, whose mind and training were so very different. Miss Jane took it as she had learned to take (though not till after many struggles) her brother's illness, as a matter of course. She was aware that there were rich people in the world. She saw them even, the Burtons, for instance, who passed her every day, and whose life was full of luxury; but this did not move her, any more than the sight of a great beauty would have moved her to impatience of her own plain and homely face. The wealth, like the beauty, was exceptional. The homeliness and the poverty were the natural rule. And Helen saw that the lines of pain were softened in Stephen's face, and that he had begun to feel something like pleasure in those alleviations of his loneliness which have been described. All this produced a soothing, quieting influence upon her. She was hushed, as a child is who is not satisfied, whose cry is ready to burst forth at any moment, but upon whom the very atmosphere, the stillness of the air, has produced a certain calm. The wrong which had burnt her heart like a fire was not extinguished; it burned low, not for want of fuel, but because the air was soft and humid, and kept down the flame. And she herself was subdued. She was weary of suffering, and the routine of the new life acted upon her like an opiate, and the sense that all this was accepted as ordinary and natural by others, kept her down. And then Norah had cast away those bonds which oppress a child—the bonds of conventional quiet, which remain when natural grief has passed away in the order of things. Norah had begun to sing about the house, to dance when she should have walked, to wake up like the flowers, to live like the birds, spending her days in a chatter and flutter of life and gladness. All this calmed down and suppressed the feelings which had swayed Helen after her husband's death. Though her old sense of suspicion in respect to her cousin had succeeded the momentary relenting which his kindness had produced in her, even that was suppressed in the artificial calm. She blamed herself for shrinking from his presence, for disliking his friendliness; she even made an effort to go to his house, to overcome what she said to herself was her mean envy of his prosperity. She made friends with his wife, as far as two women so different could make friends, and tried to believe that Reginald Burton himself had never meant but well. It was in October, when she had first begun fully to realise the strange quietness that had come upon her, that it was suddenly broken up, never in that same fashion to return again.

There were visitors at the time at Dura House, visitors of importance, great county people, potentates whom, it was said, Mrs Burton was specially bent on conciliating in order to open the way into Parliament—a glory upon which her heart was set—to her husband. Mr Burton had himself taken a holiday from business, and on this particular day had gone up, after a long interval, 'to see,' he said, with that cheerful, important laugh of his, 'how things were going on.' That evening, however, Dura village was disappointed of its usual amusement. The phaeton with the bays went slowly past, driven by the groom, with a certain consternation in every line of the horses, and in every splendid tail and high-stepping hoof.

'Has not your master come?' Mrs Burton asked, when she met this forlorn equipage in the avenue. Such a thing had been known; sometimes business was so urgent that Mr Burton had lost his train, or waited for one that went later. But that which had happened this evening had never happened before.

'He is walking, ma'am,' said the groom, with gloomy signification. It gave even Mrs Burton a start, though she was usually so self-possessed; and as for the groom, he spread it about through the house that there had been 'a smash' in the City. Nothing else could account for so extraordinary a step.

Mr Burton walked, and his countenance was clouded. There was a shade on it, which the people about Dura, stupefied in the first instance by seeing him afoot at that hour, interpreted as the groom did. They thought 'something must have happened.' The Bank of England must have faltered on its throne; half the merchants, at home and abroad, must have fallen to the dust, like Dagon. Some one of weak mind, who suggested that the ministry might be out, was snubbed by everybody with a contempt proportioned to his foolishness. Would Mr Burton look like that for any merely political misfortune? But no one ventured even to suggest that Burton & Co. themselves might have sustained some blow. Such treason might be in men's thoughts, but no one dared to hint at an event which more than a revolution or a lost empire would have convulsed Dura. There are some things which it is impious even to speculate about.

Mr Burton went direct to the Gatehouse. He had not his usual condescending word to Susan, nor did he remember to wave his hand to Stephen as he passed the window. He went straight into the drawing-room, where Helen and Norah were sitting. They had just come in from their walk, and were going to have tea; and such a visit at this hour startled them. There was something more than gloom on his face; there was suppressed anger, and he had the look of a man who had come to speak his mind. He shook hands in the slightest, most hasty way, not caring evidently to waste time in salutations, and he did not take the chair that was offered to him. He kept standing, looking first at Helen and then at Norah, with glances which he seemed to expect would be understood; but as Norah had been present at every discussion in the house all her life, it did not occur to her to go away, nor to her mother to send her. At last he was obliged to speak plainly.

'I am anxious to talk to you by yourself,' he said. 'I have something very important to say. Norah, perhaps, would run out to the garden, or somewhere—for half an hour, I should not ask for more.'

'Norah!' said Helen, with surprise. 'But she has heard everything that any one can have to say to me. She knows as much as I do. You may say anything before Norah.'

'By—!' said Mr Burton. He did not put any word in the vacant place. He swore by Blank, as we do in books, contenting himself with the 'By—!' 'I don't mean to speak of my affairs before Norah,' he said, walking to the window and looking out. 'Send her away.'

He waited there with his back turned to the two, who gazed at each other amazed.

'Go up-stairs till I send for you, Norah,' said Helen, with a trembling voice. It must be some new pain, some new terror, something about Norah's father. She put her hand on her heart to keep it still. This was how her calm was broken all in a moment. She put her child away with the other hand. And Norah, astonished, indignant, choking with sudden rage and mortification, flew out of the room and rushed up-stairs. The sound of her hurried, angry retreat seemed to ring through all the house. And it was not till her foot was heard overhead that her mother found breath to speak. 'What is it? tell me! There can be nothing now so very hard to bear.'

'I don't know what you mean about hard to bear,' said Mr Burton, turning pettishly round and seating himself on a chair in front of her. 'Helen, I have done all I could to be kind to you. You will say it has not cost me very much, but it has cost me more than you think. I have put myself to a great deal of trouble, and—'

'Is this all you have to tell me?' she asked faintly, still holding her hand upon her heart.

'All!' he repeated; and then, changing his tone suddenly, 'do you know anything about this new folly Maurice has taken in hand? Don't prevaricate, Helen; answer me yes or no.'

'I do not know what you mean,' she said, and paused for breath. Her fright, and the strange assault that had been made upon her, confused her mind. Then gradually with Maurice's name came a sudden gleam of light.

'That is a pretence,' he said. 'I can see in your face that you understand. You that I have been, so to speak, nourishing in my bosom—you—Helen! There is still time to think better of it. Have you given your consent to it? Has he got your name?'

'If it is anything Dr Maurice is doing,' she said, 'yes, he has got my consent, and more than my consent.'

'Good heavens, why? Are you in your senses? I thought it was some idiotic woman's notion. What good can it possibly do to rake up that business all over again? What the deuce do you mean by it? What can it ever be to you?'

'What is it to you?' she said.

'To me!' She was looking at him, and his voice fell. He had begun loudly, as if with the intention of declaring that to him it was less than nothing; but he was caught by her look, and only grew confused, and stammered out again, 'To me!'

'Yes,' said Helen. 'You are not a Director. You have said you were a loser only, you had no responsibility. Then what does it matter to you?'

Mr Burton turned away his head; he stamped his foot slightly on the floor in impatience. 'What is the use?' he said, as if to himself, 'you might teach an elephant to fly sooner than make a woman understand about business. Without being anything to me, it might be something to my friends.'

'Is that man—that—Golden—is he your friend?'

'Of course he is,' said Mr Burton roughly, with a certain defiance. 'You are prejudiced against him unjustly. But he is my friend, and a very good fellow too.'

'Then it is better not to say any more,' said Helen rising, trembling in every limb. 'It is best not to say any more. Oh don't venture to name his name to me! If I had not been a woman, I should have—not killed him. That would have been too good. Innocent men are killed, and you others look on, and never lift a finger. I would have pursued him till his last breath—crushed him—made him feel what he has done. And I will—if I have the power!'

She stood up confronting her cousin, trembling, yet glowing with that passion which the name of her husband's slanderer always roused within her. She was almost as tall as Burton was, and he felt as if she towered over him, and was cowed by the strength of her emotion. He rose too, but he shrank back a step, not knowing how to meet the spirit he had roused.

'These are nice Christian sentiments,' he said, with an attempt at a sneer; but in his heart the man was afraid.

'I ask nobody what kind of sentiments they are,' she cried. 'If he had wronged me only, I would have forgiven him. But no man shall say his name before me—no man! I may not have the power; my friends may not have the power; but it is that, and not the will, which will fail if we fail. I will never give up trying to punish him, never in my life!'

'Then you will be acting like a fool,' Mr Burton said; but he changed his tone, and took a great deal of trouble to persuade her to take her seat again, and discuss the matter calmly with him.

Norah stood up-stairs by the window, watching till he should go. The child's heart was bursting with rage and pain. She had never been sent away before; she had heard everything, had been always present whatever was going on. Her father, Dr Maurice, Mr Haldane, every one of them had spoken in her presence all that they had to say. And she remembered words that no one else remembered, scraps of talk which she could put together. She did so with a violent exercise of her memory as she stood there drumming on the window, and wondering when he would go. 'He thinks I am only a child,' she said to herself, in the fiery commotion of her spirits, and thought of a hundred things she could do to prove the contrary. She would go to Dr Maurice; she would let 'everybody' know. He was no friend; he was a conspirator against them—one of those who killed her father. Every moment that passed inflamed Norah more. She stood at the window and watched, thinking would he never be gone, thinking, oh why could not she make herself grow—make herself a woman! What her mother had done was nothing to what Norah felt herself capable of doing. Every vein in her body, and every nerve had begun to thrill and tremble before she heard the sound down-stairs of the door opening, and saw him go hastily away.

This was what he said when he opened the door of the sitting-room down-stairs—

'You will do what you please, of course. I have found out before now what it is to struggle with an unreasonable woman. Do what you like. Drag your husband's name through the dirt again. Throw all sorts of new light on his motives. That is what you will do. People might have forgotten it; but after what you are going to do, they will never forget. And that is all you will have for your pains—you may be sure you can do nothing to us.'

'Us?' said Helen. 'You told me you were not concerned.'

And then Mr Burton changed colour and lost his temper.

'You drive a man wild,' he cried. 'You make me that I don't know what I am saying. Of course you know what I mean, though you pretend you don't. I mean my friends. And you know that; and you know how much you owe to me, and yet the answer I get is—this!'

He slammed the door after him like an angry maid-servant; he strode hastily away to his own house, with a face which of itself gave a new paralytic seizure to old John at the lodge. He filled everybody with consternation in his own house. And Helen stood still after he had left her, half exultant, half stupefied. Us! Had she found his cunning manœuvres out?

CHAPTER V

Dr Maurice came down next day. He was a man of very quiet manners, and yet he was unable to conceal a certain excitement. He walked into the Gatehouse with an air of abstraction, as if he did not quite know what he was about.

'I have come to talk about business,' he said, but he did not send Norah away. Probably had he not been so glad to see her once more, it would have surprised him to see the child whom he had never beheld apart from a book, standing up by her mother's chair, watching his face, taking in every word. Norah's rôle had changed since those old days. She had no independent standing then; now she was her mother's companion, champion, supporter. This changes as nothing else can do a child's life.

'Our case is to be heard for the first time,' he said. 'I believe they are all very much startled. Golden was brought before the magistrate yesterday; he has been admitted to bail, of course. If I could have had the satisfaction of thinking that rascal was even one night in prison! But that was too much to hope for. Mrs Drummond, can you guess who was his bail?'

Helen shook her head, not understanding quite what he meant; but all the same she knew what his answer would be. He brought it out with a certain triumph—

'Why, Burton—your precious cousin! I knew it would be so. As sure as that sun is shining, Burton is at the bottom of it all. I have seen it from the first.'

'Dr Maurice,' said Helen, 'where have I seen, where have I read, "Burton and Golden have done it"? The words seem to haunt me. It cannot be fancy.'

Dr Maurice took out his pocket-book. He took a folded paper from an inner pocket, and held it to her without a word. Poor Helen, in the composure which she had attained so painfully, began to shake and tremble; the sight of it moved her beyond her self-control. She could not weep, but her strained nerves quivered, her teeth chattered, her frame was convulsed by the shock. 'Ah!' she cried, as people do when they receive a blow; and yet now she remembered it all—every word; it seemed to be written on her heart.

The physician was alarmed. Human emotion has many ways of showing itself, but none more alarming than this. He put the letter hastily away again, and plunged into wild talk about the way she was living, the house, and the neighbourhood.

'You are taking too little exercise. You are shutting yourself up too much,' he said, with something of that petulance which so often veils pity. He was not going to encourage her to break down by being sorry for her; the other way, he thought, was the best. And then he himself was on the very borders of emotion too, the sight of these words had brought poor Robert so keenly to his mind. And they had brought to his mind also his own hardships. Norah in her new place was very bewildering to him. He had noted her closely while her mother was speaking, and with wonder and trouble had seen a woman look at him through the girl's brown eyes—a woman, a new creature, an independent being, whom he did not know, whom he would have to treat upon a different footing. This discovery, which he had not made at the first glance, filled him with dismay and trouble. He had lost the child whom he loved.

'Norah, come and show me the house,' he said, with a certain despair; and he went away, leaving Helen to recover herself. That was better than going back upon the past, recalling to both the most painful moments of their life.

He took Norah's hand, and walked through the open door into the garden, which was the first outlet he saw.

'Come and tell me all about it,' he said. 'Norah, what have you been doing to yourself? Have you grown up in these three months? You are not the little girl I used to know.'

'Oh, Dr Maurice, do you think I have grown?' cried Norah, with her whole heart in the demand.

And it would be impossible to describe what a comfort this eager question was to him. He laughed, and looked down upon her, and began to feel comfortable again.

'Do you know, I am afraid you have not grown,' he said, putting his other hand fondly on her brown hair. 'Are you vexed, Norah? For my part, I like you best as you are.'

'Well, it cannot be helped,' said Norah, with resignation. 'I did not think I had; but for a moment I had just a little hope, you looked so funny at me. Oh, Dr Maurice, I do so wish I was grown up!—for many things. First, there is Mr Burton, who comes and bullies mamma. I hate that man. I remember at home, in the old days, when you used to be talking, and nobody thought I paid any attention—'

'What do you remember, Norah?'

'Oh, heaps of things. I can scarcely tell you. They would look at each other—I mean Mr Golden and he. They would say things to each other. Oh, I don't remember what the words were; how should I remember the words? but things—just as you might look at me, and give a little nod, if we had something that was a secret from mamma. I know they had secrets, these two. If I were grown up, and could speak, I would tell him so. Dr Maurice, can't we punish them? I cannot imagine,' cried Norah passionately, 'what God can be thinking of to let them alone, and let them be happy, after all they have done to—poor papa!'

'Norah, these are strange things for you to be thinking of,' said Dr Maurice, once more disturbed by a development which he was not acquainted with.

'Oh, no. If you knew how we live, you would not think them strange. I am little; but what does that matter? There is mamma on one side, and there is Mr Haldane. How different we all used to be! Dr Maurice, I remember when poor Mr Haldane used to take me up, and set me on his shoulder; and look at him now! Oh, how can any one see him, and bear it? But it does no good to cry.'

'But, Norah, that is not Mr Burton's fault.'

'No, not that; but, oh, it is God's fault,' said Norah, sinking her voice to a whisper, and ending with a burst of passionate tears.

'Hush, hush, hush!' He took her hand into both of his, and soothed her. Thoughts like these might float through a man's mind involuntarily, getting no utterance; but it horrified him to hear them from the lips of a child. Was she a child? Dr Maurice said to himself once more, with an inward groan, that his little Norah, his dream-child of the fairy tales, was gone, and he should find her no more.

'And then it rather vexes one to be so little,' she said, suddenly drying her eyes, 'because of Clara. Clara is not twelve yet, and she is much bigger than I am. She can reach to these roses—look—while I can't get near them; and they are the only roses we have now. But, after all, though it may be nice to be tall, it doesn't matter very much, do you think, for a woman? So mamma says; and girls are just as often little as tall—in books.'

'For my part, I am fond of little women,' said Dr Maurice, and this time he laughed within himself. She kept him between the two, changing from childhood to womanhood without knowing it. 'But tell me, who is Clara? I want to know about your new friends here.'

'Clara is Clara Burton, and very like him,' said Norah. 'I thought I should be fond of her at first, because she is my cousin; but I am not fond of her. Ned is her brother. I like him better. He is a horsey, doggy sort of boy; but then he has always lived in the country, and he knows no better. One can't blame him for that, do you think?'

'Oh, no,' said Dr Maurice, with great seriousness; 'one can't blame him for that.' The man's heart grew glad over the child's talk. He could have listened to her running on about her friends for ever.

'And then there was—some one else,' said Norah, instinctively drawing herself up; 'not exactly a boy; a—gentleman. We saw him in town, and then we saw him here; first with that horrible man, Mr Golden, and another day with the Burtons. But you are not to think badly of him for that. He was—on our side.'

'Who is this mysterious personage, I wonder?' said Dr Maurice smilingly; but this time it was not a laugh or a groan, but a little shivering sensation of pain that ran through him, he could not tell why.

'He was more like Fortunatus than any one,' said Norah. 'But he could not be like Fortunatus in everything, for he said he was poor, like us—though that might be only, as I say it myself, to spite Clara. Well, he was grown up—taller than you are, Dr Maurice—with nice curling sort of hair, all in little twists and rings, and beautiful eyes. They flashed up so when mamma spoke. Mamma was very, very angry talking to that horrible man at our own very door. Fancy, he had dared to go and call and leave his horrid card. I tore it into twenty pieces, and stamped upon it. It was silly, I suppose; but to think he should dare to call—at our own very house—'

'I am getting dreadfully confused, Norah, between the beautiful eyes and the horrible man. I don't know what I am about. Which was which?'

'Oh, Dr Maurice, how could you ask such a question? Are there two such men in the world? It was that Mr Golden whom I hate; and Mr Rivers—Cyril Rivers—was with him, not knowing—but he says he will never go with him again. I saw it in his eyes in a moment; he is on our side.'

'You are young to read eyes in this way. I do not think I quite like it, Norah,' said Dr Maurice, in a tone which she recognised at once.

'Why, you are angry. But how can I help it?' said Norah, growing a woman again. 'If you were like me, Dr Maurice—if you felt your mamma had only you—if you knew there was nobody else to stand by her, nobody to help her, and you so little! I am obliged to think; I cannot help myself. When I grow up, I shall have so much to do; and how can I know whether people are on our side or against us, except by looking at their eyes?'

'Norah, my little Norah!' cried the man pitifully, 'don't leave your innocence for such fancies as these. Your mother has friends to think for her and you—many friends; I myself, for example. As long as I am alive, do you require to go and look for people to be on your side? Why, child, you forget me.'

Norah looked at him searchingly, penetrating, as he thought, to the bottom of his heart.

'I did not forget you, Dr Maurice. You are fond of me and of—poor papa. But I have to think of her. I don't think you love her. And she has the most to bear.'

Dr Maurice did not make any reply. He did not love Helen; he even shrank from the idea with a certain prudish sense of delicacy—an old bachelor's bashfulness. Love Mrs Drummond! Why, it was out of the question. The idea disconcerted him. He had been quite pained and affected a moment before at the thought that his little Norah—the child that he was so fond of—should want other champions. But now he was disconcerted, and in front of the grave little face looking up at him, he did not even dare to smile. Norah, however, was as ready to raise him up as she had been to cast him down.

'Do you think Cyril is a pretty name, Dr Maurice?' she asked. 'I think it sounds at first a little weak—too pretty for a boy. So is Cecil. I like a rough, round sort of name—Ned, for instance. You never could mistake Ned. One changes one's mind about names, don't you think? I used to be all for Geralds and Cyrils and pretty sounds like that; now I like the others best. Clara is pretty for a girl; but everybody thinks I must be Irish, because I'm called Norah. Why was I called Norah, do you know? Charlie Dalton calls me Norah Creina.'

'Here is some one quite fresh. Who is Charlie Dalton?' said Dr Maurice, relieved.

'Oh, one of the Rectory boys. There are so many of them! What I never can understand,' cried Norah suddenly, 'is the difference among people. Mr Dalton has eight children, and mamma has only one; now why? To be sure, it would have been very expensive to have had Charlie and all the rest on so little money as we have now. I suppose we could not have done it. And, to be sure, God must have known that, and arranged it on purpose,' the child said, stopping short with a puzzled look. 'Oh, Dr Maurice, when He knew it all, and could have helped it if He pleased, why did He let them kill poor papa?'

'I do not know,' said Dr Maurice under his breath.

It was a relief to him when, a few minutes after, Helen appeared at the garden door, having in the mean time overcome her own feelings. They were all in a state of repression, the one hiding from the other all that was strongest in them for the moment. Such a thing is easily done at twelve years old. Norah ran along the garden path to meet her mother, throwing off the shadow in a moment. But for the others it was not so easy. They met, and they talked of the garden, what a nice old-fashioned garden it was, full of flowers such as one rarely sees now-a-days. And Dr Maurice told Norah the names of some of them, and asked if the trees bore well, and commented upon the aspect, and how well those pears ought to do upon that warm wall. These are the disguises with which people hide themselves when that within does not bear speaking of. There was a great deal more to be told still, and business to be discussed; but first these perverse hearts had to be stilled somehow in their irregular beating, and the tears which were too near the surface got rid of, and the wistful, questioning thoughts silenced.

After a while Dr Maurice went to pay Stephen Haldane a visit. He, too, was concerned in the business which brought the doctor here. The two men went into it with more understanding than Helen could have had. She wanted only that Golden should be punished, and her husband's name vindicated—a thing which it seemed to her so easy to do. But they knew that proof was wanted—proof which was not forthcoming. Dr Maurice told Haldane what Helen gave him no opportunity to tell her—that the lawyers were not sanguine. The books which had disappeared were the only evidence upon which Golden's guilt and Drummond's innocence could be either proved or disproved. And all the people about the office, from the lowest to the highest, had been summoned to tell what they knew about those books. Nobody, it appeared, had seen them removed; nobody had seen the painter carry them away; there was this negative evidence in his favour, if no other. But there was nothing to prove that Golden had done it, or any other person involved, and, so far as this was concerned, obscurity reigned over the whole matter—an obscurity not pierced as yet by any ray of light.

'At all events, we shall fight it out,' said Dr Maurice. 'The only thing to be risked now is a little money more or less, and that, I suppose, a man ought to be willing to risk for the sake of justice—myself especially, who have neither chick nor child.'

He said this in so dreary a way that poor Stephen smiled. The man who was removed from any such delights—who could never improve his own position in any way, nor procure for himself any of the joys of life, looked at the man who thus announced himself with a mixture of gentle ridicule and pity.

'That at least must be your own fault,' he said; and then he thought of himself, and sighed.

No one knew what dreams might have been in Stephen Haldane's mind before he became the wreck he was. Probably no one ever would know. He smiled at the other, but for himself he could not restrain a sigh.

'I don't see how it can be said to be my own fault,' said Dr Maurice with whimsical petulance. 'There are preliminary steps, of course, which one might take—but not necessarily with success—not by any means certainly with success. I tell you what, though, Haldane,' he added hastily, after a pause, 'I'd like to adopt Norah Drummond. That is what I should like to do. I'd be very good to her; she should have everything she could set her face to. To start a strange child from the beginning, even if it were one's own, is always like putting into a lottery. A baby is no better than a speculation. How do you know what it may turn out? whereas a creature like Norah—Ah, that is what I should like, to adopt such a child as that!'

'To adopt—Norah?' Stephen grew pale. 'What! to take her from her mother! to carry away the one little gleam of light!'

'She would be a gleam of light to me too,' said Dr Maurice, 'and I could do her justice. I could provide for her. Her mother, if she cared for the child's interest, ought not to stand in the way. There! you need not look so horror-stricken. I don't mean to attempt it. I only say that is what I should like to do.'

But the proposal, even when so lightly made, took away Stephen's breath. He did not recover himself for some time. He muttered, 'Adopt—Norah!' under his breath, while his friend talked on other subjects. He could not forget it. He even made Dr Maurice a little speech when he rose to go away. He put out his hand and grasped the other's arm in the earnestness of his interest.

'Look here, Maurice,' he said, 'wealth has its temptations as well as poverty; because you have plenty of money, if you think you could make such a proposition—'

'What proposition?'

'To take Norah from her mother. If you were to tempt Mrs Drummond for the child's sake to give up the child, by promising to provide for her, or whatever you might say—if you were to do that, God forgive you, Maurice—I know I never could!'

'Of course I shall not do it,' said Maurice hastily. And he went away with the feeling in his mind that this man, too, was his rival, and his successful rival. The child was as good as Stephen's child, though so far removed from himself. Dr Maurice was so far wrong that it was Helen Stephen was thinking of, and not Norah. The child would be a loss to him; but the loss of her mother would be so much greater that the very thought of it oppressed his soul. He had grown to be Helen's friend in the truest sense; he had felt her sympathy to be almost too touching to him, almost too sweet; and he could not bear the possibility of seeing her deprived of her one solace. He sat alone after Maurice had gone away (for his mother and sister had left them to have their conversation unfettered by listeners), and pondered over the possible fate of the mother and child. The child would grow up; in a very few years she would be a woman; she would marry, in all likelihood, and go away, and belong to them no more; and Helen would be left to bear her lot alone. She would be left in the middle of her days to carry her burden as she might, deserted by every love that had once belonged to her. What a lot would that be!—worse, even, than his own, who, amid all his pains, had two hearts devoted to him never to be disjoined from him but by death. Poor Stephen, you would have supposed, was himself in the lowest depths of human suffering and solitude; but yet he looked down upon a lower still, and his heart bled for Helen, who, it might be, would have to descend into that abyss in all the fulness of her life and strength. What a sin would that man's be, he thought, who arbitrarily, unnaturally, should try to hasten on that separation by a single day!

Dr Maurice went back to the other side of the house, and had his talk out quietly with Mrs Drummond; he told her what he had told Haldane, while Norah looked at him over her mother's chair, and listened to every word. To her he said that it was the lawyers' opinion that they might do good even though they proved nothing—they would stir up public opinion; they might open the way for further information. And with this, perhaps, it might be necessary to be content.

'There is one way in which something might be possible,' he said. 'All the people about the office have been found and called as witnesses, except one. That was the night-porter, who might be an important witness; but I hear he lives in the country, and has been lost sight of. He might know something; without that we have no proof whatever. I for my own part should as soon think the sun had come out of the skies, but Drummond, for some reason we know nothing of, might have taken those books—'

'Are you forsaking him too?' cried Helen in her haste.

'I am not in the least forsaking him,' said Dr Maurice; 'but how can we tell what had been said to him—what last resource he had been driven to? If we could find that porter there might be something done. He would know when they were taken away.'

Helen made no answer; she did not take the interest she might have done in the evidence. She said softly, as if repeating to herself—

'Burton and Golden, Burton and Golden!' Could it be? What communication could they have had? how could they have been together? This thought confused her, and yet she believed in it as if it were gospel. She turned it over and over like a strange weapon of which she did not know the use.

'Yes, something may come out of that. We may discover some connection between them when everything is raked up in this way. Norah thinks so too. Norah feels that they are linked together somehow. Will you come with me to the station, Norah, and see me away?'

'We are both going,' said Helen. And they put on their bonnets and walked to the railway with him through the early twilight. The lights were shining out in the village windows as they passed, and in the shops, which made an illumination here and there. The train was coming from town—men coming from their work, ladies returning, who had been shopping in London, meeting their children, who went to carry home the parcels in pleasant groups. The road was full of a dozen little domestic scenes, such as are to be seen only in the neighbourhood of London. A certain envy was in the thoughts of all three as they passed on. Norah looked at the boys and girls with a little sigh, wondering how it would feel to have brothers and sisters, to be one of a merry happy family. And Helen looked at them with a different feeling, remembering the time when she, too, had gone to meet her own people who were coming home. As for Dr Maurice, of course it was his own fault. He had chosen to have nobody belonging to him, to shut himself off from the comfort of wife and child. Yet he was more impatient of all the cheerful groups than either of the others.

'Talk of the country being quiet! it is more noisy than town,' he said; he had just been quietly pushed off the pavement by a girl like Norah, who was running to meet her father. That should have been nothing to him, surely, but he felt injured. 'I wish you would come with me and keep my house for me, Norah,' he said, with a vain harping on his one string; and Norah laughed with gay freedom at the thought.

'Good night, Dr Maurice; come back soon,' she said, waving her hand to him, then turned away with her mother, and did not even look back. He was quite sure about this, as he settled himself in the corner of the carriage. So fond as he was of the child; so much as he would have liked to have done for her! And she never so much as looked back!

CHAPTER VI

When Helen and Norah emerged again out of the lights of the little railway station to the darkness glimmering with a few lamps of the road outside, Mr Burton's phaeton was standing at the gate. The air was touched with the first frost, there was a soft haze over the distances, the lamps shone with a twinkling glow, and the breath of the horses was faintly visible in the sharpened air. Mr Burton was standing talking to some one on the pathway accompanied by his son Ned, who though he was but a year older than Norah was nearly as tall as his father. Helen's last interview with her cousin had been pleasant enough to tempt her to linger now for any greeting, and her heart was sore and wroth against him. She put her veil down over her face, and hurried past. But Mr Burton had seen her, and long before this he had repented of his rudeness of last night. Had it been successful, had he succeeded in bullying and frightening her, he would have been perfectly satisfied with himself; but he had not succeeded, and he was sorry for the cruelty which had been in vain. It was so much power wasted, and his wisest course now was to ignore and disown what he had done. He stopped short in his conversation, and made a step after her.

'Ah, Helen! 'he cried, 'you out this cold evening! Wait a moment, I will take you with me. I am going to pass your door.'

'Thanks,' said Helen, 'I think we prefer to walk.' And she was going resolutely on; but she was not to be allowed so easily to make her escape.

'One moment. I have something to say to you. If you will not drive with me, I will walk with you,' said Mr Burton, in his most genial mood. 'Good evening, Tait, we can finish our talk to-morrow. Well, and where have you been, you two ladies?—seeing some one off by the train? Ned, see if you can't amuse your cousin Norah while I talk to her mother. Helen, when you and I were that age I think we found more to say.'

'I do not think we were great friends—at that age,' said Helen.

She had meant to say at any age; but the gravity of her thoughts made such light utterances of her anger impossible. When people are going to serious war with each other, they may denounce and vituperate, but they rarely gibe.

'No; I suppose it was at a later period we were friends,' Mr Burton said, with a laugh. 'How strangely circumstances alter! I am afraid I made myself rather disagreeable last night. When a man is bilious, he is not accountable for his actions; and I had been worried in town; but it was too bad to go and put it out on you; what I really wanted to ask last night was if the house was quite in order for the winter? But something brought on the other subject, and I lost my temper like an idiot. I hope you won't think any more of it. And it is really important to know if the house is in order—if you are prepared to run the risk of frost, and all that. I was speaking to Tait, the carpenter, this moment. I think I shall send him just to look over the house.'

Helen made no reply; this talk about nothing, this pretence of ease and familiarity, was an insult to her. And Norah clung close to her arm, enclosing it with both hands, calling her mother's attention to every new sentence with a closer pressure. They went on for a few minutes before Mr Burton could invent anything more to say, and Ned stalked at Norah's other side with all a boy's helplessness. He certainly was not in a condition to help his father out.

'Ned has been up to town with me to-day,' said Mr Burton, still more cheerfully. 'It will be a loss, but we must make up our minds to send him to school. It is a disadvantage to him being so tall; everybody thinks he is fifteen at least. It is handy for you that Norah is so small. You can make a baby of her for three or four years yet.'

Here Norah squeezed her mother's arm so tight that Helen winced with the pain, yet took a kind of forlorn amusement too from the fury of the child's indignation.

'Norah is no baby,' she said, 'happily for me; Norah is my best companion and comfort.'

'Ah, yes; she is in your confidence; that is charming,' said Mr Burton; 'quite like a story-book; whereas Ned, the great blockhead, cares for nothing but his dogs and nonsense. But he shall be packed off to Eton directly. The house is so full at present, my wife has been regretting we have seen nothing of you, Helen. I suppose it is too early to ask you to come to us under present circumstances? But after a while, I hope, when we are alone—And Norah must come before Ned goes away. There is to be a children's party. What did your mother settle about that, Ned?'

'Don't know,' growled Ned at Norah's other side.

'Don't know! Well you ought to know, since it's in your honour. Clara will send you word, Helen. Now, I suppose, I must be off, or I shall not have time to dress. Why, by Jove, there goes the bell already!' cried Mr Burton.

He looked round, and the bays, which had been impatiently following at a foot-pace, held in with difficulty by the groom, stopped at the sign he made, while the sonorous dinner-bell, which rang twice every evening through all seasons, sounded its first summons through the darkness. There was something very awe-inspiring in the sound of that bell. That, as much as anything, impressed the village and neighbourhood with a sense of the importance of the master of Dura. The old Harcourts had used it only on very great occasions; but the Burtons used it every evening. All the cooks in Dura village guided themselves by its sound. 'Lord, bless us! there's the bell a-going at the great house, and my chickens not put down to roast yet,' Mrs Witherspoon at the Rectory would say, giving herself such 'a turn' as she did not get over all the evening. Mr Burton, too, got 'a turn' when he heard it.

He cried, 'Good night, Helen! Ned, come along,' and jumped into his phaeton.

'I'll walk,' shouted Ned.

And then there was a jingle, a flash, a dart, and the two bays flew, as if something had stung them, along the frosty road.

'It will be a long walk for you up that dark avenue,' said Helen, when the boy, with his hands in his pockets, stood by them at the door of the Gatehouse, hesitating with the awkwardness natural to his kind.

'Oh, I don't mind,' said Ned.

'Will you come in—and have some tea?'

Never was an invitation more reluctantly given. When his mother heard of it, it flashed through her mind that Mrs Drummond had constructed the first parallel, and that already the siege of Ned, the heir of Dura, had begun; but Helen had no such idea. And Norah squeezed her arm with a force of indignation which once more, though she was not merry, made her mother smile.

'Mamma, how could you?' Norah cried, when the boy had come in, and had been left by the bright little fire in the drawing-room to watch the flickering of the lights while his entertainers took off their bonnets; 'how could you? It is I who will have to talk to him and amuse him. It was selfish of you, mamma!'

And Ned sat by the drawing-room fire alone, repenting himself that he had been seduced, in his big boots, with mud on his stockings, into this unknown place. It was not actually unknown to him; he had broken the old china cups and thumped upon the piano, and done his best to put his fingers through the old curtains more than once while the place was empty. But he did not understand the change that had passed upon it now. He sat by the fire confused; wondering how he had ever had the courage to come in; wondering if Mrs Drummond would think him dirty, and what Norah would say. He would not have to put himself into velvet and silk stockings and show himself in the drawing-room at home, that was a comfort. But what unknown mazes of conversation, what awful abysses of self-betrayal might there be before him here! Norah came in first, which at once frightened and relieved him. And the room was pretty—the old homely neutral-tinted room, with the lively gleam of firelight lighting it up, and all the darkness made rosy in the corners, which was so different from the drawing room at the great house, with its gilding and grandeur, its masses of flowers and floods of light. Ned's head felt very much confused by the difference; but the strangeness awed him in spite of himself.

'I am always frightened in this room,' said Norah, drawing the biggest chair into the circle of the firelight, and putting herself into it like a little queen. She was so small that her one foot which hung down did not reach the floor; the other, I am sorry to say, so regardless was Norah of decorum, was tucked under her in the big chair.

'What a funny girl you are! Why?'

'Do you see that cupboard?' said Norah. 'I know there is an old woman who lives there, and spins and spins, and keeps looking at me, till I daren't breathe. Oh, I think sometimes if I look up it will turn me to stone, that eye of hers. If you weren't here I shouldn't dare to say it; I am most frightened for her in the day, when the light comes in at all the windows, and all the pictures and things say, 'What's that little girl doing here?' And then the mirror up on the wall—There's two people in it I know, now. You will say its you and me; but it isn't you and me. It's our ghosts, perhaps, sitting so still, and looking at each other and never saying a word.'

Ned felt a shiver run over him as he listened. He thought of the dark avenue which he had to go through all by himself, and wished he had driven with his father instead. And there where he was sitting he just caught that curious little round mirror, and there were two people in it—never moving, never speaking, just as Norah said.

'There is always a feeling as if somebody were by in this house,' Norah went on, 'somebody you can't see. Oh, it is quite true. You can't go anywhere, up or down, but they always keep looking and looking at you. I bear it as long as I can, and then I get up and run away. I should not mind so much if I could see them, or if they were like the ladies that walk about and rustle with long silk trains going over the floor, as they do in some old houses. But the ones here are so still; they just look at you for hours and hours together, till you get into such a dreadful fright, and feel you can't bear it any longer and rush away.'

Just then there was the sound of a little fall of ashes from the fire which made Ned start; and then he laughed hoarsely, frightened, but defiant.

'You are making it all up out of your own head to frighten a fellow,' he said.

'To frighten—a fellow!' said Norah, with gentle but ineffable contempt. 'What have I to do with—fellows? It frightens me.'

And she gave a little shudder in her big chair, and shook her head, waving her brown hair about her shoulders. Perhaps the colour in her hair would not have showed so much but for the black frock with its little white frill that came to the throat; and the firelight found out Norah's eyes, and kindled two lamps in them. She was all made up of blackness and brightness, a shadow child, not much of her apparent except the pale face and the two lights in her eyes—unless, indeed, it were that one leg, hanging down from under the black frock, with a white stocking on it, and a varnished, fire-reflecting shoe.

Never in Ned's life had he experienced anything like this before; the delicious thrill of visionary terror made the actual pleasantness of the warm corner he sat in all the pleasanter; he had thought himself past the age to have stories told to him; but nothing like Norah's visions had ever come in his way. No happiness, however, is perfect in this world. The dark avenue would come across him by moments with a thrill of terror. But the old woman could not sit and spin, that was certain, in the dark, windy, lonely avenue; there would be no mirror there to reflect his passing figure; and he would run; and if the dogs were about they would come to meet him; so the boy took courage and permitted himself to enjoy this moment, which was a novelty in his life. Then Mrs Drummond came in with her black dress like Norah's, and the long white streamers to her cap, which looked like wings, he thought. Her sorrowful look, her soft voice, that air about her of something subdued and stilled, which had not always been so, impressed the boy's imagination. Ned was an honest, single-hearted boy, and he looked with awe upon any suffering which he could understand. He explained afterwards that Helen looked as if she were very sorry about something. 'Awfully sorry—but not bothering,' he said, and the look of self-control impressed him, though he could not tell why. Altogether it was so different from home; so much more attractive to the imagination. There was no dimness, no shadows, at the great house. There nobody ever sat in the firelight, nor 'took things into their heads;' and here everything was so shadowy, so soft, so variable; the firelight gleaming suddenly out now and then, the air so full of mystery. Everything that is strange is attractive to the young fancy to begin with; and there was more than simple novelty here.

Helen brought the lamp in her hand and set it down on the table, which to some extent disturbed his picture; and then she came and sat down by the children, while Susan—old Susan, who was a landmark to Ned, keeping him to reality in the midst of all this wonderfulness—brought in and arranged the tea.

'Are you sure they will not be anxious?' said Helen. 'I am afraid your mother will be unhappy about you when she finds you don't come.'

'Oh, she'll never find out,' said Ned. 'Unhappy! I don't suppose mamma would be unhappy for that; but I'll get home before they come out from dinner. I sha'n't dress though, it would be absurd, at nine o'clock.'

'It will be a dark walk for you up the avenue,' said Helen kindly; and when she said this Ned shrank into his corner and shivered slightly. She added, 'You are not afraid?'

'Oh no—I should hope not!' said Ned.

'I should be afraid,' said Norah tranquilly; 'the wind in the trees always makes me feel strange. It sounds so moaning and dreary, as if it were complaining. We don't do it any harm that it should complain. It is like something that is in prison and wants to get out. Do you know any stories about forest spirits? I don't like them very much; they are always dwarfs, or trolls, or something grim—funny little men, hairy all over, that sit under the trees with their long arms, and dart out when you pass.'

Ned gave another suppressed shiver in his corner, and Helen came to his aid.

'Norah has read nothing but fairy tales all her life,' she said; 'but I dare say you know a great deal more than she does, and don't care for such foolish things. You are going to Eton? I was once there when all the boats were out, and there were fireworks at night. It was so pretty. I dare say when you are there you will get into the boats.'

'I shall try,' said Ned, lighting up. 'I mean to be very good at athletics if I can. It does not matter if I work very hard, for I am going into papa's business, where I sha'n't want it. I am not going to Eton to work, but to get among a good set, and to do what other people do.'

'Ah!' said Helen, with a smile. She took but a languid interest in Ned, and she was scarcely sorry that Mr. Burton's son showed no likelihood of distinguishing himself. She accepted it quite quietly, without any interest in the matter, which somehow troubled Ned, he could not have told why.

'At least, they say you're not obliged to work,' he said, a little abashed. 'I shall do as much as I can at that too.'

And then there was a momentary silence, broken only by the ring of the teacups as Susan put them down. Ned had a feeling that no very profound interest was shown in his prospect and intentions, but he was used to that. He sat quite quiet, feeling very shy, and sadly troubled to find that Susan had placed the lamp where it threw its strongest light upon himself. He drew his muddy boots and stockings as much as he could under his chair, and hoped Mrs Drummond would not notice them; how foolish he had been to come, making an exhibition of himself! and yet it was very pleasant, too.

'Now you must come to the table and have some tea,' said Helen, placing a chair for him with her own hand. Ned knew it was a gentleman's duty to do this for a lady, but he was so confused he did not feel capable of behaving like anything but a loutish boy; he turned everything he could think of as a pleasant subject of conversation over in his mind, with the idea of doing what he could to make himself agreeable; but nothing would come that he could produce. He sat and got through a great deal of bread and butter while he cudgelled his brains in this way. There was not much conversation. Helen was more silent than usual, having so much to think of; and Norah was amused by the unusual specimen of humanity before her, and distracted from the monologue with which she generally filled up all vacant places. At last Ned's efforts resolved themselves into speech.

'Oh, Mrs Drummond, please, should you like to have a dog?' he said.

'I knew he was a doggy sort of a boy,' Norah said to herself, throwing a certain serious pity into her contemplation of him. But yet the offer was very interesting, and suggested various excitements to come.

'What kind of a dog?' said Helen, with a smile.

'Oh, we have two or three different kinds. I was thinking, perhaps, a nice little Skye—like Shaggy, but smaller. Or if you would like a retriever, or one of old Dinah's pups.'

'Thanks,' said Helen. 'I don't know what we should do with it, Ned; but it is very kind of you.'

'Oh, no,' said the boy with a violent blush. 'It would be a companion for—her, you know. It is so nice to have a dog to play with. Why, Shaggy does everything but talk. He knows every word I say. You might have Shaggy himself, if you like, while I am away.'

'Oh, what a nice boy you are!' said Norah. 'I should like it, Ned. Mamma does not want anything to play with; but I do. Give it to me! I should take such care of him! And then when you came home for the holidays, I should promise to take him to the station to meet you. I love Shaggy—he is such fun. He can't see out of his eyes; and he does so frisk and jump, and make an object of himself. I never knew you were such a nice boy! Give him to me.'

And then the two fell into the most animated discussion, while Helen sat silent and looked on. She forgot that the boy was her enemy's son. He was her cousin's son; some drops of blood-kindred to her ran in his veins. He was an honest, simple boy. Mrs Drummond brightened upon him, according to her nature. She was not violently fond of children, but she could not shut her heart against an ingenuous, open face. She scarcely interfered with the conversation that followed, except to subdue the wild generosity with which Ned proposed to send everything he could think of to Norah. 'There are some books about dogs, that will tell you just what to do. I'll tell John to bring them down. And there's—Are you very fond of books? You must have read thousands and thousands, I am sure.'

'Not so many as that,' Norah said modestly. 'But I have got through—some.'

'I could lend you—I am sure I could lend you—Papa has got a great big library; I forget how many volumes. They are about everything that books were ever written about. We never read them, except mamma, sometimes; but if you would like them—'

'You must not give her anything more,' said Helen; 'and even the dog must only come if your people are willing. You are too young to make presents.'

'I am not so very young,' cried Ned, who had found his voice. 'I am near fourteen. When Cyril Rivers was my age, he was captain of fourth form;—he told me himself. But then he is very clever—much cleverer than me. Norah! if I should only be able to send Shaggy's puppy, not Shaggy himself, shall you mind?'

'Are you sure you will not be afraid to walk up the avenue alone?' said Mrs Drummond, rising from the table. 'I fear it will be so very dark; and we have no one to send with you, Ned.'

'Oh, I don't want any one,' said the boy; and he stumbled up to his feet, and put out his hand to say good night, feeling himself dismissed. Norah went to the door with him to let him out. 'Oh, I wish I could go too,' said Norah; 'it is so lonely walking in the dark; but then I should have to get back. Oh, I do so wish you could stay. Don't you think you could stay? There are hundreds of rooms we don't use. Well, then, good night. I will tell you what I shall do. I shall stand at the door here and watch. If you should be frightened, you can shout, and I will shout back; and then you will always know that I am here. It is such a comfort when one is frightened to know there is some one there.

'I shan't be frightened,' said Ned boldly. And he walked with the utmost valour and the steadiest step to the Hall gates, feeling Norah's eyes upon him. Then he stopped to shout—'Good night; all right!'

'Good night!' rang through the air in Norah's treble. And then, it must be allowed, when he heard the door of the Gatehouse shut, and saw by the darkness of the lodge windows that old John and his daughter had gone to bed, that Ned's heart failed him a little. A wild recollection crossed his mind of the dwarfs, with their long arms, under the trees; and of the old woman spinning, spinning, with eyes that fixed upon you for hours together; and then, with his heart beating, he made one plunge into the gloom, under the overarching trees.

This is how Ned and Norah, knowing nothing about it, made, as they each described the process afterwards, 'real friends.' The bond was cemented by the gift of Shaggy's puppy some days after, and it was made permanent and eternal by the fact that very soon afterwards Ned went away to school.

Meanwhile the great case of Rivers's bank came before the law courts and the public. It was important enough—for there was no war in those days—to be announced in big capitals on the placards of all the newspapers. The Great Bank Case—Arrest of the Directors—Strange Disclosures in the City—were the headings in the bills, repeated from day to day, and from week to week, as the case went on. It was of course doubly attractive from the fact that it was founded upon a tragedy, and that every writer in the papers who referred to it at all was at liberty to bring in a discussion of the motives and intentions of 'the unhappy man' who had introduced 'a watery grave' into the question. A watery grave may not be pleasant for the occupant of it, but it is a very fine thing for the press. The number of times it appeared in the public prints at this period defies reckoning. In some offices the words were kept permanently in type. The Daily Semaphore was never tired of discussing what the feelings of the wretched man must have been when he stole down to the river just as all the world was going to rest, and plunged himself and his shame, and the books of the company, under the turbid waters. The Daily Semaphore held this view of the matter very strongly, and people said that Mr Golden belonged to the same club as its editor, and that the two were intimate, which of course was a perfectly natural reason for its partisanship. Other journals, however, held different opinions. The weekly reviews, less addicted to fine writing, leaned to the side of the unfortunate painter. Their animadversions were chiefly upon the folly of a man interfering with business who knew nothing about it. When would it come to be understood, they said, that every profession required a training for itself, and that to dabble in the stocks without knowing how, was as bad, or at least as foolish, and more ruinous than to dabble in paint without knowing how. There was a great deal about the sutor, who should stick to his last, in these discussions of the subject; but, except in this particular, neither the Sword nor the Looker-on had a stone to throw at poor Drummond. Peace to his ashes, they said, he was a good painter. 'During his lifetime we thought it our duty to point out the imperfections which lessened the effect of his generally most conscientious and meritorious work. It is the vocation of a critic, and happy is he who can say he has never exceeded the legitimate bounds of criticism, never given utterance to a hasty word, or inflicted unnecessary pain. Certain we are, for our own part, that our aim has always been to temper judgment with charity; and now that a gap has been made in so melancholy a manner in the ranks of the Academy, we may venture to say that no man better deserved his elevation to the first rank of his profession than Robert Drummond; no man we have ever known worked harder, or threw himself more entirely into his work. His feeling for art was always perfect. Now and then he might fail to express with sufficient force the idea he intended to illustrate; but for harmony of conception, true sense of beauty, and tender appreciation of English sentiment and atmosphere, he has been surpassed by no painter of our modern school. We understand that an exhibition of his collected works is in contemplation, a plan which has been lately adopted with great success in so many cases. We do not doubt that a great many of our readers will avail themselves at once of the opportunity of forming a comprehensive judgment of the productions of a most meritorious artist, as well as of paying their tribute of sympathy to the, we firmly believe undeserved, misfortunes of an honest and honourable man.'

It was thus the Looker-on expressed its sentiments. The Sword did not attempt to take up the same tone of melancholy superiority and noble-mindedness—qualities not in its way; but it made its stand after its own fashion against the ruthless judgments of the public. 'No one can respect the British public more than we do,' said that organ of the higher intellect; 'its instincts are so unerring, and its good taste so unimpeachable, that, as a matter of course, we all bow to a decision more infallible than that of the Holiest Father that ever sat in Papal See. But after we have rendered this enlightened homage, and torn our victim to pieces, an occasional compunction will make itself audible within the most experienced bosom. After all, there is such a thing as probability to be taken into account. Truth, as we all know, is stranger than fiction; but yet the cases are so few in which fact outrages every likelihood that we are justified in looking very closely into the matter before we give an authoritative assent. So far as our personal knowledge goes, we should say that a painter is as much afraid of the money market as a woman is (or rather used to be) of a revolver, and that the dramatic completeness of the finale which the lively commercial imagination has accepted as that of poor Drummond, quite surpasses the homelier and milder invention of the daughters of art. A dramatic author, imbued with the true modern spirit of his art, might indeed find an irresistible attraction in the "situation" of the drowning director, tossing the books of a joint-stock company before him into the abyss, and sardonically going down into Hades with the proofs of his guilt. But though the situation is fine, we doubt if even the dramatist would personally avail himself of it, for dramatists have a way of being tame and respectable like their neighbours. In our days your only emulator of the piratical and highway heroes of the past is the commercial man pur sang, who has not an idea in his head unconnected with business. It is he who convulses society with those witticisms and clevernesses of swindling which charm everybody; and it is he who gives us now and then the example of such a tragical conclusion as used to belong only to poetry. It is no longer the Bohemian, it is the Philistine, smug, clean, decorous, sometimes pious, who is the criminal of the nineteenth century.'

This article made a great sensation in many circles. There were people who thought it was almost a personal libel, and that Golden would be justified in 'taking steps' against the paper, for who could that smug, clean, decorous Philistine be but he? But the manager was better advised. He was the hero of the day to all readers and writers. He was kept under examination for a whole week, badgered by counsel, snubbed by the judge, stared at by an audience which was not generally favourable; but yet he held his own. He was courageous, if nothing else. All that could be done to him in the way of cross-examination never made him falter in his story. Other pieces of information damaging to his character were produced by the researches of the attorneys. It was found that the fate of all the speculations in which he had been involved was suspiciously similar, and that notwithstanding those business talents which everybody allowed to be of the highest order, ruin and bankruptcy had followed at his heels wherever he went. The counsel for the prosecution paid him unbounded compliments on his ability, mingled with sarcastic condolence on this strange and unfailing current of misfortune. He led the witness into a survey of his past life with deadly accuracy and distinctness, damning him before all the world, as history only can damn. 'It is unfortunate that this should have happened to you again after your previous disappointments,' he said. 'Yes, it was unfortunate,' said the unhappy man. But he held such head against the torrent of facts thus brought up, that the sympathy of many people ran strongly in his favour for the moment. 'Hang it all! which of us could stand this turn-up of everything that ever happened to him?' some said. Golden confronted it all with the audacity of a man who knew everything that could be said against him; and he held steadily by his story. He admitted that Drummond had done nothing in the business, and indeed knew next to nothing about it until that day in autumn, when, in the absence of all other officials, he had himself had recourse to him. 'But the more inexperienced a man may be, the more impetuous he is—in business; when once he begins,' said the manager. And that there was truth in this, nobody could deny. But gradually as the trial went on, certain mists cleared off and other mists descended. The story about poor Drummond and the books waned from the popular mind; it was dropped out of the leading articles in the Semaphore. If they had not gone into the river with the painter, where were they? Who had removed them? Were they destroyed, or only hidden somewhere, to be found by the miraculous energy of the police? This question began to be the question which everybody discussed after a while; for by this time, though proof was as far off as ever, and nobody knew who was the guilty party, there had already fallen a certain silence, a something like respect, over that 'watery grave.'

And something more followed, which Helen Drummond scarcely understood, and which was never conveyed in words to the readers of the newspapers—a subtle, unexpressed sentiment, which had no evidence to back it but only that strange thrill of certainty which moves men's minds in spite of themselves. 'I would just like to know what state Rivers's was in before it became a joint-stock company,' was the most distinct expression of opinion any one was guilty of in public; and the persons to whom this speech was addressed would shake their heads in reply. The consequence was one which nobody could have distinctly accounted for, and which no one ventured to speak of plainly. A something, a breath, a mist, an intangible shadow, gathered over the names of the former partners who had managed the whole business, and transferred it to the new company. These were Mr Burton and another, who has nothing to do with this history. In what condition had they handed it over? What induced them to dispose of such a flourishing business? And why was it that both had got so easily out of it with less loss than many a private shareholder? These were very curious questions, and took an immense hold on the public mind, though they were not discussed in the newspapers; for there are many things which move the public mind deeply, which it would not answer to put in the newspapers. As for Lord Rivers, he was a heavy loser, and nobody suspected for a moment that he knew anything about it. The City men were sorry for him as a victim; but round the names of Mr Burton and his colleague there grew that indefinable shadow. Not a word could be said openly against them; but everybody thought the more. They were flourishing, men in great business—keeping up great houses, wearing all the appearance of prosperity. No righteous critic turned his back upon them. At kirk and at market they were as much applauded, as warmly received, to all outward appearance, as ever. But a cold breath of distrust had come round them, like an atmosphere. The first prick of the canker had come to this flower.

This was the unrecorded, undisclosed result of the inquiry, with which Helen Drummond, and the Haldanes, and all uninstructed, were so deeply dissatisfied. It had ended in nothing, they said. The managers and directors were acquitted, there being no proof against them. No authoritative contradiction had been or could be given to the theory of Robert Drummond's guilt. The Semaphore was still free to produce that 'watery grave' any time it was in want of a phrase to round a paragraph. Their hearts had been wrung with the details of the terrible story all over again, and—nothing had come of it. 'I told you it would be so,' Mr Burton said, who knew so much better. 'It would have been much more sensible had you persuaded Maurice to leave it alone.' But Maurice had a different tale to tell when he came to make his report to his anxious clients. He bewildered them with the air of triumph he put on. 'But nothing is proved,' said Helen sadly. 'No, nothing is proved,' he said; 'but everything is imputed.' She shook her head, and went to her room, and knelt down before the Dives, and offered up to it, meaning no harm, what a devout Catholic would call an acte de reparation—an offering of mournful love and indignation—and, giving that, would not be comforted. 'They cannot understand you, but I understand you, Robert,' she said, in that agony of compunction and tenderness with which a true woman tries to make up to the dead for the neglect and coldness of the living. This was how Helen, in her ignorance, looked upon it. But Stephen Haldane understood better when he heard the tale. Golden, at least, would never hold up his head again—or, at least, if ever, not for long years, till the story had died out of men's minds. And the reputation of the others had gone down as by a breath. No one could tell what it was; but it existed—the first shadow, the beginning of suspicion. 'I am satisfied,' Dr Maurice said, with a stern smile of triumph. The man had thrown himself entirely into the conflict, and took pleasure in that sweet savour of revenge.

'But Mrs Drummond?' said Stephen, whose mind was moved by softer thoughts.

'That woman cannot understand,' said Dr Maurice. 'Oh, I don't mean any slight to your goddess, your heroine. I may say she is not my heroine, I suppose? She can't understand. Why, Drummond is clear with everybody whose opinion is worth having. We have proved nothing, of course. I knew we could prove nothing. But he is as clear as you or I—with all people who are worth caring for. She expected me to bring her a diploma, I suppose, under the Queen's hand and seal.'

'I did not expect that,' said Haldane; 'but I did look for something more definite, I allow.'

'More definite! It is a little hard to deal with people so exigent,' said Dr Maurice, discomfited in the midst of his enthusiasm. 'Did you see that article in the Looker-on? The Drummond exhibition is just about to open; and that, I am confident, will be an answer in full. I believe the public will take that opportunity of proving what they think.'

And so far Maurice turned out to be right. The public did show its enthusiasm—for two days. The first was a private view, and everybody went. The rooms were crowded, and there were notices in all the papers. The next day there was also a very fair attendance; and then the demonstration on the part of the public stopped. Poor Drummond was dead. He had been a good but not a great painter. His story had occupied quite as much attention as the world had to give him—perhaps more. He and his concerns—his bankruptcy, his suicide, and his pictures—had become a bore. Society wanted to hear no more of him. The exhibition continued open for several weeks, not producing nearly enough to pay its expenses, and then it was closed; and Drummond's story came to an end, and was heard of no more.

This is the one thing which excited people, wound up to a high pitch by personal misfortune or suffering, so seldom understand. They are prepared to encounter scurrility, opposition, even the hatred or the enmity of others; but they are not prepared for the certain fact that one time or other, most likely very soon, the world will get tired of them; it is their worst danger. This was what happened now to the Drummonds; but fortunately at Dura, in the depths of the silent country, it was but imperfectly that Helen knew. She was not aware how generally public opinion acquitted her husband, which was hard; and she did not know that the world was tired of him, which was well for her. He was done with, and put aside like a tale that is told; but she still went on planning in her own mind a wider vindication for him, an acquittal which this time it should be impossible to gainsay.

And quietness fell upon them, and the months began to flow on, and then the years, with no incident to disturb the calm. When all the excitement of the trial was over, and everything done that could be done, then the calm reign of routine began. There were times, no doubt, in which Helen chafed and fretted at it; but yet routine is a great support and comfort to the worn and weary. It supplies a kind of dull motive to keep life going when no greater motives exist. The day commenced always with Norah's lessons. Helen was not an intellectual woman, nor did she feel herself consciously the better for such education as she had herself received; but such as she had received she transmitted conscientiously to Norah. She heard her read every morning a little English and a little French. She made her write a succession of copies, and do exercises in the latter language, and she gave her an hour's music. I fear none of this was done with very much spirit; but yet it was done conscientiously every morning of their lives except Sunday, when they went to church. She did it because it was right, because it was necessary, and her duty; but not with any strong sense of the elevated character of her employment, or expectation of any vast results from it. It had not produced very great results in herself. Her mind had worked busily enough all her life, but she did not believe that her music, or her French, or anything else she had learnt, had done her much good. Therefore she proceeded very calmly, almost coldly, with the same process, with Norah. It was necessary—it had to be done just as vaccination had to be done when the child was a baby; that was about all.

Then after the lessons they had their homely dinner, which Susan did not always cook to perfection; and then they took their walk; and in the evening there were lessons to be learned and needlework to do. When the child went to bed, her mother read—not anything to improve her mind. She was not bent upon improvement, unfortunately; indeed, it did not occur to her. She read, for the most part, novels from the circulating library. The reader, perhaps, is doing the same thing at this moment, and yet, most likely, he will condemn, or even despise, poor Helen. She had one or two books besides, books of poetry, though she was not poetically disposed in any way. She had 'In Memoriam' by her, which she did not read (does any one who has ever lived in the valley of the shadow of death read 'In Memoriam?'), but pored over night and day, thinking in it, scarcely knowing that her own mind had not spoken first in these words. And then there was Mr Browning's poem of 'Andrea,' the painter who had a wife. Helen would sit over her fire and watch it dying out at her feet, and ponder on Andrea's fate—wondering whether, perhaps, a woman might do badly for her husband, and yet be a spotless woman, no Lucrezia; whether she might sap the strength out of him with gentle words, and even while she loved him do him harm? Out of such a question as this she was glad to escape to her novel, the first that might come to hand.

And so many people in Helen's state of mind read novels—people who fly into the world of fiction as a frightened child flies into a lighted room, to escape the ghosts that are in the dark passages and echoing chambers—that it is strange so little provision is made for them, and that the love-story keeps uppermost in spite of all. Yet perhaps the love-story is the safest. The world-worn sufferer is often glad to forget all that reminds him of his own trouble, and even when he is not touched by the fond afflictions of the young people, finds a little pleasure in smiling at them in the exuberance of their misery. They think it is so terrible, poor babies, to be 'crossed in love.' The fact that they cannot have their own way is so astounding to them, something to rouse earth and heaven. Helen ran over a hundred tales of this description with a grave face, thankful to be interested in the small miseries which were to her own as the water spilt from a pitcher is to the sea. To be sure, there were a great many elevating and improving books which Helen might have had if she pleased, but nobody had ever suggested to her that it was necessary she should improve her mind.

And thus the time went on, and Mrs Drummond dropped, as it were, into the background, into the shade and quietness of life. She was still young, and this decadence was premature. She felt it creeping upon her, but she took no pains to stop the process. So long as Norah was safe there was nothing beside for which she was called upon to exert herself; and thus with all her powers subdued, and the stream of life kept low, she lived on, voluntarily suppressing herself, as so many women do. And in the mean time new combinations were preparing, new personages coming upon the scene. While the older people stood aside, the younger ones put on their singing garments, and came forward with their flowery wreaths, with the sunshine upon their heads, to perform their romance, like the others before them. And so it happened that life had stolen imperceptibly away, so noiseless and soft that no one knew of its going, until all at once there came a day when its progress could be no longer ignored. This was the day when Norah Drummond, eighteen years old, all decked and dressed by her mother's hands, spotless and radiant as the rose in her hair, with her heart full of hopes, and her eyes full of light, and no cloud upon her from all the tragic mists through which her youth had passed, went up the long avenue at Dura to the House which was brilliant with lamps and gay with music, to make her first appearance, as she thought, in the world. Norah's heart was beating, her gay spirit dancing already before she reached the door.

'Oh, I wonder, mamma, I wonder,' she said, 'what will happen? will anything happen to-night?' What could happen to her by her mother's side, among her old friends? She did not know; she went to meet it gaily. But Norah found it impossible to believe that this first triumphant evening, this moment of glory and delight, could pass away like the other evenings; that there should not be something in it, something unknown, sweet, and yet terrible, which should affect all her life.

A girl's first ball! What words more full of ecstasy could be breathed in this dull world! A vague, overwhelming vision of delight before she goes into it—all brightness, and poetry, and music, and flowers, and kind, admiring faces; everything converging towards herself as a centre, not with any selfish sense of exclusive enjoyment, but sweetly, spontaneously, as to the natural queen. A hundred unexpected, inexpressible emotions go to make up this image of paradise. There is the first glow and triumph of power which is at once a surprise to her and a joy. The feeling that she has come to the kingdom, that she herself has become the fair woman whose sway she has read of all her life; the consciousness, at last, that it is real, that womanhood is supreme in her person, and that the world bows down before her in her whiteness and brightness, in her shamefacedness and innocent confidence, in her empire of youth. She is the Una whose look can tame the lion; she is the princess before whose glance the whole world yields; and yet at the same time, being its queen, is she not the world's sweet handmaid, to scatter flowers in its path, and dance and sing to make it glad? All these thoughts are in the girl's mind, especially if she be a fanciful girl—though, perhaps, she does not find words to express any of them; and this it is which throws such a charm to her upon the pleasure-making, which to us looks sometimes so stale and so poor.

And it is only after a long interval—unless her case be an exceptionally hard one—that she gets disenchanted. When she goes into the fairy palace, she finds it all that she thought; all, with the lively delight of personal enjoyment added, and that flattery of admiring looks, of unspoken homage, not to the ideal princess, or representative woman, but to her, which is so sweet and so new. Thus Norah Drummond entered the ball-room at Dura House, floating in, as it were, upon the rays of light that surrounded her—the new woman, the latest successor of Eve in the garden, unexacting queen of the fresh world she had entered into, fearing no rivals—nay, reigning in the persons of her rivals as well as in her own. And when she had thus made her entrance in an abstract triumph, waking suddenly to individual consciousness, remembering that she was still Norah, and that people were looking at her, wondering at her, admiring her—her, and not another—she laughed as a child laughs for nothing, for delight, as she stood by her mother's side. It was too beautiful and wonderful to be shy of it.

'Pinch me, mamma, and it will all pass away like the other dreams,' she whispered, holding fast by her mother's arm. But the curious thing, the amazing thing, was, that it continued, and warmed her and dazzled her, and lighted her up, and did not pass away.

'Norah, come! you are to dance this dance with me,' cried Ned, rushing up. He had seen them come in, though he was at the other end of the room; he had watched for them since the first note of the music struck; he had neglected the duty to which he had been specially appropriated, the duty of looking after and amusing and taking care of the two fair daughters of the Marchioness, who was as good as Lady Patroness of Mrs Burton's ball. To keep up the proper contrast, I am aware that Lady Edith and Lady Florizel should have been young women of a certain age, uninviting, and highly aristocratic, while Norah Drummond had all the beauty and sweetness, as well as poverty and lowliness, to recommend her; but this, I am sorry to confess, was not the case. The Ladies Merewether were very pretty girls, as pretty as Norah; they were not 'stuck-up,' but as pleasant and as sweet as English girls need be—indeed, except that they were not Norah, I know no fault they had in Ned's eyes. But they were not Norah, and he forsook his post. Nobody noticed the fact much except Mrs Burton. As for Lady Florizel, she had the most unfeigned good-humoured contempt for Ned. He was a mere boy, she said; she had no objection to dance with him, or chatter to him; but she had in her reach two hundred as good, or better than him, and she preferred men to boys, she did not hesitate to say. So that when Ned appeared by Norah's side, Lady Florizel, taking her place with her partner, smiled upon him as he passed, and asked audibly, 'Oh, who was that pretty girl with Mr Burton? oh, how pretty she was! Couldn't anybody tell her?' Lady Florizel was not offended. But Mrs Burton saw, and was wroth.

Many changes had happened in those six years. At the time of the trial and after it there had been many doubts and speculations in Helen's mind as to what she should do. Suspecting her cousin as she did, and with Robert's judgment against him, as recorded in that last mournful letter, how was she to go on accepting a shelter from her cousin, living at his very gates in a sort of dependence upon him? But she had nowhere else to go, for one thing, and the shade of additional doubt which had been thrown upon Burton by the trial, was not of a kind to impress her mind; nothing had been brought forward against him, no one had said openly that he was to blame, and Helen was discouraged when it all ended in nothing as she thought, and had not energy enough to uproot herself from the peaceful corner she had taken refuge in. Where could she go? Then she had the Haldanes to keep her to this spot, which now seemed the only spot in the world where pity and friendship were to be found. Stephen, whom she contemplated with a certain reverence in his great suffering and patience, was the better for her presence and that of Norah, and their kind eyes and the voices that bade her welcome whenever she crossed their threshold was a comfort to her. She kept herself apart from the Burtons for a long time, having next to no intercourse with them, and so she would have done still had the matter been in her hands. But the matter was no longer in her hands. The children had grown up, all of them together. They had grown into those habits which fathers and mothers cannot cross, which insensibly affect even their own feelings and relations. Clara Burton and Norah Drummond were cousins still, though so great a gulf of feeling lay between their two houses. Both of them had been, as it were, brought up with the Daltons at the Rectory. They were all children together, all boys and girls together. Insensibly the links multiplied, the connection grew stronger. When Ned Burton was at Dura there was never a day in his life that he did not spend, or attempt to spend, part of it in the Gatehouse. And Clara ran in and out—she and Mary Dalton; they were all about the same age; at this moment they ranged from twenty to seventeen, a group of companions more intimate than anything but youth and this long and close association could have made them. They were like brothers and sisters, Mrs Dalton said anxiously, veiling from herself the fact that some of them perhaps had begun to feel and think as brothers and sisters do not feel. Charlie Dalton, for instance, who was the eldest of all—one-and-twenty—instead of falling in love with Norah, who was as poor as himself—a thing which would have been simple madness, of course, but not so bad as what had happened—had seen fit to go and bestow his heart upon Clara Burton, whose father dreamed of nothing less than a duke for her, and who had not as much heart as would lie on a sixpence, the rector's wife said indignantly; and Heaven knows how many other complications were foreshadowing through those family intimacies, and the brother and sister condition which had been so delightful while it lasted. Mrs Drummond and Mrs Dalton went together on this particular evening watching from a distance over their respective children. Helen's face was calm, for Norah was in no trouble; but the rector's wife had a pucker on her brow. She could see her Charlie watching so wistfully the movements of Clara Burton through the crowd, hanging about her, stealing to her side whenever he could, following her everywhere with his eyes. Charlie was especially dear to his mother, as the eldest boy of a large family, when he is a good boy, so often is. She had been able to talk to him many a day about her domestic troubles when she could not speak to his father. She had felt herself strengthened by his sympathy and support, that backing up which is so good for everybody, and it broke her heart to see her boy breaking his for that girl. What could he see in her? the mother thought. If it had been Norah Drummond! and then she tried to talk to her friend at her side. They had come to be very fast friends; they had leant upon each other by turns, corners, as it were, of the burdens which each had to bear, and Mrs Dalton knew Mrs Drummond could guess what the sigh meant which she could not restrain.

'How nice Norah is looking,' she said, 'and how happy! I think she has changed so much since she was a child. She used to have such a dreamy look; but now there is no arrière pensée, she goes into everything with all her heart.'

'Yes,' said Helen; but she did not go on talking of Norah, she understood the give and take of sympathy. 'I like Mary's dress so much. She and Katie look so fresh, and simple, and sweet. But they are not such novices as Norah; you know it is her first ball.'

'Poor children, how excited it makes them! but dressing them is a dreadful business,' said Mrs Dalton, with her anxious look still following her Charlie among all the changing groups. 'I need not disguise it from you, dear, who know all about us. It was sometimes hard enough before, and now what with evening dresses! And when they come to a dance like this they want something pretty and fresh. You will feel it by-and-by even with Norah. I am sure if it were not for the cheap shops, where you can buy tarlatan for so little, and making them up ourselves at home, I never could do it. And you know, whatever sacrifices one makes, one cannot refuse a little pleasure to one's children. Poor things, it is all they are likely to have.'

'At least they are getting the good of it,' said Helen. Norah's dress was the first task of this kind that had been put upon her, and she had been forced to make her sacrifices to dress the child who had grown a woman; but Helen, too, knew that she could not buy many ball dresses off her hundred a year. And it was so strange to think such thoughts in this lavish extravagant house, where every magnificence that could be thought of adorned mother and daughter, and the room and the walls. Mrs Dalton answered to the thought before it had been expressed.

'It is curious,' she said, 'there is Clara Burton, who might dress in cloth of gold if she liked—but our girls look just as well. What a thing it is to be rich!—for the Burtons you know are—' Here Mrs Dalton stopped abruptly, remembering that if the Burtons were nobodies, so was also the friend at her side. She herself was connected with the old Harcourts, and had a right to speak.

'Now, ladies, I know what you are doing,' said Mr Burton, suddenly coming up to them; 'you are saying all sorts of sweet things to each other about your children, and privately you are thinking that there is nobody in the room fit to be seen except your own. Oh don't look so caught! I know, because I am doing the same thing myself.'

Doing the same thing himself—comparing his child to my Norah—to my Mary, the ladies inwardly replied; but no such answer was made aloud. 'We were saying how they all enjoy themselves,' said Mrs Dalton, 'that was all.'

Mr Burton laughed that little laugh of mockery which men of vulgar minds indulge in when they talk to women, and which is as much as to say, you can't take me in with your pretences, I see through you. He had grown stouter, but he did not look so vigorous as of old. He was fleshy, there was a furtive look in his eye. When he glanced round him at the brilliant party, and all the splendour of which he was the owner, it was not with the complacency of old. He looked as if at any moment something disagreeable, something to be avoided, might appear before him, and had acquired a way of stretching out his neck as if to see who was coming behind. The thing in the room about which he was most complacent was Clara. She had grown up, straight, and large, and tall in stature, like our Anglo-Saxon queen with masses of white rosy flesh and gold-coloured hair. The solid splendid white arm, laden with bracelets, which leaned on her partner's shoulder, was a beauty not possessed by any of the slight girls whose mothers were watching her as she moved past them. Clara's arm would have made two of Norah's. Her size and fulness and colour dazzled everybody. She was a full-blown Rubens beauty, of the class which has superseded the gentler, pensive, unobtrusive heroine in these days. 'I don't pretend to say anything but what I think,' said Mr Burton, 'and I do feel that that is a girl to be proud of. Don't dance too much, Clary, you have got to ride with me to-morrow.' She gave him a smile and a nod as she whirled past. The man who was dancing with her was dark, a perfect contrast to her brilliant beauty. 'They make a capital couple,' Mr Burton said with a suppressed laugh. 'I suppose a prophet, if we had one, would see a good many combinations coming on in an evening like this. Why, by Jove, here's Ned.'

And it was Ned, bringing Norah back to her mother. 'I thought you had been dancing with one of—' said his father, pointing with his thumb across his shoulder. 'Have you no manners, boy? Norah, I am sure, will excuse you when she knows you are engaged—people that are stopping in the house.'

'Oh, of course I will excuse him,' said Norah. 'I did not want him at all. I would rather sit quiet a little and see everybody. And Charlie has promised to dance with me. I suppose it was not wrong to ask Charlie, was it? He might as well have me as any one, don't you think, mamma?'

'If you take to inviting gentlemen, Norah, I shall expect you to ask me,' said Mr Burton, who was always jocular to girls. Norah looked at him with her bright observant eyes. She always looked at him, he thought, in that way. He was half afraid of her, though she was so young. He had even tried to conciliate her, but he had not succeeded. She shook her head without making any reply, and just then something happened which made a change in all the circumstances. It was the approach of the man with whom Clara had been dancing; a man with the air of a hero of romance; bearded, with very fine dark eyes and hair that curled high like a crest upon his head. Norah gave a little start as he approached, and blushed. 'It is the hero,' she said to herself. He looked as if he had just walked out of a novel with every sign of his character legibly set forth. But though it may be very well to gibe at beautiful dark eyes and handsome features, it is difficult to remain unmoved by their influence. Norah owned with that sudden flush of colour a certain curiosity, to say the least of it. Mr Burton frowned, and so did his son and daughter simultaneously, as if by touching of a spring.

'I am afraid you don't remember me, Mrs Drummond,' the stranger said; 'but I recollect you so very well that I hope you will let me introduce myself—Cyril Rivers. It is a long time since we met.'

'Oh, I remember!' cried impulsive Norah, and then was silent, blushing more deeply than ever. To ask Charlie Dalton to dance with her was one thing, but meeting the hero was entirely different. It took away her breath.

And two minutes after she was dancing with him. It was this he had come to her mother for—not asking any one to introduce him. He was no longer a boy, but a man travelled and experienced, who knew, or thought he knew, society and the world. But he had not yet dismissed from his mind that past episode—an episode which had been fixed and deepened in his memory by the trial and all the discussions in the newspapers. To say that he had continued to think about the Drummonds would have been foolish; but when he came back to Dura to visit the Burtons, they were the first people who recurred to his mind. As his host drove him past the Gatehouse on the night of his arrival, he had asked about them. And Mr Burton remembered this now, and did not like it. He stood and looked after the pair as they went away arm-in-arm. Norah did not answer as Clara did as a complete foil and counter to Mr Rivers's dark handsomeness. It was a mistake altogether. It was Clara who should have been with him, who was his natural companion. Mr Burton reflected that nothing but kindness could have induced him to invite his cousin's penniless girl to the great ball at which Clara made her début in the world as well as Norah. He felt as he stood and looked on that it was a mistake to have done it. People so poor and so lowly ought not to be encouraged to set themselves up as equals of the richer classes. He said to himself that his system had been wrong. Different classes had different duties, he felt sure. His own was to get as much of the good things of this world, as much luxury and honour, as he could have for his money. Helen's was to subsist on a hundred a year; and to expect of her that she could anyhow manage to buy ball dresses, and put her child in competition with his! It was wrong; there was no other word. Mr Burton left his neighbours, and went off with a dissatisfied countenance to another part of the room. It was his own fault.

'I should have known you anywhere,' said Mr Rivers in the pause of the waltzing. 'You were only a child when I saw you last, but I should have known you anywhere.'

'Should you? How very strange! What a good memory you must have!' said Norah. 'Though, indeed, as soon as you said who you were, I remembered you.'

'But nobody told me who you were,' he said, 'when I saw you just now, dancing with that young fellow, the son of the house.'

'Did you see us then?'

'Yes, and your mother sitting by that stand of flowers. You are half yourself as I remember you, and half her.'

'What a good memory you must have!' said Norah, very incredulous; and then they floated away again to the soft dreamy music, he supporting her, guiding her through the moving crowd as Norah had never dreamt of being guided. She had felt she was on her own responsibility when dancing with Ned and Charlie; with, indeed, a little share of responsibility on account of her partners too. But Mr Rivers danced beautifully, and Norah felt like a cloud, like a leaf lightly carried by the breeze. She was carried along without any trouble to herself. When they had stopped, instead of feeling out of breath, she stopped only from courtesy's sake, to let the others go on.

'How well you dance, Mr Rivers!' she cried. 'I never liked a waltz so much before. The boys are so different. One never feels sure where one is going. I like it now.'

'Then you must let me have as many waltzes as you can,' he said, 'and I shall like it, too. Who are the boys? You have not any—brothers? Boys are not to be trusted for waltzing; they are too energetic—too much determined to have everything their own way.'

'Oh, the boys! they are chiefly Ned and—Charlie Dalton. They are the ones I always dance with,' said Norah. 'And oh, by-the-bye, I was engaged to Charlie for this dance.'

'How clever of me to carry you off before Mr Charlie came!' said the hero. 'But it is his own fault if he was not up in time.'

'Oh, I don't know,' said Norah, with a blush. 'The fact is—he did not ask me; I asked him. I never was at a ball before, and I don't know many people, and of course I wanted to dance. I asked him to take me if he was not engaged, so if he found any one he liked better, he was not to be blamed if he forgot. Why do you laugh? Was it a silly thing to do?'

'I don't know Charlie,' said Mr Rivers; 'but I should punch his head with pleasure. What has he done that he should have you asking him to dance?'

And then that came again which was not dancing, as Norah understood it, an occasion which had always called for considerable exertion, but a very dream of delightful movement, like flying, like—she could not tell what. By this time she was a little ashamed about Charlie; and the waltz put it out of Mr Rivers's mind.

'Do you think I may call to-morrow?' he said, when they stopped again. 'Will your mother let me? There are so many things I should like to talk over with her. You are too young, of course, to remember anything about a certain horrid bank.'

'Ah, no, I am not too young,' said Norah, and the smiles with which she had been looking up at him suddenly vanished from her face.

'I beg your pardon. I had forgotten that it was of more importance to you than to any one. I want to talk to your mother about that. Do you think I may come? Look here; is this Charlie? He is just the sort of youth whom a young lady might ask to dance with her. And good heavens, how he waltzes! I don't wonder that you felt it a painful exercise. Are Miss Burton and her guests friends?'

'We are all great friends,' said Norah, half-displeased. And Clara Burton as she passed gave her an angry look. 'Why Clara is cross,' she said pathetically. 'What can I have done?'

Mr Rivers laughed. Norah did not like the laugh; it seemed a little like Mr Burton's. There was a certain conscious superiority and sense of having found some one out in it, which she did not either like or understand.

'You seem to know something I don't know,' she said, with prompt indignation. 'Perhaps why Clara is cross; but you don't know Clara. You don't know any of us, Mr Rivers, and you oughtn't to look as if you had found us out. How could you find out all about us, who have known each other from babies, in one night?'

'I beg your pardon,' he said, with an immediate change of tone. 'It is one of the bad habits of society that nobody can depend on another, and everybody likes to grin at his neighbours. Forgive me; I forgot I was in a purer air.'

'Oh, it was not that,' said Norah, a little confused. He seemed to say things (she thought) which meant nothing, as if there was a great deal in them. She was glad to be taken back to her mother, and deposited under her shelter; but she was not permitted to rest there. Ned came and glowered at her reproachfully, as she sat down, and other candidates for her hand arrived so fast that the child was half intoxicated with pleasure and flattery. 'What do they want me for?' she wondered within herself. She was so much in request that Ned did not get another dance till the very end of the evening: and even Mr Rivers was balked in at least one of the waltzes he had engaged her for. He drew back with a smile, seeing it was Mr Burton himself who was exerting himself to find partners for Norah. But Norah was all smiles; she danced the whole evening, coming little by little into her partner's way. Pleased to be so popular, delighted with everybody's 'kindness' to her, and dazzled with this first opening glimpse of 'the world.'

'If this is the world, I like it,' she said to her mother as they drove home. 'It is delightful; it is beautiful; it is so kind! Oh, mamma, is it wrong to feel so? I never was so happy in my life.'

'No, my darling, it is not wrong,' Helen said, kissing her. She was not insensible to her child's triumph.

CHAPTER IX

'It is vanity, my dear, vanity. You must not set your mind upon it,' said Mrs Haldane.

'Oh, but it was delightful,' said Norah, 'it was wonderful! if you had been there yourself you would have liked it as much as I did. Everybody looked so nice, and everybody was so nice, Mrs Haldane. A thing that makes every one kind and pleasant and smiling must be good, don't you think so? We were all as amiable, as charming, as fascinating as ever we could be.'

'And whom did you dance with?' said Miss Jane.

'I danced with everybody. It is quite true. You cannot think how kind the people were. When we went in first,' said Norah, with a laugh and a blush, 'I saw so many strange faces, I was afraid I should have no dancing at all; so I whispered to Charlie Dalton, 'Do take me out for the next dance, Charlie!' and he nodded to say yes. I suppose it was dreadfully wrong and ignorant; but I did so want to have a good dance!'

'Well, then, that is one,' said practical Miss Jane, beginning to count on her fingers.

'Oh, no! it is not one at all. Mr Rivers came and asked me, and I forgot all about Charlie. He forgot too, I suppose; for I did not dance with him the whole evening. And then there was Ned, and young Mr

Howard, and Captain Douglas, and Mrs Dalton's brother, and—I told you, everybody; and, to be very grand, Lord Merewether himself at the end.'

'Lord Merewether!' Miss Jane was deeply impressed, and held the finger on which she had counted this potentate for a full minute. 'Then, Norah, my dear, you had the very best of the great county folks.'

'Yes,' said Norah, 'it was very nice; only he was a little—stupid. And then Ned again, and Mr Rivers; Mr Rivers was always coming; mamma made me say I was engaged. It did not turn out to be a fib, for some gentleman always came to ask me; but one always shows it in one's face when one says a thing that is not quite true.'

'Oh, Norah!' said Mrs Haldane, 'is not that just what I told you? Do you think anything can be good or right for a young girl in a Christian land that makes you say what is not quite true? There may be no harm in the dancing by itself, though in my day we were of a different way of thinking; but to tell—lies—'

'Not lies, mother,' said Stephen. 'When Norah told Mr Rivers she was engaged, he understood, of course, that she did not want to dance with him.'

'Well,' said Norah slowly, 'I don't know. To tell the very, very truth, I did want very much to dance with him. He dances like an angel—at least, I don't know how an angel dances—Oh, please don't look so shocked, Mrs Haldane; I did not mean any harm. He is just simply delightful to dance with. But mamma thought something—I don't know what. It is etiquette, you know; a girl must not dance very often with one man.'

'And who is this Mr Rivers?' said Stephen. 'Is he as delightful in other ways?'

'Don't you remember?' said Norah. 'It is so funny nobody seems to remember but me. When we came here first, he was here too, and mamma and I met him one day at our old home in London. Mr Stephen, I am sure I have told you; the boy, I used to call him, that was on our side.'

'Ah, I remember now,' said Stephen; 'and he seems to be on your side still, from what you say. But who is he, Norah, and what is he, and why did he want to dance so often with you?'

'As for that,' said Norah, laughing, 'I suppose he liked me too; there was not any other reason. He is so handsome!—just exactly like the hero in a novel. The moment I saw him I said to myself, "Here is the hero." He is almost too handsome: dark, with hair that curls all over his head, and the most beautiful dark eyes. You never saw such beautiful eyes! Oh, I am not speaking because I like him. I think I should almost like him better if he was not quite so—don't you know? If I were writing a novel, I should take him for the hero. I should make everybody fall in love with him—all the ladies, one after another. When one sees a man like that in real life,' said Norah, with gravity, 'it puts one directly on one's guard.'

'Are you on your guard, Norah?' said Stephen, with a smile. The incipient fun in his eyes was, however, softened by a tenderer alarm, a wistful curiosity. The child! Since poor Drummond used to call her so, regarding her as the child par excellence—the type and crown of childhood—this was the name that had seemed most appropriate to Norah. And it meant so much—not only Robert's child, who was gone, and had left her to the love of his friends, but the very embodiment of youth and innocence—the fresh, new life, to be made something better of than any of the older lives had been. Should she, too, fall just into the common snare—just into the vulgar pitfalls, as everybody did? The thought disturbed her self-appointed guardian—her father's friend.

'Me!' said Norah, and her colour rose, and she laughed, with a light in her eyes which had not been there before. It was not the glance of rising excitement, as Stephen feared, but only a merry glow of youthful temerity—that daring which loves to anticipate danger. 'Oh, what fun it would be! But no, Mr Stephen; oh, no! that was not what I meant in the least. I am not that sort of girl. Mr Rivers,' she added, with a certain solemnity, 'had something to do with that bank, you know. I don't know what he had to do with it. He is Lord Rivers's son, and it is to talk over that that he is coming to see mamma.'

'Oh, to talk over that!' said Stephen, half amused.

'Yes, to talk it over,' said Norah, with great gravity; and then she made a sudden leap from the subject. 'The Merewethers are all staying at the great house—the Marchioness herself, and Lord Merewether, and the girls; I think they are very nice girls. But, oh! Miss Jane, I must tell you one thing; she had on her diamonds. I never saw diamonds before. They are like light. They change, and they glimmer, and they make little rainbows. I never saw anything so beautiful! They are like a quantity of dewdrops when the sun is shining—only you never could get dewdrops to keep still in one place.'

'And I suppose they are worth a mint of money,' said Miss Jane, with a sigh of admiration. 'I have never seen them but in the shops, Norah; but I don't think I should like to wear as much as would keep half-a-dozen poor families round my neck.'

Norah paused doubtfully, not feeling equal to this question.

'I suppose they belong to the family, and she dare not sell them, and then, perhaps—Would God have made diamonds if He did not mean people to wear them?' she asked, with hesitation. 'Oh, do you know, I think I should like so much to wear them, if they were mine!'

'Ah, my dear,' said old Mrs Haldane, 'see how vanity comes into the mind. Yesterday you had never thought of diamonds; now you would like—you know you would like—to have them; and from that to trying to get them is but a step, Norah, but a step—if you don't mind.'

'I could only try to get them by stealing them,' said Norah; 'and, after all, I don't care so much as that. Besides, girls don't wear diamonds. But I'll tell you what I should like. I should like to take those lovely things of the Marchioness's, and put them upon mamma.'

'There, I told you!' said the old lady. 'Norah, don't go to these places any more. You have begun to covet them in your heart.'

'Oh, how beautiful mamma would look in them!' cried Norah. 'Mr Stephen, is it vanity to admire one's mother? I suppose it must be really; for if there is anything in the world that belongs to you, of course it is your mother. I think mamma is beautiful: even in her black silk, made square, and not so fresh as it once was, she was the most beautiful in the room—I don't mean pretty, like us girls. And if I could have put her into black velvet instead, with lovely lace, like Mrs Burton's, and the Marchioness's diamonds—oh!' cried Norah, expanding in her proud imagination, 'she would have been like a queen!'

'Oh, Norah, Norah!' cried Mrs Haldane, shaking her head.

'And so she would,' said Stephen. 'Norah is quite right.'

He spoke low, and there was a melancholy tone in his voice. He was thinking sadly how she had been buried like himself in the middle of her days—shut out from all those triumphs and glories which are pleasant to a woman. A less human-hearted man in Stephen Haldane's position would no doubt have pronounced it happy for Helen that she was thus preserved from vanity and vain-glory. But he had learned to feel for all the deprivations of life. This was what he was really thinking, but not what he was supposed to think. Miss Jane gave a glance of her eye at him from her sewing, half-indignant, half-sorrowful. She had fancied something of the sort often, she said to herself. Stephen, poor Stephen! who could never have a wife, or any other love different from her own. She thought that the other woman whom she had admitted in all the confidence of friendship had stolen from him her brother's heart.

'Well, and if she had,' said Miss Jane, with some sharpness, 'what good would that have done her? I never heard that to be like a queen made anybody the happier yet.'

'I was not thinking of what made her happier,' said Norah, coming behind Miss Jane's chair, and stealing an arm round her neck, 'but of what would make me happier. Shouldn't you like to have everything that was nice for Mrs Haldane and Mr Stephen, even if they didn't want it? Oh, I know you would! and so should I.'

'You coaxing child! you would make one swear black was white! What has that to do with lace and diamonds?' said Miss Jane; but she was vanquished, and had no more to say.

'Mary and Katie were in white tarletane,' said Norah. 'They looked so pretty! Clara looked very much the same. You can't have much better than fresh white tarletane, you know; only she had the most beautiful silk underneath, and heaps of ornaments. She is so big she can stand a great deal of decoration; but it would not have done for any of us little things. How anxious I used to be to grow big!' Norah went on. 'Now, on the whole, I think it is best not; one does not take up so much room; one does not require so much stuff for a dress; one can do without a great many things. If I had been as big as Clara, now, for instance, I never could have done with those little bits of bracelets and mamma's one string of pearls.'

'So you see good comes from evil,' said Stephen, with a smile.

'Oh, Stephen, don't talk so to encourage the child! With your upbringing, Norah, and with all the advantages you have had, to give up your mind to such follies! If I were your poor mamma—'

'She is saying nothing wrong, mother,' said Miss Jane. 'It is a great gain to Norah, you know, that she is little, and can get a pretty dress out of twelve yards of stuff, when Clara Burton takes twenty. That is thrift, and not vanity. I am very glad you are little, Norah; big women are always in the way. That Clara Burton, for instance—if she were in a small house she would fill it all up; there would not be room for any one else. What does Mr Rivers see in her, I wonder? She is not half so nice as some people I know.'

'Mr Rivers?' said Norah.

'Yes, my dear. They say it is almost a settled thing between the two families. She will have quantities of money, and he will be Lord Rivers when his father dies. They say that is why he is here.'

It did not matter anything to Norah. She did not care; why should she? Her very admiration of him had been linked with a gibe. He was too handsome; he was a man out of a book. Nevertheless, she looked at Miss Jane for a moment aghast. 'The boy that was on our side!' she said to herself.

'Who are they, and what do they know about it?' said Stephen. 'People don't make such arrangements now-a-days. If this were intended, you may be sure nothing at all would be said.'

Stephen made this little speech partly out of a real regard for Norah's cheerfulness, which he thought was affected, and partly to rouse her to self-defence.

'But it would be quite nice,' said Norah, recovering her dismay. 'Oh, how funny it would be to think of one of us being married! It should be Clara the first; she is the youngest, but she is the biggest, and she was always the one who would be first, you know. She is very, very handsome, Miss Jane. You never were fond of Clara; that is why you don't see it. It would be the very thing!' cried Norah, clapping her hands. 'She is not one of the girls that would go and make him vain, falling in love with him. She will keep him in his right place; she will not let him be the hero in the novel. The only thing is, I am a little disappointed—though it is very foolish and stupid; for of course all that is over long ago, and Clara is like my sister; and if Mr Burton was wicked, I hope he has repented. But still, you know, I have always thought of Mr Rivers as one that was on our side.'

'Hush, child!' cried Miss Jane. 'Don't be the one to keep up old quarrels. That is all over now, and we have no sides.'

'So I suppose,' said Norah; 'but I feel a little as if he were a deserter. I wonder if Clara likes him. I wonder if—It is all so very funny! One of us girls! But I must go now to mamma. Mr Stephen, I will come back in the evening, and tell you what mamma thinks, and if Mr Rivers had anything to tell her—that is, if he comes to-day.'

And Norah ran away unceremoniously, without leave-taking. She was the child of both the households. Sometimes she went and came a dozen times in a day, carrying always a little stream of youth, and life, and freshness into the stagnant places. Stephen laid down his book with a smile at the sight of her; he took it up now with a little sigh. He had sat there all these six years, a motionless, solemn figure, swept aside from the life of man, and Norah's comings and goings had been as sweet to him as if she had been his own child. Now he feared that a new chapter of life was opening, and it moved him vaguely, with an expectation which was mingled with pain; for any change must bring pain to him. To others there would be alternations—threads twisted of dark and bright, of good and evil; but to him in his chair by the window, no change, he felt, could bring anything but harm.

'Oh, mamma,' said Norah, rushing into the drawing-room at the other side of the house, 'fancy what I have just heard! They say it is all but settled that Clara is to marry Mr Rivers. They say that is why he is here.'

'It is very likely, dear,' said Helen. 'I thought something of that kind must be intended from what I saw last night.'

'What did you see, mamma? How odd I should never have thought of it! I feel a little disappointed,' said Norah; 'because, you know, I always made up my mind that he was on our side.'

'We don't want him on our side,' said Mrs Drummond, with a decision which surprised her daughter. 'And, Norah, I am glad you have spoken to me. Be sure you don't forget this when you meet Mr Rivers: he is very agreeable, and he seems very friendly; but you must take care never to say anything, or to let him say anything, that you would not wish Clara to hear.'

Norah paused, and looked at her mother with considerable bewilderment. 'How very strange of you to say this, mamma! How very disagreeable—never to say anything, nor let him say anything! But I should hate to have Clara, or any one, listening to all I say. I will not talk to him at all. I will close my lips up tight, and never say a word. I suppose that will be best.'

'Not to-day, however,' said Mrs Drummond; 'for I see him coming, Norah. You must be as you always are—neither opening your mouth too much, nor closing it up too tight.'

'I hate the juste milieu,' said naughty Norah; but at that moment the door-bell rang, and, before she could speak again, Mr Rivers was shown in, looking more like the hero of a novel than ever. He was tall, slender, well-proportioned. He had those curls about his temples which go to a girl's heart. He had the most ingratiating nose, the beautifullest eyes. 'For one thing,' said Norah to herself savagely, 'Clara will not go and fall in love with him and make him vain!' Clara had too great an opinion of herself; she was not likely to be any man's worshipper. There was consolation in that.

'It is a long time since we met,' Mr Rivers said; 'but you must pardon me for thrusting myself upon you all at once, Mrs Drummond. I have never forgotten what passed when I saw you last. I doubt whether I ought to speak of it after all these years.'

'Perhaps it is better not,' said Helen.

'Perhaps; but I should like to say one thing—just one thing. I do not know if you thought my father to blame. He is a quiet man; he never makes any public appearance; he was a sufferer only. He had nothing to do with the bank. He was one of those who were wronged, not of those who did the wrong.'

'I have always known that,' said Mrs Drummond; and then there was a pause. ('He is on our side still,' Norah thought to herself; but her mother changed the subject abruptly.) 'The children have all grown up since you were here. Time has made more change upon them than upon you.'

'Do you think so?' said the hero. 'I am not sure. Time has made a great deal of difference in me. I am not half so sure of the satisfactoriness of life and the good qualities of the world as I used to be. I suppose it is a sign that age is coming on; whereas these young people, these fairy princes and princesses, who were babies when I was here—'

At this point Norah was seized with one of those irrestrainable, seductive laughs which lead the spirit astray. 'Oh, I beg your pardon,' she said; 'but I was puzzled to think how poor dear Ned could be a fairy prince! He is such a dear fellow, and I am so fond of him; but Prince Charmant, mamma!'

'If he is a dear fellow, and you are fond of him, I should think it did not matter much whether he looked like Prince Charmant or not,' said Mr Rivers; and then he added, with a smile—'There are other kinds of princes besides Charmant. Riquet, with the tuft, for instance; and he with the long nose—'

Now Ned, poor fellow, had a long nose. He had not grown up handsome, and Norah was strongly conscious of the fact. She felt that she had been the first to laugh at him, and yet she hated this stranger for following her example. She grew very red, and drew herself up with the air of an offended queen.

'They all got charmant at the last,' she said stiffly; 'that is better than beginning by being charmant, and turning out very disagreeable in the end.'

Mrs Drummond gave her daughter a warning glance. 'It was a pretty party last night,' she said; 'I hope you liked it. We thought it very grand; we have so little gaiety here.'

'Was it gaiety?' said the young man. 'I suppose it was; but a ball is always rather a solemn affair to me, especially when you are staying in the house. The horror that comes over you lest you have danced with some one you ought not to have danced with, or left some one whom you ought. I broke away for a little while last night when I saw you, and went in for simple pleasure—but duty always drags one back at the end.'

'Duty at a ball! Why it is all pleasure,' cried Norah. 'It may be foolish and frivolous, or it may even be—wrong; but I never was so happy in my life.'

Then the hero of romance turned upon her, and smiled. 'You told me it was your first ball,' he said; 'and that, I suppose, would naturally make it look like Paradise.'

'It was very nice,' said Norah. His smile and his look drove her back into the shelter of commonplace. Somehow when he looked at her, her energy seemed to turn into exaggeration, and her natural fervour into pretence. Then she plunged into the heart of a new subject with all a child's temerity. 'Don't you think Clara is very handsome?' she said.

Mr Rivers did not shrink from a reply. 'She is very handsome—if she knew how to dress.'

'Dress! why, she had the loveliest dress—'

'It was all white and puffy—like yours,' he said. 'Fancy that girl having no more perception than to dress herself like you! What has she to do with shadows, and clouds, and mystery? She should be in heavy silks or satins, like the Juno she is.'

Norah did not quite make out what this meant; whether it was the highest admiration or a covert sneer. She took it for granted it must be the former. 'Yes; I know she is like a Juno,' she said, somewhat doubtfully; adding, with a slightly faltering tone, 'and she is very nice too.'

'She is your cousin, Norah,' said Mrs Drummond quietly; and then the child grew redder than ever, and felt herself put on her defence.

'I did not mean to gossip, mamma. I don't know what Mr Rivers likes to talk about. When any one is quite a stranger, how can you tell, unless you are very, very clever, what to talk about? And then I have been with Mr Stephen, telling them all about the ball. It is in my head. I can't think of anything else. How pretty the Merewether girls are! Oh, I beg your pardon. I did not mean to go back to the same subject. But I had to tell them everything—what people were there, and whom I danced with, and—'

'Mr Stephen always encourages your chatter,' said Helen, with a smile.

'What a sensible man Mr Stephen must be! May I know who he is?' said young Rivers; and thus a new topic presented itself. Stephen Haldane's name and his story brought up an unintentional reference to the misfortunes which linked the two households together, and which had given Cyril Rivers a certain hold upon them. When this chance was afforded him, he told them, very simply and shortly, what sacrifices his father had made; how he had mortgaged some of his property, and sold some, and was living very quietly now, in retirement, till his children were all educated. 'I am sent out into the world, to see how it looks after the waters have abated,' he said, laughing. 'I have got to find out how the land lies, and if there is any green showing above the flood; but I don't know whether I am most likely to turn out the raven or the dove.'

'Oh, I should like to find an olive leaf for you to fly back with,' said Norah, obeying her first impulse, in her foolish way. Mrs Drummond looked at him very gravely, without any of her daughter's enthusiasm.

'Mr Rivers must find the olive leaf in some warmer corner,' she said. 'They don't grow in our garden, Norah. We have none to give.'

'That is true,' said the heedless girl; 'but, if the olive would do, Mr Rivers, there is one in the conservatory at the great house—a poor, little, wee, stunted thing; but there is one, I know.'

Did she mean it? or was it mere innocence, heedlessness? It was not wonderful if Cyril Rivers was puzzled, for even Mrs Drummond could not make quite sure.

CHAPTER X

It was natural that there should be nothing talked about that morning throughout Dura except the ball. All the young people were late of getting up, and they were all full of the one subject—how this one and that one looked; how Charlie haunted Clara all the evening; how young Mr Nicholas, the curate, whom decorum kept from waltzing, stood mournfully and gazed at Mary Dalton through all the round dances. Things were getting very serious between Mary and Mr Nicholas; though waltzing was such a temptation to her, poor child, and though she had plenty of partners, she sat still half the evening out of pity for the curate's wistful eyes; and yet he had been ungrateful all the same, and reproachful on the way home. Katie Dalton, to her own great comfort, was still quite loverless and hampered by nobody's looks. 'I would not put up with it,' she said to her sister; 'because a man chooses to make himself disagreeable, can you not be allowed to enjoy yourself? It is not so often we have a dance. I should let him know very plainly, if it were me.'

'Oh, Katie dear,' said her sister, 'you don't know what you would do if it were you.'

'Well, then, I am very glad it isn't me. I hate parsons!' cried Katie. This was but a specimen of the commotion made by the ball. The sudden incursion of quantities of new people into the limited little society in which everybody had appropriated a companion to his or herself was at the first outset as disagreeable as it was bewildering. The Dura boys and girls had each a sore point somewhere. They had each some reproaches to make, if not audibly, yet in their hearts. Norah and Katie, who were quite fancy-free, were the only ones who had received no wound. At the moment when Mr Rivers sat in the drawing-room at the Gatehouse, Ned and Clara Burton were walking down the avenue together, discussing the same subject. They were both of them somewhat sulky; and both with the same person. It was Norah who had affronted both the brother and sister; and to Clara, at least, the affront was doubly bitter, from her consciousness of the fact that, but for the kindness, nay, charity, of the Burtons, Norah never could have come into such a scene of splendour at all. Clara was her father's child, and this was a thing which she never forgot.

'I have never been so fond of Norah Drummond as the rest of you were,' she said. 'I think she is a heartless little thing. I am sure what she and her mother want is to be revenged on us because we are so much better off. I am sure papa thinks so. It is the shabbiest, the most wretched thing in the world, to hate people because they are better off.'

'Trust to you girls for imputing bad motives,' said Ned. He was very sulky, and rather unhappy, and consequently ready to quarrel with his best friend. In his heart he had no such bad opinion of 'girls;' but at this moment he felt that nothing was too disagreeable to be said.

'We girls know better what we are about a great deal than you do,' said Clara. 'We see through things. Now that you begin to have your eyes opened about Norah Drummond, I may speak. She is a dreadful little flirt. I have seen it before, though you never did. Why, I have seen her even with Mr Nicholas; and she asked Charlie Dalton to dance with her last night—asked him! Would any girl do that who had a respect for herself, or cared for what people think?'

'Did Charlie tell you?' said Ned with deeper wrath and wretchedness still. 'She never asked me,' he said to himself; though he would have been ready to dance himself half dead in her service had she but taken the trouble to ask.

'I heard her,' said Clara; 'and then, as soon as something better came, she forgot all about Charlie. She made Cyril Rivers dance with her, claiming acquaintance because she met him once when we were all little. Ned, I would never think of that girl more, if I were you. In the first place, you know it never could come to anything. Papa would not allow it—a girl without a penny, without any position even, and all that dreadful story about her father!'

'The less we say of that dreadful story the better,' said Ned.

'Why? We have nothing to do with it—except that papa has been so very kind. I don't think it is wise to have poor relations near,' said Clara. 'You are obliged to take some notice of them; and they always hate you, and try to come in your way. I know mamma was quite wild to see you, the very first thing—before you had danced with Lady Florizel, or any one—taking Norah out.'

'Mamma is too sensible to think anything about it,' said Ned.

'You may suppose so, but I know to the contrary. Mamma was very anxious you should be attentive to Lady Florizel. We are rich, but we have not any connections to speak of; only rich people, like poor grandpapa. I don't mean to say I am not very fond of grandpapa; but the exhibition he always makes of himself at those meetings and things, and the way he throws his money away—money that he ought to be saving up for us. Papa says so, Ned! Why should you look so fierce at me?'

'Because it is odious to hear you,' said Ned. 'You have no right to repeat what papa says—if papa does say such things. I hope my grandfather will do exactly what he likes with his money. I am sure he has the best right.'

'Oh, that is all very well,' said Clara. 'I never had college debts to be paid. It suits you to be so independent, but it is chiefly you that the rest of us are thinking of. You know we have no connections, Ned. Grandpapa and his Dissenters are enough to make one ill. If he had only been philanthropic, one would not have minded so much; but fancy having, every month or two, Mr Truston from the chapel to dinner! So you are bound to make a high marriage when you marry.'

'I wish, Clara, you would talk of things you understand. I marry—is it likely?' said Ned.

'Very likely—if you ask Lady Florizel. Papa would not ask you to go into the business, or anything. Oh, I know! He does not say much about his plans, but he cannot hide a great deal from me. But you spoil it all, Ned,' said Clara severely. 'You put everything wrong, and make your own people your enemies. Instead of seeing how nice and how sweet and how charming the right young lady is, you go and throw yourself away on Norah Drummond—who leaves you in the lurch the moment she sees some one else better worth her pains.'

'And who might that be?' asked Ned. He tried to laugh, poor fellow, but his laugh and his voice were both unsteady. There was truth in it all; that was what made him so tremulous with anger and suppressed passion.

'As if you could not see for yourself,' said Clara, herself flushing with indignation. 'Why, Cyril Rivers, of course. No doubt they had decided he was the best man to pitch upon. Lord Merewether was too grand; they could not venture upon him—and the Marchioness was there to take care of her son. But poor Cyril had nobody to take care of him. I saw Mrs Drummond look at him in her languid way. She has some magnetism about her, that woman. I have seen her look at people before, and gradually something drew them that they had to go and talk to her. That was how it was last night. Of course, Norah thought no more of you. She had bigger game. She knew very well, if things changed, and Cyril Rivers escaped from her, that, so far as you were concerned, she had only to hold out a finger.'

'You don't seem to make very much of me,' said Ned with an angry blush.

'No, I should not make much of—any boy,' said Clara calmly. 'What could you do? You would fall into the net directly. You are such a simpleton, such a baby, that, of course, Norah would not need even to take any trouble. If she only held up her finger—'

'That is what you mean to do to Charlie, I suppose?' said Ned, with concentrated brotherly malice; and then it was Clara's turn to flash crimson, not so much with shame as with anger. Her complexion was so beautiful, her white so white, and her red so rosy, that the deeper colour which flushed all over her face in a moment seemed to dye the wavy, downy, velvety surface. Her blue eyes flashed out, deepening in colour like the sea under the wind.

'What does it matter to you what I mean to do?' she cried, and turned her back upon him in her wrath, and went back again up the avenue without a word of warning. Ned, in his surprise, stood and looked after her. She was like a Juno, as Mr Rivers had said. She was the youngest of the whole band; but yet the great scale on which she was formed, her imperious manner and looks, gave her a certain command among them. The others were pretty girls; but Clara was splendid, and a woman. She had to be judged on a different standard. Poor Ned's heart was very sore; he was very angry, and wounded, and unhappy; and yet he recognised the difference as he stood and looked after his sister. It was natural that she should make up her mind to marry whosoever pleased her—and break a heart as she would cast away a flower. There was nothing out of character in the superior tone she had taken with her elder brother. On the contrary, it was natural to her; and as for Norah, poor little Norah, what would befall her should she come in the way of this queen? Ned went upon his own way down the village with a hankering in his heart which all Clara's worldly wisdom and all his wounded pride could not quite subdue. Norah had been unkind to him. She had danced with him but twice all that long evening. She had danced with everybody but him. He had seen her—was it a dozen times?—with Rivers—confound him! And then he wondered whether there was any truth in Clara's theory about Rivers. Had Mrs Drummond herself fallen into that way of matchmaking which was natural to mothers? He breathed a little more freely when he presumed that it must be she, and she only, who was to blame, not Norah. He strolled on with his hands in his pockets, thinking if, perhaps, he could meet her, or see her at a window, or persuade Katie Dalton to fetch her; there was always a hundred chances of an accidental meeting in Dura. But he could not with his own sore heart and wounded temper go to the Gatehouse.

Just as Ned reached the lodge going out, Mr Rivers entered the gates coming back. He had a condescending, friendly way of accosting Ned which the young fellow could not bear.

'Ah, going into the village?' he said. 'I am glad to be able to assure you that nobody has suffered from last night.'

'I didn't suppose they had. I am going to the post,' said Ned, surly as a young bear.

'Don't let me detain you, in that case. The post is too important to wait for anything,' Rivers said, stepping aside.

Ned looked at him, and would have liked to knock him down. He thought what an effeminate puppy the fellow was, what a curled darling—the sort of thing that girls admire and think very fine, and all men despise. In short, the feelings with which a washed-out young woman contemplates the creature who is recognised as 'a gentleman's beauty' were a trifle to those which governed Ned. Such feelings, it would appear, must be natural. Ned despised the man for being handsome, and the women for thinking him so, with a virulence which no neglected maiden ever surpassed.

'Do you want me, Burton?' Mr Rivers said pleasantly, seeing that the other did not pass on.

'Oh, good heavens, no! not the least in the world,' cried boorish Ned, and went on without another word.

'Country lout!' the hero said quietly, with a smile to himself. If he could but have heard the comments upon him which were passing through the mind of Ned!

Clara, for her part, went home with her mind full of angry thoughts. She had no personal feeling about Cyril Rivers. If she liked any one it was poor Charlie, who was her slave. But Clara knew with precocious worldly wisdom that that would never come to anything. It might be all very well for the moment. It was pleasant enough to have him hanging about, watching her every look, attentive to her lightest word. But it never could come to anything. The highest prosperity which the future could bring to Charlie would be advancement in the public office where he was now a junior clerk. And that was no lot for her to share: she, Mr Burton's daughter, might (her father said) pick and choose among the most eligible men in England. Mr Burton was in the habit of speaking in this unguarded way. Clara was his favourite in the family, his chosen companion, his almost confidante. He was proud of her beauty and 'style,' and fond of thinking that, in mind at least, she resembled himself. It was he who had settled that Cyril Rivers should be invited to Dura, and should, as a natural consequence, offer all that remained to the Riverses to Clara. The idea of this alliance pleased his mind, though the Riverses were not so rich as they used to be. 'They are still very well off, and the title must be taken into consideration,' he had said to his wife. And when Clara returned home she found her parents sitting together in the library, which was not very common, and discussing their children's prospects, which was less common still. It was October, and there was a fire over which Mrs Burton was sitting. She was a chilly woman at all times. She had not blood enough, nor life enough physically, to keep her warm, and she had been up late, and was tired and not disposed to be on her best company behaviour in the big drawing-room on the chance that the Marchioness might come down-stairs. Mrs Burton was not quite so placid as she once had been. As her children had grown up there had been complications to encounter more trying to the temper than the naughtiness of their childhood; and it sometimes happened that all the advantages to be gained from a succession of fine visitors would be neutralized, or partially neutralized, by the reluctance of the mistress of the house to devote her personal attention to them. Or so, at least, Mr Burton thought. His wife, on the other hand, was of opinion that it was best to leave the visitors sometimes to themselves; and this was what she had done to-day. She had established herself over the library fire with a book after luncheon, leaving the Marchioness and the young ladies to drive or to repose as they pleased. And this piece of self-will had procured her a reprimand, as forcible as Mr Burton dared to deliver, when he came in and found her there.

'You are throwing away our chances, Clara,' he said. 'You are setting the worst example to the children. If the Marchioness had not been resting in her own rooms—'

'The Marchioness is very well, Mr Burton,' said his wife. 'You may be sure I know what I am doing so far as she is concerned. She does not want me to follow her about and make a fuss, as some people do.'

'I have always told you,' said Mr Burton, 'that I wished the utmost civility to be shown to people of her rank in my house. Why, Clara, what can you be thinking of? With all the ambitious ideas you have in your head for Ned—'

'My ambition is very easily satisfied,' she said, 'if you will let the boy follow his own inclinations. He has no turn for business; all that he would do in business would be to lose what you have made.'

'If he makes a good match—if he marries into the Merewether family—I should not say another word about business,' said Mr Burton. Looking at him in daylight, it was still more easy to perceive the change that had come over him. His clothes, those well-made, light-coloured clothes which had once been a model of everything that clothes should be, had begun to look almost shabby, though they were in themselves as glossy and as spotless as ever. Anxiety was written in the lines about his eyes. 'Should the children do well, Clara—should they do as we wish them—I should be tempted myself to get out of the business, when I have an opportunity,' he said. 'It is wearing work, especially when one has nobody to help, nobody to sympathize;' and the man who had been always the incarnation of prosperity, needing no props of external support, puffed out from his bosom a real sigh.

Mrs Burton took no notice; she was perfectly calm and unmoved, either unaware that her husband had displayed anything like emotion, or indifferent to it.

'I cannot say that I have ever been fond of these matchmaking schemes,' she said, 'and Ned is only a boy; but there is one thing that must be taken into consideration, whatever you may do in this matter; that is Norah Drummond. If she thinks differently, you may as well give up the conflict.'

'Norah Drummond!' said Mr Burton, grinding his teeth. 'By Jove! they talk about a man's pleasant sins being against him; but there is nothing so bad in that way as his unpleasant virtues, I can tell you. If all the annoyance I have had through these two women could be reckoned up—'

'I do not know what annoyance you may have had yourself,' said Mrs Burton, in her cold, judicial way. 'I have seen nothing to complain of. But now I confess it begins to be unpleasant. She has more influence over Ned than any of us. He danced with her last night before any one else. He is always there, or meeting her at other places. I have observed it for some time. But you have done nothing to stop it, Mr Burton. Sometimes I have thought you approved, from the way you have allowed things to go on.'

'I approve!' he cried, with something like horror.

'How was I to know? I do not say it is of very much importance. Ned, of course, will follow his own taste, not ours.'

'But, by Jove, he sha'n't!' cried Mr Burton. 'By Jove, he shall take himself out of this, and make his own way, if I hear any more nonsense. What! after all I have done to set them up in the world—after all I have gone through!'

He was affected, whatever was the cause. There was something like agitation about him. He was changed altogether from the confident man of former times. His wife looked at him with a little surprise, and came to this conclusion quite suddenly. She had not noticed it when he was among other people, playing his part of host with an offensive hospitality which often annoyed her, and which the Marchioness, for example, scarcely hesitated to show her contempt of. But now, when there was no one present, when he was free to look as he pleased, Mrs Burton found out all at once that her husband was changed. Was it merely that he was older, tired with last night's dissipation, not so able to defy late hours, and supper and champagne, as he had once done? She was not a woman to rest in so superficial a view of affairs; but for the moment these were the questions she asked herself, as she looked at him with calm yet undeniable surprise.

'You seem to be excited, Mr Burton,' she said.

'Excited!' he cried; 'and good reason, too; with you sitting there as cold as a little fish, never thinking of the interests of your family, talking of Ned thwarting me as if it was nothing! If I were excited it would be little wonder, I think.'

'I have no desire that Ned should thwart you,' she said; 'on the contrary, it is my own wish. He will never make a good man of business. A marriage with one of the Merewethers, or a girl in that position, with your money, Mr Burton, would be the best thing for him. He might get into Parliament, and do all that I once hoped for you; but what I hoped is neither here nor there.'

Mrs Burton was only human, though she was so philosophical; and this was a stroke in her own defence.

'See that Ned does it, then,' he said. 'Perhaps it was what I hoped too; but business has swallowed me up, instead of leaving me more free. You ought to make it your duty to see that Ned does what we both wish. What is there to stand in the way?'

'Not much,' said Mrs Burton, shrugging her shoulders. 'Norah Drummond—not a very large person—that is all.'

'Confound Norah Drummond! A man is always a fool when he thinks of other people. I am finding that out too late. But you may compose yourself about Ned,' added the father, with irony. 'That little thing has other fish to fry. She is poking herself into Clara's way, confound her! That sentimental ass, Rivers, who is unfit to touch my child's hand—'

'I heard of that too,' said Mrs Burton, in a low voice.

'I should think you did hear of it; but you never interfered, so far as I could see. He would have danced with her all night, if I had not taken it into my own hands. The ass! a poor little chit like that, when he might have had Clary! But, however, understand me, Clara, this is a woman's business. I want these children settled and put out in life. Ned may be rather young, but many a young fellow in his position is married at one-and-twenty. And, by Jove, I can't go on bearing this infernal strain! I should give it up if it was not for them.'

'Is there anything going wrong, Mr Burton?' asked his wife.

'What should be going wrong? I am tired of working and never getting any sympathy. I want a son-in-law and a daughter-in-law who will do us credit—but, above all, a son-in-law. And I don't see any obstacle in the way which you cannot overcome, if you choose.'

'I wonder,' said Mrs Burton, 'can I overcome Norah Drummond?—and her mother? They are the obstacles in the way.'

'Thanks to my confounded good-heartedness,' said her husband.

And it was at this moment Clara came in and joined their deliberations. Little more, however, was said, and she was sent away to seek out Lady Florizel, and do her duty to the young visitors as the daughter of the house should. Mr Burton went off himself to see if the Marchioness had made herself visible, and do his best to overwhelm her with fussy hospitality. But Mrs Burton sat still on the library fire and warmed her cold little feet, and set her mind to work out the problem. It was like a game of chess, with two skilfully-arrayed, scientific lines of attack all brought to nothing by a cunning little knight, of double movement-power, in the centre of the board. Either of the schemes on which her husband had set his heart, or both—and one of them was dear to herself also if she would have acknowledged it—might be brought to a satisfactory issue, if this little Norah, this penniless child, this poor little waif, who had grown up at their gates, could but be put out of the way. Was the part of Nemesis, so unlike her childish appearance and character, reserved for Norah? or was the mother using her child as the instrument of a deep, and patient, and long-prepared vengeance? It was the latter view of the question which was most congenial to Mrs Burton's mind; but whether it was that or fate, the greatest combinations which the family at the great house had yet ventured on, the things most concerning their comfort and happiness, were suddenly stopped short by this little figure. It was Norah Drummond, only Norah, who was the lion in the way.

Ned Burton went to the post, as he had said. He had to pass the Gatehouse on his way; and his business was not of so important a description that he should make any haste about it, or tire himself with walking. He loitered along, looking into the windows, sore at heart and wistful. There was no one, to be sure, at Mrs Drummond's end of the Gatehouse. He tried to get a glimpse at the interior through the chinks of the little green Venetian blinds which veiled the lower panes; but they were turned the wrong way, and he could not see anything. He had made up his mind he should be sure to see Norah, for no particular reason except that he wanted so much to see her. But no Norah was visible. At the other end of the house, however, Stephen Haldane's window was open as usual, and he himself sat within, looking almost eagerly for that interview with the outside world which his open window permitted. The summer was over, with all its delights, and soon the window would have to be closed, and Stephen's chair removed into winter quarters. What a deprivation this was to him no one knew;—but just at the fall of the year, when the transparent lime-leaves had turned into yellow silk instead of green, and littered the flags under the window, Stephen looked out more eagerly than he was wont for some one to talk to him. It was his farewell, in a measure, to life. And Ned was but too glad to stop and lean against the outer sill, keeping always an eye upon the door, and Mrs Drummond's windows. He was not handsome. He had a large nose—too large for the rest of his face—which his aunt, Mrs Everest, sometimes comforted him by suggesting was a sign of character and energy, but which Ned had been used to hear all his friends laugh at. The young community at Dura had brought themselves up in all the frankness of family relations, and were wont to laugh freely at Ned's nose, as they laughed at Katie's large teeth, and as, while they were children, they had laughed at Clara's red hair. On that last particular they were undeceived now, and gloried in it, as fashion required; but Katie's teeth and Ned's nose were still amusing to everybody concerned. Poor boy! he had not any feature which was so good as to redeem this imperfection. He had 'nice' eyes, a tolerable mouth, and was well-grown and strong; but nobody could say he was handsome. And then, though he was a gentleman in thought and heart, he was a gentleman of twenty, whose real refinement had not yet had time to work out to the surface, and soften away the early asperities. This was why he looked boorish and loutish in the presence of Cyril Rivers, who had not only the easy confidence which springs from good looks, but that inevitable surface suavity which can only be attained by intercourse with the world.

'You are not shooting to-day,' said Stephen, from within.

'No; we were all late this morning. I don't know why we should be such muffs,' said Ned. 'Merewether had to go off to town to get his leave extended; and Rivers is too fine a gentleman, I suppose, to take much trouble. That's not fair, though. I did not mean it. He is a very good shot.'

'Who is he?' said Stephen. 'I have been hearing a great deal about him this morning.'

'Oh, have you?' Ned looked yellow as the lime leaves which came tumbling about his head, and his nose was all that was visible under the hat, which somehow, in his agitation, he pulled over his brows. 'He is a man about town, I suppose. He is member for somewhere or other—his father's borough. He is an æsthetic sort of politician, diplomatist, whatever you like to call it: a man who plays at setting all the world right.'

'But who does not please Ned Burton, I am afraid,' said Stephen, with a smile. 'I hear you all enjoyed yourselves very much last night.'

'Did we?' said Ned. 'The girls did. I suppose they don't think of much else. But as one grows older, one sees the absurdity of things. To think of a man, a rational being, putting his brains in his pocket, and giving himself up to the cultivation of his legs! Oh, yes; we all did our fetish worship, and adored the great god Society, and longed to offer up a few human sacrifices; though there are enough, I suppose, without any exertion of ours,' said Ned, leaning both his arms on the window. He heaved such a sigh, that the leaves fluttered and whirled before the mighty breath. And Stephen Haldane suppressed a laugh, though he was not very gay. It was hardly possible to help being amused by this juvenile despair. And yet, poor Stephen going back into those old memories, which looked a thousand years off, could not but recollect, with a smile and a sigh, similar hours and moments, in which he too had sounded the very depths of tragedy and endured all the tortures of despair.

'My poor boy,' he said, with a tone which was half comic, half pathetic, 'I feel for you. Did you ever hear of ces beaux jours quand j'étais si malheureux?

Ned looked up in a blaze of sudden resentment.

'I did not think I had said anything funny—though it is always pleasant to have amused you, Mr Haldane,' he said, with desperate politeness. 'I am going to the post-office. I rather think I shall have to be postman, and carry out the bags to-day. Good morning. I ought not to have stood so long keeping you from your book.'

But Stephen's laugh was very low and tender when the young fellow went on, walking at the rate of six miles an hour. Poor Ned! There was not so much to laugh at, for he had serious difficulties in his way—difficulties of which he tried to remind himself as he turned up the village street, by way of making himself a little more unhappy. But the attempt did not succeed. The fact was that his real troubles counted for nothing in the mixture of misery and anger which filled his youthful bosom. The shadow which filled the air with blackness, and made life intolerable, was—Norah. She had slighted him, wounded him, preferred some one else. In presence of this terrible sorrow, all the doubts about his future career, the serious question about the business, the discussions of which he had been the subject, faded into insignificance. It seemed to Ned even that he would gladly consent to go into the business at half an hour's notice if only that half hour would procure him the chance of making himself more miserable still by an interview with Norah. What a fool he was, poor boy! how wretched he was! and what poor creatures those people are who are never wretched and never fools!

Ned Burton lounged about into half the shops in the village in his unhappiness. He bought an ugly little mongrel from a lying porter at the station, who swore to its purity of blood. Ned, in an ordinary way, knew a great deal more about this subject than the porter did, but it gained him a little time, and Norah might, for anything he knew, become visible in the mean time. He went into Wigginton's and bought a rose-coloured ribbon for his straw hat. It was quite unsuitable; but Norah wore rose-coloured ribbons, and it was a forlorn profession of allegiance, though nobody would ever know it. He went to the confectioner's, and bought a bag of cakes, with which he fed half a dozen gaping children outside. In short, he visited as many tradespeople as Mother Hubbard did. But it was all in vain. No Norah passed by; no one like her went into any of the shops. When he passed the Gatehouse once more, the windows were all vacant still. Then Ned took a desperate resolution, and went and paid a visit at the Rectory. He sat with Mrs Dalton in the drawing room, and then he strolled round the garden with the girls. When things had come to this pass, Providence befriended him, and sent a special messenger, in the shape of Mr Nicholas, to take up Mary's attention. As soon as he was alone with her sister, Ned seized the opportunity.

'Katie,' he said, breathless, 'you might do me such a favour.'

'Might I?' said friendly Katie; 'then of course I will, Ned.'

'You are always the nicest and the kindest! Katie, I have something to say to Norah Drummond; something I—have to tell her—by herself. I can't go to the house, for it is something—a kind of a secret.'

'I'll run and fetch her. I know what you have got to say to her,' said Katie, laughing. 'Oh, how funny you are! Why didn't you say it right out, you silly boy.'

'It is not what you mean at all,' said Ned, with great gravity.

But Katie laughed, and ran across the road.

And this was how the interview came about. Norah came over to the Rectory in all innocence, fearing nothing. She said, 'Oh, Ned is here too!' as if nothing had happened. Indeed, she was not aware that anything had happened—only that a game at croquet would be the best way of spending the listless afternoon after the dissipation of the previous night. They sat down on a bench behind that clump of laurel which hid a portion of the lawn from the windows of the Rectory. Mary and Mr Nicholas were walking up and down, round and round. The red geraniums were still bright in the borders, with all manner of asters, and salvias, like scarlet velvet. The autumn leaves were dropping singly, now one, now another, without any sound; the air was very still and soft, the sun shining through a pleasant haze. A sheaf of great, splendid, but dusty gladiolus, stood up against the dark green laurel. They were like Clara in her full and brilliant beauty—not like little Norah in her gray frock, sitting quite still and happy, thinking of nothing, on the warm bench in the sunshine, with her hands folded in her lap, waiting for Katie to come back with the croquet mallets, and altogether unconscious of the dark looks Ned was casting upon her from under his hard brows.

'I suppose Katie will come when she is ready,' he said, in reply to some question. 'She is not always at your word and beck, like me.'

'Are you at my word and beck?' she said, looking round upon him with some surprise. 'How funny you look, Ned! Is anything the matter? Are you—going away?'

'I often think I had best go away,' said Ned, in Byronic melancholy. 'That would be better than staying here and having every desire of my heart trampled on. It seems hard to leave you; and I am such a fool—I always stay on, thinking anything is better than banishment. But after being crushed to the earth, and having all my wishes disregarded, and all my feelings trampled on—'

'Oh, Ned! what can you mean? Who has done it? Is it that dreadful business again?'

'Business!' said Ned, with what he would have described as the hollow laugh of despair. 'That seemed bad enough when I had nothing worse to bear. But now I would embrace business; I would clasp it in my arms. Business! No! That affected only my inclinations; but this goes to my heart.'

'Ned,' said Norah, growing pale, 'you must be over-tired. That is it. You shoot all day—and then the ball last night. Poor boy! you are taking fancies in your head. You don't know what you are saying. You have been over-tired.'

Upon which Ned shook his head, and laughed again, this time 'wildly.' He was very miserable, poor fellow, and yet it cannot be said that he was quite indifferent to the effect he produced. It gave him a certain satisfaction in the midst of his despair.

'If you were to ask yourself, Norah, what is the matter, instead of suggesting so far less than the reality—so much less—' he began.

Then Norah took courage.

'Is that all!' she said. 'Oh, what a fright you gave me! Is it only something I have done without knowing it? You ridiculous, silly boy! Why can't you tell me plainly what it is, without all this nonsense? You know it is nonsense,' Norah continued, warming as she went on. 'What can I have done? Besides, however disagreeable I might have been, what right have you to mind? Nobody else minds. I am not a slave, never to be allowed to make myself unpleasant. There! I will be disagreeable if I like! I am not to be always bound to do what is pleasant to you.'

'If you take me up in this spirit, Norah—'

'Yes, I mean to take you up in this spirit. You have no right to feel everything like a ridiculous sensitive plant. Why should you? If I were a sensitive plant I might have some cause. I am little, I am friendless, I am very poor; I have nothing in the world but mamma. But for you to set up to have feelings, Ned! you, a boy! that can go where you like, and do what you like, and have heaps of money, and everybody bowing down before you! It is because you have nothing really to vex you, that you are obliged to invent things. Oh, you wicked, ungrateful boy, to pretend that you are unhappy! Look at Mr Stephen, and look at mamma!'

'But, Norah,' said Ned hurriedly; 'Norah dear! listen to me only one moment.'

'You ought to be ashamed of yourself,' she said. 'I won't listen to you. I have plenty of things to bother me, and you have nothing. You never had to think whether you could spend this or that—whether you could have a new coat, or go a journey, or anything; and you go and make troubles because you have not got any.' Here she made a pause, turning her head away, so that poor Ned was more miserable than ever. And then all at once she turned and looked up kindly at him. 'What was it I did, Ned?'

This sudden revolution overwhelmed him altogether. He felt the water leap to his eyes. He was so young. And then he laughed unsteadily.

'What a girl you are, Norah!' he said.

'Was I cross last night? What did I do? I didn't mean it, I am sure. I came over quite innocently, never thinking Katie was bringing me to be scolded. It was not friendly of Katie. She ought to have told me. But, Ned, what was it? Tell me what I did.'

'Norah, things must not go on like this. I cannot do it. It may be as much as my life is worth,' said the youth. 'Look at those two over there; they may quarrel sometimes—'

'They quarrel every day of their lives,' said Norah, breathless, in a parenthesis.

'But they know that they belong to each other,' said Ned; 'they know that right or wrong nobody will part them. But, Norah, think how different I am. You may not mind, but it kills me. Once you said you loved me—a little.'

'I love—everybody; we, all of us, love each other,' said Norah, in a subdued voice.

'But that is not what I want. I love you very differently from that, Norah; you know I do. I want you to belong to me as Mary belongs to Nicholas. Next year I will be of age, and something must be settled for me, Norah. How do you think I can face all this talking and all this advising if I don't know what you are going to do? Give me your hand, Norah; give it me into mine; it is not the first time. Now, am I to keep it always? Tell me yes or no.'

'Oh! you hurt me—a little, Ned!'

'I cannot help it,' he said; 'not so much, not half so much, as you hurt me. Oh, Norah, put yourself in my place! Think, only think, how I can bear to see you talking to other people, smiling at them, looking up as you look at me. Is it possible, Norah? And perhaps I may have to go away to fight with the world, and make my own career. And would you send me away all in the dark without knowing? Oh, Norah, it would be cruel; it would not be like you.'

'Please, please, Ned! Mary and Mr Nicholas are coming. Let go my hand.'

'Not until you give me some sort of answer,' said Ned. 'I have loved you since ever I remember—since I was a boy, frightened to speak to you. You have always laughed and gibed; but I never minded. I love you more than all the world, Norah! I can't help thinking it would be so easy for you to love me, if you only would try. You have known me since we were children. You have always had me to order about, to do whatever you liked with.'

'Wait till they have passed,' said Norah in a whisper, drawing her hand out of his.

And then the elder pair, who were engaged, and had a right to walk about together, and hold long private conferences, and quarrel and make friends, passed slowly, suspending their talk also out of regard for the others.

'Are you waiting for Katie?' Mary said. 'She is so tiresome; always finding something unexpected to do.'

'Oh, I am talking to Ned. We are in no hurry,' Norah replied.

And then those full-grown lovers, the pair who had developed into actuality, whom Ned envied, and who had been having a very sharp little quarrel, passed on.

Ned was very much in earnest, poor fellow. His face was quite worn and full of lines. There was a strain and tremulous tension about him which showed how high his excitement was.

'It isn't as if this was new to you, Norah,' he cried piteously. 'You have known it ever so long. And I cannot help thinking you might love me so easily, if you would, Norah, you are so used to me—if you only would!'

Norah was very sympathetic, and his emotion moved her much. She cast down her eyes; she could not bear to look at him, and she nearly cried.

'Oh, Ned,' she said, 'I do love you. I am very fond of you; but how can I tell if it is in that way? How can you tell? We are just like brother and sister. We have never known anybody else all our lives.'

'I have,' said Ned, 'I have known hundreds. And there is no girl in all the world but one, and that is you. Oh, Norah, that is you!'

'But I have never seen any one,' said Norah again. She spoke so very softly that he could scarcely hear. 'I have never seen any one,' she repeated, heaving a gentle sigh—a sigh which was half regret for Ned and half for herself. 'Dear Ned, I do love you. But how could I tell until I saw—?'

'Ah!' he cried, and let her hand drop in his youthful impatience and mortification. 'If that is all your answer, Norah, the best thing for me is to rush away. Why should I stay here any longer? There will be nothing to live for, nothing to hope for!'

'Oh, don't talk nonsense, Ned!'

'It is not nonsense,' said Ned, rising up. 'Norah, if you hear I am gone you will know why it is. If you hear of anything happening to me, I hope you will be sorry. Oh, Norah, Norah!' he cried, the tears forcing themselves to his eyes, 'is it all to end like this?'

He was so young. His despair was real, though it might be too tragical in its outward form. He was capable of going away, as he said, and making himself hugely uncomfortable, and for a time intensely unhappy; and yet perhaps being all the better for it in the end. But Norah, who was not much wiser than himself, was driven to her wit's end by this adjuration, and did not know what to say.

'Ned, don't be so sorry,' she said, taking his hand in her turn. 'Oh, dear Ned, I do love you; but your people would be very angry, and we are so young. We must not think of such things yet. Oh, I am sure I did not mean to make you unhappy. Don't cry. I could not bear to see you crying, Ned!'

'I am not crying,' he said roughly. He had to be rough, he had been so near it. And just at this moment Katie came smiling up with the mallets over her shoulders. He could not come down from that elevation of feeling into this. 'I am afraid I must go now,' he said, almost turning his back upon them. 'I am going to the—to the station now. Merewether is coming by this train.'

'Oh, Ned, how unkind of you, when everything is ready for a game!' cried Katie. But Norah said nothing as he strode away, giving a nod at them over his shoulder. He had not been boorish while he was pleading his own cause; but he had not the heart to be civil when it was over. Cæsars of twenty do not pull their cloaks gracefully about them when they are going to die.

Then Norah suddenly turned upon her companion, and metaphorically gagged and bound her.

'How tiresome it was of you to be so long!' she cried. 'Here we have been waiting and waiting, till Ned's time was up; and so is mine. I must go back to mamma.'

'Why, I have not been gone ten minutes!' cried indignant Katie.

But Norah, too, waved her hand, and moved majestically away. She could scarcely keep from crying. Her heart was full, something was quivering in her throat. It was not so much her own emotion as the reflection of his. Poor Ned! how hard it was that he should be so miserable! She wanted to get safely to her own room, that she might think it over! She walked across the road as if she had been in a dream. She did not hear Mr Stephen call to her in her abstraction. She went in enveloped, as it were, in a cloud of sad and curious fancies, wondering—Was it all over? Would he never say any more about it? Would he go away, and never be heard of more? Would it—and the very thought of this thrilled through Norah's veins, and chilled her heart—would it do him harm? Would he die?

CHAPTER XII

Mrs Burton had taken a very serious piece of work in hand. No wonder that she lingered over the fire in the library, or in her drawing-room, or wherever she could find a fire, in those early chills of October, to warm her little cold toes, and to make up her plan of warfare. She was a chilly little woman, as I have said. She had not much except a mind to keep her warm, and mind is not a thing which preserves the caloric thoroughly unless it is comforted by the close vicinity of other organs. Mrs Burton had no body to speak of; and, so far as has been seen, not very much heart. Her mind had to fulfil all the functions usually performed by these other properties, and to keep her warm besides; so that it was not wonderful if she sat over the fire.

It was not to be expected, however, that the Marchioness would always be so obliging as to remain in her room till three o'clock; and consequently Mrs Burton's thinking had to be done at odd moments when the cares of her household could be lawfully laid aside. She was rather in bondage to her distinguished guest; and as she was a little republican, a natural democrat at heart, the bondage was hard to her. She was a great deal cleverer than the Marchioness of Upshire; her mind went at railroad speed, while that great lady jogged along at the gentlest pace. Where the heart is predominant, or even a good, honest, placid body, there is tolerance for stupidity; but poor intellect is always intolerant. Mrs Burton chafed at her noble companion, and suffered tortures inwardly; but she was very civil, so far as outward appearance went, and did her duty as hostess in a way which left nothing to be desired.

But it took all her powers to master the problem before her. She had an adversary to overcome; an adversary whom she did not despise, but whom everybody at the first glance would have thought too slight a creature to merit so much as a thought. Mrs Burton knew better. She looked at Norah Drummond not in her simple and evident shape as a little girl of eighteen, the daughter of a poor mother, who lived upon a hundred pounds a year. This was what Norah was; and yet she was a great deal more. She was the commander of a little compact army, of which the two chief warriors, love and nature, were not much known to Mrs Burton; but which was reinforced by youth, and supreme perverseness and self-will, powers with which she was perfectly acquainted. Ned's love his mother might perhaps have laughed at; but Ned's obstinacy, his determination to have his own way, were opponents at which she could not laugh; and they were arrayed against her. So was the capricious fancy, the perverse individuality of Cyril Rivers, who was a man accustomed to be courted, and not over-likely to fall into an arrangement made for him by his family. Mrs Burton pondered much upon all these things. She found out that her guest was seen at the Gatehouse almost every day, and she saw from her son's aspect that he too knew it, and was beginning to hate his rival. Then there arose a little conflict in her mind as to which of her two children she should make herself the champion of. A mother, it may be thought, would incline most to the daughter's side; but Mrs Burton was not an emotional mother. She was not scheming how she could save her children pain. The idea of suffering on their part did not much affect her—at least, suffering of a sentimental kind. She formed her plan at last with a cold-blooded regard to their advantage, founded on the most careful consideration. There was no particular feeling in it one way or another. She had no desire to injure Norah, or even Norah's mother, more than was inevitable. She had not even any harsh or revengeful feelings towards them. To confound their projects was necessary to the success of her own—that was all; but towards themselves she meant no harm. With an equal impartiality she decided that her operations should be on Ned's side. If she could be said to have a favourite, it was Ned. Clara was self-seeking and self-willed to a degree which was disagreeable to Mrs Burton. Such strenuous sentiments were vulgar and coarse to the more intellectually constituted nature. And Clara had so much flesh and blood, while her mother had so little, that this, too, weakened the sympathy between them. The mother, who was all mind, could not help having a certain involuntary unexpressed contempt for the daughter whose overwhelming physique carried her perpetually into a different world. But what was vulgar in Clara was allowable in Ned; and then Ned had talent in his way, and had taken his degree already, and somewhat distinguished himself, though he was careful, as he himself said, to 'put his brains in his pocket,' and refrain from all exhibition of them when he got home. Then, it would not have flattered Mrs Burton's vanity at all to see her daughter the Hon. Mrs., or even Lady Rivers; but it was a real object with her to see her son in Parliament. She had tried hard to thrust her husband into a seat, with a little swell of impatience and ardour in her heart, to have thus an opportunity of exercising her own powers in the direction of the State. It was a thing she could have done, and she would have given half her life to have it in her power. But this had turned out an impossible enterprise, and now all her wishes were set upon Ned. With the Merewethers' influence, in addition to their own, Ned, almost as soon as he had come of age, might be a legislator. With the talents he had derived from her, and which she would stimulate and inspire, he might be of service to his country. It was not an ungenerous aspiration; it was rather, on the contrary, as noble a wish as mere intellect could form. And to attain this it was necessary that Ned should gain his father's favour by bringing a splendid connection to the house of Dura; and that, on the other hand, he should obtain that influence which was his shortest way to the coveted position. What did it matter if a temporary heart-break were the price he had to pay, or even a temporary humiliation in the shape of giving up his own will? His mother decided for him that such a price was a very small matter to pay. She made up her mind accordingly that he should pay it at once, and in its most unquestionable form. That Clara should be humbled, too, and exposed to tortures of wounded pride and mortification, was a pity; but there was no other way.

This, then, was Mrs Burton's plan: to encourage young Rivers, the suitor whom her husband had chosen for her daughter, to devote himself to Norah; to throw him continually in the girl's way; to make him display his admiration, and if possible his devotion to her; to delude Norah into satisfaction, even response, to the assiduities of her new suitor; and by these means to disgust and detach Ned from the object of his youthful affection. It was a bold scheme, and at the same time it promised to be an easy one. As to what might follow in respect to Clara, the risk would have to be run; but it did not seem a very great risk. In the first place, Clara's 'feelings' (a word at which her mother smiled) were not engaged; and in the second place, Cyril Rivers, though he might be foolish enough, was not such a fool as to throw his handsome self away upon a penniless girl without connections or anything to recommend her. There was very little fear that it would ever come to that. He might fall in love with Norah, might flatter and woo, and even break (Mrs Burton smiled again, the risk seemed so infinitesimal) the girl's heart; but he was not likely, as a man of the world, to commit himself. And if after her end was served it might be thought expedient still that he should marry Clara, why a flirtation of this kind could make very little difference; it might put a stop to Mr Burton's ideas at the moment, but it need not affect them in the future. She made this plan, with her toes warming at the library fire, and she did not confide it to any one. Such schemes sound a great deal worse when they are put into words than they feel in the recesses of the bosom that gave them birth. She felt very well satisfied when she had thus settled what to do. It seemed the minimum of pain for the maximum of advantage; and then it was a kind of pain which Mrs Burton could not but contemplate with a certain mockery, and which she could but faintly realize.

At luncheon that day it turned out, as she supposed, that Mr Rivers was not one of the shooting party. He had been writing letters, he said; he was going to call at the Rectory in the afternoon to see Mr Dalton. In short, he had an appointment. Mr Dalton was a member of the Anthropological Society, to which he also belonged.

'I wonder if I might ask you to do something for me,' said Mrs Burton. 'It is just to leave a note at the Gatehouse. You know the Gatehouse? Mrs Drummond's, just opposite the Rectory.'

'Certainly. I know Mrs Drummond,' said Rivers. He answered very promptly, feeling that there was a covert attack intended, and that this was meant to remind him of the allegiance he owed elsewhere. His reply had thus quite an unnecessary degree of promptitude and explanatoriness. 'I have known her for many years. In fact, I called there yesterday.' He felt it was expedient for his own independence to assert his freedom of action at once.

'Then you won't mind leaving my note,' said Mrs Burton. 'We are getting up a picnic for Wednesday, you know; and I should like Norah to be with us. She has rather a dull life at home, poor child.'

'That is the pretty girl you were dancing with, Mr Rivers,' said Lady Florizel, 'with dark hair and hundreds of little flounces. I should have said she was too little for so many flounces, if she had consulted me.'

'That is the mistake girls always make,' said the Marchioness, 'especially girls who are not in society. They follow the fashion without ever thinking whether it suits them or not.'

'But, under correction, I think it did suit her,' said Mr Rivers. 'Do not let us call them flounces—call them clouds, or lines of soft white mist. I am not sufficiently learned in chiffons to speak.'

'Oh, but you are delightful on chiffons!' said Lady Florizel. 'Men always are when they know just a little. Sometimes, you know, one can actually derive an idea from you; and then you make the most delicious mistakes. Clara, let us make him talk chiffons; it is the greatest fun in the world.'

'I have more confidence in my maid,' said Clara. She was not in the habit of controlling herself or hiding her emotions. She contracted her white forehead, which was not very high by nature, with a force which brought the frizzy golden fringe of hair over her very eyebrows—and pouted with her red lips. 'Besides, Mr Rivers has something better to do,' she said, getting up from the table.

She was the first to get up—a thing which filled the Marchioness with consternation. Clara was a girl of the nineteenth century, feeling that her youth, and her bloom, and riotous, luxurious beauty made her queen of the more gently toned, gently mannered company. She broke up the party with that pout and frown.

Rivers went away with the note in his pocket, believing devoutly that it had been intended for a snare for him, a way of interfering with his freedom. 'Let her wait at least till I am in her toils, which will not be just yet,' he said to himself while he went down the avenue; while Clara pursued her mother, who had gone to put on her bonnet to accompany the Marchioness on her drive, up-stairs.

'How could you, mamma?' she cried. 'Oh, how could you? It is because you think nothing of me; you don't care for me. To ask the Drummonds at all was bad enough; but to send Cyril Rivers to ask them. It seems too bad even for you.'

'Clara, what is Cyril Rivers to you?'

'To me?' Clara faltered, stopped short, was silent, gazing at her mother with blue, wide-open eyes, which astonishment made round. Even to a dauntless girl, accustomed to speak her mind, the question was a hard one. She could not answer, 'Papa means him to marry me. He is my property; no one has any right to him but me,' as she might have done had she spoken at all. It requires a very great deal of hardihood to put such sentiments into speech, and Clara, with all her confidence, was not quite bold enough. She gazed at her mother, with angry blue eyes, speaking with them what she could not say in words; but all she could do audibly was to murmur again, 'To me!'

'Yes, to you. I don't know what right you have to interfere. If you consider that you have any just right, state it to me; and if I find it reasonable I will tell you what I am doing; but, otherwise, not a word. In the circumstances composure and patience are the best things for you. I am acting, and I shall act, towards Mr Rivers according to principles of my own, and a system of my own; and I don't mean to be interfered with, Clara. You understand that.'

'I shall speak to papa,' said Clara, in her anger. 'I shall just tell it all to papa.'

'Do, my dear,' said her mother calmly, and put on her bonnet. It was clear that now, at least, there was not another word to be said.

Clara went away in her anger to Lady Florizel for sympathy.

'Mamma has made up her mind to ask those people,' she said. 'And I hate them. They are low people—people that ought not to be asked to meet you.'

'Oh, as for us, never mind! They will not hurt us,' said Lady Florizel shrugging her shoulders; 'but I thought you told me you were great friends with the people in the village before the ball.'

'That is the worst of all,' said Clara. 'We are great friends. They were all the company I ever had before I came out. But now, when I don't require them any longer, they have grown disagreeable; and yet there is the old habit existing all the same.'

'Poor Clara!' said her new companion, 'what a bore for you! Village companions are so apt to be a bore. But I am sure if you were to talk to your mamma she would find some way of getting rid of them. That would be the best.'

'Why, it is she that is asking them,' said Clara.

And it became more and more apparent that her injury was past help; for in the face of her mother's invitation what could even papa do?

Mr Rivers carried the note with much fidelity to its destination. 'I should not have ventured to come,' he said when he went in and met Mrs Drummond's look of suspicion, 'but for this. And I hope it will find favour in your eyes. I suppose I am to wait and take an answer? And it will be a favourable answer, I hope.'

Helen and her child had been talking of him before he appeared, and Norah had been a little agitated, half-pleasurably, half-painfully, by her mother's warning.

'I do not like him to come so often,' Mrs Drummond had said. 'Whether he means anything or not, I would much rather he did not come.'

'Mean, mamma! What could he mean, except to talk to you a little? I am sure he does not mean anything,' Norah had cried, with the premature confidence of her age.

And then he had made his appearance, and with the knowledge of that brief discussion in her mind she was embarrassed, and felt as if he must read all about it in her eyes.

'May I tell you what it is, Miss Drummond?' he asked, turning to her, while her mother opened the note, and sinking his voice. 'It is a picnic to the old tower of Dura. I suppose you know all about it. It is to be on Wednesday, and I hope you will come.'

'Oh, a picnic!' said Norah, with a flush of joyful anticipation. 'I never was at a real grown-up picnic. I should like it so much, if mamma thinks we may.'

'But perhaps you could influence mamma.'

'No, no. I don't think it. I would rather not bother her,' said Norah, with a little hesitation, feeling all her embarrassment return. 'Of course she must know best.'

'Oh, of course,' said Mr Rivers. He smiled as he looked at her, and Norah, giving a wistful, furtive glance at him, was suddenly seized with spontaneous wonder as to what he meant—a question not arising from what her mother had said, but from herself. The thought sprung up in her mind unawares, bringing with it a blush. What could he mean? Why did he come so often? Why did he wish that she should have this new pleasure? What could it matter to him? There would be plenty of people at the picnic—young people, nice people, pretty people, people all dressed in purple and fine linen—who would be much more like him than Norah. And why should he care? A delicious doubt, a delicious suspicion came into her thoughts. Could it be possible? Might it really, really—? She shut some little trap-door down upon it resolutely in her mind, and would not look at, would not consider that suggestion; but it ran through all her veins when she cast it out of her thoughts. Could it be possible? And this was not Ned Burton, a boy whom she had known all her life, but the hero of romance himself—he who looked as if he had walked out of a book. It flattered her—she could not tell why. She cast down her eyes, for he had been looking at her all the time, and it seemed to her as if he must be able to tell her thoughts.

But he did not. He took up the cotton with which she was working, and wound and unwound it upon his fingers.

'I have to run over to the Rectory,' he said. 'Perhaps I had better do that now, and come back to get my answer. Perhaps then I might have a cup of tea? This room is the very sort of room to drink tea in. The first dish of tea must have been made here.'

'It is not so old as that.'

'Oh, it is as old as we like to believe it,' said Mr Rivers. 'Don't disturb Mrs Drummond. I will go away now, and in half an hour I shall come back.' And he let himself out like a child of the house, assuming a familiarity to which he had not any right.

Norah sat quite tremulous, yet perfectly quiet, after he was gone, wondering, and trying to stop herself from wondering—feeling somehow that this must be that power of which she had read, which made the strongest and best of men subject to a girl—and feeling that it was not possible, seeing the girl was 'only me.'

'It is another invitation,' Mrs Drummond said, with a little sigh. 'You must decide about it, Norah. It will be a pleasure to you, and it seems hard you should not have a little pleasure. But, on the other hand, my dear, after all you told me about Ned, and how Mr Rivers—'

'There is nothing about Mr Rivers, mamma.'

'Perhaps not, perhaps not, dear. I do not say there is—anything, Norah; but still it is not comfortable that he should come so often. There is the note. I will not say yes or no, my darling. You shall decide whether we shall go or stay.'

Norah read the note over with glowing eyes. The blood came hot to her face. It seemed to open up before her a day out of Paradise. The children had made picnics among themselves often enough to Dura Tower. They had gone in the height of the summer for a long day; the boys walking, the girls packed into Mrs Dalton's pony-carriage, or the little donkey-chair, which lived in the village. Bread and butter, and fruit, and hard-boiled eggs, and bottles of milk was what they used to take with them; and they would come home laden with garlands of the lush woodbine, with honeysuckles in sheaves, and basketfuls of those fragile wild-flowers which never survive the plucking, but which children cannot resist. These old days rose before her with all their sweetness. But this was different;—one of the Dura carriages to take them up; a few hours among the woods, and luncheon out of doors, if it was warm enough; 'to show the Marchioness and the young ladies what little antiquities we have.' Perhaps the grandeur and the glory of the society would make up for the absence of the brilliant summer, and the freedom of the childish party; but yet—She looked up shyly at her mother with cheeks that were crimson upon her dark eyelashes.

'I suppose, mamma, it would be selfish of me to want to go?'

'That means you do want to go, Norah,' said Helen, shaking her head softly, with a half-reproachful smile.

'Is it wrong?' said Norah, stealing behind her mother's chair with a coaxing arm round her neck. 'I never saw anything like it. I should like, just this once. Our old little parties were such baby affairs, mamma. That donkey-chair, what fun it was! And oh! do you remember how it always ran away, and that time when little Jenny fell asleep? But this will be grand—something to see. And you will like the drive; it is such a pretty drive; and the woods will be lovely. I never was there in October before.'

'You coaxing child, as Miss Jane says; you want to go.'

'Yes, please, mamma.'

And Norah dropt a little curtsey demurely, like the child she was no longer. And yet as she stood there in her gray frock, she was so very like a child that Helen had to rub her eyes and ask herself what was this wonderful difference. Yesterday or so Norah had trudged along among the boys, taking her share, pushing them about, carrying her own basket in all the bon camaraderie of childhood. Now she was the princess, drawing their wistful looks after her, breaking poor Ned's heart, attracting the other hero out of his natural sphere. How was it? The mother sighed a little, wondering, and smiled, with a sense that the world, which had so long neglected her, was offering to her, to herself, not to Norah, the sweetest, strangest flatteries. She was anxious as to how it might all end, and sometimes was unhappy; and yet she was pleased—what mother ever was otherwise?—'to see her bairn respected like the lave.'

And then Mr Rivers came back for his cup of tea. What did he want, haunting the old house? He came back for the answer, he said; and called himself Mrs Burton's man, and the penny-post, and made very merry over the whole transaction. But in all this he made it very apparent that any excuse for coming was sweet to him. And Norah laughed at the joke, and cast down her pretty eyes, and her colour went and came like the wind. What did he mean? Did he mean anything? Or was it for mere amusement that on every pretext possible he came to the Gatehouse?

CHAPTER XIII

There was, however, another point to be considered before Wednesday, and that was the question of dress, which convulses a poor household when unusual festivities are in progress. Mrs Drummond's black silk was, as Mrs Dalton said, 'always nice.' It had lasted from Helen's prosperous days till now; it had changed its form half-a-dozen times, and now, thanks to the beneficent fashion which prevailed, short walking dresses had 'come out quite fresh,' as Norah declared in triumph. But Norah did not possess that toilette fraîche which is indispensable for a young lady at a picnic. Her gray frock was very pretty at home; but amid all the shining garments of the great young ladies, their perfect ribbons, and hats, and boots, and gloves, all those wonderful accessories which poor people cannot hope for, how could she look anything but a poor little Cinderella? 'My dress would do, mamma—it is not the dress,'

Norah said, looking at herself in dismay in the old-fashioned long glass in its ebony frame, as they discussed this matter; 'and all that I have is well enough; good enough, you know, very nice for common wear. Short dresses are a blessing, but then they show one's boots; and the cuffs, and the collars, and the ribbons! Perhaps we ought not to have said we would go.'

'That is what I feared,' said Helen. 'It is hard you should not have a little amusement when it comes in your way; and then there are other things to think of; but to live among people who are richer, much richer than one is one's self—'

'What are the other things that have to be thought of?' said Norah, with that sudden fantastic jealousy of ulterior motives which affects the young.

'My dear Norah, I am not mercenary. I would not sacrifice your happiness for any worldly motive. I would not even suggest—But, my darling, you must see people—you must have it in your power at least to meet those whom—you must go into the world.'

Norah gazed at her mother with dilated eyes. They had come down into the drawing-room after their inspection of the poor boots and gloves that suggested Cinderella. And the child was standing against the light, against the old brown-gray curtains, which threatened to crumble into dust any day, and yet held out miraculously. The round mirror made a little picture of her standing there alone, like an old miniature in dim enamel. But Norah was not dim in herself at that moment—her brown eyes were dilated and shining—her cheeks mantled with the overwhelming blush of mingled indignation and shame. 'To meet—people!—oh! mamma, mamma, how can you!—is it all true, then, what people say?'

'Yes,' said Helen, gravely, 'or at least it is half true. I am ashamed, and yet I should not be ashamed. I want you to meet those who can appreciate you, who may love you, Norah, and make your life happy. Why should you look at me so indignantly? it is my duty. But I do not wish to speak of it to you.'

'Then I am going—to be inspected—to be offered in the market—to be—oh! mamma, I would rather die!'

'You are going for nothing of the kind. I shall have to put away my companion and friend who was such a comfort to me; and send you back into the place of a silly, impatient child.'

'So I am,' said Norah, throwing herself at her mother's feet, and hiding her tears and burning cheeks in Helen's gown. 'So I am. Oh, mamma, can't I work or do something? is there nothing, nothing in the world for a girl, but that?'

'Hush, my darling, hush!' said Helen, and it was upon this group that some one came in suddenly, whose indignation was prompt at the sight, and unhesitating. It was Dr Maurice, who had come down from London, as he did periodically to see the child, whom he considered as his ward; and who instinctively, seeing tears, made up his mind that Norah had been suffering cruelty, and that the mother was in fault.

'What is the matter?' he said. 'Norah crying! I have not seen her cry before since she was a baby—there must be a good cause.'

'She is growing a woman,' said her mother, 'and learning something about life, poor child; but fortunately this time the cause is not very grave.'

Norah sprang to her feet and dried her tears. She had divined long ere now that her old friend loved her a great deal better than he loved her mother. And Norah was ready to take up arms for her mother, à outrance, night or day.

'No, it was not very much,' she said, all glowing with tears, and blushes, and excitement; 'it was something you will laugh at—you will think it so like a silly woman. You know you hate us all, Dr Maurice, and that is what you will say.'

'Yes, I hate you all,' said the doctor, looking at her with eyes that softened and brightened unconsciously, and a voice that sounded caressing in spite of himself.

'I know it,' said Norah. 'Well, then, Dr Maurice, this is what I was crying about. We are going to a picnic with the Burtons, and the Marchioness of Upshire, and all kinds of fine people, and I was crying because I have not got a pretty dress.'

Dr Maurice gave a short laugh, and then he turned away his head, and his eyes glistened under their heavy brows. 'Poor child!' he said with a tremble in his voice—if it had been any one else probably he would have sneered, as Norah said, at the frivolity of woman's nature; but because it was Norah his heart melted within him, and the water came to his eyes.

'When is it going to come off?' he said.

'Oh, to-day—at one o'clock they were to call for us. Dear doctor,' said Norah, looking up at him laughing, yet with the tears still on her eyelashes, 'won't you say that, after all, I look very nice in my gray frock?'

'Go away, child,' he said, almost angrily, 'go and dress yourself and let me look at you after. I want to speak to your mamma.'

When she heard this, Helen was afraid. She believed in Dr Maurice because he had been substantially kind, and because he was her husband's friend; but she did not like him, and she had that fear of him which came from the conviction that he disliked and distrusted her.

'Why is this?' he said, as Norah went away. 'Mrs Drummond, I thought you knew that I look upon Norah as if she was my own. She should not want anything if you would let me know—I think you ought for Norah's sake to get over any feeling—and put pride aside.'

'It is not so easy,' said Helen, with a smile. 'Pride, if you call it so, sticks very close. You are very, very kind—'

'I am not kind—I don't mean to be; but I look upon Norah as if she were my own.'

'She is not your own, Dr Maurice,' said Helen with spirit. 'I cannot put a feeling in the place of a right. Nothing in the world would make me appeal to a stranger for finery for my child. We can live with what we have of our own.'

'Pride, pride!' said the doctor hastily. 'I don't mean to give offence; but I am not a stranger—I have known the child from her cradle. Why shouldn't you be so yielding—so kind if you will—as to tell me when she wants a dress? My little Norah! she has been a delight to me all my life. If I had my will, she should rustle with the best.'

Helen was angry, but she was moved. A man who loved her child could scarcely shut her heart even by disliking herself. She put out her hand to the surly critic who had never trusted her—'Thanks,' she said, 'many thanks. I accept your love for Norah; but I could not accept anything else. Why, you must know that! My child, Robert's child, appealing to your charity! Dr Maurice, I am not ungrateful, but surely Cinderella's frock is better than that.'

The doctor was silent, he could not reply. 'Poor little Cinderella!' he said; but just then there appeared a vision at the door, which took away his breath. Men are poor creatures where a woman's dress is concerned. To Dr Maurice, who knew no better, Norah's pretty rose-coloured ribbons, the little end of rose-coloured feather, which relieved the black in her hat, and the fresh little pair of gray gloves, which she had indulged in, made Cinderella at once, without more ado, into the fairy princess. 'Why, good heavens, child, what would you have more?' he said, almost with offence. He had been taken in, he thought, and betrayed into an unnecessary warmth of sympathy. It is true that, after a little, even Dr Maurice saw points which might be improved: but he could not look upon Norah's toilette with the instructed eyes which Clara Burton and Lady Florizel turned upon it; and it was the other girls, the Marchioness, the ladies who knew, not a mere man, ignorant as a baby, whom Norah feared.

However, it was grand to see the carriage glide up to the door, and the ladies get into it. Mrs Ashurst and her niece were in it already, two highly respectable persons with claims to belong to the county. The Rectory people were not asked, and Katie stood at the window and watched with somewhat wistful looks, waving her hand as they drove away. And Dr Maurice put them into the carriage, and stood on the steps with his hat off watching them too. There was a splendour about it certainly, whether it was delightful or not. Norah thought of the donkey-chaise loaden with children, and for a moment sighed; she had worn brown holland in those days—but now brown holland all embroidered and decorated was a great deal too expensive—far more costly than her gray—and she had not cared what she wore then, which was far better; whilst now she felt that Miss Ashurst was looking at her, and saw that her cuffs were rather coarse in texture and her feather nothing but a tip. Neither was the drive very lively in the society of these respectable ladies, the younger of whom was older than Norah's mother. But when the carriage approached the end of the pilgrimage, Norah's sky began to brighten. All the others had already arrived, and on a green knoll in front of the old tower the luncheon was being arranged. It was a prettier, gayer sight than the old parties with the donkey chaise. Lady Florizel and her sister were standing at one of the windows in the tower with Ned Burton, looking down; but among the trees near the gate Cyril Rivers was waiting on the outskirts of a group, looking round with evident anxiety, waiting to open the carriage door and hand the ladies out. 'I am so glad you have come,' he whispered into Norah's ear. His very face brightened up at the sight of them. There is no girl living who could withstand such delicate flattery, and that not from any nobody, not from an old friend and faithful slave like Ned Burton, but from the hero, the prince of romance. Norah's heart grew light in spite of herself; she might be indifferently dressed, she might even look as she felt, a poor relation: but this distinction all the same was hers—the prince had found Cinderella out, and none of the others could get a word from him. He took them to Mrs Burton, who was doing the honours of the old tower to the Marchioness, and who received them very graciously, giving thanks to some heathenish deity of her own for the success of her plans; and then he found a shady spot for them where they could command everything. 'I suppose you do not care to go over the tower,' he said. 'I know it as well as my A B C,' said Norah; and then he placed them under the great ash-tree and took up his own position by Mrs Drummond's side.

Mrs Burton gave thanks to her gods for her success. She looked up and saw Ned's eyes peering out of the window above as if he were about to swoop down upon her. 'What are you doing, Ned,' she said in momentary alarm.

'Getting this for Lady Florizel,' he said, holding out a tuft of wild flowers from the old wall. And Mrs Burton thanked that fetish, whoever he was. But she did not see that between the line of Ned's hat and his nose, were a pair of eyes glancing fiercely down upon the ash-tree. If lightning could have come out of mortal eyes, that tree would have shrivelled up and borne no more foliage. The spell was beginning to work. Perhaps Cyril Rivers would not have so committed himself had he not believed that the Burtons had made some scheme to detach him from Norah's side, and to slight and scorn her. He thought they had attempted to make him privy to a plot against her comfort and honour, and that she had been asked here on purpose to be insulted by that impertinence of society which women cannot struggle against. This was the conclusion he came to, and all that was chivalrous and kind was stirred within him. If everybody else neglected them, he at least would show that a man's proper place was by the side of the weak. And then the weak who had to be succoured was so pretty, so charming, so sweet! A man's generous impulses are immensely strengthened in such cases. Miss Ashurst, who was as well-born as anybody there, and as well dressed, was really neglected by the whole company: but Mr Rivers did not feel himself impelled to her side by his desire to succour those who were in need.

'Look there, papa,' said Clara Burton, going to her father and thrusting her hand through his arm, 'only look there!'

'Rivers!' said Mr Burton, gazing through the branches, 'with that girl again!'

'And whose fault is it? Mamma's! It is all mamma. I told you; she actually sent him there—sent him to their house!'

'I will soon put a stop to all that; don't be disturbed, Clara,' said her father, and he went off with great vehemence to where his wife was standing. He put his hand on her arm and drew her away from the Marchioness. 'One moment—a thousand pardons,' he said, bowing to the great lady, and then turned to his wife with the air of a suppressed volcano. 'Clara, what on earth do you mean? there's Rivers with those Drummonds again!'

'He has been with them ever since they came, Mr Burton; probably he will drive home with them. He seems to have made himself their attendant for the day.'

'But, good Lord, Clara! what do you mean? Do you mean to drive your daughter out of her senses—don't you intend to interfere?'

'I am acting for the best,' said Mrs Burton, 'and it will be at your peril if you meddle. Take it in hand if you please; but if the work is to be mine I must do it my own way.'

'But, Clara, for heaven's sake—'

'I have no time for any more, Mr Burton. I must be allowed to work, if I work at all, in my own way.'

And with this poor satisfaction Mr Burton had to be content. He went away fuming and secretly smarting with indignation, through the groups of people who were his own guests, gathered together to make him merry. A mixture of rage and bewilderment filled his bosom. He could no more bear to have his Clara crossed than Mrs Drummond could bear to cross Norah; and his wife's silence was far beyond his comprehension. Clara met him as he came up, with a fluctuating colour, now pale, now crimson, and her white low forehead almost lost under the fringe of hair. She clasped his arm energetically with both hands. 'Tell me, papa! what has she got to say?'

'Well, Clary, we must not interfere. Your mother has her own way of acting; she says it is all right. There are dozens more that would be glad of a look from you, Clary. For to-day we are not to interfere.'

Clara, who was not in the habit of disguising her feelings, tossed his arm from her, pulling away her hands; she was half wild with injured pride and self-will. She went up to the group under the tree with anger in her step and in her eye.

'Oh Norah!' she said, 'I did not know you were coming. Good morning, Mrs Drummond. Mr Rivers, I thought you were altogether lost. You disappeared the moment we set you down. I suppose you had something more agreeable in hand.'

'I had nothing in hand, Miss Burton, except like everybody else—to amuse myself, I suppose.'

'And you have found a charming way of doing that, I am sure,' said poor jealous, foolish Clara; her face was flushed, her voice slightly elevated. She could not bear it; if it had been one of the Ladies Merewether, or even one of the Daltons from the Rectory—but Norah! It was more than she could put up with. Mrs Drummond, who was decorous, the very soul of good order and propriety, rose up instinctively to cover this little outbreak. 'Let us walk about a little,' she said. Let us hide this unwomanly self-betrayal, was what she meant.

Norah, too, was wounded and ashamed, though without feeling herself involved. Clara was 'in a temper,' Norah thought. They all knew that Clara in a temper was to be avoided. She was sorry Mr Rivers should see it. 'Oh Clara! isn't it strange to be here with everything so different,' she said. 'Don't you remember our pranks on the grass when we were children? and your pony which we all envied so much? How odd it is in some ways to be grown up!'

Clara took no notice of this conciliatory speech, but Mr Rivers did. 'I hope it is not less pleasant,' he said.

'I don't know—we walk about now, instead of running races and playing games. Do you remember, Clara—'

'I have not time to talk over all that old nonsense,' said Clara. 'The Marchioness is calling me;' and she turned sharply off and joined her mother, who was with that great lady. She was quite pale with anger and dismay. She walked up to Mrs Burton and looked her in the face. It was her doing! and then she drew back a step, and stood behind, doing all she could to make her vexation visible. She wanted to punish her mother. The others had all dispersed into groups; but Clara stood alone, determined to be unhappy. Mrs Burton, however, was not punished at all; her scheme had succeeded. Her daughter's temper could not last above an hour or two; and her son was safe. He was walking about with Lady Florizel, 'paying her,' as Miss Ashurst said, 'every attention,' under her satisfied eyes.

The picnic ran its course like other picnics. It was very delightful to some, and very wretched—a day to date from, as the unhappiest ever known—to others. Cyril Rivers did not, as Mrs Burton had predicted, leave the Drummonds all day. Had he suspected that this was the very result she aimed at, and that Ned's lowering brows and unhappy looks were the very things the party had been given for, the chances are that he would have resisted the temptation which was stealing over him; but he did not know this, and he did not resist. He thought they were laying vulgar visible claim to him, before he had made up his mind one way or another; and this was a thing his pride refused to allow; while at the same time Norah was very sweet. She was a 'rosebud set about with wilful thorns;' she would not agree with him, nor yield in argument; she was not a shadowless beauty all in broad blaze of sunshine and complacency, like Clara; there were clouds and shadows about her, and a veil of soft mystery, spontaneous movements of fancy, wayward digression out of one thing into another. Mrs Drummond, who was the spectator at the banquet, grew alarmed. She tried to separate them, to lead Norah away among the other people. But she was balked in that by every means. The other people were chiefly county people, too grand for the Drummonds, who were civil to the handsome mother and pretty daughter, but not anxious for their further acquaintance. Wherever they turned Mr Rivers met them. He was not cold, nor slow to see when Helen wanted to seat herself, when she wanted to move about. At last, when the afternoon was beginning to wane, and the elder ladies to think of their shawls, some of the younger ones proposed a dance on the green. Mrs Drummond was left sitting by herself, while Norah went to dance with Mr Rivers, and it was then for the first time that Mr Burton came up to her. She could not but suppose that he had been taking too much wine.

'Well, Helen,' he said, in his loud voice, 'this is an unusual sort of scene for you—like it? I don't suppose you know many people, though; but that little girl of yours is going too fast; mind my word, she is going too fast.'

'I think, Mr Burton, you mistake—'

'No, I don't mistake;—going too fast—trying to lead Cyril Rivers off his feet as she did my Ned. What am I talking of? No, not Ned; Ned has more sense—some other of the lads. But Cyril Rivers, mind you, ain't such a fool as he looks.'

He went on, but Helen did not hear him. Suddenly the whole situation glanced upon her. If a flash of lightning had illuminated everything it could not have been more clear. It was not a good light or a friendly that blazed over that scene, which was confused by so many shades of good and evil feeling. Helen's whole spirit had been moved in her by the tone and words of her cousin in respect to her child. He had touched her daughter—and a woman is as a tigress when a finger is laid upon her cub, people say.

I don't know if this was any excuse for her; but certainly, all in a moment, something appeared within her reach which made her heart beat. Revenge! Whatever his degree of guilt had been, this man had been her husband's evil angel; he had put him in the way which had led him to his destruction—with how much or how little guilt who could say? And Helen looked over the bright scene—the dancers on the grass, the groups standing round, the autumn trees dressed out in all their beauty, like their human brethren—and suddenly saw, or thought she saw, that she had the happiness of her adversary's home in her hand. Little Norah, all unaware of her tragic task, was the Nemesis who was to accomplish their overthrow. There was Ned, heart-broken, but defiant—Ned whom she had seen watching all day, miserable as youth only is; and Clara, furious, making a show of herself in her passion. Was it the sin of the father that was being visited on the children? Helen's heart gave one loud, angry throb; the time of her temptation had come. She did not use the word revenge; all that was brought before her in the sudden tumult of her thoughts was punishment—retribution for sin.

While this terrible suggestion flashed into Helen's mind and took sudden possession of it, another idea had begun to germinate in another bosom, which was to bear fruit also. Dr Maurice went to see the Haldanes, and had a great deal of conversation with them. This conversation ran chiefly upon the one subject on which they were both so much interested—'the child.' From them he learnt that Norah had 'come out,' that she had made a great succès, that everybody (to wit the Daltons) were raving of her prettiness and sprightliness, and how much admired she was; and that since the ball Cyril Rivers had 'never been out of the house.'

'Find out what sort of fellow he is, Maurice,' said Stephen Haldane; 'it would be hard to see our little Norah throw herself away. I thought it would have been Ned.'

'Ned! Ned? Burton's son—a mere City fellow! Good heavens! has it come to that?' said Dr Maurice.

He left the Gatehouse, and walked slowly to the station, and went home just about the time when the dance began on the green. 'The child wants some one to take care of her,' he said over and over again to himself. When he got home he went over all his house, and looked at it with a half comic, half puzzled look. The idea perhaps had gleamed across his mind before; it was an idea he did not half like. It would be a trouble to him—more trouble than anybody could imagine. But still if such a sacrifice should be necessary—for Norah's sake.

CHAPTER XIV

The thought of revenge which had thus entered Helen's mind might have died out of it naturally, or it might have been overcome by better thoughts. All the passion and conflict of her life had died into stillness; six years had come and gone since the great storm had passed over her, which had changed her existence, and though that had not come to any satisfactory conclusion, but only raged itself out, leaving germs that might grow into tumultuous life again—so long an interval of quiet had buried these germs very deep. She had grown tranquil in spite of herself; the calm routine of her life had taken hold upon her, and she had made that change which is so imperceptible while in progress, so real and all influencing when once accomplished—the change which steals away the individuality of existence, and introduces that life by proxy, to which we all—or at least to which, all women—must come. Insensibly, without knowing it, Helen had grafted herself into her child. She had lived for Norah, and now she lived in Norah, regarding the events of the world and the days as they passed solely in reference to the new creature who had a new career to weave out of them. This change has a wonderful effect upon the mind and being. Her sphere of interests was altered, her hopes and wishes were altered, her very modes of thought. The gravity of her nature gave way before this potent influence. Had she been in the way of it, Helen, who had lived through her own youth with a certain serious dignity, accepting her pleasures as a necessity rather than entering into them with enthusiasm, would have acquired for herself, no doubt, the character of a frivolous woman, fond of balls and gaiety, all because of the gayer temper of her child. She felt with Norah that thrill of wonder about Cyril Rivers; her own heart began to beat a little quicker when she heard him coming; a reflection of Norah's blush passed over her. She had to make an effort now and then not to be altogether carried away by this strange entry she had made into another nature; for Norah was not like her mother in nature; training and constant association had made them alike, and it was quite possible that Norah in later life might become Helen, as Helen for the moment had become Norah. But this wondrous double life that ebbs and flows from one heart to another as from one vessel to another—the same blood, the same soul—is not very explicable in words. It was only when Helen sat, as she did at the moment we are now describing, all by herself over her little fire, and felt the silence round her, and realized her own individuality separate from the rest of the world, that the old strain of her thoughts came back to her, and for half an hour at a time she became herself once more.

It was a month after the day of the picnic. The guests at Dura had departed, or rather had been succeeded by new ones, of whom the Drummonds knew nothing. A breach had been made between the great house and the village—a breach which the Daltons murmured and wondered at, but which no one attributed distinctly to its true cause. That cause, Mrs Drummond knew very well, was Norah. They had been invited once more to Dura after the picnic, and Mr Rivers once more had constituted himself their attendant. By this time all other motives except one had ceased to influence the young man. He had ceased to think of the Burtons' claims or of Clara's fury—things which, no doubt, had at first made the pursuit of Norah piquant and attractive to him. What he thought of now was Norah herself. He had no intention of committing himself—no thought of compromising his future by a foolish match; but he fell in love—he could not help it. It is a thing which men of the best principles, men incapable of ruining themselves by an absurd marriage, will nevertheless do from time to time. How he should get out of it he did not know, and when he ventured to think at all, he was very sorry for himself for the fatality which made Norah impossible. But impossible or not, this was what had happened to him; he had fallen in love. The sensation itself was sweet; and Clara's perpetual angry pout, her flash of wrath when he approached Norah, her impatient exclamation at the sound of her name, amused him immensely, and at the same time flattered his vanity. So did Ned's lowering brows and unhappy looks. Mr Rivers was tickled with his own position, flattered and amused by the effect his erratic proceedings had produced. And he had fallen in love. I am sorry to say that Mrs Drummond encouraged him on that evening which she and her daughter spent at Dura after the picnic. She waved him, as it were, in the faces of the Burtons like a flag of triumph. She took pleasure in Ned's misery, though she liked Ned—and in Clara's wrath. They had scorned her child; but her child was able to turn all their plans to confusion, and break up their most skilful combinations. Norah was the queen of the moment, and the others were crushed under her little foot. She was able to make Ned's life a burden to him and destroy Clara's prospects. I am very sorry to have to say this of Helen; but I have never set her up as possessing the highest type of character, and it was true.

She was heartily sorry for it afterwards, however, it must be added. When she got home she felt ashamed, but rather for having done something that did not come up to her own ideal of womanly or lady-like behaviour, than for the pain she had helped to inflict. Even while she was sorry for having 'encouraged' (women are so conscious of all that word means) Mr Rivers, she was not sorry for Ned's despair, which rather amused her—nor for Clara's fury, which made her so angry that she would have liked to whip Clara. She was only ashamed of the deed; she did not dislike the results. Norah, as so often happens, did not know half, nor nearly half, of what it all meant. She was flattered by Mr Rivers's attention; she admired him, she liked him. He was the hero, and he had taken her for his heroine. The thought entranced her girlish fancy, and seduced her into a thousand dreams. She wondered would he 'speak' to her, and what should she answer him? She framed pictures to herself of how he should be brought to the very verge of that 'speaking,' and then by chance prevented and sent away, and longing and anxious, while Norah herself would get a respite. She imagined the most touching scenes—how somebody unknown would be found to watch over her, to bring wonderful good fortune to her, to be at hand when she was in any danger, to save her life, and perform all kinds of wonders; and how at last, suddenly turning upon this anonymous guardian angel, she should find that it was he. Everything that a true knight had ever done for his lady she dreamt of having done for her, and a sweet exultation, a grateful sense of her own humility and yet grandeur would fill her foolish little mind. But still, even in her fancy, Norah held as far off as possible the inevitable response. No lady, of course, could accept such devotion without sooner or later bestowing the reward; but the devotion, and not the reward, was the thing it pleased her to contemplate. It surrounded with a halo of glory not only herself, the recipient, but even in a higher degree the man who was capable of bestowing such exquisite, and delicate, and generous service. Such are the fantastic fancies of a girl when she finds herself wafted into the land of old romance by the astounding, delicious, incomprehensible discovery that some one has fallen in love with her. She was not in the very least in love with him.

All this is a long way from the November evening when Helen sat over her fire, and became for the periodical half-hour herself, and not simply Norah's mother. Thinking it all over, she blushed a little over her own conduct. Mr Rivers had left Dura, but he kept writing to her on one absurd pretext after another. Mrs Drummond had answered very briefly one of these notes, and she was taking herself to task for it now. Was she right to 'encourage' Cyril Rivers? It had punished the Burtons, and she was not sorry for that. But was such a mode of revenge permissible? Was it consistent with her own dignity, or such a thing as ought to be? Susan had not yet brought in the lamp, and she was sitting in the ruddy darkness, scarcely illuminated, yet made rosy by the brilliant not-flaming redness of the fire. Norah even now would have been frightened to sit so in that haunted room; but it was not haunted to Helen. It was a clear, moonlight evening out of doors, and the thin long lines of window at the other end of the room let in each a strip of dark wintry blue between the brown-gray curtains. This cold light, and the ruddy, suppressed glow of the fire, balanced each other, holding each their own half of the room like two armies, of which the red one made continual sorties upon the realm of the other, and the blue one stood fast without a movement. It was a curious little interior, but Helen did not see it. She sat, as thoughtful people so often sit, with her eyes fixed upon the red glow of the embers. In a variation of the same attitude, half visible as the light rose and fell, like a spell-bound woman, her image shone in the round mirror.

Norah was at the Rectory spending the evening, and Norah's mother had changed into Helen herself, and not another. How many old thoughts came and went through her mind it is needless to say; but they resolved themselves into this, that she had sacrificed her own dignity, that what she was doing was not the thing she ought to do. What was the punishment of the Burtons to her? Why should she like to give a heart-ache to a boy and girl who had done her no harm? It was to get at their father, and give him a stab through their means; but was that a kind of warfare for a woman—a lady? Helen started in the dark, though no one could see her. She had a high, almost fantastic, sense of honour and generosity, yet in this she was sacrificing both.

I do not know what impulse it was which made her, when the fire began to burn low and wanted refreshment, go to the window and look out—no reason in particular—because it was a beautiful night. She stood looking out on the moonlight, on the silent country road, and the lively lights which shone in the Rectory windows opposite. She had rung for the lamp; she was going to have her woman's meal, her cup of tea, in the solitude which was not grievous, for to be sure it would last but an hour or two. On the table there was a basket full of work, some dress-making for Norah, and a novel, for still Helen loved the novels which took her into other lives. All these placid details gave an air of profoundest peace to the scene, and the white, clear moonlight shone outside, and the stars, sharpened and brightened by frost, fluttered, as if they had wings or a heart that throbbed, out of the blue of the sky; when suddenly the place became clamorous, the silence fled, the echoes carried circles of sound all over the unseen country. Mr Burton was coming home. A slight smile came upon Helen's face. All this ostentation and noise of wealth did not irritate her as it used to do. The phaeton came dashing along, and paused a moment at the corner, where Williams's shop threw out a stream of illumination. Some one else sat by Mr Burton's side—some one who suddenly, as they passed, turned his face full into the light.

In a moment Helen's heart had begun to beat like an engine suddenly set in motion; the blood mounted up into her ears, to her heart, like its moving wheels and piston. She clenched her hand, and a sudden demon seemed to wake up and come into existence all in a moment. It was the man whom she believed to be her husband's murderer—the destroyer of her own happiness and of Robert's good name. She stood as if spell-bound while they drove past the window, laughing and talking. Nay, there was even a half pause, and Mr Burton made some explanation, and pointed to the Gatehouse, not seeing the secret spectator. She heard the sound of their voices—the laugh; and clenched her hands tighter, and through her mind there passed words which a woman should not say.

It was then that Susan came into the room with the lamp. When she had set it down on the table, and turned round to close the window, it startled her to see where Helen was standing. Susan uttered an exclamation; it gave her 'a turn;' and she had a still greater turn when she perceived the change in Mrs Drummond's face. But for the moment she did not say anything. It was only when she had arranged the tea and put everything ready that she ventured to look again, and encountered Helen's eyes, which were fixed, and did not see her.

'Lord bless us!' said Susan, 'if something has happened, 'm, don't look dreadful like that, but say it out.'

Helen woke up at the sound of her voice. She tried to smile and clear her countenance.

'Nothing has happened,' she said; and it startled her to find how hoarse she was. 'I was thinking only about old times.'

'That comes o' Miss Norah being out to tea,' said Susan. 'I'd think of old times fast enough if I could do any good. But what's the use? Thinking and thinking only moiders a body's brain. I've give it up for my part.'

'It is the wisest way,' said Helen, trying to smile.

'Shall I ask Miss Jane to come and stay with you a bit? or shall I run for Miss Norah?' asked Susan, who was practical-minded, and felt that something ought to be done.

'Never mind, Susan. It is very kind of you to think of me. It will pass over directly,' said Helen; and she was so decided and imperative that Susan was forced to yield.

When she was gone, Mrs Drummond rose and walked about the room with hasty, tremulous steps. She was not sick nor sorry, as the woman thought, but burning with wild indignation, sudden rage. Her better feelings were overwhelmed by the tide of passion that rushed into her mind. 'Golden and Burton! Golden and Burton!' When she had last repeated these words she had felt herself powerless, helpless, unable to inflict any punishment upon them, compelled to subside into silence, knowing that neither her voice nor anything she could do would reach them. It was different now, she said to herself, with fierce satisfaction. Now she had indeed something in her power; now she could indeed reach the very heart of one of them. Her cheek glowed, her eyes blazed in her solitude. She would do it. She would abstract Mr Rivers from them utterly, and she would break the heart of their boy. She seemed to hold it in her hand, and crush it, as she pursued these thoughts. This was the horrible effect produced upon a reasonable woman by the appearance of a man who had wronged her. It is not easy to bear the seeming prosperity of the wicked. He had taken from Helen all, except Norah, that made life worth having, and he himself had appeared to her full of jovial talk and laughter, going to visit at Dura, evidently a favoured guest. The difficulty was one which David felt even more deeply, and has argued with himself upon in many a strain which religion has made familiar to us as the air we breathe. In the Psalms it is never said that it is wrong to chafe at the prosperity of evil-doers, but only that that prosperity is short-lived, and that ruin is coming. When Helen suddenly saw her enemy, the wicked man par excellence, the incarnation of wrong and cruelty, flourishing like the green bay-tree, gay and confident as he had always been, it was not wonderful if she took the Old Testament rather than the New for her guide. The only strange thing was, that with the curious inconsistency of human nature, she grasped the weapon that she had suddenly found at her side, to strike, not him, but his companion. Golden and Burton! Once more they had become one to her; her enemies—the incarnation of murder, slander, and wrong!

'Mamma, Ned has walked across with me,' said Norah, running in all fresh from the outer air, with a red hood over her brown hair. 'May I ask him to come in? He looks so unhappy, mamma.'

'I don't see that we have anything to do with his unhappiness,' said Helen; but already he was standing at the door, looking in very wistfully. Norah was rather wistful too; her heart was relenting over her old vassal; and now there was no Mr Rivers in the way to take possession of her, and come between her and the looks of others.

Ned came in with very doubtful step, not knowing whether to be frightened or glad. He was not afraid of Mrs Drummond; she had never been unkind to him, and there seemed a possibility now that his misery might be over, and that Norah might relent. But it was a shock to Ned to find that she did not offer him her hand, but only bowed stiffly, and began to speak to her daughter.

'You are early to-night,' she said. 'I did not expect you so soon.'

'Oh, mamma, soon! Why, it is eleven; and you have the tea-things still on the table. Mamma, I shall never be able to go anywhere, if you behave so. You have not had any tea.'

'I have not wanted it. I did not observe that it was there,' said Helen, seating herself on her former seat by the fire. In doing this, she turned her back upon Ned, who, startled and wounded, did not know what to do. Norah was alarmed too. She made a sign to him to sit down, and then went to her mother, taking her hand,

'Mamma, you are not well,' she said.

'I am quite well. I fear, however, I shall not be good company for—Mr Burton to-night.'

'Mamma! Why it is only Ned!'

'He is Mr Burton's son,' said Helen, trembling with emotion. 'Norah, do you remember the man who murdered your father, and tried to disgrace him—Golden—that man? Well, I have just seen him drive up with Mr Burton to Dura. They paused, and pointed out this house to each other—the place where their victims were living. You may understand why I am not fit company for—Mr Burton to-night.'

'Oh, my poor, dear mother! have you had this to bear, with no one to support you? I will never go out and leave you again.'

'The sight of his face is like a curse to me,' said Helen, scarcely knowing what she said. 'I have had as much as I can bear for one night.'

'Yes, dear mamma, so you have,' said soothing Norah. And then behind her mother's back she made an imperative sign to poor Ned, whispering, 'Go away; go away!'

He stumbled up to his feet, poor fellow! so dreadfully disappointed that he could scarcely find voice enough to speak. But yet his instinct was to strike one blow in self-defence.

'Mrs Drummond,' he said, clearing his voice, 'I don't know much about Mr Golden; but if he is such a man as you say, my father must be deceived; and I have nothing at all to do with it. Is it fair to punish me?'

'Oh, your father!' said Helen, facing suddenly round upon him, with a flush on her face, and the tremulous movement of passion in all her frame. If she had not been so agitated, she would not have spoken so, let us hope, to the man's son. 'Your father is not deceived. I don't say you know. But you are his son.'

'Good evening, Norah!' said Ned; he crushed his hat between his hands, and went straight out without another word. What a change from the hopeful spirit in which he had crossed the threshold two minutes before! But like many a man who makes an abrupt retreat, Ned found he fared the worse for his impetuosity when he had got outside. He might have stayed and asked some questions about it, fathomed it somehow, tried to discover what was the meaning of it. He walked up the avenue, upon which the moon was shining bright, so confused and troubled that he could not tell certainly which was the cloud floating along at a break-neck pace before the wind and which the true shadows, themselves immovable, which his rapid progress made almost as wildly fugitive. He thought he had been on the eve of renewed happiness, and lo! now he found himself pushed further off than ever; repulsed, he could not tell how. A tide of wild fancy rushed through his mind, carrying a hundred thoughts upon it as the wind carried the cloud. Sometimes it was the image of Mrs Drummond which was uppermost, sometimes a wondering puzzled question about his father, sometimes the name of Golden. He remembered dimly the trial and the comments upon the latter, and how his own young mind had glowed half with indignation, half with sympathy. He was better able to judge now; but Helen's language sounded violent and exaggerated to him. 'The man who murdered your father'—'the sight of his face is like a curse.' What language was this for any one in their senses to use?

A stormy night with a full moon is perhaps the most dramatic spectacle in nature. The world was flooded with light as Ned, a dark speck in all that whiteness, came out into the open lawns amid which his father's house stood. The wind was driving the clouds across the clear blue at such a desperate pace as might become the pursued and terrified stragglers of a great army; and the army itself, piled up in dark confused masses in the north, loomed behind the house of Dura, which was inundated by the white radiance. These angry forces were turning to bay, heaping themselves in a threatening mass, glooming in silent opposition to all the splendour and glory of the light. Ned's heart was so sick and sore that he gazed at this sight with unusual force of fancy, wondering if it could mean anything? The moon and the wind were doing all they could to disperse these vapours; they were driven back upon each other, heaped up in masses, pursued off the face of the sky, which over Ned's head was blue and clear as a summer noon. But yet the clouds gathered, held together, stood, as it were, at bay. Did it mean anything? Was that storm about to burst over the house, which stood so tranquilly, whitened over by the moon, below. This was what Ned asked himself (though he was not usually imaginative) as he went in with an ache in his heart to his father's house.

VOLUME III

CHAPTER I

The drawing-room within was very different from the wild conflict of light and darkness outside. There was music going on at one end, some people were reading, some talking. There were flirtations in hand, and grave discussions. In short, the evening was being spent as people are apt to spend the evening when there is nothing particular going on. There had been a good deal of private yawning and inspection of watches throughout the evening, and some of the party had already gone to bed, or rather to their rooms, where they could indulge in the happiness of fancying themselves somewhere else—an amusement which is very popular and general in a country house.

But seated in an easy-chair by the fire was a tall man, carefully dressed, with diamond studs in his shirt, and a toilette which, though subdued in tone as a gentleman's evening dress must be, was yet too elaborate for the occasion. The fact that this new guest was a stranger to him, and that his father was seated by him in close conversation, made it at once apparent to Ned that it must be Golden. Clara was close to them listening with a look of eager interest to all they said. These three made a little detached group by one side of the fire. At the other corner sat Mrs Burton, with her little feet on a footstool, as near as possible to the fender. She had just said good-night to the dignified members of the party, the people who had to be considered; the others who remained were mere young people, about whose proceedings she did not concern herself. She was taking no part in the talk at the other side of the fire. She sat and warmed her little toes and pondered; her vivid little mind all astir and working, but uninfluenced by, and somewhat contemptuous of, what was going on around; and her chilly little person basking in the ruddy warmth of the fire.

Ned came up and stood by her when he came in. No one took any notice of him, the few persons who remained in the room having other affairs in hand. Ned was fond of his mother, though she had never shown any fondness for him. She had done all for him which mere intellect could do. She had been very just to the boy all his life; when he got into scrapes, as boys will, she had not backed him up emotionally, it is true, but she had taken all the circumstances into account, and had not judged him harshly. She had been tolerant when his father was harsh. She had never lost her temper. He had always felt that he could appeal to her sense of justice—to her calm and impartial reason. This is not much like the confidence with which a boy generally throws himself upon his mother's sympathy, yet it was a great deal in Ned's case. And accordingly he loved his mother. Mrs Burton, too, loved him perhaps more than she loved any one. She was doing her best to break his heart; but that is not at all uncommon even when parents and children adore each other. And then Ned was not aware that his mother had any share intentionally or otherwise in the cruel treatment he had received.

'Who is that?' he asked under his breath.

'A Mr Golden, a friend of your father's,' said Mrs Burton, lifting her eyes and turning them calmly upon the person she named. There was no feeling in them of one kind or another, and yet Ned felt that she at least did not admire Mr Golden, and it was a comfort to him. He went forward to the fire, and placed himself, as an Englishman loves to do, in front of it. He stood there for ten minutes or so, paying no particular attention to the conversation on his right hand. His father, however, looked more animated than he had done for a long time, and Clara was bending forward with a faint rose-tint from the fire tinging the whiteness of her forehead and throat, and deeper roses glowing on her cheeks. Her blue eyes were following Mr Golden's movements as he spoke, her hair was shining like crisp gold in the light. She was such a study of colour, of splendid flesh and blood, as Rubens would have worshipped; and Mr Golden had discrimination enough to perceive it. He stopped to address himself to Clara. He turned to her, and gave her looks of admiration, for which her brother, bitterly enough biassed against him on his own account, could have 'throttled the fellow!' Ned grew more and more wrathful as he looked on. And in the mean time the late young ladies came fluttering to say good-night to their hostess; the young men went off to the smoking-room, where Ned knew he ought to accompany them, but did not, being too fully occupied; and thus the family were left alone. Notwithstanding, however, his wrath and his curiosity, it was only the sound of one name which suddenly made the conversation by his side quite articulate and intelligible to Ned.

'I hear the Drummond has a pretty daughter; that is a new weapon for her, Burton. I wonder you venture to have such a family established at your gates.'

'The daughter is not particularly pretty; not so pretty by a long way as Helen was,' said Mr Burton. 'I don't see what harm she can do with poor little Norah. We are not afraid of her, Clara, are we?' and he looked admiringly at his daughter, and laughed.

As for Clara she grew crimson. She was not a girl of much feeling, but still there was something of the woman in her.

'I don't understand how we could be supposed to be afraid of Norah Drummond,' she said.

'But I assure you I do,' said Mr Golden. 'Pardon me, but I don't suppose you have seen the Drummond herself, the Drummond mamma—in a fury.'

'Father,' said Ned, 'is Mr Golden aware that the lady he is speaking of is our relation—and friend? Do you mean to suffer her to be so spoken of in your house?'

'Hold your tongue, Ned.'

'Ned! to be sure it is Ned. Why, my boy, you have grown out of all recollection,' said Golden, jumping up with a great show of cordiality, and holding out his hand.

Ned bowed, and drew a step nearer his mother. He had his hands in his pockets; there were times, no doubt, when his manners left a great deal to be desired.

'Ah, I see! there are spells,' said Mr Golden, and he took his seat again with a hearty laugh—a laugh so hearty that there seemed just a possibility of strain and forced merriment in it. 'My dear Miss Burton,' he said, in an undertone, which however Ned could hear, 'didn't I tell you there was danger? Here's an example for you, sooner than I thought.'

'Mother,' said Ned, 'can I get your candle? I am sure it is time for you to go up-stairs.'

'Yes, and for Clara too. Run away, child, and take care of your roses; Golden and I have some business to talk over; run away. As for you, Ned, to-morrow morning I shall have something to say to you.'

'Very well, sir,' said Ned solemnly.

He lighted his mother's candle, and he gave her his arm, having made up his mind not to let her go. The sounds of laughter which came faintly from the smoking-room did not tempt him; if truth must be told, they tempted Clara much more, who stood for a moment with her candle in her hand, and said to herself, 'What fun they must be having!' and fretted against the feminine fetters which bound her. Such a thought would not have come into Norah's head, nor into Katie Dalton's, nor even into that of Lady Florizel, though it was a foolish little head enough; but Clara, who was all flesh and blood, and had been badly brought up, was the one of those four girls who probably would have impressed most deeply a journalist's fancy as illustrating the social problem of English young womanhood.

Ned led his mother not to her own room, but to his. He made her come in, and placed a chair for her before the fire. It is probable that he had sense enough to feel that had he asked her consent to his marriage with Norah Drummond he would have found difficulties in his way; but short of this, he had full confidence in the justice which indeed he had never had any reason to doubt.

'Do you like this man Golden, mother?' he asked. 'Tell me, what is his connection with us?'

'His connection, I suppose, is a business connection with your father,' said Mrs Burton. 'For the rest, I neither like him nor hate him. He is well enough, I suppose, in his way.'

'Mrs Drummond does not think so,' said Ned.

'Ah, Mrs Drummond! She is a woman of what are called strong feelings. I don't suppose she ever stopped to inquire into the motives of anybody who went against her in her life. She jumps at a conclusion, and reaches it always from her own point of view. According to her view of affairs, I don't wonder, with her disposition, that she should hate him.'

'Why, mother?'

'Well,' said Mrs Burton, I am not in the habit of using words which would come naturally to a mind like Mrs Drummond's. But from her point of view, I should say, she must believe that he ruined her husband—drove him to suicide, and then did all he could to ruin his reputation. These are things, I allow, which people do not readily forget.'

'And, mother, do you believe all this? Is it true?'

'I state it in a different way,' she said. 'Mr Golden, I suppose, thought the business could be redeemed, to start with. When he drew poor Mr Drummond into active work in the concern, he did it in a moment when there was nobody else to refer to. And then you must remember, Ned, that Mr Drummond had enjoyed a good deal of profit, and had as much right as any of the others to suffer in the loss. He was ignorant of business, to be sure, and did not know what he was doing; but then an ignorant man has no right to go into business. Mr Golden is very sharp, and he had to preserve himself if he could. It was quite natural he should take advantage of the other's foolishness. And then I don't suppose he ever imagined that poor Mr Drummond would commit suicide. He himself would never have done it under similar circumstances—nor your father.'

'Had my father anything to do with this?' said Ned hoarsely.

'That is not the question,' said Mrs Burton. 'But neither the one nor the other would have done anything so foolish. How were they to suppose Mr Drummond would? This sort of thing requires a power of realising other people's ways of thinking which few possess, Ned. After he was dead, and it could not be helped, I don't find anything surprising,' she went on, putting her feet nearer the fire, 'in the fact that Mr Golden turned it to his advantage. It could not hurt Drummond any more, you know. Of course it hurt his wife's feelings; but I am not clear how far Golden was called upon to consider the feelings of Drummond's wife. It was a question of life and death for himself. Of course I do not believe for a moment, and I don't suppose anybody whose opinion is worth considering could believe, that a poor, innocent, silly man destroyed those books—'

'Mother, I don't know what you are speaking of; but it seems to me as if you were describing the most devilish piece of villany—'

'People do employ such words, no doubt,' said Mrs Burton calmly; 'I don't myself. But if that is how it appears to your mind, you are right enough to express yourself so. Of course that is Mrs Drummond's opinion. I have something to say to you about the Drummonds, Ned.'

'One moment, mother,' he cried, with a tremor and heat of excitement which puzzled her perhaps more than anything she had yet met with in the matter. For why should Ned be disturbed by a thing which did not concern him, and which had happened so long ago? 'You have mentioned my father. You have said they, speaking of this man's infamous—Was my father concerned?'

Mrs Burton turned, and looked her son in the face. The smallest little ghost of agitation—a shadow so faint that it would not have showed upon any other face—glided over hers.

'That is just the point on which I can give you least information,' she said; and then, after a pause, 'Ned,' she continued, 'you are grown up; you are capable of judging for yourself. I tell you I don't know. I am not often deterred by any cause from following out a question I am interested in; but I have preferred not to follow up this. I put away all the papers, thinking I might some day care to go into it more deeply. You can have them if you like. To tell the truth,' she added, sinking her voice, betrayed into a degree of confidence which perhaps she had never given to human creature before, 'I think it is a bad sign that this man has come back.'

'A sign of what?'

Mrs Burton's agitation increased. Though it was the very slightest of agitations, it startled Ned, so unlike was it to his mother.

'Ned,' she said, with a shiver that might be partly cold, 'nobody that I ever heard of is so strong as their own principles. I do not know, if it came to me to have to bear it, whether I could bear ruin and disgrace.'

'Ruin and disgrace!' cried Ned.

'I don't know if I have fortitude enough. Perhaps I could by myself; I should feel that it was brought about by natural means, and that blame was useless and foolish. But if we had to bear the comments in the newspapers, the talk of everybody, the reflections on our past, I don't know whether I have fortitude to bear it; I feel as if I could not.'

'Mother, has this been in your mind, while I have been thinking you took so little interest? My poor little mamma!'

The wicked little woman! And yet all that she had been saying was perfectly true.

'Ned,' she said, with great seriousness, 'this dread, which I can never get quite out of my mind, is the reason why I have been so very earnest about the Merewethers. I have never, you know, supported your father's wish that you should go into the business. On the contrary, I have always endeavoured to secure you your own career. I have wished that you at least should be safe—'

'Safe!' he cried. 'Mother, if there is a possibility of disgrace, how can I, how can any of us, escape from it—and more especially I? And if there is a chance of ruin, why I should be as great a villain as that man is, should I consent to carry it into another house.'

'It is quite a different case,' she cried with some eagerness, seeing she had overshot her mark. 'I hope there will be neither; and you have not the least reason to suppose that either is possible. Look round you; go with your father to the office, inspect his concerns as much as you please; you will see nothing but evidences of prosperity. So far as you know, or can know, your father is one of the most prosperous men in England. Nobody would have a word to say against you, and I shall be rich enough to provide for you. If there is any downfall at all, which I do not expect, nobody would ever imagine for a moment that you knew anything of it; and your career and your comfort would be safe.'

'O mother! mother!' Poor Ned turned away from her and hid his face in his hands. This was worse to him than all the rest.

'You ought to think it over most carefully,' she said; 'all this is perfectly clear before you. I may have taken fright, though it is not very like me. I may be fanciful enough' (Mrs Burton smiled at herself, and even Ned in his misery half smiled) 'to consider this man as a sort of raven, boding misfortune. But you know nothing about it; there is abundant time for you to save yourself and your credit; and this is the wish which, above everything in the world, I have most at heart, that, if there is going to be any disaster,—I don't expect it, I don't believe in it; but mercantile men are always subject to misfortune,— you might at least be safe. I will not say anything more about it to-night; but think it over, Ned.'

She rose as she spoke and took up her candle, and her son bent over her and touched her little cold face with his hot lips. 'I will send you the papers,' she said as she went away. Strange little shadow of a mother! She glided along the passage, not without a certain maternal sentiment—a feeling that on the whole she was doing what was best for her boy. She could provide for him, whatever happened; and if evil came he might so manage as to thrust himself out from under the shadow of the evil. She was a curious problem, this woman; she could enter into Mr Golden's state of mind, but not into her son's. She could fathom those struggles of self-preservation which might lead a man into fraud and robbery; but she could not enter into those which tore a generous, sensitive, honourable soul in pieces. She was an analyst, with the lowest view of human nature, and not a sympathetic being entering into the hearts of others by means of her own.

No smoking-room, no jovial midnight party, received Ned that night. He sat up till the slow November morning dawned reading those papers; and then he threw himself on his bed, and hid his face from the cold increasing light. A bitterness which he could not put into words, which even to himself it was impossible to explain, filled his heart. There was nothing, or at least very little, about his father in these papers. There was no accusation made against Mr Burton, nothing that any one could take hold of—only here and there a word of ominous suggestion which chilled the blood in his veins. But Golden's character was not spared by any one; it came out in all its blackness, more distinct even than it could have done at the moment these events occurred. Men had read the story at the time with their minds full of foregone conclusions on the subject—of prejudices and the heat of personal feeling. But to Ned it was history; and as he read Golden's character stood out before him as in a picture. And this man, this deliberate cold-blooded scoundrel, was sleeping calmly under his father's roof—a guest whom his father delighted to honour. Ned groaned, and covered his eyes with his hands to shut out the hazy November morning, as if it were a spy that might find out something from his haggard countenance. Sleep was far from his eyes; his brain buzzed with the unaccustomed crowd of thoughts that whirled and rustled through it. A hundred projects, all very practicable at the first glance and impossible afterwards, flashed before him. The only thing that he never thought of was that which his mother had called the wish of her heart—that he should escape and secure his own career out of the possible fate that might be impending. This, of all projects, was the only one which, first and last, was impossible to Ned.

The first step which he took in the matter was one strangely different. He had to go through all the ordinary remarks of the breakfast-table upon his miserable looks; but he was too much agitated to be very well aware what people were saying to him. He watched anxiously till he saw his father prepare to leave the house. Fortunately Mr Golden was not with him. Mr Golden was a man of luxury, who breakfasted late, and had not so much as made his appearance at the hour when Mr Burton, who, above everything, was a man of business, started for the station. Ned went out with him, avoiding his mother's eye. He took from his father's hand a little courier's bag full of papers which he was taking with him.

'I will carry it for you, sir,' he said.

Mr Burton was intensely surprised; the days were long gone by when Ned would strut by his side, putting out his chest in imitation of his father.

'Wants some money, I suppose!' Mr Burton—no longer the boy's proud progenitor, but a wary parent, awake to all the possible snares and traps which are set for such—said to himself.

They had reached the village before Ned had began to speak of anything more important than the weather or the game. Then he broke into his subject quite abruptly.

'Father,' he said, 'within the last few days I have been thinking of a great many things. I have been thinking that for your only son to set his face against business was hard lines on you. Will you tell me frankly whether a fellow like me, trained so differently, would be of real use to you? Could I help you to keep things straight, save you from being cheated?—do anything for you? I have changed my ideas on a great many subjects. This is what I want to know.'

'Upon my word, a wonderful conversion,' said his father with a laugh; 'there must be some famous reason for a change so sudden. Help me to keep things straight!—Keep ME from being cheated! You simpleton! you have at least a capital opinion of yourself.'

'But it was with that idea, I suppose, that you thought of putting me into the business,' said Ned, overcoming with an effort his first boyish impulse of offence.

'Perhaps in the long-run,' said Mr Burton jocularly; 'but not all at once, my fine fellow. Your Greek and your Latin won't do you much service in the city, my boy. Though you have taken your degree—and a deuced deal of money that costs, a great deal more than it's worth—you would have to begin by singing very small in the office. You would be junior clerk to begin with at fifty pounds a year. How should you find that suit your plans, my fine gentleman Ned?'

'Was that all you intended me for?' asked Ned sternly. A rigid air and tone was the best mask he could put upon his bitter mortification.

'Certainly, at first,' said Mr Burton; 'but I have changed my mind altogether on the subject,' he added sharply. 'I see that I was altogether deceived in you. You never would be of any use in business. If you were in Golden's hands, perhaps—but you have let yourself be influenced by some wretched fool or other.'

'Has Mr Golden anything to say to your business?' asked Ned.

The question took his father by surprise.

'Confound your impudence!' he cried, after a keen glance at his son and sputter of confused words, which sounded very much like swearing. 'What has given you so sudden an interest in my business, I should like to know? Do you think I am too old to manage it for myself?'

'It was the sight of this man, father,' said Ned, with boyish simplicity and earnestness, 'and the knowledge who he was. Couldn't I serve you instead of him? I pledge you my word to give up all that you consider nonsense, to settle steadily to business. I am not a fool, though I am ignorant. And then if I am ignorant, no man could serve you so truly as your son would, whose interests are the same as yours. Try me! I could serve you better than he.'

'You preposterous idiot!' cried Mr Burton, who had made two or three changes from anger to ridicule while this speech was being delivered. 'You serve me better than Golden!—Golden, by Jove! And may I ask if I were to accept this splendid offer of yours, what would you expect as an equivalent? My consent to some wretched marriage or other, I suppose, allowance doubled, home provided, and my blessing, eh? I suppose that is what you are aiming at. Out with it—how much was the equivalent to be?'

'Nothing,' said Ned. He had grown crimson; his eyes were cast down, not to betray the feeling in them—a choking sensation was in his throat. Then he added slowly—'not even the fifty pounds a year you offered me just now—nothing but permission to stand by you, to help to—keep danger off.'

Mr Burton took the bag roughly out of his hand. 'Go home,' he said, 'you young ass; and be thankful I don't chastise you for your impudence. Danger!—I should think you were the danger if you were not such a fool. Go home! I don't desire your further company. A pretty help and defender you would be!'

And Ned found himself suddenly standing alone outside the station, his fingers tingling with the roughness with which the bag had been snatched from him. He stood still for half a minute, undecided, and then he turned round and strolled listlessly back along the street. He was very unhappy. His father was still his father, though he had begun to distrust, and had long given over expecting any sympathy from him. And the generous resolution which it had cost him so much pain to make, had not only come to nothing, but had been trampled under foot with derision. His heart was very sore. It was a hazy morning, with a frosty, red sun trying hard to break through the mist; and everything moved swiftly to resist the cold, and every step rang sharp upon the road; except poor Ned's, who had not the heart to do anything but saunter listlessly and slowly, with his hands in his pockets and his eyes fixed wistfully upon nothing. Everything in a moment had become blank to him. He wondered why the people took the trouble to take off their hats to him—to one who was the heir of misery and perhaps of disgrace and ruin, as his mother had said. Ruin and disgrace! What awful words they are when you come to think of it—dreadful to look forward to, and still more dreadful to bear if any man could ever realise their actual arrival to himself!

Norah was standing at the open door of the Gatehouse. He thought for a moment that he would pass without taking any notice; and then it occurred to him in a strange visionary way that it might be the last time he should see her. He stopped, and she said a cold little 'Good morning' to him, without even offering her hand. Then a sudden yearning seized poor Ned.

'Norah,' he said, in that listless way, 'I wish you would say something kind to me to-day. I don't know why I should be so anxious for it, but I think it would do me good. If you knew how unhappy I am—'

'Oh Ned, for heaven's sake don't talk such nonsense,' cried impatient Norah. 'You unhappy, that never knew what it was to have anything go wrong! It makes me quite ill to hear you. You that have got everything that heart can desire; because you can't just exactly have your own way—about—me—Oh, go away; I cannot put up with such nonsense—and to me, too, that knows what real trouble means!'

Poor Ned made no protest against this impatient decision. He put on his hat in a bewildered way, with one long look at her, and then passed, and disappeared within his father's gates. Norah did not know what to make of it. She stood at the door, bewildered too, ready to wave her hand and smile at him when he looked round; but he never looked round. He went on slowly, listlessly, as if he did not care for anything—doing what both had told him—the father whom he had been willing to give up his life to—the girl who had his heart.

That afternoon he carried out their commands still more fully. He went away from his father's house. On a visit, it was said; but to go away on a visit in the middle of the shooting season, when your father's house is full of guests, was, all the young men thought, the most extraordinary thing which, even in the freedom of the nineteenth century, an only son, deputy master of the establishment, had ever been known to do.

CHAPTER II

It was a long time before it was fully understood in Dura what had become of Ned. At first it was said he had gone on a visit, then that he had joined some of his college friends in an expedition abroad; but before spring it began to be fully understood, though nobody could tell how, that Ned had gone off from his home, and that though occasional letters came from him, his family did not always know where he was, or what he was about. There was no distinct authority for this, but the whole neighbourhood became gradually aware of it. The general idea was that he had gone away because Norah Drummond had refused him; and the consequence was that Norah Drummond was looked upon with a certain mixture of disapproval and envy by the youthful community. The girls felt to their hearts the grandeur of her position. Some were angry, taking Ned's part, and declaring vehemently that she had 'led him on;' some were sympathetic, feeling that poor Norah was to be pitied for the tragical necessity of dismissing a lover; but all felt the proud distinction she had acquired by thus driving a man (they did not say boy) to despair. The boys, for the most part, condemned Ned as a muff—but in their hearts felt a certain pride in him, as proving that their side was still capable of a great act of decision and despair. As for Norah, when the news burst upon her, her kind little heart was broken. She cried till her pretty eyes were like an old woman's. She gave herself a violent headache, and turned away from all consolation, and denounced herself as the wickedest and cruellest of beings. It was natural that Norah should believe it implicitly. After that scene in the Rectory garden, when poor Ned, in his boyish passion, had half thrown the responsibility of his life upon her shoulders, there had been other scenes of a not unsimilar kind; and there was that last meeting at the door of the Gatehouse, when she had dismissed him so summarily. Oh, if he had only looked round, Norah thought; and she remembered, with a passing gleam of consolation, that she had intended to wave her hand to him. 'What shall I do? Oh, what shall I do?' she said, 'if—anything should happen to him, mamma, I shall have killed him! If anybody calls me a murderess, I shall not have a word to say.'

'Not so bad as that, my darling,' Helen said, soothing her; but Helen herself was very deeply moved. This was the revenge, the punishment she had dreamt of. By her means, whom he had injured so deeply, Reginald Burton's only son had been driven away from him, and all his hopes and plans for his boy brought to a sudden end. It was revenge; but the revenge was not sweet. Christianity, heaven knows, has not done all for us which it might have done, but yet it has so far changed the theories of existence that the vague craving of the sufferer for punishment to its oppressors gives little gratification when it is fulfilled. Helen was humbled to the dust with remorse and compunction for the passing thought, which could scarcely be called an intention, the momentary, visionary sense of triumph she had felt in her daughter's power (as she believed) to disturb all the plans of the others. Now that was done which it had given her a vague triumph to think of; and though her tears were not so near the surface as Norah's, her shame and pain were deeper. And this was all the more the fact because she dared not express it. A word of sympathy from her (she felt) would have looked like nothing so much as the waving of a flag of triumph. And, besides, from Ned's own family there came no word of complaint.

The Dura people put the very best face upon it possible. Mrs Burton, who had never been known to show any emotion in her life, of course made none of her feelings visible. Her husband declared that 'my young fool of a son' preferred amusing himself abroad to doing any work at home. Clara was the only one who betrayed herself. She assured Katie Dalton, in confidence, that she never could bear to see that hateful Norah again—that she was sure it was all her fault. That Ned would never have looked at her had not she done everything in her power to 'draw him on'—and then cast him off because somebody better worth having came in her way. Clara's indignation was sharp and vehement. It was edged with her own grievance, which she was not too proud to refer to in terms which could not disguise her feelings. But she was the only one of her house who allowed that Ned's disappearance had any significance. His mother said nothing at all on the subject even to her husband and her child; but in reality it was the severest blow that fate had ever aimed at her. Her hopes for his 'career' toppled over like a house of cards. The Merewethers, astounded at the apology which had to be sent in reply to their invitation to Ned for Christmas, suddenly slackened in their friendship. Lady Florizel ceased to write to Clara, and the Marchioness sent no more notes, weighted with gilded coronets, to her dear Mrs Burton. So far as that noble household was concerned, Ned's prospects had come to an end. The son of so rich a man, future proprietor of Dura, might have been accepted had he been on the spot to press his suit; but the Ladies Merewether were young and fair, and not so poor as to be pressed upon any one. So Lady Florizel and the parliamentary influence sunk into the background; and keenly to the intellectual machine, which served Mrs Burton instead of a heart, went the blow. This was the moment, she felt, in which Ned could have made himself 'safe,' and disentangled himself from the fatal web which instinct told her her husband was weaving about his feet. There was no confidence on business matters between Mr Burton and his wife; but a woman cannot be a man's constant companion for twenty years without divining him, and understanding, without the aid of words, something of what is going on in his mind. She had felt, even before Golden's arrival, a certain vague sense of difficulty and anxiety. His arrival made her sure of it. He had been abroad, withdrawn from the observation of English mercantile society for all these years; but his talents as the pilot of a ship, desperately making way through rocks and sandbanks, were sufficiently well known; and his appearance was confirmation sure to Mrs Burton of all her fears. Thus she felt in her reticent, silent breast that her boy had thrown up his only chance. The son of the master of Dura could have done so much—the son of a bankrupt could do nothing. He might have withdrawn himself from all risk—established himself in a sure position—had he taken her advice; and he had not taken it. It was the hardest personal blow she had ever received. It did not move her to tears, as it would have done most women. She had not that outlet for her sorrow; but it disarranged the intellectual machinery for the moment, and made her feel incapable of more thinking or planning. Even her motherhood had thus its anguish, probably as deep an anguish as she was capable of feeling. She was balked once more—her labour was in vain, and her hopes in vain. She had more mind than all of her family put together, and she knew it; but here once more, as so often in her experience, the fleshly part in which she was so weak overrode the mind, and brought its counsels to nought. It would be hard to estimate the kind and degree of suffering which such a conviction brought.

Time went on, however, as it always does; stole on, while people were thinking of other things, discussing Ned's disappearance and Norah's remorse, and Mr Nicholas's hopes of a living, and Mary's trousseau. When the first faint glimmer of the spring began, they had another thing to talk of, which was that Cyril Rivers had appeared on the scene again, often coming down from London to spend a day, and then so ingratiating himself with the Rectory people, and even with Nicholas, the bridegroom elect, that now and then he was asked to spend a night. This time, however, he was not invited to the great house; neither would Mrs Drummond ask him, though he was constantly there. She was determined that nobody should say she drew him on this time, people said. But the fact was that Helen's heart was sick of the subject altogether, and that she would have gone out of her way to avoid any one who had been connected with the Burtons, or who might be supposed to minister to that revenge of which she was so bitterly ashamed. While Cyril Rivers went and came to Dura village, Mr Golden became an equally frequent visitor at the House. The city men in the white villas had been filled with consternation at the first sight of him; but latterly began to make stiff returns to his hearty morning salutations when he went up to town along with them. It was so long ago; and nothing positively had been proved against him; and it was hard, they said, to crush a man altogether, who, possibly, was trying to amend his ways. Perhaps they would have been less charitable had he been living anywhere else than at the great house. Gradually, however, his presence became expected in Dura; he was always there when there were guests or festivities going on. And never had the Burtons been so gay. They seemed to celebrate their son's departure by a double rush of dissipation. The idea of any trouble being near so pleasant, so brilliant a place was ridiculous, and whatever Mrs Burton's thoughts on the subject might have been, she said nothing, but sent out her invitations, and assembled her guests with her usual calm. The Rectory people were constantly invited, and so indeed were the Drummonds, though neither Norah nor her mother had the heart to go.

Things were in this gay and festive state when Mr Baldwin suddenly one morning paid his daughter a visit. It was not one of his usual visits, accompanied by the two aunts, and the old man-servant and the two maids. These visits had grown rarer of late. Mrs Burton had so many guests, and of such rank, that to arrange the days for her father on which the minister of the chapel could be asked to dinner, and a plain joint provided, grew more and more difficult; while the old people grew more and more alarmed and indignant at the way Clara was going on. 'Her dress alone must cost a fortune,' her aunt Louisa said. 'And the boy brought up as if he were a young Lord; and the girl never to touch a needle nor an account-book in her life,' said Mrs Everest; and they all knew by experience that to 'speak to' Clara was quite futile. 'She will take her own way, brother, whatever you say,' was the verdict of both; and Mr Baldwin knew it was a true one. Nevertheless, there came a day when he felt it was his duty to speak to Clara. 'I have something to say to Haldane; and something to arrange with the chapel managers,' he said apologetically to his sisters; and went down all alone, in his black coat and his white tie with his hat very much on the back of his head, to his daughter's great house.

'I have got some business with Haldane and with the chapel managers,' he said, repeating his explanation; 'and I thought as I was here, Clara, I might as well come on and see you.'

'You are very welcome always, papa.'

'But I don't know if I shall be welcome to-day,' he went on, 'because I want to speak to you, Clara.'

'I know,' she said, with a faint smile, 'about our extravagance and all that. It is of no use. I may as well say this to you at once. I cannot stop it if I would; and I don't know that I would stop it if I could.'

'Do you know,' he said, coming forward to her, and laying his hand on her shoulder; for though he wore his hat on the back of his head, and took the chair at public meetings, he was a kind man, and loved his only child. Do you know, Clara, that in the City—you may despise the City, my dear, but it is all-important to your husband—do you know they say Burton is going too fast? I wish I could contradict it, but I can't. They say he's in a bad way. They say—'

'Tell me everything, papa. I am quite able to bear it.'

'Well, my dear, I don't want to make you unhappy,' said Mr Baldwin, drawing a long breath, 'but people do begin to whisper, in the best-informed circles, that he is very heavily involved.'

'Well?' she said looking up at him. She too drew a long breath, her face, perhaps, paled by the tenth of the tint. But her blue eyes looked up undaunted, without a shadow in them. Her composure, her calm question, drove even Mr Baldwin, who was used to his daughter's ways, half out of himself.

'Well?' he cried. 'Clara, you must be mad. If this is so, what can you think of yourself, who never try to restrain or to remedy?—who never made an attempt to retrench or save a penny? If your husband has even the slightest shadow of embarrassment in his business, is this great, splendid house, full of guests and entertainments, the way to help him through?'

'It is as good a way as any other,' she said, still looking at him. 'Papa, you speak in ignorance of both him and me. I don't know his circumstances; he does not tell me. It is he that enjoys all this; not me. And if he really should be in danger, I suppose he thinks he had better enjoy it as long as he can; and that is my idea too.'

'Enjoy it as long as he can! Spend other people's money in every kind of folly and extravagance!' cried Mr Baldwin aghast. 'Clara, you must be mad.'

'No, indeed,' she said quietly. 'I am very much in my senses. I know nothing about other people's money. I cannot control Mr Burton in his business, and he does not tell me. But don't suppose I have not thought this all over. I have taken every circumstance into consideration, papa, and every possibility. If we should ever be ruined, we shall have plenty to bear when that comes. There is Clary to be taken into consideration too. If there were only two days between Mr Burton and bankruptcy I should give a ball on one of those days. Clary has a right to it. This will be her only moment if what you say is true.'

To describe Mr Baldwin's consternation, his utter amazement, the eyes with which he contemplated his child, would be beyond my power. He could not, as people say, believe his ears. It seemed to him as if he must be mistaken, and that her words must have some other meaning, which he did not reach.

'Clara,' he said, faltering, 'you are beyond me. I hope you understand yourself—what—you mean. It is beyond me.'

'I understand it perfectly,' she said; and then, with a little change of tone, 'You understand, papa, that I would not speak so plainly to any one but you. But to you I need not make any secret. If it comes to the worst, Clary and I—Ned has deserted us—will have enough to bear.'

'You will always have your settlement, my dear,' said her father, quite cowed and overcome, he could not tell why.

'Yes. I shall have my settlement,' she said calmly; 'but there will be enough to bear.'

It was rather a relief to the old man when Clary came in, before whom nothing more could be said. And he was glad to hurry off again, with such astonishment and pain in his heart as an honest couple might have felt who had found a perverse fairy changeling in their child's cradle. He had thought that he knew his daughter. 'Clara has a cold exterior,' he had said times without number; 'but she has a warm heart.' Had she a heart at all? he asked himself; had she a conscience? What was she?—a woman or a—The old man could have stopped on the way and wept. He was an honest old man, and a kind, but what kind of a strange being was this whom he had nourished so long in his heart? It was a relief to him to get among his chapel managers, and regulate their accounts; and then he took Mr Truston, the minister, by the arm, and walked upon him. 'Come with me and see Haldane,' he said. Mr Truston was the same man who had wanted to be faithful to Stephen about the Magazine, but never had ventured upon it yet.

'I am afraid you are ill,' said the minister. 'Lean upon me. If you will come to my house and take a glass of wine.'

'No, no; with my daughter so near I should never be a charge to the brethren,' said Mr Baldwin. 'And so poor Haldane gets no better? It is a terrible burden upon the congregation in Ormond Road.'

'It must be indeed. I am sure they have been very kind; many congregations—'

'Many congregations would have thrown off the burden utterly; and I confess since they have heard that he has published again, and has been making money by his books—'

'Ah, yes; a literary man has such advantages,' said the minister with a sigh.

He did not want to favour the congregation in Ormond Road to the detriment of one of his own cloth; and at the same time it was hard to go against Mr Baldwin, the lay bishop of the denomination. In this way they came to the Gatehouse. Stephen had his proofs before him, as usual; but the pile of manuscripts was of a different complexion. They were no longer any pleasure to him. The work was still grateful, such as it was, and the power of doing something; but to spend his life recording tea-meetings was hard. He raised his eyes to welcome his old friend with a certain doubt and almost alarm. He too knew that he was a burden upon the congregation in Ormond Road.

'My dear fellow, my dear Stephen!' the old man said, very cordially shaking his hand, 'why you are looking quite strong. We shall have him dashing up to Ormond Road again, Mrs Haldane, and giving out his text, before we know where we are.'

Stephen shook his head, with such attempt at smiling as was possible. Mr Baldwin, however, was not so much afraid of breaking bad news to him as he had been at the great house.

'It is high time you should,' he continued, rubbing his hands cheerfully; 'for the friends are falling sadly off. We want you there, or somebody like you, Haldane. How we are to meet the expenses next year is more than I can say.'

A dead silence followed. Miss Jane, who had been arranging Stephen's books in the corner, stopped short to listen. Mrs Haldane put on her spectacles to hear the better; and poor Mr Truston, dragged without knowing it into the midst of such a scene, looked around him as if begging everybody's forbearance, and rubbed his hands faintly too.

'The fact is, my dear Haldane—it was but for five years—and now we've come to the end of the second five—and you have been making money by your books, people say—'

It was some little time before Stephen could answer, his lips had grown so dry. 'I think—I know—what you mean,' he said.

'Yes. I am afraid that is how it must be. Not with my will—not with my will,' said Mr Baldwin; 'but then you see people say you have been making money by your books.'

'He has made sixteen pounds in two years,' said Miss Jane.

Stephen held up his hand hurriedly. 'I know how it must be,' he said. 'Everybody's patience, of course, must give way at last.'

'Yes—that is just about how it is.'

There was very little more said. Mr Baldwin picked up his hat, which he had put on the floor, and begged the minister to give him his arm again. He shook hands very affectionately with everybody; he gave them, as it were, his blessing. They all bore it as people ought to bear a great shock, with pale faces, without any profane levity. 'They take it very well,' he said, as he went out. 'They are good people. Oh, my dear Truston, I don't know a greater sign of the difference between the children of this world and the children of the light than the way in which they receive a sudden blow.'

He had given two such blows within an hour; he had a right to speak. And in both cases, different as was the mien of the sufferers, the blow itself had all the appearance of a coup de grâce. It had not occurred to Mr Baldwin, when he made that classification, that it was his own child whom he had taken as the type of the children of wrath. He thought of it in the railway, going home; and it troubled him. 'Poor Clara! her brain must be affected,' he thought; he had never heard of anything so heathenish as her boldly-professed determination to give a ball, if need was, on the eve of her husband's bankruptcy, and for the reason that they would have a right to it. It horrified him a great deal more than if she had risked somebody else's money in trade and lost. Poor Clara! what might be coming upon her? But, anyhow, he reflected, she had her settlement, and that she was a child of many prayers.

Mrs Burton said nothing of this stroke which had fallen upon her. It made her fears into certainty, and she took certain steps accordingly, but told nobody. In Stephen's room at the Gatehouse there was silence, too, all the weary afternoon. They had lost the half of their living at a blow. The disaster was too great, too sudden and overwhelming, to be spoken of; and to one of them, to him who was helpless and could do nothing, it tasted like the very bitterness of death.

CHAPTER III

Mrs Burton said nothing about her troubles to any one: she avoided rather than sought confidential intercourse with her husband. She formed her plans and declined to receive any further information on the subject. Her argument to herself was that no one could have any right to suppose she knew. When the crash came, if come it must, she would be universally considered the first of the victims. The very fact of her entertainments and splendours would be so much evidence that she knew nothing about it— and indeed what did she know? her own fears and suspicions, her father's hints of coming trouble— nothing more. Her husband had never said a warning word to her which betrayed alarm or anxiety. She stood on the verge of the precipice, which she felt a moral certainty was before her, and made her arrangements like a queen in the plenitude of her power. 'There will be enough to bear,' she repeated to herself. She called all the county about her in these spring months before people had as yet gone to town. She made Dura blaze with lights and echo with music: she filled it full of guests. She made her entertainments on so grand a scale, that everything that had hitherto been known there was thrown into the shade. The excitement, so far as excitement could penetrate into her steady little soul, sustained and kept her up; or at least the occupation did, and the thousand arrangements, big and little, which were necessary. If her husband was ever tempted to seek her sympathy in these strange, wild, brilliant days which passed like a dream—if the burden on his shoulders ever so bowed the man down that he would have been glad to lean it upon hers, it is impossible to say; he looked at her sometimes wondering what was in her mind; but he was not capable of understanding that clear, determined intelligence. He thought she had got fairly into the whirl of mad dissipation and enjoyed it. She was playing into his hands, she was doing the best that could be done to veil his tottering steps, and divert public attention from his business misfortunes. He had no more idea why she was doing it, or with what deliberate conscious steps she was marching forward to meet ruin, than he had of any other incomprehensible wonder in heaven or earth.

The Haldanes made no secret of the distress which had fallen upon them. It was a less loss than the cost of one of Mrs Burton's parties, but it was unspeakable to them who had no way of replacing it. By one of those strange coincidences, however, which occur so often when good people are driven to desperation, Stephen's publisher quite unexpectedly sent him in April a cheque for fifty pounds, the produce of his last book, a book which he had called 'The Window,' and which was a kind of moral of his summer life and thoughts. It was not, he himself thought, a very good book; it was a medley of fine things and poor things, not quite free from that personal twaddle which it is so difficult to keep out of an invalid's or a recluse's view of human affairs. But then the British public is fond of personal twaddle, and like those bits best which the author was most doubtful about. It was a cheap little work, published by one of those firms which are known as religious publishers; and nothing could be more unexpected, more fortunate, more consoling, than this fifty pounds. Mrs Haldane, with a piety which, perhaps, was a little contemptuous of poor Stephen's powers, spoke of it, with tears in her eyes, as an answer to prayer; while Miss Jane, who was proud of her brother, tried to apportion the credit, half to Providence and half to Stephen; but anyhow it made up the lost allowance for the current year, and gave the poor souls time to breathe.

All this time the idea which had come into Dr Maurice's mind on the day of the picnic in October had been slowly germinating. He was not a man whose projects ripened quickly, and this was a project so delicate that it took him a long time to get it fully matured, and to accustom himself to it. It had come to full perfection in his mind when in the end of April Mrs Drummond received a letter from him, inviting Norah and herself to go to his house for a few days, to see the exhibitions and other shows which belong to that period of the year. This was an invitation which thrilled Norah's soul within her. She was at a very critical moment of her life. She had lost the honest young lover of her childhood, the boy whose love and service had grown so habitual to her that nobody but Norah knew how dreary the winter had been without him; and she was at present exposed to the full force of attentions much more close, much more subtle and skilful, but perhaps not so honest and faithful. Norah had exchanged the devotion of a young man who loved her as his own soul, for the intoxicating homage of a man who was very much in love with her, but who knew that his prospects would be deeply injured, and his position compromised, did he win the girl whom he wooed with all the fascinations of a hero in a romance, and all the persistency of a mind set upon having its own way. His whole soul was set upon winning her; but what to do afterwards was not so clear, and Rivers, like many another adventurer in love and in war, left the morrow to provide for itself. But Norah was very reluctant to be won. Sometimes, indeed, capitulation seemed very near at hand, but then her lively little temper would rise up again, or some hidden susceptibility would be touched, or the girl's independent soul would rise in arms against the thought of being subjugated like a young woman in a book by this 'novel-hero!' What were his dark eyes, his speaking glances, his skilful inference of a devotion above words, to her? Had not she read about such wiles a thousand times? And was it not an understood rule that the real hero, the true lover, the first of men, was never this bewitching personage, but the plainer, ruder man in the background, with perhaps a big nose, who was not very lovely to look upon? These thoughts contended in Norah with the fascinations of him whom she began to think of as the contre-heros. The invitation to London was doubly welcome to her, insomuch that it interrupted this current of thought and gave her something new to think about. She was fond of Dr Maurice: she had not been in town since she was a child: she wanted to see the parks and the pictures, and all the stir and tumult of life. For all these six years, though Dura was so near town, the mother and daughter had never been in London. And it looked so bright to Norah, bright with all the associations of her childhood, and full of an interest which no other place could ever have in its associations with the terrible event which ended her childhood. 'You will go, mamma?' she said, wistfully reading the letter a second time over her mother's shoulder. And Helen, who felt the need of an interruption and something new to think of as much as her child did, answered 'Yes.'

Dr Maurice was more excited about the approaching event than they were, though he had to take no thought about his wardrobe, and they had to take a great deal of thought; the question of Norah's frocks was nothing to his fussiness and agitation about the ladies' rooms and all the arrangements for their comfort. He invited an old aunt who lived near to come and stay with him for the time of the Drummonds' visit, a precaution which seemed to her, as it seems to me, quite unnecessary. I do not think Helen would have had the least hesitation in going to his house at her age, though there had been no chaperon. It was he who wanted the chaperon: he was quite coy and bashful about the business altogether: and the old aunt, who was a sharp old lady, was not only much amused, but had her suspicions aroused. In the afternoon, before his visitors arrived, he was particularly fidgety. 'If you want to go out, Henry, I will receive your guests,' the old lady said, not without a chuckle of suppressed amusement; 'probably they will only arrive in time to get dressed before dinner. You may leave them to me.'

'You are very kind,' said the doctor, but he did not go away. He walked from one end of the big drawing-room to the other, and looked at himself in the mirror between the windows, and the mirror over the mantelpiece. And then he took up his position before the fireplace, where of course there was nothing but cut paper. 'How absurd are all the relations between men and women,' he said, 'and how is it that I cannot ask my friend's widow, a woman in middle life, to come to my house—without—'

'Without having me?' said the aunt. 'My dear Henry, I have told you before—I think you could. I have no patience with the freedom of the present day in respect to young people, but, so far as this goes, I think you are too particular—I am sure you could—'

'You must allow me to be the best judge, aunt, of a matter that concerns myself,' said Dr Maurice, with gentle severity. 'I know very well what would happen: there would be all sorts of rumours and reports. People might not, perhaps, say there was anything absolutely wrong between us—Pray may I ask what you are laughing at?'

For the old lady had interrupted him by a low laugh, which it was beyond her power to keep in.

'Nothing, my dear, nothing,' she said, in a little alarm. 'I am sure I beg your pardon, Henry. I had no idea you were so sensitive. How old may this lady be?'

'The question is not about this lady, my dear aunt,' he answered in the dogmatic impatient tone which was so unlike him, 'but about any lady. It might happen to be a comfort to me to have a housekeeper I could rely on. It would be a great pleasure to be able to contribute to the comfort of Robert Drummond's family, poor fellow. But I dare not. I know the arrangement would no sooner be made than the world would say all sorts of things. How old is Mrs Drummond? She was under twenty when they were married, I know—and poor Drummond was about my own age. That is, let me see, how long ago? Norah is about eighteen, between eighteen and nineteen. Her mother must be nearly, if not quite, forty, I should think—'

'Then, my dear Henry—' began the old lady.

'Why, here they are!' he said, rushing to the window. But it was only a cab next door, or over the way. He went back to his position with a little flush upon his middle-aged countenance. 'My dear aunt,' he resumed, with a slight tremor in his voice, 'it is not a matter that can be discussed, I assure you. I know what would happen; and I know that poor Helen—I mean Mrs Drummond—would never submit to anything that would compromise her as Norah's mother. Even if she were not very sensitive on her own account, as women generally are, as Norah's mother of course she requires to be doubly careful. And here am I, the oldest friend they have, as fond of that child as if she were my own, and prevented by an absurd punctilio from taking them into my house, and doing my best to make her happy! As I said before, the relations between men and women are the most ridiculous things in the world.'

'But I do think, Henry, you make too much of the difficulties,' said the old aunt, busying herself with her work, and not venturing to say more.

'You must allow me to be the best judge,' he said, with a mixture of irritation and superiority. 'You may know the gossip of the drawing-rooms, which is bad enough, I don't doubt; but I know what men say.'

'Oh, then, indeed, my poor Henry,' said the old lady, with vivacity, eagerly seizing the opportunity to have one shot on her own side, 'I can only pray, Good Lord deliver you; for everybody knows there never was a bad piece of scandal yet, but it was a man that set it on foot.'

Aunt Mary thus had the last word, and retired with flying colours and in very high feather from the conflict; for at this moment the Drummonds arrived, and Dr Maurice rushed down-stairs to meet them. The old aunt was a personage very well worth knowing, though she has very little to do with this history, and it was with mingled curiosity and amusement that she watched for the entrance of Mrs Drummond and her daughter. It would be a very wise step for him anyhow to marry, she thought. The Maurice family were very well off, and there were not many young offshoots of the race to contend for the doctor's money. Was he contemplating the idea of a wife young enough to be his daughter? or had he really the good sense to think of a woman about his own age? Aunt Mary, though she was a woman herself, and quite ready to stand up for her own side, considered Helen Drummond, under forty, as about his own age, though he was over fifty. But as the question went through her mind, she shook her head. She knew a great many men who had made fools of themselves by marrying, or wishing to marry, the girl young enough to be their daughter; but the other class who had the good sense, &c., were very rare indeed.

There was, however, very little light thrown upon the subject by Aunt Mary's observations that evening. Mrs Drummond was very grave, almost sad; for the associations of the house were all melancholy ones, and her last visit to it came back very closely into her memory as she entered one room—the great old gloomy dining-room—where Norah, a child, had been placed by Dr Maurice's side at table on that memorable occasion, while she, unable even to make a pretence of eating, sat and looked on. She could not go back now into the state which her mind had been in on that occasion. Everything was calmed and stilled, nay, chilled by this long interval. She could think of her Robert without the sinking of the heart— the sense of hopeless loneliness—which had moved her then. The wound had closed up: the blank, if it had not closed up, had acquired all the calmness of a long-recognized fact. She had made up her mind long since that the happiness which she could not then consent to part with, was over for her. That is the great secret of what is called resignation: to consent and agree that what you have been in the habit of calling happiness is done with; that you must be content to fill its place with something else, something less. Helen had come to this. She no longer looked for it—no longer thought of it. It was over for her, as her youth was over. Her heart was tried, not by active sorrow, but by a heavy sense of past pain; but that did not hinder her from taking her part in the conversation—from smiling at Norah's sallies, at her enthusiasm, at all the height of her delight in the pleasure Dr Maurice promised her. Norah was the principal figure in the scene. She was surrounded on every side by that atmosphere of fond partiality in which the flowers of youth are most ready to unfold themselves. Dr Maurice was even fonder than her mother, and more indulgent; for Helen had the jealous eye which marks imperfections, and that intolerant and sovereign love which cannot put up with a flaw or a speck in those it cherishes. To Dr Maurice the specks and flaws were beauties. Norah led the conversation, was gay for every one, talked for every one. And the old aunt laughed within herself, and shook her head: 'He cannot keep his eyes off her; he cannot see anything but perfection in her,—but she is a mere excited child, and her mother is a beautiful woman,' said Aunt Mary to herself; 'man's taste and woman's, it is to be supposed, will be different to the end of time.' But after she had made this observation, the old lady was struck by the caressing, fatherly ways of her nephew towards this child. He would smooth her hair when he passed by her; would take her hand into his, unconsciously, and pat it; would lay his hand upon her shoulder; none of which things he would have ventured to do had he meant to present himself to Norah as her lover. He even kissed her cheek, when she said good-night, with uncontrollable fondness, yet unmistakable composure. What did the man mean?

He had sketched out a very pretty programme for them for their three days. Next evening they were to go to the theatre; the next again, to an opera. Norah could not walk, she danced as she went up-stairs. 'The only thing is, will my dress do?' she said, as she hung about her mother in the pretty fresh room, new-prepared, and hung with bright chintz, in which Mrs Drummond was lodged. Could it have been done on purpose? For certainly the other rooms in the house still retained their dark old furniture; dark-coloured, highly-polished mahogany, with deep red and green damask curtains—centuries old, as Norah thought. Mrs Drummond was surprised, too, at the aspect of this room. She was more than surprised, she was almost offended, by the presence of the old aunt as chaperon. 'Does the man think I am such a fool as to be afraid of him?' she wondered, with a frown and a smile, but gave herself up to Norah's pleasure, rejoicing to see that the theatre and the opera were strong enough to defeat for the moment and drive from the field both Cyril and Ned. And the next day, and the next, passed like days of paradise to Norah. She drove about in Dr Maurice's carriage, and laughed at her own grandeur, and enjoyed it. She called perpetually to her mother to notice ladies walking who were like themselves. 'That is what you and I should be doing, if it were not for this old darling of a doctor! trudging along in the sun, getting hot and red—'

'But think, you little sybarite, that is what we shall be doing to-morrow,' cried Helen, half amused and half afraid.

'No, the day after to-morrow,' said Norah, 'and then it will be delightful. We can look at the people in the carriages, and say, "We are as good as you;—we looked down upon you yesterday." And, mamma, we are going to the opera to-night!'

'You silly child,' Helen said. But to eyes that danced so, and cheeks that glowed so, what could any mother say?

It was the after-piece after that opera, however, which was what neither mother nor daughter had calculated upon, but which, no doubt, was the special cause of their invitation, and of the new chintz in the bed-rooms, and of all the expense Dr Maurice had been at. Norah was tired when they got home. She had almost over-enjoyed herself. She chatted so that no one could say a word. Her cheeks were blazing with excitement. When the two elder people could get a hearing, they sent her off to bed, though she protested she had not said half she had to say. 'Save it up for to-morrow,' said Dr Maurice, 'and run off and put yourself to bed, or I shall have you ill on my hands. Mrs Drummond, send her away.'

'Go, Norah, dear, you are tired,' said Helen.

Norah stood protesting, with her pretty white cloak hanging about her; her rose-ribbons a little in disorder; her eyes like two sunbeams. How fondly her old friend looked at her; with what proud, tender, adoring, fatherly admiration! If Aunt Mary had not been away in bed, then at least she must have divined. Dr Maurice lit her candle and took her to the door. He stooped down suddenly to her ear and whispered, 'I have something to say to your mother.' Norah could not have explained the sensation that came over her. She grew chill to her very fingers' ends, and gave a wondering glance at him, then accepted the candle without a word, and went away. The wonder was still in her eyes when she got up-stairs, and looked at herself in the glass. Instead of throwing off her cloak to see how she looked, as is a girl's first impulse, she stared blankly into the glass, and could see nothing but that surprise. What could he be going to talk about? What would her mother say?

Helen had risen to follow her daughter, but Dr Maurice came back, having closed the door carefully, and placed a chair for her. 'Mrs Drummond, can you give me ten minutes? I have something to say to you,' he said.

'Surely,' said Helen; and she took her seat, somewhat surprised; but not half so much surprised as Norah was, nor, indeed, so much as Dr Maurice was, now that matters had finally come to a crisis, to find himself in such an extraordinary position. Helen ran lightly over in her mind a number of subjects on which he might be going to speak to her; but the real subject never entered her thoughts. He did not sit down, though he had given her a chair. He moved about uneasily in front of her, changing his attitude a dozen times in a minute, and clearing his throat. 'He is going to offer me money for Norah,' was Helen's thought.

'Mrs Drummond,' he said—and his beginning confirmed her in her idea—'I am not a—marrying man, as you know. I am—past the age—when men think of such things. I am on the shady side of fifty, though not very far gone; and you are—about forty, I suppose?'

'Thirty-nine,' said Helen, with more and more surprise, and yet with the natural reluctance of a woman to have a year unjustly added to her age.

'Well, well, it is very much the same thing. I never was in love that I know of, at least not since;—and—and—that sort of thing, of course, is over for—you.'

'Dr Maurice, what do you mean?' cried Helen in dismay.

'Well, it is not very hard to guess,' he said doggedly. 'I mean that you are past the love-business, you know, and I—never came to it, so to speak. Look here, Helen Drummond, why shouldn't you and I, if it comes to that—marry? If I durst do it I'd ask you to come and live here, and let Norah be child to both of us, without any nonsense between you and me. But that can't be done, as you will easily perceive. Now, I am sure we could put up with one another as well as most people, and we have one strong bond between us in Norah—and—I could give her everything she wishes for. I could and I would provide for her when I die. You are not one to want pretences made to you, or think much of a sacrifice for your child's sake. I am not so vain but to allow that it might be a sacrifice—to us both.'

'Dr Maurice,' said Helen, half laughing, half sobbing, 'if this is a joke—'

'Joke! am I in the way of making such jokes? Why, it has cost me six months to think this joke out. There is no relaxation of the necessary bonds that I would not be ready to allow. You know the house and my position, and everything I could offer. As for settlements, and all business of that kind—'

'Hush,' she said. 'Stop!' She rose up and held out her hand to him. There were tears in her eyes; but there was also a smile on her face, and a blush which went and came as she spoke. 'Dr Maurice,' she said, 'don't think I cannot appreciate the pure and true friendship for Robert and me—'

'Just so, just so!' he interposed, nodding his head; he put his other hand on hers, and patted it as he had patted Norah's, but he did not again look her in the face. The elderly bachelor had grown shy—he did not know why; the most curious sensation, a feeling quite unknown to him was creeping about the region of his heart.

'And the love for Norah—' resumed Helen.

'Just so, just so.'

'Which have made you think of this. But—but—but—' She stopped; she had been running to the side of tears, when suddenly she changed her mind. 'But I think it is all a mistake! I am quite ready to come and stay with you, to keep house for you, to let you have Norah's company, when you like to ask us. I don't want any chaperon. Your poor, dear, good aunt! Dr Maurice,' cried Helen, her voice rising into a hysterical laugh, 'I assure you it is all a mistake.'

He let her hand drop out of his. He turned away from her with a shrug of his shoulders. He walked to the table and screwed up the moderator lamp, which had run down. Then he came back to his former position and said, 'I am much more in the world than you are; you will permit me to consider myself the best judge in this case. It is not a mistake. And I have no answer from you to my proposal as yet.'

Then Helen's strength gave way. The more serious view which she had thrust from her, which she had rejected as too solemn, came back. The blush vanished from her face, and so did the smile. 'You were his friend,' she said with quivering lips. 'You loved him as much as any one could, except me. Have you forgotten you are speaking to—Robert's wife?'

'Good lord!' cried Dr Maurice with sudden terror; 'but he is dead.'

'Yes, he is dead; but I do not see what difference that makes; when a woman has once been a man's wife, she is so always. If there is any other world at all, she must be so always. I hate the very name of widow!' cried Helen vehemently, with the tears glittering in her eyes. 'I abhor it; I don't believe in it. I am his wife!'

Dr Maurice was a man who had always held himself to be invincible to romantic or high-flown feelings. But somehow he was startled by this view of the question. It had not occurred to him before; for the moment it staggered him, so that he had to pause and think it over. Then he said, 'Nonsense!' abruptly. 'Mrs Drummond, I cannot think that such a view as this is worth a moment's consideration; it is against both reason and common sense.'

She did not make any reply; she made a movement of her hand, deprecating, expostulating, but she would not say any more.

'And Scripture, too,' said Dr Maurice triumphantly, 'it is quite against Scripture.' Then he remembered that this was not simply an argument in which he was getting the better, but a most practical question. 'If it is disagreeable to you, it is a different matter,' he said; 'but I had hoped, with all the allowances I was ready to make, and for Norah's sake—'

'It is not disagreeable, Dr Maurice; it is simply impossible, and must always be so,' she said.

Then there was another silence, and the two stood opposite to each other, not looking at each other, longing both for something to free them. 'In that case I suppose there had better be no more words on the subject,' he said, turning half away.

'Except thanks,' she cried; 'thanks for the most generous thoughts, the truest friendship. I will never forget—'

'I do not know how far it was generous,' he said moodily, and he got another candle and lighted it for her, as he had done for Norah; 'and the sooner you forget the better. Good night.'

Good night! When he looked round the vacant room a moment after, and felt himself alone, it seemed to Dr Maurice as if he had been dreaming. He must have fallen down suddenly from some height or other—fallen heavily and bruised himself, he thought—and so woke up out of an odd delusion quite unlike him, which had arisen he could not tell how. It was a very curious sensation. He felt sore and downcast, sadly disappointed and humbled in his own conceit. It had not even occurred to him that the matter might end in this way. He gave a long sigh, and said aloud, 'Perhaps it is quite as well it has ended so. Probably we should not have liked it had we tried it,' and then went up to his lonely chamber, hearing, as he thought, his step echo over all the vacant house. Yes, it was a vacant house. He had chosen that it should be years ago, and yet the feeling now was dreary to him, and it would never be anything but vacant for all the rest of his life.

CHAPTER IV

It was difficult for the two who had thus parted at night to meet again at the breakfast-table next morning without any sign of that encounter, before the sharp eyes of Aunt Mary, and Norah's youthful, vivacious powers of observation. Dr Maurice was the one who found the ordeal most hard. He was sullen, and had a headache, and talked very little, not feeling able for it. 'You are bilious, Henry; that is what it is,' the aunt said. But though he was over fifty, and prided himself on his now utterly prosaic character, the doctor felt wounded by such an explanation. He did not venture to glance at Helen, even when he shook hands with her; though he had a lurking curiosity within him to see how she looked, whether triumphant or sympathetic. He knew that he ought to have been gay and full of talk, to put the best face possible upon his downfall; but he did not feel able to do it; not to feel sore, not to feel small, and miserable, and disappointed, was beyond his powers. Helen was not gay either, nor at all triumphant; she felt the embarrassment of the position as much as he did; but in these cases it is the woman who generally has her wits most about her; and Mrs Drummond, who was conscious also of her child's jealous inspection, talked rather more than usual. Norah had demanded to know what the doctor had to say on the previous night; a certain dread was in her mind. She had felt that something was coming, something that threatened the peace of the world. 'What did he say to you, mamma?' she had asked anxiously. 'Nothing of importance,' Helen had replied. But Norah knew better; and all that bright May morning while the sunshine shone out of doors, even though it was in London, and tempted the country girl abroad, she kept by her mother's side and watched her with suspicious eyes. Had Norah known the real state of affairs, her shame and indignation would have known no bounds; but Helen made so great an effort to dismiss all consciousness from her face and tone, that the child was balked at last, and retired from the field. Aunt Mary, who had experience to back her, saw more clearly. Whatever had been going to happen had happened, she perceived, and had not been successful. Thus they all breakfasted, watching each other, Helen being the only one who knew everything and betrayed nothing. After breakfast they were going to the Exhibition. It had been deferred to this day, which was to be their last.

'I do not think I will go,' said Dr Maurice; and then he caught Norah's look full of disappointment, which was sweet to him. 'You want me, do you, child?' he asked. There was a certain ludicrous pathos in the emphasis which was almost too much for Helen's gravity, though, indeed, laughter was little in her thoughts.

'Of course I want you,' said Norah; 'and so does mamma. Fancy sending us away to wander about London by ourselves! That was not what you invited us for, surely, Dr Maurice? And then after the pictures, let us have another splendid drive in the carriage, and despise all the people who are walking! It will be the last time. You rich people, you have not half the pleasure you might have in being rich. I suppose, now, when you see out of the carriage window somebody you know walking, it does not make you proud?'

'I don't think it does,' said the doctor with a smile.

'That is because you are hardened to it,' said Norah. 'You can have it whenever you please; but as for me, I am as proud—'

'I wish you had it always, my dear,' said Dr Maurice; and this time his tone was almost lachrymose. It was so hard-hearted of Helen to deny her child these pleasures and advantages, all to be purchased at the rate of a small personal sacrifice on her part—a sacrifice such as he himself was quite ready to make.

'Oh, I should not mind that,' cried Norah; 'if I had it always I should get hardened to it too. I should not mind; most likely then I should prefer walking, and think carriages only fit for old ladies. Didn't you say that one meets everybody at the Academy, mamma?'

'A great many people, Norah.'

'I wonder whom we shall meet,' said the girl; and a sudden blush floated over her face. Helen looked at her with some anxiety. She did not know what impression Cyril Rivers might have made on Norah's heart. Was it him she was thinking of? Mrs Drummond herself wondered, too, a little. She was half afraid of the old friends she might see there. But then she reflected to herself dreamily, that life goes very quickly in London, that six years was a long time, and that her old friends might have forgotten her. How changed her own feelings were! She had never been fond of painters, her husband's brothers-in-arms. Now the least notable of them, the most painty, the most slovenly, would look somehow like a shadow of Robert. Should she see any of those old faces? Whom should she meet? Norah's light question moved many echoes of which the child knew nothing; and it was to be answered in a way of which neither of them dreamed.

The mere entrance into those well-known rooms had an indescribable effect upon Helen. How it all rushed back upon her, the old life! The pilgrimages up those steps, the progress through the crowd to that special spot where one picture was hung; the anxiety to see how it looked—if there was anything near that 'killed' it in colour, or threw it into the shade in power; her own private hope, never expressed to any one, that it might 'come better' in the new place. Dr Maurice stalked along by her side, but he did not say anything to her; and for her part, she could not speak—her heart and her eyes were full. She could only see the other people's pictures glimmering as through a mist. It seemed so strange to her, almost humiliating, that there was nothing of her own to go to—nothing to make a centre to this gallery, which had relapsed into pure art, without any personal interest in it. By-and-by, when the first shock had worn off, she began to be able to see what was on the walls, and to come back to her present circumstances. So many names were new to her in those six years; so many that she once knew had crept out of sight into corners and behind doorways. She had begun to get absorbed in the sight, which was so much more to her than to most people, when Mr Rivers came up to them. He had known they were to be in town; he had seen them at the opera the previous night, and had found out a good deal about their plans. But London was different from Dura; and he had not ventured to offer his attentions before the eyes of all the world, and all the cousins and connections and friends who might have come to a knowledge of the fact that an unknown pretty face had attracted his homage. But of a morning, at the Royal Academy, he felt himself pretty safe; there every one is liable to meet some friend from the county, and the most watchful eyes of society are not on the alert at early hours. He came to them now with eager salutations.

'I tried hard to get at you at the opera last night,' he said, putting himself by Norah's side; 'but I was with my own people, and I could not get away.'

'Were you at the opera last night?' said Norah, with not half the surprise he anticipated; for she was not aware of the facilities of locomotion in such places, nor that he might have gone to her had he so desired; and besides, she had seen no one, being intent upon the stage. Yet there was a furtive look about him now, a glance round now and then, to see who was near them, which startled her. She could not make out what it meant.

'Come, and I will show you the best pictures,' he said; and he took her catalogue from her hand and pointed out to her which must be looked at first.

They made a pretty group as they stood thus,—Norah looking up with her sunshiny eyes, and he stooping over her, bending down till his silky black beard almost touched her hair. She little, and he tall—she full of vivacity, light, and sunshine; he somewhat quiet, languishing, Byronic in his beauty. Norah was not such a perfect contrast to him as Clara was—Rubens to the Byron; but her naturalness, the bright, glowing intelligence and spirit about her—the daylight sweetness of her face, with which soul had as much to do as feature, contrasted still more distinctly with the semi-artificiality of the hero. For even granting that he was a little artificial, he was a real hero all the same; his handsomeness and air of good society were unmistakable, his conversation was passable; he knew the thousand things which people in society know, and which, whether they understand them or not, they are in the habit of hearing talked about. All these remarks were made, not by Norah, nor by Norah's mother, but by Dr Maurice, who stood by and did not pretend to have any interest in the pictures. And this young fellow was the Honourable Cyril, and would be Lord Rivers. Dr Maurice kept an eye upon him, wondering, as Helen had done, Did he mean anything? what did he mean?

'But there is one above all which I must show you—every one is talking of it,' said Mr Rivers. 'Come this way, Miss Drummond. It is not easy to reach it; there is always such a crowd round it. Dr Maurice, bring Mrs Drummond; it is in the next room. Come this way.'

Norah followed him, thinking of nothing but the pictures; and her mother and Dr Maurice went after them slowly, saying nothing to each other. They had entered the great room, following the younger pair, when some one stepped out of the crowd and came forward to Helen. He took off his hat and called her by her name—at first doubtfully, then with assurance.

'I thought I could not be mistaken,' he cried, 'and yet it is so long since you have been seen here.'

'I am living in the country,' said Helen. Once more the room swam round her. The new-comer's voice and aspect carried her back, with all the freshness of the first impression, to the studio and its visitors again.

'And you had just been in my mind,' said the painter. 'There is a picture here which reminds us all so strongly of poor dear Drummond. Will you let me take you to it? It is exactly in his style, his best style, with all that tenderness of feeling—It has set us all talking of you and him. Indeed, none of his old friends have forgotten him; and this is so strangely like his work—'

'Where is it?—one of his pupils, perhaps,' said Helen. She tried to be very composed, and to show no emotion; but it was so long since she had heard his name, so long since he had been spoken of before her! She felt grateful, as if they had done her a personal service, to think that they talked of Robert still.

'This way,' said the painter; and just then Norah met her, flying back with her eyes shining, her ribbons flying, wonder and excitement in her face.

Norah seized her mother by the hands, gasping in her haste and emotion. 'Oh, mamma, come; it is our picture,' she cried.

Wondering, Helen went forward. It was the upper end of the room, the place of honour. Whether it was that so many people around her carried her on like a body-guard making her a way through the crowd, or that the crowd itself, moved by that subtle sympathy which sometimes communicates itself to the mass more easily than to individuals, melted before her, as if feeling she had the best right to be there, I cannot tell. But all at once Helen found herself close to the crimson cord which the pressure of the throng had almost broken down, standing before a picture. One picture—was there any other in the place? It was the picture of a face looking up, with two upward-reaching hands, from the bottom of an abyss, full of whirling clouds and vapour. High above this was a bank of heavenly blue, and a white cloud of faintly indistinct spectators, pitiful angel forms, and one visionary figure as of a woman gazing down. But it was the form below in which the interest lay. It was worn and pale, with the redness of tears about the eyes, the lips pressed closely together, the hands only appealing, held up in a passionate silence. Helen stood still, with eyes that would not believe what they saw. She became unconscious of everything about her, though the people thronged upon her, supporting her, though she did not know. Then she held out her hands wildly, with a cry which rang through the rooms and penetrated every one in them—'Robert!'—and fell at the foot of the picture, which was called 'Dives'—the first work of a nameless painter whom nobody knew.

It would be impossible to describe the tumult and commotion which rose in the room to which everybody hastened from every corner of the exhibition, thronging the doorways and every available corner, and making it impossible for some minutes to remove her. 'A lady fainted! Is that all?' the disappointed spectators cried. They had expected something more exciting than so common, so trifling an occurrence. 'Fortunately,' the newspapers said who related the incident, 'a medical man was present;' and when Helen came to herself, she found Dr Maurice standing over her, with his finger on her pulse. 'It is the heat, and the fatigue—and all that,' he said; and all through the rooms people repeated to each other that it was the heat, and the dust, and the crowd, and that there was nothing so fatiguing as looking at pictures. 'Both body and mind are kept on the strain, you know,' they said, and immediately thought of luncheon. But Dr Maurice thought of something very different. He did not understand all this commotion about a picture; if his good heart would have let him, he would have tried to think that Helen was 'making a fuss.' As it was he laid this misfortune to the door of women generally, whom there was no understanding; and then, in a parenthesis, allowed that he might himself be to blame. He should not have agitated her, he thought; but added, 'Good Lord, what are women good for, if they have to be kept in a glass-house, and never spoken to? The best thing is to be rid of them, after all.'

I will not attempt to describe what Helen's thoughts were when she came to herself. She would not, dared not betray to any one the impression, which was more than an impression—the conviction that had suddenly come to her. She put up her hand, and silenced Norah, who was beginning, open-mouthed, 'Oh, mamma!' She called the old friend to her, who had attended the group down into the vestibule, and begged him to find out for her exactly who the painter was, and where he was to be heard of; and there she sat, still abstracted, with a singing in her ears, which she thought was only the rustle of the thoughts that hurried through her brain, until she should be able to go home. It was while they were waiting thus, standing round her, that another event occurred, of which Helen was too much absorbed to take any but the slightest cognizance. She was seated on a bench, still very pale, and unable to move. Dr Maurice was mounting guard over her. Norah stood talking to Mr Rivers on the other side; while meanwhile the stream of the public was flowing past, and new arrivals entering every moment by the swinging doors. Norah had grown very earnest in her talk. 'We have the very same subject at home, the same picture,' she was saying; her eyelashes were dewy with tears, her whole face full of emotion. Her colour went and came as she spoke; she stood looking up to him with a thrill of feeling and meaning about her, such as touch the heart more than beauty. And yet there was no lack of beauty. A lady who had just come in, paused, having her attention attracted to the group, and looked at them all, as she thought she had a right to do. 'The poor lady who fainted,' she heard some one say. But this girl who stood in front had no appearance of fainting. She was all life, and tenderness, and fire. The woman who looked on admired her fresh, sweet youthfulness, her face, which in its changing colour was like a flower. She admired all these, and made out, with a quick observant eye, that the girl was the daughter of the pale beautiful woman by the wall, and not unworthy of her. And then suddenly, without a pause, she called out, 'Cyril!' Young Rivers started as if a shot had struck him. He rushed to her with tremulous haste. 'Mother! you don't mean to say that you have come here alone?'

'But I do mean it, and I want you to take care of me,' she said, taking his arm at once. 'I meant to come early. We have no time to lose.'

Norah stood surprised, looking at the woman who was Cyril's mother; in a pretty pause of expectation, the blush coming and going on her face, her hand ready to be timidly put out in greeting, her pretty mouth half smiling already, her eyes watching with an interest of which she was not ashamed. Why should she be ashamed of being interested in Cyril's mother? She waited for the approach, the introduction—most likely the elder woman's gracious greeting. 'For she must have heard of me too,' Norah thought. She cast down her eyes, pleasantly abashed; for Lady Rivers was certainly looking at her. When she looked up again, in wonder that she was not spoken to, Cyril was on the stair with his mother, going up. He was looking back anxiously, waving his hand to her from behind Lady Rivers. He had a beseeching look in his eyes, his face looked miserable across his mother's shoulders, but—he was gone. Norah looked round her stupefied. Had anything happened?—was she dreaming? And then the blood rushed to her face in a crimson flush of pride and shame.

She bore this blow alone, without even her mother to share and soften it; and the child staggered under it for the moment. She grew as pale as Helen herself after that one flash. When the carriage came to the door, two women, marble-white, stepped into it. Dr Maurice had not the heart to go with them; he would walk home, he said. And Norah looked out of the window, as she had so joyfully anticipated doing in her happiness and levity, but not to despise the people who walked. The only thought of which she was capable was—Is everybody like that? Do people behave so naturally? Is it the way of the world?

This is what they met at the Academy, where they went so lightly, not knowing. The name of the painter of the 'Dives' reached them that same night; it was not in the catalogue. His name was John Sinclair, Thirty-fifth Avenue, New York.

CHAPTER V

'You must be dreaming,' cried Dr Maurice with energy. 'You must be dreaming! With my—folly—and other things—you have got into a nervous state.'

'I am not dreaming,' she said very quietly. There was no appearance of excitement about her. She sat with her hands clasped tightly together, and her eyes wandering into the unknown, into the vacant air before her. And her mind had got possession of one burden, and went over and over it, repeating within herself, 'John Sinclair, Thirty-fifth Avenue, New York.'

'I will show you the same picture,' she went on. 'The very same, line for line. It was the last he ever did. And in his letter he spoke of Dives looking up—John Sinclair, Thirty-fifth Avenue, New York!'

'Helen, Helen!' said Dr Maurice with a look of pity. He had never called her anything but Mrs Drummond till the evening before, and now the other seemed so natural; for, in fact, she did not even notice what he called her. 'How easy is it to account for all this! Some one else must have seen the sketch, who was impressed by it as much as you were, and who knew the artist was dead, and could never claim his property. How easy to see how it may have been done, especially by a smart Yankee abroad.'

She shook her head without a word, with a faint smile; argument made no difference to her. She was sure; and what did it matter what any one said?

'Then I will tell you what I will do,' he said. 'I have some friends in New York. I will have inquiries made instantly about John Sinclair. Indeed it is quite possible some one may know him here. I shall set every kind of inquiry on foot to-morrow, to satisfy you. I warn you nothing will come of it—nothing would make me believe such a thing; but still, to prevent you taking any rash steps—'

'I will take no rash steps,' she said. 'I will do nothing. I will wait till—I hear.'

'Why this is madness,' he said. And then all at once a cold shudder passed over him, and he said to himself, 'Good God! what if she had not refused last night!'

But the very fact that she had refused was a kind of guarantee that there was nothing in this wild idea of hers. Had there been anything in it, of course she would have accepted, and all sorts of horrors would have ensued. Such was Dr Maurice's opinion of Providence, and the opinion of many other judicious people. The fact that a sudden re-appearance would do no harm made it so much less likely that there would be any re-appearance. He tried hard to dismiss the idea altogether from his mind. It was not a comfortable idea. It is against all the traditions, all the prejudices of life, that a man should come back from the dead. A wild, despairing Dives might wish for it, or a mourner half frantic with excess of sorrow; but to the ordinary looker-on the idea is so strange as to be painful. Dr Maurice had a true affection for Robert Drummond; but he could not help feeling that it would be out of all character, out of harmony, almost an offence upon decency, that he should not be dead.

It was curious, however, what an effect this fancy of Helen's had in clearing away the cloud of embarrassment which had naturally fallen between her and him. All that produced that cloud had evidently disappeared from her mind. She remembered it no more. It was not that she had thrust it away of set will and purpose, but that without any effort it had disappeared. This was, it is true, somewhat humiliating to Dr Maurice; but it was very convenient for all the purposes of life that it should be so. And she sat with him now and discussed the matter, abstracted in the great excitement which had taken possession of her, yet calmed by it, without a recollection that anything had ever passed between them which could confuse their intercourse. This unconsciousness, I say, was humiliating in one sense, though in another it was a relief, to the man who did not forget; but it confused him while it set Helen at her ease. It was so extraordinary to realise what was the state of affairs yesterday, and what to-day—to enter into so new and wonderful a region of possibilities, after having lived so long in quite another; for, to be sure, Helen had only known of Dr Maurice's project as regarded herself since last night; whereas, he had known it for six months, and during all that time had been accustoming himself to it, and now had to make a mental spring as far away from it as possible—a kind of gymnastic exercise which has a very bewildering effect upon an ordinary mind.

It was a relief to all the party when the Drummonds went home next morning; except, perhaps, to the old aunt, who had grown interested in the human drama thus unexpectedly produced before her, and who would have liked to see it out. The mother and daughter were glad to go home; and yet how life had changed to them in these three days! It had given to Helen the glow of a wild, incomprehensible hope, a something supernatural, mixed with terror and wonder, and a hundred conflicting emotions; while to Norah it had taken the romance out of life. To contemplate life without romance is hard upon a girl; to have a peep, as it were, behind the scenes, and see the gold of fairy-land corroding itself into slates, and the beauty into dust and ashes. Such a revolution chills one to the very soul. It is almost worse than the positive heart-break of disappointed love, for that has a warm admixture of excitement, and is supported by the very sharpness of its own suffering; whereas in Norah's pain there was but disenchantment and angry humiliation, and that horrible sense that the new light was true and the other false, which takes all courage from the heart. She had told her mother, and Helen had been very indignant, but not so wroth as her daughter. 'Lady Rivers might have no time to wait—she might have wanted him for something urgent—there might be something to explain,' Helen said; but as for Norah, she felt that no explanation was possible. For months past this man had been making a show of his devotion to her. He had done everything except ask her in words to be his wife. He had been as her shadow, whenever he could come to Dura, and his visits had been so frequent that it was very evident he had seized every opportunity to come: yet the moment his mother appeared on the scene, the woman whom in all the world he ought to have most wished to attach to the girl whom he loved, he had left her with shame and embarrassment—escaped from her without even the politeness of a leave-taking. Norah had wondered whether she cared for him in the old days; she had asked herself shyly, as girls do, whether the little flutter of her heart at his appearance could possibly mean that sacredest, most wonderful and fascinating of mysteries—love? Sometimes she had been disposed to believe it did: and then again she had surprised herself in the midst of a sudden longing for poor Ned with his big nose, and had blushed and asked herself angrily, was the one compatible with the other? In short, she had not known what to make of her own feelings; for she was not experienced enough to be able to tell the difference—a difference which sometimes puzzles the wisest—between the effect produced by gratified vanity, and pleasure in the love of another, and that which springs from love itself. But she was in no doubt about the anger, the mortification, the indignant shame with which her whole nature rose up against the man who had dared to be ashamed of her. Of this there could be no explanation. She said to herself that she hoped he would not come again or attempt to make any explanation, and then she resented bitterly the fact that he did not come. She had made up her mind what she would say, how she would crush him with quiet scorn, and wonder at his apologies. 'Why should you apologise, Mr Rivers? I had no wish to be introduced to your mother,' she meant to say; but as day after day passed, and he gave her no opportunity of saying this, Norah's thoughts grew more bitter, more fiery than ever. And life was dull without this excitement in it. The weather was bright, and the season sweet, and I suppose she had her share of rational pleasure as in other seasons; but to her own consciousness Norah was bitterly ill-used, insomuch as she had not an opportunity to tell, or at least to show Cyril Rivers what she thought of him. It had been an immediate comfort to her after the affront he had put upon her, that she would have this in her power.

The change that had come upon the lives of the two ladies in the Gatehouse was, however, scarcely apparent to their little world. Norah was a little out of temper, fitful, and ready to take offence, the Daltons at the Rectory thought; and Mrs Drummond was more silent than usual, and had an absorbed look in her eyes, a look of abstraction for which it was difficult to account. But this was all that was apparent outside. Perhaps Mr Rivers was a little longer than usual in visiting Dura; he had not been there for ten days, and Katie Dalton wondered audibly what had become of him. But nobody except Norah supposed for a moment that his connection with Dura was to be broken off in this sudden way. And everything else went on as usual. If Mrs Drummond was less frequently visible, no one remarked it much. Norah would run over and ask Katie to walk with her, on the plea that 'mamma has a headache,' and Mrs Dalton would gather her work together, and cross the road in the sunshine and 'sit with' the sufferer. But the only consequence of this visit would be that the blinds would be drawn down over the three windows in front, Mrs Dalton having an idea that light was bad for a headache, and that when she returned she would tell her eldest daughter that poor dear Mrs Drummond was very poorly, and very anxious for news of a friend whom she had not heard of for years.

And the picture of Dives, which had been hung in a sacred corner, where Helen said her prayers, was brought out, and placed in the full light of day. It was even for a time brought down-stairs, while the first glow of novel hope and wonder lasted, and placed in the drawing-room, where everybody who saw it wondered at it. It was not so well painted as the great picture in the Academy. It was even different in many of its details. There was no hope in the face of this, but only a haggard passionate despair, while the look of the other was concentrated into such an agony of appealing as cannot exist where there is no hope. Dr Maurice even, when he came down, declared forcibly that it was difficult for him to trace the resemblance. Perhaps the leading idea was the same, but then it was so differently worked out. He looked at the picture in every possible light, and this was the conclusion he came to;—No; no particular resemblance,—a coincidence, that was all. And John Sinclair was a perfectly well-known painter, residing in New York, a man known to Dr Maurice's friends there. Why there was no name to the picture in the catalogue nobody could tell. It was some absurd mistake or other; but John Sinclair, the painter, was a man who had been known in New York for years. 'Depend upon it, it is only a coincidence,' Dr Maurice said. After that visit, from what feeling I cannot say, the picture was taken back up-stairs. Not that Mrs Drummond was convinced, but that she shrank from further discussion of a matter on which she felt so deeply. She would sit before it for hours, gazing at it, careless of everything else; and if I were to reproduce all the thoughts that coursed through Helen's mind, I should do her injury with the reader, who, no doubt, believes that the feelings in a wife's mind, when such a hope entered it, could only be those of a half-delirious joy. But Helen's thoughts were not wildly joyful. She had been hardly and painfully trained to do without him, to put him out of her life. Her soul had slid into new ways, changed meanings; and in that time what change of meaning, what difference of nature, might have come to a man who had returned from death and the grave? Could it all be undone? Could it float away like a tale that is told, that tale of seven long years? Would the old assimilate with the new, and the widow become a wife again without some wrench, some convulsion of nature? Not long before she had denounced the name vehemently, crying out against it, declaring that she did not believe in it: but now, when perhaps it might turn out that her widowhood had been indeed a fiction and unreal—now! How she was to be a wife again; how her existence was to suffer a new change, and return into its old channel, Helen could not tell. And yet that Robert should live again, that he should receive some recompense for all his sufferings; that even she who had been in her way so cruel to him, should be able to make up for it—for that Helen would have given her life. The news about John Sinclair was a discouragement, but still it did not touch her faith. She carried her picture up-stairs again, and put it reverently, not in its old corner, but where the sunshine would fall upon it and the full light of day. The fancifulness of this proceeding did not occur to her, for grief and hope, and all the deeper emotions of the heart, are always fanciful: and in this time of suspense, when she could do nothing, when she was waiting, listening for indications of what was coming, that silent idol-worship which no one knew of, did her good.

Meanwhile Dura went on blazing with lights, and sweet with music, making every day a holiday. Mrs Burton did not walk so much as she used to do, but drove about, giving her orders, paying her visits, with beautiful horses which half the county envied, and toilettes which would have been remarked even in the park. 'That little woman is losing her head,' the Rector said, as he looked at an invitation his wife had just received for a fête which was to eclipse all the others, and which was given in celebration of Clara's birthday. It was fixed for the 6th of July, and people were coming to it from far and near. There was to be a garden party first, a sumptuous so-called breakfast, and a ball at night. The whole neighbourhood was agitated by the preparations for this solemnity. It was said that Ned, poor Ned, whose disappearance was now an old story, was to be disinherited, and that Clara was to be the heiress of all. The importance thus given to her birthday gave a certain colour to the suggestion; it was like a coming of age, people said, and replaced the festivities which ought to have taken place on the day when Ned completed his twenty-first year, a day which had passed very quietly a few weeks before, noted by none. But to Clara's birthday feast everybody was invited. The great county people, the Merewethers themselves, were coming, and in consideration of Clara's possible heiress-ship, it was whispered that the Marchioness had thoughts of making her son a candidate for the place deserted by Cyril Rivers. Cyril, too, moreover, was among the guests; he was one of a large party which was coming from town; and the village people were asked, the Daltons and the Drummonds, beside all the lesser gentry of the neighbourhood. It was to Katie Dalton's importunate beseechings, seconded, no doubt, by her own heart, which had begun to tire of seclusion and long for a little pleasure, that Norah relinquished her first proud determination not to go; and Dr Maurice had just sent a box from town containing two dresses, one for the evening, and one for out-of-doors, which it was beyond the powers of any girl of nineteen to refuse the opportunity of wearing. When Norah had made up her own mind to this effort, she addressed herself to the task of overcoming her mother's reluctance; and, after much labour, succeeded so far that a compromise was effected. Norah went to the out-door fête, under the charge of Mrs Dalton, and Helen with a sigh took out her black silk gown once more, and prepared to go with her child in the evening. The Daltons were always there, good neighbours to support and help her; and seated by Mrs Dalton's side, who knew something of her anxiety about that friend whom she had not heard of for years, Mrs Drummond felt herself sustained. When Norah returned with the Daltons from the garden party, Mr Rivers accompanied the girls. He came with them to the door of the Gatehouse, where Katie, secretly held fast by Norah, accompanied her friend. He lingered on the white steps, waiting to be asked in; but Norah gave no such invitation. She went back to her mother triumphant, full of angry delight.

'I have been perfectly civil to him, mamma! I have taken the greatest care—I have not avoided him, nor been stiff to him, nor anything. And he has tried so hard, so very hard, to have an explanation. Very likely! as if I would listen to any explanation.'

'How did you avoid it, Norah, if you were neither angry nor stiff?'

'Katie, mamma, always Katie! I put her between him and me wherever we went. It was fun,' cried Norah, with eyes that sparkled with revengeful satisfaction. Her spirits had risen to the highest point. She had regained her position; she had got the upper hand, which Norah loved. The prospect of the evening which was still before her, in which she should wear that prettiest ball-dress, which surely had been made by the fairies, and drag Cyril Rivers at her chariot-wheels, and show him triumphantly how little it mattered to her, made Norah radiant. She rushed in to the Haldanes' side of the house to show herself, in the wildest spirits. Mrs Haldane and Miss Jane—wonder of wonders—were going too; everybody was to be there. The humble people were asked to behold and ratify the triumph, as well as the fine people to make it. As for Mrs Haldane, she disapproved, and was a great deal more grim than ordinary; but, for once in a way, because it would be a great thing to see, and because Mr Baldwin and his sisters were to be there too,—'as much out of their proper place as we,' she said, shaking her head,—she had allowed herself to be persuaded. Miss Jane required no persuading. She was honestly delighted to have a chance of seeing anything—the dresses and the diamonds, and Norah dancing with all the grandees. When Norah came in, all in a cloud of tulle and lace, Miss Jane fairly screamed with delight. 'I am quite happy to think I shall see the child have one good dance,' she said, walking round and round the fairy princess. 'Were you fond of dancing yourself, Miss Jane?' said Norah, not without the laugh of youth over so droll an idea. But it was not droll to Miss Jane; she put her hands, which were clothed in black with mittens, on the child's shoulders, and gave her a kiss, and answered not a word. And Stephen looked on from that immovable silent post of his, and saw them both, and thought of the past and present, and all the shadowy uncertain days that were to come. How strange to think of the time when Miss Jane, so grave and prosaic in her old-maidish gown, had been like Norah! How wonderful to think that Norah one day might be as Miss Jane! And so they all went away to the ball together, and Stephen in his chair immovable till his nurses came back, and Susan bustling about in the kitchen, were left in the house alone.

One ball is like another; and except that the Dura ball was more splendid, more profuse in ornament, gayer in banks of flowers, richer in beautiful dresses and finery, more ambitious in music, than any ball ever known before in the country, there is little that could be said of it to distinguish it from all others, except, perhaps, the curious fact that the master of the house was not present. He had not been visible all day. He had been telegraphed for to go to town that morning, and had not returned; but then Mr Golden, who was a far more useful man in a ball-room than the master of the house, was present, and was doing all that became a man to make everything go off brilliantly. He was the slave of the young heroine of the feast to whom everybody was paying homage; and it was remarked by a great many people, that even when going on the arm of Lord Merewether to open the ball, Clara had a suggestion to whisper to this amateur majordomo. 'He is such an old friend; he is just the same as papa,' she said to her partner with a passing blush; but then Clara was in uncommonly brilliant looks that evening, even for her. Her beautiful colour kept coming and going; there was an air of emotion, and almost agitation, about her, which gave a charm to her usually unemotional style of beauty. Lord Merewether, who was under his mother's orders to be 'very attentive,' almost fell in love with Clara, in excess of his instructions, when he noticed this unusual fluctuation of colour and tone. It supplied just what she wanted, and made the Rubens into a goddess—or so at least this young man thought.

But Helen had not been above an hour in this gay scene when a strange restlessness seized upon her. She did her best to struggle against it; she tried hard to represent to herself that nothing could have happened at home, no post could have come in since she left it, and that Norah needed her there. She saw Mr Rivers hovering about with his explanation on his lips trying to get at her, since Norah would have nothing to say to him; and felt that it was her duty to remain by her child at such a moment. But, after a while, her nerves, or her imagination, or some incomprehensible influence was too much for her. 'You look as if you would faint,' Mrs Dalton whispered to her. 'Let Mr Dalton take you to the air—let Charlie get you something; I am sure you are ill.'

'I am not ill; but I must get home. I am wanted at home,' said Helen with her brain swimming. How it was that she did it, she never could tell afterwards; but she managed to retain command of herself, to recommend Norah to Mrs Dalton's care, and finally to steal out; no one noticing her in the commotion and movement that were always going on. When she got into the open air with her shawl wrapped about her, her senses came back. It was foolish, it was absurd—but the deed was done; and, though her restlessness calmed down when she stepped out into the calm of the summer night, it was easier then to go on than to go back; and Norah was in safe hands. It was a moonlight night, as is indispensable for any great gathering in the country. To be sure it was July, and before the guests went home, the short night would be over; but still, according to habit, a moonlight night had been selected. It was soft, and warm, and hazy,—the light very mellow, and not over bright,—the scent of the flowers and the glitter of the dew filling the air. There was so much moon, and so much light from the house, that Helen was not afraid of the dark avenue. She went on, relieved of her anxiety, feeling refreshed and eased, she could not tell how, by the blowing of the scented night-air in her face. But before she reached the shade of the avenue, some one rushed across the lawn after her. She turned half round to see who it was, thinking that perhaps Charlie or Mr Dalton had hurried after her to accompany her home. The figure, however, was not that of either. The man came hurriedly up to her, saying, in a low but earnest tone, 'Mrs Burton, don't take any rash step,' when she, as well as he, suddenly started. The voice informed her who spoke, and the sight of her upturned face in the moonlight informed him who listened. 'Mrs Drummond!' he exclaimed. They had not met face to face, nor exchanged words since the time when she denounced him in the presence of Cyril Rivers in St Mary's Road. 'Mrs Drummond,' he repeated, with an uneasy laugh; 'of all times in the world for you and me to meet!'

'I hope there is no reason why we should meet,' said Helen impetuously. 'I am going away. There can be nothing that wants saying between you and me.'

'But, by Jove, there is though,' he said; 'there is reason enough, I can tell you—such news as will make the hair stand upright on your head. Ah! they say revenge is sweet. I shall leave you to find it out to-morrow when everybody knows.'

'What is it?' she asked breathlessly, and then stopped, and went on a few steps, horrified at the thought of thus asking information from the man she hated most. He went on along with her, saying nothing. He had no hat on, and the rose in his coat showed a little gleam of colour in the whitening of the light.

'You ought to ask me, Mrs Drummond,' he said; 'for revenge, they say, is sweet, and you would be glad to hear.'

'I want no revenge,' she said hurriedly; and they entered the gloom of the avenue side by side, the strangest pair. Her heart began to beat and flutter—she could not tell why; for she feared nothing from him; and all at once there rose up a gleam of secret triumph in her. This man believed that Robert Drummond was dead, knew no better. What did she care for his news? if indeed she were to tell him hers!

'Well,' he said, after an interval, 'I see you are resolved not to ask, so I will tell you. I have my revenge in it too, Mrs Drummond; this night, when they are all dancing, Burton is off, with the police after him. It will be known to all the world to-morrow. You ought to be grateful to me for telling you that.'

'Burton is off!—the police—after him!' She did not take in the meaning of the words.

'You don't believe me, perhaps—neither did his wife just now; or at least so she pretended; but it is true. There was a time when he left me to bear the brunt, now it is his turn; and there is a ball at his house the same night!'

She interrupted him hurriedly. 'I don't know what you mean. I cannot believe you. What has he done?' she said.

Mr Golden laughed; and in the stillness his laugh sounded strangely echoing among the trees. He turned round on his heel, waving his hand to her. 'Only what all the rest of us have done,' he said. 'Good night; I am wanted at the ball. I have a great deal to do to-night.'

She stood for a moment where he had left her, wondering, half paralysed. And then she turned and went slowly down the avenue. She felt herself shake and tremble—she could not tell why. Was it this man's voice? Was it his laugh that sounded like something infernal? And what did it all mean? Helen, who was a brave woman by nature, felt a flutter of fear as she quickened her steps and went on. A ball at his house—the police after him. What did it mean? The silence of the long leafy road was so strange and deep after all the sound and movements; the music pursued her from behind, growing fainter and fainter as she went on; the world seemed to be all asleep, except that part of it which was making merry, dancing, and rejoicing at Dura. And now the eagerness to get home suddenly seized upon her again,—something must have happened since she left; some letter; perhaps—some one—come back.

When she got within sight of the Gatehouse, the moon was shining right down the village street as it did when it was at the full. All was quiet, silent, asleep. No, not all. Opposite her house, against the Rectory gates, two men were standing. As she went up into the shadow of the lime-trees, and rang the bell at her own door, one of them crossed the road, and came up to her touching his hat. 'Asking your pardon, ma'am,' he said, 'there is some one in your house, if you're the lady of this house, as oughtn't to be there.'

A thrill of great terror took possession of Helen. Her heart leapt to her mouth. 'I don't understand you. Who are you? And what do you want?' she asked, almost gasping for breath.

'I'm a member of the detective force. I ain't ashamed of my business,' said the man. 'We seen him go in, me and my mate. With your permission, ma'am, we'd like to go through the house.'

'Go through my house at this hour!' cried Helen. She heard the door opened behind her, but did not turn round. She was the guardian of the house, she alone, and of all who were in it, be they who they might. Her wits seemed to come to her all at once, as if she had found them groping in the dark. 'Have you any authority to go into my house? Am I obliged to let you in? Have you a warrant?'

'They've been a worriting already, ma'am, and you out,' said Susan's voice from behind. 'What business have they, I'd like to know, in a lady's house at this hour of the night?'

'Has any one come, Susan?' Helen said.

'Not a soul.'

She was standing with a candle in her hand, holding the door half open. The night air puffed the flame; and perhaps it was that too that made the shadow of Susan's cap tremble upon the panel of the door.

'I cannot possibly admit you at this hour,' said Mrs Drummond. 'To-morrow, If you come with any authority; but not to-night.'

She went into her own house, and closed the door. How still it was and dark, with Susan's candle only flickering through the gloom! And then Susan made a sudden clutch at her mistress's arm. She held the candle down to Helen's face, and peered into it, 'I've atook him into my own room,' she said.

CHAPTER VI

The Gatehouse was full of long, rambling, dark passages with mysterious closets at each elbow of them, or curious little unused rooms—passages which had struck terror to Norah's soul when she was a child, and which even now she thought it expedient to run through as speedily as possible, never feeling sure that she might not be caught by some ghostly intruder behind the half-shut doors. Mrs Drummond followed Susan through one of these intricate winding ways. It led to a corner room looking out upon the garden, and close to the kitchen, which was Susan's bed-chamber. For some forgotten reason or other there was a sort of window, three or four broad panes of glass let into the partition wall high up between this room and the kitchen, the consequence of which was that Susan's room always showed a faint light to the garden. This was her reason for taking it as the hiding-place for the strange guest.

Mrs Drummond went down the dark passage, feeling herself incapable of speech and almost of thought; a vague wonder why he should be so hotly pursued, and how it was that Susan should have known this and taken it upon herself to receive and shelter one who was a stranger to her, passed through Helen's mind. Both these things were strange and must be inquired into hereafter, but in the mean time her heart was beating too high with personal emotion to be able to think of anything else. Was it possible that thus strangely, thus suddenly, she was to meet him again from whom she had been so long parted? Their last interview rushed back upon her mind, and his appearance then. Seven years ago!—and a man changes altogether, becomes, people say, another being in seven years. This thought quivered vaguely through Helen's mind. So many thoughts went pursuing each other, swift and noiseless as ghosts. It was not above two minutes from the time she came into the hall until she stood at the threshold of Susan's room; but a whole world of questions, of reflections, had hurried through her thoughts. She trembled by intervals with a nervous shiver. Her heart beat so violently that it seemed at once to choke and to paralyse her. To see him again—to stand face to face with him who had come back out of the grave,—to change her whole being,—to be no more herself, no more Norah's mother, but Robert's wife again! Her whole frame began to shake as with one great pulse. It was not joy, it was not fear; it was the wonder of it, the miracle, the strange, strange, incomprehensible, incredible—Could he be there?—nothing more between the two who had been parted by death and silence but that closed door?

Susan turned round upon her just before they reached it. Susan, too, hard, bony woman, little given to emotion, was trembling. She wiped her eyes with her apron and gave a sniff that was almost a groan, and thrust the candle into Helen's hand.

'Oh, don't you be hard upon him, Miss Helen as was!' cried Susan with a sob; and turned and fled into her kitchen.

Helen stopped for a moment to steady herself—to steady the light of the poor candle which, held by such agitated, unsteady hands, was flickering wildly in her grasp. And then she opened the door.

Some one started and rose up suddenly with a movement which had at once fear and watchfulness in it. Her agitation blinded her so that she could not see. She held up the light,—if her misty eyes could have made him out,—and then all at once there came a voice which made her nerves steady in a moment, calmed down her pulses, restored to her self-command.

'Helen, is it you? I thought it must be my wife.'

The blood rushed back to Helen's heart with an ebb as sudden as the flow had been, making her faint and sick. But the revulsion of feeling was as strong, and gave her strength. The light gave a leap in her hand as she steadied herself, and threw a wild broken gleam upon him.

'Mr Burton,' she said, 'what are you doing here?'

'Then the news had not come,' he cried, with a certain relief; 'nobody knows as yet? Well, well, things are not so bad, then, as I thought.'

She put the candle on the table and looked at him. He was dressed in his morning clothes, those light-coloured summer garments which made his full person fuller, but which at this hour, and after the scene from which she had just come, looked strangely disorderly and out of place. His linen was crushed and soiled, and his coat, which was of a colour and material which showed specks and wrinkles as much as a woman's dress, had the look of having been worn for a week night and day. The air of the vagabond which comes so rapidly to a hunted man had come to him already, and mixed with his habitual air of respectability, of wealth and self-importance, in the most curious, almost pitiful way.

'Tell me,' she said, repeating her question almost without knowing what she said, 'why are you here?'

He did not answer immediately. He made an effort to put on his usual jaunty look, to speak with his usual jocular superiority. But something—whether it was the flickering, feeble light of the candle which showed him her face, or some instinct of his own, which necessity had quickened into life—made him aware all at once that the woman by his side was in a whirl of mental indecision, that she was wavering between two resolves, and that this was no time to trifle with her. In such circumstances sometimes a man will seize upon the best argument which skill could select, but sometimes also in his haste and excitement he snatches at the one which makes most against him. He said—

'I will tell you plainly, Helen. I am as your husband was when he went down to the river—that night.'

She gave a strange and sudden cry, and turning round made one quick step to the door. If she had not seen that Dives in the exhibition, if she had not been in the grip of wild hope and expectation, I think she would have gone straightway, driven by that sudden probing of the old wound, and given him up to his pursuers. At least that would have been her first impulse; but something turned her back. She turned to him again with a sudden fire kindled in her eyes.

'It was you who drove him there,' she said.

He made a little deprecating gesture with his hands, but he did not say anything. He saw in a moment that he had made a mistake.

'You drove him there,' she repeated, 'you and—that man; and now you come to me and think I will save you—to me, his wife. You drove him to despair, to ruin, and you think I am to save you. Why should I? What have you done that I should help you? You had no pity on him; you let him perish, you let him die. You injured me and mine beyond the reach of recovery; and now you put yourself into my hands—with your enemies outside!'

He gave a shudder, and looked at the window as if with a thought of escape; and then he turned round upon her, standing at bay.

'Well,' he said, 'you have your revenge; I am ruined too. I don't pretend to hide it from you; but I have no river at hand to escape into to hide all my troubles in,—but only a woman to taunt me that I have tried to be kind to—and my wife and my child dancing away close by. Listen; that is what you call comfort for a ruined man, is it not?'

He pointed towards Dura as he spoke. Just then a gust of the soft night-wind brought with it the sound of the music from the great house, that house ablaze with gaiety, with splendour, and light, where Clara Burton all jewelled and crowned with flowers was dancing at this moment, while her mother led the way to the gorgeous table where princes might have sat down. No doubt the whole scene rose before his imagination as it did before Helen's. He sat down upon Susan's rush-bottomed chair with a short laugh. One candle flickering in the dim place revealing all the homely furniture of the servant's bed-room. What a contrast! what a fate! Helen felt as every generous mind feels, humbled before the presence of the immediate sufferer. He had injured her, and she, perhaps, had suffered more deeply than Reginald Burton was capable of suffering; but it was his turn now; he had the first place. The sorrow was his before which even kings must bow.

While she stood there with pity stealing into her heart, he put down his head into his hands with a gesture of utter weariness.

'Whatever you are going to do,' he said faintly, 'let Susan give me something to eat first. I have had nothing to eat all day.'

This appeal made an end of all Helen's enmity. It had been deep, and hot, and bitter when all was well with him—but the first taste of revenge which Ned's disappearance gave her had appeased Mrs Drummond. It had been bitter, not sweet. And now this appeal overcame all her defences. If he had asked her to aid in his escape she might have resisted still. But he asked her for a meal. Tears of humiliation, of pitying shame, almost of a kind of tenderness came into her eyes. God help the man! Had it come to this?

She turned into the kitchen, where Susan sat bolt upright in a hard wooden chair before the fire, with her arms folded, the most watchful of sentinels. They had a momentary discussion what there was to set before him, and where it was to be served. Susan's opinion was very strongly in favour of the kitchen.

'Those villains 'ud see the lights to the front,' said Susan. 'And then Miss Norah, she'll be coming home, and folks with her. Them policemen is up to everything. The shutters don't close up to the very top; and if they was to climb into one o' the trees! And besides, there's a fire here.'

'It is too warm for a fire, Susan.'

'Not for them as is in trouble,' said the woman; and she had her way.

Helen arranged the table with her own hands, while Susan made up with her best skill an impromptu meal—not of the richest or choicest, for the larder at the Gatehouse was poorly enough supplied; but fortunately there had been something provided for next day's dinner which was available. And when the fugitive came in to the warm kitchen—he who the day before had made all the household miserable in Dura over the failure of a salmi—he warmed his hands with a shiver of returning comfort, and sniffed the poor cutlet as it cooked, and made a wretched attempt at a joke in the sudden sense of ease and solace that had come to him.

'He was always one for his joke, was Mr Reginald,' Susan said with a sob; and as for Helen, this poor pleasantry completed her prostration. The sight of him warming himself on this July night, eating so eagerly, like a man famished, filled her with an indescribable pity. It was not so much magnanimity on her part as utter failure on his. How could she lay sins to this man's charge, who was not great enough in himself to frighten a fly? The pity in her heart hurt her like an ache, and she was ashamed.

But what was to be done? She went softly, almost stealthily (with the strange feeling that they might hear her out of doors, of which she was not herself aware), up to her bed-room, which was over the drawing-room, and looked out into the moonlight. The men still kept their place, opposite at the Rectory gate—and now a third man, one of the Dura police, with his lantern in his hand, joined them. Helen was a woman full of all the natural prejudices and susceptibilities. Her pride received such a wound by the appearance of this policeman as it would be difficult to describe. Reginald Burton was her enemy, her antagonist; and yet now she remembered her cousin. The Burtons had been of unblemished good fame in all their branches till now. The shame which had been momentarily thrown upon her husband had been connected with so much anguish that Helen's pride had not been called uppermost. But now it seized upon her. The moment the Dura policeman appeared, it became evident to her that all the world knew, and the pang ran through her proud heart like a sudden arrow. Her kindred were disgraced, her own blood, the honest, good people in their graves; and Ned—poor, innocent Ned!—at the other end of the world. The pang was so sharp that it forced tears from her, though she was not given to weeping. A policeman! as if the man was a thief who was her own cousin, of her own blood! And then the question returned, What was to be done? I don't know what horrible vision of the culprit dragged through the street, with his ignominy visible to the whole world, rose before Helen's imagination. It did not occur to her that such a capture might be very decorously, very quietly made. She could think of nothing but the poor ragged wretch whom she had once seen handcuffed, his clothes all muddy with the falls he had got in struggling for his liberty, and a policeman on either side of him. This was the only form in which she could realise an arrest by the hands of justice. And to see the master of Dura thus dragged through the village, with all the people round, once so obsequious, staring with stupid, impudent wonder! Anything, anything rather than that! Helen ran down-stairs again, startling herself with the sound she made. In the quiet she could hear the knife and fork which were still busy in the kitchen, and the broken talk with Susan which the fugitive kept up. She heard him laugh, and it made her heart sick. This time she turned to the other side, to the long passage opposite to that which led to the kitchen, which was the way of communication with the apartments of the Haldanes. The door there, which was generally fastened, was open to-night, and the light was still in Stephen's window, and he himself, for the first time for years, had been left to this late hour in his chair. He was seated there, very still and motionless, when Helen entered. He had dropped asleep in his loneliness. The candles on the table before him threw a strange light upon the pallor of his face, upon the closed eyes, and head thrown back. His hair had grown grey in these seven years; his face had refined and softened in the long suffering, in the patient, still, leaden days which he had lived through, making no complaint. He looked like an apostle in this awful yet gentle stillness—and he looked as if he were dead.

But even Mrs Drummond's entrance was enough to rouse him—the rustle of her dress, or perhaps even the mere sense that there was some one near him. He opened his eyes dreamily.

'Well, mother, I hope you have enjoyed it,' he said, with a smile. Then suddenly becoming aware who his companion was, 'Mrs Drummond! I beg your pardon. What has happened?'

She came and stood by him, holding out her hand, which he took and held between his. There was a mutual pity between these two—a sympathy which was almost tenderness. They were so sorry for each other—so destitute of any power to help each other! Most touching and close of bonds!

'Something has happened,' she said. 'Mr Haldane, I have come to you for your advice.'

He looked up at her anxiously.

'Not Norah—not—any one arrived—'

'Oh, no, no; something shameful, painful, terrible. You know what is going on at the great house. Mr Haldane, Reginald Burton is here in Susan's kitchen, hidden, and men watching for him outside. Men—policemen! That is what I mean. And oh! what am I to do?'

He held her hand still, and his touch kept her calm. He did not say anything for a minute, except one low exclamation under his breath.

'Sit down,' he said. 'You are worn out. Is it very late?'

'Past midnight. By-and-by your mother will be back. Tell me first, while we are alone and can speak freely, what can I do?'

'He is hiding here,' said Stephen, 'and policemen outside? Then he is ruined, and found out. That is what you mean. Compose yourself, and tell me, if you can, what you know, and what you wish to do.'

'Oh, what does my wish matter?' she cried. 'I am asking you what is possible. I know little more than I tell you. He is here, worn-out, miserable, ruined, and the men watching to take him. I don't know how it has happened, why he came, or how they found it out; but so it is. They are there now in front of the house. How am I to get him out?'

'Is that the only question?' Stephen asked.

She looked at him with an impatience she could not restrain.

'What other question can there be, Mr Haldane? In a few minutes they will be back.'

'But there is another question,' he said. 'I believe this man has been our ruin—yours and mine—yours, Mrs Drummond, more fatally than mine. Golden was but one of his instruments, I believe—as guilty, but not more so. He has ruined us, and more than us—'

She wrung her hands in her impatience.

'Mr Haldane, I hear steps. We may but have a moment more.'

He put his hand upon her arm.

'Think!' he cried. 'Are we to let him go—to save him that he may ruin others? Is it just? Think what he has made us all suffer. Is there to be no punishment for him?'

'Oh, punishment!' she cried. 'Do you know what punishment means, when you make yourself the instrument of it? It means revenge; and there is nothing so bitter, nothing so terrible, as to see your own handiwork, and to think, "It was not God that did this; it was me."'

'How can you tell?'

'Oh, yes, I can tell. There was his son. I thought it was a just return for all the harm he had done when his poor boy—But Ned went away, and left everything. It was not my fault; it was not Norah's fault. Yet she had done it, and I had wished she might. No; no more revenge. How can I get him away?'

'I am not so forgiving as you,' he said.

Helen could not rest. She rose up from the seat she had drawn to his side, and went to the window. There were steps that frightened her moving about outside, and then there was the sound of voices.

'Come in and go over the house! Come in at this hour of the night!' said a voice. It was Miss Jane's voice, brisk and alert as usual. Helen hurried into the hall, to the door, where she could hear what was said.

'But Jane, Jane, if any one has got in? A thief—perhaps a murderer! Oh, my poor Stephen!'

'Nonsense, mother! If you like to stay outside there, I'll go over all the house with Susan, and let you know. Why, Mrs Drummond! Here are some men who want to come in to search for some one at this time of night.'

'I have told them already they should not come in,' said Helen.

She had opened the door, and stood in front of it with a temerity which she scarcely felt justified in; for how did she know they might not rush past her, and get in before she could stop them? Such was her idea—such was the idea of all the innocent people in the house. The Dura policeman was standing by with his truncheon and his lantern.

'I've told 'em, mum, as it's a mistake,' said that functionary; 'and that this 'ere is the quietest, most respectablest 'ouse—'

'Thanks, Wilkins,' said Helen.

It was a positive comfort to her, and did her good, this simple testimony. And to think that Wilkins knew no better than that!

'Will you keep near the house?' she said, turning to him, with that feeling that he was 'on our side' which had once prepossessed Norah in favour of Mr Rivers. 'My daughter will be coming back presently, and I don't want to have her annoyed or frightened with this story. No one except the people who belong to it shall enter this house to-night.'

'As you please, ma'am; but I hope you knows the penalty,' said the detective.

Helen did not know of any penalty, nor did she care. She was wound up to so high a strain of excitement, that had she been called upon to put her arm in the place of the bolt, or do any other futile heroic piece of resistance, she would not have hesitated. She closed the door upon Mrs Haldane and her daughter, one of whom was frightened and the other excited. As they all came into the hall, Susan became visible, with her candle in her hand, defending the passage to the kitchen. Something ludicrous, something pathetic and tragic and terrible was in the aspect of the house, and its guardians—had one been wise enough to perceive what it meant.

'If Susan will come with me,' said Miss Jane briskly; 'after that idiot of a man's romance, my mother will think we are all going to be murdered in our beds. If Susan will come with me, I'll go over all the house.'

'We have examined ours,' said Helen. 'Susan, go with Miss Jane. Mrs Haldane, Mr Stephen is tired, I think.'

'Stephen must not be alarmed,' said Mrs Haldane with hesitation. 'But are you sure it is safe? Do you really think it is safe? You see, after all, when our door is open it is one house. A man might run from one room to another. Oh, Jane—Mrs Drummond—if you will believe me, I can see a shadow down that passage! Oh, my dear, you are young and rash! The men will know better; let them come in.'

'I cannot allow them to come in. There is no one, I assure you, except your son, who wants your help.'

'You are like Jane,' said the old lady; 'you are so bold and rash. Oh, I wish I had begged them to stay all night. I wouldn't mind giving a shilling or two. Think if Stephen should be frightened! Oh, yes, I am going; but don't leave me, dear. I couldn't be alone; I shall be frightened of my life.'

This was how it was that Helen was in Stephen's room again when Miss Jane came down, bustling and satisfied.

'You may make yourself perfectly easy, mother. We have gone over all the rooms—looked under the beds and in the cupboards, and there is not a ghost of anything. Poor Susan is tired sitting up for us all; I told her I'd wait up for Norah. Well, now you don't ask any news of the ball, Stephen. Norah has danced the whole evening; I have never seen her sitting down once. Her dress is beautiful; and as for herself, my dear! But everybody was looking their best. I don't admire Clara Burton in a general way; but really Clara Burton was something splendid—Yes, yes, mother; of course we must get Stephen to bed.'

'Good-night,' said Helen, going up to him. She looked in his face wistfully; but now the opportunity was over, and what could he say? He held her hand a moment, feeling the tremor in it.

'Good-night,' he said; and then very low he added hurriedly, 'The gate into the Dura woods—the garden door.'

'Thanks,' she said, with a loud throb of her heart.

The excitement, the suspense, were carrying Helen far beyond her will or intention. She had been sensible of a struggle at first whether she would not betray the fugitive. Now her thoughts had progressed so fast and far, that she would have fought for him, putting even her slight strength in the way to defend him or protect his retreat. He was a man whom she almost hated; and yet all her thoughts were with him, wondering was he safe by himself, and what could be done to make him safer still. She left the Haldanes' side of the house eagerly, and hurried down the passage to the kitchen. He was there, in Susan's arm-chair before the fire. His meal was over, and he had turned to the fire again, and fallen into a doze. While she was moving about in a fever of anxiety, he himself with his head sunk on his breast, was unconscious of his own danger. Helen, who felt incapable of either resting or sleep, stood still and looked at him in a sort of stupor.

'Poor dear, poor dear!' said Susan, holding up her hand in warning, 'he's been worrited and worn out, and he's dozed off—the best thing he could do.'

He might rest, but she could not. She went down the few steps to the garden, and stole out into the night, cautiously opening and closing the door. The garden was walled all round. It was a productive, wealthy garden, which, even when the Gatehouse had been empty, was worth keeping up, and its doors and fastenings were all in good order. There was no chance of any one getting in by that side. Mrs Drummond stole out into the white moonlight, which suddenly surged upon her figure, and blazoned it all over with silver, and crept round, trembling at every pebble she disturbed, to the unused door which opened into the Dura woods. It had been made that there might be a rapid means of communication between the Gatehouse and the mansion, but it had never been used since the Drummonds came. She had forgotten this door until Stephen reminded her of its existence. It was partially hid behind a thicket of raspberry-bushes, which had grown high and strong in front. Fortunately, a rusted key was in the lock. With the greatest difficulty Helen turned it, feeling as if the sound, as it grated and resisted, raised whirlwinds of echoes all round her, and must betray what she was doing. Even when it was unlocked, it took all her strength to pull it open, for she could do no more. For one moment she pressed out into the dark, rustling woods. Through the foliage she could see the glance of the lights from the house and the moving flicker of carriage-lamps going down the avenue. The music came upon her with a sudden burst like an insult. Oh, heaven! to think that all this should be going on, the dancing and laughter, and him dozing there by Susan's kitchen fire!

She paused a little in the garden in the stillness—not for rest, but that she might arrange her thoughts, without interruption. But there was no stillness there that night. The music came to her on the soft wind, now lower, now louder; the sound of the carriage wheels coming and going kept up a low, continuous roll; now and then there would come the sound of a voice. It was still early; only a few timid guests who feared late hours, old people and spectators like the Haldanes, were leaving the ball. It was in full career. The very sky seemed flushed over Dura House, with its numberless lights.

Helen formed her plan as she crept about the garden in the moonlight. Oh, if some kindly cloud would but rise, and veil for a little this poor earth with its mysteries! But all was clear, well seen, visible; the clear night and the blue heavens were not pitiful, like Helen. Man is often hard upon man, heaven knows, yet it is man only who can feel for the troubles of mankind.

CHAPTER VII

While her mother was thus occupied Norah was taking her fill of pleasure. She 'danced every dance'— beatific fulfilment of every girlish wish in respect to a ball. She was so young and so fresh that this perpetual motion filled up the measure of her desires, and left her little time to think. To be sure, once or twice it had come over her that Ned, poor Ned, was not here to share in all this delight; and if Norah had been destitute of partners, or less sought than she thought her due, no doubt her heart would have been very heavy on account of Ned. But she had as many partners as any girl could desire, and she had no time to think. She was as happy as the night was long. The dancing was delightful to her for itself, the music was delightful, and the 'kindness' of everybody, which was Norah's modest, pretty synonym for the admiration she received; and she asked no more of heaven than this, which she was receiving in such full measure. To be sure, her mother's disappearance disturbed her for the moment. But when Mrs Dalton had sworn by all her gods that Mrs Drummond was not ill, Norah resigned herself once more to her happy fate.

There was, at the same time, a special point which exhilarated Norah, satisfied her pride, and raised her spirits. During all the festivities of the afternoon she had kept Cyril Rivers at arm's length. Perhaps if he had not shown so much anxiety to approach nearer, Norah would not have felt the same satisfaction in this—but his explanation, it was evident, was hanging on his very lips, and she had triumphantly kept him from making it. The same process was repeated in the evening. She had rushed into a perfect crowd of engagements in order to escape him. Poor Charlie Dalton, whom Clara had no longer any thought of, and who for the greater part of the evening had been standing about, dolefully gazing after her, was pressed unceremoniously into Norah's service. Once, when she happened to be disengaged and saw Rivers approaching, she was so lost to all sense of shame as to seize him breathlessly by the arm. 'Dance this dance with me, Charlie,' she whispered impatiently.

'Why must I dance?' said the poor boy, who had no heart for it.

'Because I am determined not to dance with him,' said Norah, energetically leading off her captive. And thus she kept the other at a distance, though perhaps she would have been less rigid in evasion had he been more indifferent to the opportunity. It was late in the night, after supper, when he secured her at last.

'Miss Drummond, you have avoided me all night—'

'I!' cried Norah, 'but that is ridiculous. Why should I avoid you, Mr Rivers? Indeed I am sure I have spoken to you at least a dozen times this evening. It is not one's own fault when one is engaged.'

'And I have been so anxious to see you—to explain to you,' he cried, his eagerness, and the long, tantalizing delay having overcome his wisdom. 'I have been quite miserable.'

'About what, Mr. Rivers?'

'About what you must have thought very abominable behaviour—that day at the pictures; fancy, it is two months since, and you have never allowed me a moment in which I could say it till now!'

'At the pictures?' said Norah, feigning surprise. 'I don't think we have seen you very often lately, and two months is a long time to remember. Oh, I recollect! you left us in a hurry.'

'My mother had come to look for me—there was some business in hand that I had to be consulted about. I cannot tell you what a wretched ass I felt myself, dragged away without a moment to explain—without even time to say, "This is my mother."'

'Mr Rivers,' said Norah, drawing her small person to its full height, and loosing her hold of his arm, 'I think it would have been good taste not to say anything about this. When we did not remark upon it, why should you? I am only a girl, I am nineteen, and I never disobeyed mamma that I know of; but still, do you think I should have let her carry me off like a baby from my friends whom I cared for, without a word? There are some things that one ought not to be asked to believe. You were not obliged to say anything at all about it. I should like to be polite, but I can't make myself a fool to please you. And, on the other hand, you know Lady Rivers is nothing to us. I did not ask to be introduced to her, and poor mamma was too ill even to know. Please don't say any more about it. It would have been much better not to have mentioned it at all.'

'But, Miss Drummond!—'

'Yes, I know. You wanted to be polite. But never mind. I am quite, quite satisfied,' said Norah with a gleam of triumph. 'Look here! Let us have Katie for our vis-a-vis. Don't you think Clara Burton is looking quite beautiful to-night?'

Mr Rivers did not reply. He said to himself that he had never been so completely snubbed in his life. He had never felt so small, so cowed, and that is not pleasant to a man. Her very pardon, her condonation of his offence, was humbling to him. Had she resented it, he had a hundred weapons with which to meet her resentment; but he had not one to oppose to her frank indignation, and her pardon. And yet, with curious perversity, never before had Norah seemed so sweet to him. He had felt the wildest jealousy of poor Charlie during that dance, which he went through so unwillingly; and, but for the cheerful strains of the Lancers, which commenced at this point, and set them all—so many who enjoyed it, so many who did not enjoy it—in motion, it was in his mind to commit himself as he had never yet done—to throw himself upon her mercy. This thought gave to his handsome face a look which Norah in her triumph secretly enjoyed, and called 'sentimental.' 'But I am not one of those girls that fall down and worship a man, and think him a demigod,' Norah said to herself. 'He is no demigod! he has not so much courage as I have. He is frightened of—me! Oh, if Ned were but here!' This last little private exclamation was accompanied with the very ghost of a sigh—half of a quarter of a sigh, Norah would have said, had she described it—Ned was afraid of her too, and was not the least like a demigod. I do not defend Norah for her sauciness, nor do I blame her; for, after all, the young men of the present day are very unlike demigods; and there are some honest girls left in the world capable of loving a man as his wife ought, without worshipping him as his slave, and without even bowing herself down in delicious inferiority before him, grovelling as so many heroines do. Norah was incapable of grovelling under any circumstances; but then she had been brought up by her mother, in the traditions of womanly training such as they used to be in a world which we are told is past.

This is the very worst place in the world for a digression, I allow; it is to permit of the dancing of that figure which they were just about to commence. Clara Burton was dancing in the same set, with Mr Golden. And as her own partner after this little episode was for some time anything but lively, Norah gave her mind to the observation of Clara. Clara and Mr Golden were great friends. She had said to Lord Merewether that he was like papa, but it may be doubted whether papas generally, even when most indulgent, are looked up to by their children as Clara looked up to her father's friend. All Dura had remarked upon it before now; all Dura had wondered, did the parents see it? What did Mrs Burton mean by permitting it? But it never once entered into Mrs Burton's cool, clever little head to fancy it possible that the attractions of such a man could move her child. Everybody in the neighbourhood, except those most concerned, had seen Clara wandering with this man, who was nearly as old as her father, through the Dura woods. Everybody had seen the flushed, eager, tender way in which she hung upon him, and looked up to him; and his constant devotion to her. 'If I were you I should speak to Mr Burton about it,' the rector's wife had said half a dozen times over; but the rector had that constitutional dislike to interfere in anything which is peculiar to Englishmen. That night Clara was beautiful, as Norah had said; she was full of agitation and excitement—even of something which looked like feeling; her colour was splendid, her blue eyes as blue as the sea when it is stirred, her hair like masses of living gold, her complexion like the flushings of the sunset upon snow. As for her partner, a certain air of warning mingled in his assiduity. Once Norah saw him hold up his finger, as if in remonstrance. He was wary, watchful, observant of the glances round him; but Clara, who never restrained herself, put on no trammels to-night. She stood looking up at him, talking to him incessantly, forgetting the dance, and when she was compelled to remember it, hurrying through the figure that she might resume the intermitted conversation. Gradually the attention of the other dancers became concentrated on her. It was her moment of triumph, no doubt—her birthday, her coming of age as it were, though she was but eighteen—her entry, many people thought, into the glory of heiress-ship. But all this was not enough to account for the intoxication of excitement, the passion that blazed in Clara's eyes. What did it mean? When the dance was over, the majority of the dancers made their way into the coolness of the conservatory, which was lighted with soft lamps. Mr Rivers took Norah back to Mrs Dalton. His dark eyes had grown larger, his air more sentimental than ever. He withdrew a little way apart, and folded his arms, and stood gazing at her, just, Norah reflected with impatience, as a man would do who was the hero in a novel. But very different ideas were in Norah's mind. She seized upon Charlie once more, who was sentimental too. 'Come out on the terrace with me. I want to speak to Clara,' she said. They were stopped just inside the open window by a stream of people coming in for the next dance. Norah had been pushed close to the window, half in half out, by the throng. This was how she happened to hear the whispered talk of a pair outside, who were close by her without knowing it, and whom nobody else could hear.

'At the top of the avenue, at three o'clock. Wrap a cloak round you, my darling. In the string of carriages ours will never be noticed. It is the best plan.'

'And everything is ready?' asked another voice, which was Clara's.

'Everything, my love! In an hour and a half—'

'For you! I could do it only for you!'

In a minute after the two came in, pushing past Norah and her companion, who, both pale as statues, let them pass. The others were not pale. Clara's face was dyed with vivid colour, and Mr Golden, bending over her, looked almost young in the glow of animation and admiration with which he gazed at her. Charlie Dalton had not heard the scrap of dialogue, which meant so much; but he ground his teeth and stared at his supplanter, and crushed Norah's hand which held his arm. 'That fellow!' Charlie said between his teeth. 'Had it been some one else, I could have borne it.'

'Oh, Charlie, take me back to your mother,' cried Norah. Her thoughts went like the wind; already she had made out her plan—but what was the use of saying anything to him, poor simpleton, to make him more unhappy? Norah went back, and placed herself by Mrs Dalton's side. 'I do not mean to dance any more. I am tired,' she said; and, though the music tempted her, and her poor little feet danced in spite of her, keeping time on the floor, she did not change her resolution. Mr Rivers came, finding the opportunity he sought; but Norah paid no heed to him. The men whose names were written upon her card came too, in anxiety and dismay. But to all she had the same answer. 'I am tired. I shall dance no more to-night.'

'Let me look at you, child,' said kind Mrs Dalton; 'indeed you look tired—you look as if you had seen a ghost.'

'And so I have,' said Norah. She felt as if she must cry; Clara Burton had been her play-fellow, almost her sister, as near to her as Katie, and as much beloved. What was it Clara was going to do? The child shivered in her terror. When the dancers were all in full career once more, Norah put her mouth close to Mrs Dalton's ear and whispered forth her story. 'What can we do? What shall we do?' she asked. It would be impossible to describe Mrs Dalton's consternation. She remonstrated, struggled against the idea, protested that there must be some mistake. But still Norah asked, 'What can we do? what can we do?'

'My dear Norah! see, they are not near each other—they are not looking at each other. You have made a mistake.'

'Why should they look at each other? everything is arranged and settled,' said Norah. Mrs Dalton, if you will not come with me, I will go myself. Clara must not be allowed to go. Oh, only think of it! Clara, one of us! I have made up my plan; and if you will not come, I will go myself.'

'Norah, where will you go? What can you do—a child? And, oh, how can I go after Clara and leave the girls?' replied Mrs Dalton in her distress.

'You can leave them with Charlie,' said Norah. It had struck two before this explanation was made, and already a few additional guests had begun to depart. There was very little time to lose. Before Mrs Dalton was aware she found herself hurried into the cloak-room, wrapped in some wrap which was not hers, and out under the moonlight again, scarcely knowing how she got there.

'This is not my cloak, Norah,' she said piteously; 'my cloak was white.'

'Never mind, dear Mrs Dalton; white would have been seen,' said Norah, who was far too much excited to think of larceny. And then, impetuous as a little sprite, she led her friend round the farther side of the lawn, and placed her under the shadow of a clump of evergreens. 'There is a brougham standing here which never budges,' whispered Norah, 'with a white horse. I have seen him driving a white horse. Now stand very still. Oh, do stand still, please!'

'But, Norah, I see no one. It is Mrs Ashurst's old white horse; it is the fly from the inn. Norah, it is very cold. Our carriage will be coming. If it comes while we are gone—'

Norah grasped her tremulous companion by the arm. 'You would go barefoot from here to London,' she said in her ear, with a voice which was husky with excitement, 'to save any one, you know you would; and this is Clara—Clara!'

Some one came rapidly across the grass—a dark, veiled, hooded figure, keeping in the shadow. The morning was breaking in the east and mingled mysteriously with the moonlight, making a weird paleness all about among the dark trees and bushes. There was such a noise and ceaseless roll of carriages passing, of servants waiting about, of impatient horses, pawing and tossing their heads, that the very air was full of confusion. Mrs Dalton's alarm was undescribable. She held back the impetuous girl by her side, who was rushing upon that new-comer. 'Norah! it is some lady looking for her carriage. Norah!'

Norah paid no heed; she rushed forward, and laid hold upon the long grey cloak in which the new-comer was muffled. 'Clara!' she cried. 'Oh, Clara! stop, stop! and come back.'

At this moment there suddenly appeared among them another figure, in an overcoat, with a soft felt hat slouched over his face, who took Clara by the hand and whispered, 'Quick! there is not a moment to lose.'

'Is it you, Norah?' said Clara from under her cloak. 'You spy! you prying inquisitive—! Go back yourself. You have nothing to do with me.'

'Oh, Clara!' cried the other girl, clasping her hands; 'don't go away like this. It is almost morning. They will see you—in your ball dress. Clara, Clara, dear! Hate me if you like—only, for heaven's sake, come back.'

And now Mrs Dalton crept out from the shadow of the bushes. 'Mr Golden, leave her. Let her go. How dare you over-persuade a child like that? Let her go, or I will call out to stop you. Clara!'

He pushed them apart—one to one side, one to the other. 'Quick!' he cried, with a low call to a servant who stood close by. 'Quick, Clara! don't lose a moment.' He had pushed them aside roughly, and stood guarding her retreat, facing round upon them. 'What is it to you,' he said, 'if I am employed to take Miss Burton to her father? You may call any one you please—you may go and tell her mother. I am coming—now, for your life!'

The brougham dashed off with dangerous speed, charging, as it seemed, into the mass of carriages. There was a tumult and trampling of horses, a cry as of some one hurt; but all that the two terrified women on the lawn saw was Clara's face, looking back at them from the carriage window, with an insolent, triumphant look. She had partially thrown off her cloak, and appeared from under it in her white dress, a beautiful, strange vision—and then there came the sound of the collision and conflict, and the struggle of horses, and the cry. But whoever was wounded, it was not anybody belonging to that equipage. The white horse could be traced down the avenue like a long, lessening streak of light. So far, at least, the scheme had been successful. They were gone.

Norah could not speak; she walked about upon the lawn, among the servants, wringing her hands. The morning dew, which was beginning to fall, shone wet upon her hair. 'What can we do—what can we do?' she cried.

'My dear child, we have done all we can. Oh, that foolish, foolish girl! Norah, your feet must be wet, and so I am sure are mine; and your pretty white tarlatan all spoiled. Oh, heaven help us! is this what it has all come to? I dare not send Charlie after them. Norah, run and call Mr Dalton. He might go, perhaps. Norah, oh, you must not go alone!' cried the rector's wife.

But Norah was gone. She rushed into the house, through all the departing guests, her cloak and her hair all wet with dew. She made her way into the ball-room in that plight, and rushed up to Mr Dalton, and led him alarmed out into the hall. Mrs Dalton had followed, and was slowly gathering up her dress. Her heart was full of dismay and trouble; that Clara should thus destroy herself—break her parents' hearts! and Norah must certainly have spoilt her pretty new dress. 'One would not have minded had it done any good,' she murmured within herself. When they met the rector in the hall, a hurried consultation ensued.

'Take our fly, George,' said Mrs Dalton heroically. 'We can get home somehow. Take it! They cannot be very far gone—you may overtake them yet.'

'Overtake them! Though I don't even know which way they have gone,' said the rector, fretful with this strange mission. But, all the same, he went off, and hunted out the fly, and offered the driver half a sovereign if he could overtake the brougham with a white horse. But everything retarded Mr Dalton. His horse was but a fly horse, not the most lively of his kind. The man had been drinking Miss Burton's health, and was more disposed to continue that exercise than to gallop vaguely about the roads, even with the promise of an additional half-sovereign; Mrs Dalton, in the mean while, threw off her borrowed cloak, and went into the almost deserted ball-room in search of the mistress of the house; and Mary and Katie, wondering and shivering, standing close to Charlie, who was their protector for the moment, made a group round Norah in the hall, with the daylight every moment brightening over their faces, weariness stealing over them, and mystery oppressing them, and no appearance of either father or mother, or the fly!

Norah leant against Katie's shoulder and cried. After all her impetuous exertions the reaction was sharp. She would not give any explanation, but leant upon her friend, and cried, and shivered.

'Oh, where can mamma be? Where is the fly? Oh, Norah, have my cloak too; I don't want it. How cold you are! Charlie, run and look for the fly,' cried Katie. They stood all clinging together, while the people streamed past, getting into their carriages, going away. The daylight grew clearer, the sun began to rise, while still they stood there forlorn. And what with weariness, what with wonder and anxiety and vexation, Mary and Katie were almost crying too.

Finally Mrs Dalton appeared, when almost all the guests were gone, with a flush on her kind face, and an energy which triumphed over her weariness. 'Come, children, we must pluck up our courage and walk,' she said. 'Take up your dresses, girls, and help Norah with hers. Poor child, perhaps the walk will be the best thing for her. It is of no use waiting for the fly.'

Here Charlie came back to report that the fly was nowhere visible, but that some one who had been knocked down by a runaway horse was being carried up to the house, much injured. 'A white horse in a brougham. They say it took fright, and dashed down the avenue; and they are afraid the man is badly hurt,' said Charlie. The ladies shuddered as the poor fellow was carried past them, his head bound round with a handkerchief stained with blood. They were the last to leave, and came down the steps just as this figure was being carried in. It was broad daylight now, and they all felt guilty and miserable in their ball dresses. This was how the last ball ended which was given by the Burtons in Dura House.

They walked down weary, feeling some weight upon them which the majority of the party did not understand, all the length of the leafy avenue, where the birds were singing, and the new morning sending arrows of gold. The fly, with Mr Dalton in it, very tired and fretful, met them at the gate. He had not so much as come within sight of the brougham with the white horse. But yet he was ready to go up to the great house as duty demanded, to put himself at the service of its mistress. Charlie, enlightened all in a moment as to the meaning of the night's proceedings, went with him, like a ghost of misery and wrath. The girls and the mother went home alone through the sunshine. And the echoes grew still about that centre of tumult and rejoicing. The rejoicing had ended now; and, with that feast, the reign of the Burtons at Dura had come to an end.

CHAPTER VIII

A summer night passes quickly to those who have need of darkness for their movements. When Mrs Drummond found herself at liberty to carry out the plan she had formed, the time before her was very short. She went back to the kitchen, and called Susan to her. Mr Burton woke up as she came in, and they had a hurried consultation; the consequence of which was that Susan was sent to the stables, which were not very far from the garden door of the Gatehouse, to order a carriage to be dispatched instantly to pick up Mr Burton at the north gate, two miles off, in the opposite direction from the village. He could walk thus through the grounds by paths he was familiar with, and drive to a station five miles further off on another railway. So readily do even innocence and ignorance fall into the shifty ways of guilt that this was Helen's plan. He was to wait here till Susan returned, and the experiment of her going would be a proof if the way was quite safe for him. When Susan was gone Mrs Drummond returned alone to where her guest sat before the kitchen fire. She had her blotting-book under her arm, and an inkstand in her hand. 'Before you go,' she said in a low voice, 'I want you to do something for me.'

'I will do anything for you,' he cried—'anything! Helen, I have not deserved it. You might have treated me very differently. You have been my salvation.'

'Hush!' she said. His thanks recalled her old feelings of distrust and dislike rather than the new ones of pity. She put down her writing things on the table. 'I have my conditions as well as other people,' she said. 'I want now to know the truth.'

'What truth?'

'About Rivers's,' she said.

'Helen!'

'It is useless for you to resist or deny me,' she replied, 'you are in my power. I am willing to do everything to serve you, but I will have a full explanation. Write it how you please—but you shall not leave this place till you have given me the means, when I please, and how I please, of proving the truth.'

'What is the truth, as you call it?' he said sullenly; 'what have I to do with it? Drummond and the rest went into it with their eyes open; all the accounts of the concern were open to them.'

'I do not pretend to understand it,' said Helen. 'But you do. Here are pens and paper. I insist upon a full explanation—how it was that so flourishing a business perished in three years; where those books went to, which Robert was so falsely accused of destroying. Oh, are you not afraid to tire out my patience? Do you know that you are in my power?'

He gave an alarmed look at her. He had forgotten everything but those fables about feminine weakness which are current among such men, and had half laughed in his sleeve half an hour before at her readiness to help and serve him. But now all at once he perceived that laughter was out of place, and there was no time to lose. The reflection that ran through his mind was—All must come out in a week or two—it will do her no good; but it can do me no harm. 'If I am to give an account of the whole history it will take me hours,' he said. 'I may as well give up all thought of getting away to-night.' But he drew the blotting-book towards him. Helen did not relax nor falter. She lighted another candle; she left him to himself with a serious belief in his good faith which startled him. She moved about the kitchen while he wrote, filling a small flask with wine out of the solitary bottle which had been brought out for his refreshment, and which represented the entire cellar of the Gatehouse—even brushing the coat which he had thrown aside, that it might be ready for him. The man watched her with the wonder of an inferior nature. He had loved her once, and it had given him a true pleasure to humble her when the moment came. But now the ascendancy had returned into her hands. Had he been in her place how he would have triumphed! But Helen did not triumph. His misery did not please, it bowed her down to the ground. She was sad—suffering for him, ashamed, anxious. He did not understand it. Gradually, he could not have told how, her look affected him. He tore up the first statement he had commenced, a florid, apologetic narrative. He tore up the second, in which he threw the blame upon the ignorance of business of poor Drummond and his fellow-directors. Finally he was moved so strangely out of himself that he wrote the simple truth, and no more, without a word of apology or explanation. Half-a-dozen lines were enough for that. The apology would, as he said, have taken hours.

And then Susan came back. By this time he had written not only the explanation required of him, but a letter to his wife, and was ready to try his fate once more. Helen herself went with him to the garden door; the path through the woods was dark, hidden from the moonlight by the close copses and high fence, which it skirted for many a mile. And there would not be daylight to betray him for at least an hour. He stood on the verge of the dark wood, and took her hand. 'Helen, you have saved me: God bless you,' he said. And in a moment this strange episode was over, as though it had never been. She stood under the rustling trees, and listened to his footsteps. The night wind blew chill in her face, the dark boughs swayed round her as if catching at her garments. A hundred little crackling sounds, echoes, movements among the copse, all the jars and broken tones of nature that startle the fugitive, made her heart beat with terror. If she had felt a hand on her shoulder, seizing her instead of him, Helen would not have been surprised. But while she stood and listened all the sounds seemed to die away again in the stillness of the night. And the broad moonlight shone, silvering the black trees, out of which all individuality had fled, and the music from Dura came back in a gust, and the roll of the carriages slowly moving about the avenue, waiting for the dancers. And but that Helen stood in so unusual a spot, with that garden door half open behind her, and the big key in her hand, she might have thought that all this was nothing more than a dream.

She went in, and locked the door; and then returned to Susan's kitchen. It was her turn now to feel the cold, after her excitement was over; she went in shivering, and drew close to the fire. She put her head down into her hands. The tears came to her eyes unawares; weariness had come upon her all at once, when the necessity of exertion was over. She held in her hand the paper she had made Burton write, but she had not energy enough to look at it. Would it ever be of any use to her? Would he whom it concerned ever return? Or was all this—the picture, the visit to the Exhibition, the sudden conviction which had seized upon her—were these all so many delusions in her dream? After a while Miss Jane, all unconscious, excited with her unusual pleasure, and full of everything she had seen, came and sat by her and talked. 'I told Susan to go to bed,' said Miss Jane; 'and I wish you would go too, Mrs Drummond. I will sit up for Norah. Oh, how proud I was of that child to-night! I suppose it's very wrong, you know—so my mother says—but I can't help it. It is just as well I am a single woman, and have no children of my own; for I should have been a fool about them. The worst of all is that we shan't keep her long. She will marry, and then what shall we do? I am sure to lose her would break Stephen's heart.'

'She is very young,' said Helen, who answered for civility's sake alone, and who with all the heavy thoughts in her heart and apprehensions for the fugitive, would have given much to be left to herself.

'Yes, she is young; but not too young to do a great deal of mischief. When I saw all those men on their knees before her!' cried Miss Jane, with a laugh of triumph. She had never been an object of much admiration or homage herself; men had not gone on their knees to her, though no doubt she was more worthy than many of the foolish creatures who have been so worshipped; but the result of this was that Miss Jane enjoyed heartily the revenge which other women had it in their power to take for all the slights and scorns to which she and her homely sisters had been subjected. She liked to see 'them' punished, though 'they' were an innocent, new generation, blameless, so far as she was concerned. She would not have injured a fly; but her face beamed all over with delight at the thought that it was Norah's mission to break hearts.

Thus the good soul sat and talked, while Helen listened to every sound, and wondered where was he now? what might be happening? She did not even hear what was being said to her until Miss Jane fell into a moralising vein. 'The Burtons are at the height of their splendour now,' she said. 'I never saw anything so grand as it was. I don't think anything could be grander. But oh, Mrs Drummond, people's sins find them out. There's Clara getting bewitched by that man; everybody could see it. A man old enough to be her father, without a scrap of character, and no money even, I suppose. Think of that! and oh, what will all their grandeur do for them, with Ned at the other end of the world, and Clara throwing herself away?'

'Oh, hush, hush!' cried Helen. 'Don't prophesy any more misfortune; there is enough without that.'

And five minutes after Norah came to the door, surrounded by the party from the Rectory, all pale and terror-stricken, with the news which they felt to be so terrible. 'Clara has gone away!' They stood at the door and told this tale, huddled together in the fresh sunshine, the girls crying, the elder women asking each other, 'what would the Burtons do?' 'She was almost rude to me. She sent me away,' Mrs Dalton said, 'or I should have stayed with her. And Mr Burton is not there! What will she do?' They could scarcely make up their minds to separate, worn out and miserable as they all were. And, opposite, in the morning sunshine, two men still watched the Gatehouse, as they had watched it all through the night.

These miseries all ended in a misery which was comic, had any of them had heart enough left to laugh. While she helped to undress Norah, Miss Jane suddenly uttered a scream, which made Helen tremble from head to foot. She had caught in her hands the pretty flounces of that white dress, that lovely dress, Dr Maurice's present, which had turned poor little Cinderella-Norah into an enchanted princess; but now, alas, all limp, damp, ruined! even stained with the dewy grass and gravel across which it had come. Miss Jane could have cried with vexation and dismay. This was the climax of all the agonies of that wonderful night; but, fortunately, it was not so hopeless as the others. An hour later, when the house was all silent, and even Helen lay with her eyes shut, longing to sleep, Miss Jane stole down-stairs again, carrying this melancholy garment on her arm. She went to Susan's kitchen, where the fire was still burning, and spreading it out upon the big table, took it to pieces to see what could be done. And then she made a discovery which drew from her a cry of joy. The dress was grenadine, not tarlatan! Dear, ignorant reader, perhaps you do not know what this means? but well did Miss Jane understand. 'Grenadine will wash!' she said to herself triumphantly. She was a clever woman, and she was not unconscious of the fact. She could wash and starch with any professional. Accordingly, she set to work with scissors and soap and starch and hot irons; but, above all, with love—love which makes the fingers cunning and the courage strong.

Mr Burton made his escape safely. He had reached the north gate before the dog-cart did, which came up for him just as the morning was breaking. With this delay it so happened that when he reached the station to which he was bound, a brougham with a white horse appeared in sight behind, and gave him a thrill of terror; it was not a likely vehicle certainly for his pursuers; but still it was possible that they might have found nothing more suitable had they got scent of him at Dura. He sprang out of the dog-cart accordingly, and took refuge in one of the corners of the station. It was a junction, and two early morning trains, one up and one down, passed between four and five o'clock. Both parties accordingly had some time to wait. Mr Burton skulking behind anything that would shelter him, made out, to his great amazement, that the other traveller waiting about was his friend Golden, accompanied by a cloaked and veiled woman. The fugitive grinned in ghastly satisfaction when he saw it. He had no desire just then to encounter Golden, and in such companionship he was safe. It was a lovely morning, fresh and soft, cooler than July usually is, and the pair on the platform walked about in the sun, basking in it. He watched them from behind a line of empty carriages. The woman, whoever she was, clung close to her companion, holding his arm clasped with both her hands; while Golden bent over her, with his face close to her veil. 'I wonder who she is? I wonder what they are doing here at this hour? I wonder if he has been to Dura? And, by Jove, to think of his going in for that sort of thing, as if he were five-and-twenty!' Mr Burton said to himself. He was full of curiosity, almost of amazement, and he longed to go and sun himself on that same platform too; but he was a fugitive, and he dared not. How could he tell who might be about, or what Golden's feelings were towards him? They had been very good friends once; but Burton had stood by Golden but feebly at the time of the trial about Rivers's, and Golden had not stood by Burton warmly during the time of difficulty which had culminated in ruin. He watched them with growing curiosity, with a kind of interest which he could not understand—with—yes, he could not deny it, with a curious wistfulness and envy. He supposed the fellow was happy like that, now? And as for himself, he was not happy—he was cold, weary, anxious, afraid. He had a prison before him, perhaps a felon's sentence—anyhow, at the least, a loud, hoarse roar of English society and the newspapers. If he could but succeed in putting the Channel between him and them! and there was that other man, as guilty as himself, perhaps more guilty ('for he had not my temptations,' Mr Burton said to himself; 'he had not a position to keep up, an expensive establishment, a family'), sunning himself in the full morning light, waiting for his train in the eye of day, not afraid of anybody—nay, probably at the height of pleasure and success, enjoying himself as a young man enjoys himself! When the pair approached a little closer to his hiding-place than they had yet done, Burton, in his haste to get out of the way, slipped his foot, and fell upon the cold iron rails. He rose with a curse in his heart, the poignancy of the contrast was too much for him. Had he but known that his appearance would have confounded his old friend, and set all his plans to nought! Could he but have imagined who it was that clung to Golden's arm!

But he did not. He saw the up-train arrive, and the two get into it. He had meant to go that way himself, feeling London, of all refuges, the most safe; but he had not courage to venture now. He waited for the other train going down into the country. He made a rapid calculation how he could shape his course to the sea, and get off, if not as directly, perhaps more securely. He had found a dark overcoat in the dog-cart, which was a boon to him; he had poor Helen's flask of wine in his pocket. And as he got into the train, and dashed away out of the station and over the silent, sunshiny country, where safety lay, Golden and Golden's companion went out of Mr Burton's mind. He had a hundred things to think of, and yet a hundred more. Why should he trouble himself about that?

Thus the night disappeared like a mist from the face of the world; and the 7th of July, an ordinary working day like the others,—Saturday, the end of a common week,—rose up business-like and usual upon a host of toiling folk, to whom the sight of it was sweet for the sake of the resting day that came after it. Old Ann from Dura Den drove her cart with the vegetables, and the big posy for the sick gentleman, under Stephen's window, and wondered that it should still be closed, though it was ten o'clock. Susan, very heavy-eyed and pale, was cleansing and whitening her steps, upon which there had been so many footsteps last night.

'Well, Susan, you are late,' said old Ann.

'Our folks were all at that ball last night,' said Susan, 'keeping a body up, awaiting for 'em till morning light.'

'Well, well, young folks must have their diversions. We was fond of 'em oursels once on a day,' said the charitable old woman.

Across the road the blinds were still down in the Rectory. The young people were all asleep; and even the elder people had been overcome with weariness and the excitement through which, more or less, all of them had gone. Before old Ann's cart resumed its progress, however, Stephen's window had been opened, and signs of life began to appear. About eleven Mrs Drummond came down-stairs. She had slept for an hour, and on waking had felt assured that she must have been dreaming, and that all her vision of the night was a delusion; but her head ached so, and her face was so pale when she looked at herself in the glass, that Helen trembled and asked herself if this was the beginning of a fever. Something must have happened—it could not all be a dream. She knelt down to say her prayers in front of the table, where her picture, her idol, was. And then she saw a paper, placed upright beneath it, as flowers might be put at a shrine. She read it then, for the first time, on her knees. It was the paper that Reginald Burton had written, which she had taken from him in her weariness without being able to read it. Half-a-dozen lines, no more. She did not understand it now; but it was enough, it was final. No one, after this, could throw reproach or scorn upon her Robert's name.

Robert! This night had been like a year, like a lifetime. It had made her forget. Now she knelt there, and everything came back to her. She did not say her prayers; the attitude sometimes is all that the heavy-laden are capable of; of itself that attitude is an appeal to God, such as a child might make who plucked at its mother's dress to attract her notice, and looked up to her, though it could find no words to say. Not a word came to Helen's lips. She knelt and recollected, and thought—her mind was in a whirl, yet it was silent, not even forming a wish. It was as if she held her breath and gazed upon something which had taken place before her, something with which she had no connection. 'I have seen the wicked great in power, like a green bay-tree; and I passed again, and lo! he was not.' Was that the story, written in ruin, written in tears? And Robert! Where was he—he who had stretched out his hands to her in the depths of despair, from hell, from across the Atlantic, from—where?

Helen rose up piteously, and that suspense which had been momentarily dispossessed by the urgency of more immediate claims upon her attention, came back again, and tore her heart in twain. Oh, they might think her foolish who did not know! but who else except Robert could have seized her very heart with those two up-stretched hands of Dives, hands that could have drawn her down, had she been there, out of the highest heaven? She could trust no longer, she thought, to the lukewarm interest of friends—to men who did not understand. She must bestir herself to find out. She must find out if she should die.

Thus, with dry, bright eyes, and a fire new-lit in her heart which burned and scorched her, she went down-stairs into the common world. 'I will bring your breakfast directly, 'm,' said Susan, meeting her in the passage, and Helen went in to the old, ghostly drawing-room, the place which had grown so familiar to her, almost dear.

Was it the old drawing-room she had lived in yesterday? or what strange vision was it that came across her of another room, far different, a summer evening as this was a summer morning, a child who cried 'Mamma, here is a letter!' Nothing—nothing! only a mere association, one of the tricks fancy plays us. This feverish start, this sudden swimming of the head, and wild question whether she was back in St Mary's Road, or where she was, arose from the sight of a letter which lay, awaiting her, on the centre of a little round table. It lay as that letter had lain some years ago, in which he took his leave of her—as a hundred letters must have lain since. A common letter, thrown down carelessly, without any meaning. Oh, fool, fool that she was!

Mrs Burton was alone in her deserted house. The house was not deserted in the common sense of the word. Up-stairs at this very moment it was buzzing with life and movement; and at least the young men in the smoking-room—men who had come from town, from their duties and their pleasures, expressly for the ball—were commenting to each other carelessly upon the absence of their host. 'Young Burton has been off for six months on a wandering fit, and old Burton is up to the eyes in business, as usual,' Cyril Rivers explained, who was not unfriendly to his entertainers; while the Marchioness, with Lady Florizel in the room of state up-stairs, who was commenting upon Clara's behaviour, and declaring her intention to leave next morning. 'Fortunately, Merewether has not committed himself,' the Marchioness was saying. In another room of the house, Mrs Burton's two aunts, supported by their two maids, were shaking their heads together in mingled sorrow and anger. 'Depend upon it, something will come of all this,' Mrs Everest said, as she put on her nightcap; and Aunt Louisa cried, and exclaimed that when Clara entered on such an extravagant course, she always knew that some chastisement must come. 'I would shut that child up, and feed her on bread and water,' cried the stronger-minded sister; and so said the maids, who thought Miss Clary was bewitched—and with such a man!

While all this was going on, little Mrs Burton was alone in the ball-room, which was still blazing with lights. She was seated wearily in a big chair at one end. But for her diamonds, which sought the light, and made a blaze of radiance round about her, like the aureole of a saint, she would have been invisible in the great, spacious, empty room. A deserted ball-room has been so often described, that I will not repeat the unnecessary picture. This ball-room, however, had not a dismal aspect; everything was too well managed for that. The flowers, arranged in great brilliant banks of colour, were not fading, but looked as brilliant as ever; the lights shone as brightly. Except for some flowers dropped about from the bouquets of the dancers, some shreds of lace and tulle torn from their dresses, it might have been before instead of after the ball. Mrs Burton was seated at the further end. She sat quite motionless, her hands crossed in her lap, her diamonds reflecting the light. What a night this had been for her! The other parties concerned had each had their share—her husband his ruin, her child her elopement; but this small woman with her hands clasped, with this crowded house to regulate and manage, with her part still to play in the world around her, knew all and had all to bear. She sat thus among the ruins, nothing hid from her, nothing postponed. Through her slight little frame there was a dull throbbing of pain; but her head was clear, and did not lose a jot of all that fate had done, of all it had in store. She did not complain. She had foreseen much; she had gone forward with her eyes open; she had even said that were her husband to be bankrupt in two days, she would give a ball on the intermediate night. If it was a brag, she had excelled that brag; she had given her greatest ball, and reached her apotheosis, on the very night when he was flying from justice. And no good angel had interfered to soften to her the news of these successive blows. She had herself opened the ball with old Lord Bobadil—the man of highest rank present; and it was when she had resumed her seat after that solemn ceremonial that Golden, whom she hated, approached her, and whispered in her ear the news of her husband's ruin. She had been prepared for the news, but not then, nor at such a moment; nevertheless, she stood up and received the blow without a cry, without a moment's failure of her desperate courage. And everything had gone on. She was always pale, so that there was nothing to betray her so far as that went, and her cares as hostess never relaxed. She went from side to side, dispensing her attentions, looking after everybody's comfort as if she had been a queen, and all the time asking herself had he been taken? was he a prisoner? how much shame should she have to bear? Then, when the slow hours had gone on, and the insupportable din about her seemed as if it must soon come to an end, there arrived that other messenger of woe, poor kind Mrs Dalton, with tears in her eyes, and a voice which faltered. 'The rector has gone after them. Oh, will you let me stay with you? Can I be of any use to you?' Mrs Dalton had sobbed, attracting, as the other woman—the real sufferer—knew, the attention of those groups about, who had no right to know anything of her private sorrows. 'It is not necessary. My father is here, and my aunts. I can have everything done that is wanted,' Mrs Burton replied: and she had turned round to show some one who came to ask her where the basket was with all the ribbons, and flowers, and pretty toys for the cotillion. Through all this she had stood her ground. She had shaken hands with the last of her guests and had seen the visitors to their rooms before she gave in; and even now she was not giving in. Had any one entered the empty room, Mrs Burton would have proved equal to the occasion; she would have risen to meet them—have talked on any subject with perfect self-command. But, fortunately, no one came.

Poor old Mr Baldwin had arrived at Dura only that night, he had heard a great many disquieting rumours, and he was very unhappy about his son-in-law's position, and about the way in which his daughter took it. Even the fact that she had her settlement scarcely consoled him; for he said to himself that the creditors would 'reflect' upon all this extravagance, and that even about the settlement itself a great deal would be said. He had hovered about her all the evening, looking wistfully at her, inviting her confidence; but Mrs Burton had not said a word to him, even of her daughter's disappearance. She had felt no impulse to do anything about Clary. Whether it was that all her energy was required to bear up against those successive blows, or if her pride shrank from informing even her own friends, or finally, if she felt it useless, and knew that now no power on earth could compel the self-willed girl to return, it is certain that Mrs Burton had 'taken no steps.' Even now she did not think of taking any steps. She allowed her father and her aunts to go to bed without a word. She sat and pondered, and did nothing. Alone in that great blazing deserted room—alone in the house—alone in the world: this was what she felt. Out of doors the birds were singing and the sun shining; but the closed windows admitted only the palest gleam of the daylight. When the servants came to tell her that Mr Dalton was at the door, asking to see her, she sent him a civil message: 'Many thanks; but her father was with her, and could do all she wanted.' Then her maid came to ask if Mrs Burton did not want anything, and was sent away with a wave of her hand. Then the butler came timidly to ask should they shut up? was master to be expected? At that summons Mrs Burton rose.

'I am tired,' she said, putting on her company calm; for Simmons the butler was as important in his way as old Lord Bobadil. 'I was glad to rest a little after all the worry. Yes, certainly, shut up, and let everybody go to bed. I do not expect your master to-night.'

'If I might make so bold, madam,' said Simmons, 'Tom the groom have just been in to say as orders was took to the stables to send the dog-cart for master to the north gate, and as he took him up there and drove him to Turley station, and as he gave him this note, and said as it was all right.'

'All right!' She repeated the words, looking at him with a ghastly bewilderment which frightened the man. And then she recovered herself, and resumed her former composure. 'That will do, Simmons. Your master had a—journey—to make. I was not aware he would have started so—soon. Have everything shut up as quickly as possible, and let all the servants go to bed.'

She went up-stairs, emerging all at once into the full morning sunshine in the hall, which dazzled and appalled her. The light dazzled her eyes, but not her jewels, which woke at its touch, and blazed about her with living, many-coloured radiance. A little rainbow seemed to form round her as she went up-stairs. How her temples throbbed! What a dull aching was in every limb, in every pulse! She went into Clara's room first. She was not a very tender mother, and never had been; yet almost every night for seventeen years she had gone into that room before retiring to her own. Clara's maid was seated, fast asleep, before a table on which a candle was burning pitifully in the full daylight. The room looked trim and still as a room does which has not been occupied in that early brightness. The maid woke with a shiver as Mrs Burton entered.

'Oh, Miss Clara, I beg your pardon!' she said.

'It is no matter. My daughter will not want you to-night. Go to bed, Jane,' said Mrs Burton. 'And you can tell Barnes to go to bed. Neither of you will be wanted. Go at once.'

When she was left alone, she cast a glance round to see if there was any letter. There was a little three-cornered note fastened on the pin-cushion. She took that into her hand along with her husband's note, which she held there, but did not attempt to read either. With a quick eye she noted that Clara's jewel-case and all the presents which had been showered upon her that morning—her eighteenth birthday—had gone. A faint, mechanical smile came upon her face, and then she locked the door, and went to her own room.

There she sat down again to think, with the diamonds still upon her and all her ornaments, and the two letters in her hand. Why should she read them? She knew exactly what they would be. The one she did open after a long pause was Clary's. The other—had she any interest in it? it gave her a sensation of disgust rather: she tossed it on the table. Clary's note was very short. It ran thus:—

'DEAR MAMMA,—Feeling sure you never would consent, and as we both   know we could not live without each other, I have made up my mind   to leave you. I shall be Mrs Golden when you get this, for he has   prepared everything. We start immediately for the Lakes, and I will   write you from there. Of course it would have been nicer to have   been Lady Somebody; but then I never saw any one who was half so   nice as he is, and he hopes, and so do I, that you will soon make   up your mind to it, and forgive us.

'Your affectionate CLARY.

'He bids me say it is to be at St James's, Piccadilly, and that if   you inquire, you will find everything quite right.'

Mrs Burton tossed this from her too on to the same table where the father's letter lay unopened. The scorn with which they filled her stopped for a moment the movements of that wonderful machine for thinking which nothing had yet arrested. It was 'human nature' pur et simple. Clara had taken her jewels, had made sure it was 'all right' about the wedding; and the father had sent the same message— 'all right.' All right! A smile flitted across the pale, almost stern, little face of the woman who was left to bear all this, and to bear it alone. Most other women would have made some passionate attempt to do something—to pursue the one or the other—to go to their succour. Mrs Burton had no such impulse. She was like a soldier who has fought to the last gasp; she stood still upon her span of soil, her sword broken, her banner taken from her; nothing to fight for any longer, yet still, with the instinct of battle, holding out, and standing firm. So long as there was any excuse for keeping up the conflict, she would have borne every blow like a stoic; what she could not bear was the thought of giving in; and the hour for giving in had come.

Must it be told? Must she acknowledge before the world that all had been in vain? that her husband was a fugitive, her daughter the victim of a scoundrel, her family for ever crushed down and trampled in the dust? To everything else she could have wound up her high courage. This was the only thing that was really hard for her, and this was what she had to do. How much, she wondered, would she have to suffer? Probably Mr Burton would be taken, tried, share the fate which various men whose names she knew had already borne. Should she have to go to him? to visit him in his prison? to read her own name in the papers—'Mrs Burton spent an hour with the prisoner.' 'His wife was present!' She clasped her small, thin hands together. For a long time she had wondered whether when it came she would feel it. She could have answered her own question now. Ruin, shame, public comment, sudden descent from her high estate, humiliation, sympathy, even pity—all these were before her; and it would have been hard for her to say which was the worst.

The young men roused her with their voices as they came up-stairs. It was not worth while going to bed, she heard one say; a bath, and then a long walk somewhere before breakfast was the only thing possible. This called her attention to the clock striking on the mantelpiece. Six o'clock! No longer night, but day! She rose, and took off her jewels and her evening dress. It troubled, and tired, and irritated her to do all this for herself; but she succeeded at last. A nightly vigil, and even all the emotion through which she had passed did not make the same difference to her colourless countenance which it would have done to a more blooming woman. When she knocked at her father's door, and went in to his bedside to speak to him, he thought her looking very much as usual. He thought he must have overslept himself, which was likely enough, considering how late he had been last night; and that she had come to call him and have a chat with him before all her fine people came down to breakfast. It was kind of Clara. It showed, what he had sometimes doubted, that she was still capable of recollecting that she was his child.

'I have come to tell you of some things that have happened,' she said, sitting down in the big chair by the bed, 'and to ask your advice and help. Some strange things have happened to-night. In the first place, papa, you were a true prophet. Mr Burton has been obliged to go away.'

'To go away?'

'Yes, to escape, to fly—whatever you call it. He is—ruined. I suppose he must be worse than ruined,' she added quietly; 'for—I hear—the police—'

'Oh, Clara! Oh, my poor, poor child!'

'Don't be sorry for me, papa. Let us look at it calmly. I am not one to cry, you know, and get over it in that way. So far as I have heard yet, he has got off: he reached Turley station this morning, I suppose in time for the train. Most likely he has money, as he has not asked for any, and he may get safely off. Stop, papa; that is not all I have to tell you. There is something more.'

'Clara, my own poor girl! there can be nothing so bad.'

'Some people would think it worse,' she said. 'Papa, don't say any more than you can help. Clara has—eloped. She has gone off with Mr Golden, whom you all forgave, whom I hated, who was—her father's friend.'

The old man gave a great cry. Clary was his grandchild, whom he adored. He loved her with that fond, caressing, irresponsible love which is sometimes sweeter than even a parent's love for his own child. It was for others to find fault with, to correct, her; the grandfather had nothing to do but admire, and pet, and praise. 'Clary!' it was but the other day that he told her stories as she sat on his knee!

'Yes, Clary. Here is her note, and here is—Mr Burton's. They are both gone. All this has happened since last night.'

'Clara, what o'clock is it now?'

'Half-past six,' she said, mechanically taking out her watch, 'and fortunately nobody will be stirring for some time at least. Papa, what are you going to do?'

'I am going to get up,' he said. 'Clara, there is still time. If I can get up to town by the first train, I may be in time to stop it yet.'

'To stop—what?'

'The marriage, child, the marriage! Clary's destruction! Go away, my dear, and let me get up.'

'It would be of no use,' she said. 'Papa, when Clara has made up her mind, nothing that we can say would stop her. You might do it by law, perhaps; but she will never come home again—never hear reason. I know her better. There were a great many things I wanted to ask about—'

'Leave me just now, for heaven's sake, Clara! I must try, at least, to save the child.'

She rose without another word, and went away. A smile once more stole upon her face, and stayed there, rigid and fixed. He might have been of a little help to herself; but he thought of Clary first—Clary, who was obstinate, and whom nothing could move—who was coaxing and winning to those who loved her, and would persuade the old man to anything. Well, Mrs Burton said to herself, she had hoped for his help for a moment; but now it was clear that she must do everything for herself.

She went down-stairs, and took down a cloak which hung in the hall, and wrapping it about her, stepped out into the fresh air. That, at least, might help her, though nothing else would. She walked down to the avenue, to the skirt of the woods. Like a cordial the soft air breathed about her, and gave her a certain strength. She was not a woman who cared about the meaner delights of wealth; all these she would have given up without a pang. But to exchange this large, free, lofty life which she had been leading for the restrained and limited existence of her father's house—to be no longer entire mistress of her own actions, but to be bound by her father's antiquated notions, by what Aunt Everett and Aunt Louisa thought proper—that would be hard to bend her mind to. To give up Dura for Clapham! Even that she could do stoically, and no one would ever be the wiser. But to bear all the shame, all the comments, a husband in prison, a story of romance of real life, ruin of the father, elopement of the daughter, in the newspapers! Mrs Burton gave no outward sign of the struggle that went on within her, but she clasped her little thin white hands together, and she recognised at once, wholly and clearly, without any self-deception, what she would have to bear.

She waited there till her father came up to her on his way to the station. He stopped and told her he would come back as soon as he could.

'Most likely I will take Clary to Clapham first,' he said. 'Better than here, don't you think? She might be frightened to face you after her folly. My dear, take a little courage, if you can. The innocent child has given us all the clue that is necessary—St James's, Piccadilly. No marriage could take place before eight o'clock, and I shall reach there soon after—in time to prevent that, at least. I will take her to Clapham, and then, my dear, I will come straight back to you.'

'Very well, papa,' she said.

In her heart she wondered at his simplicity, at the folly of his hopes; but what was the use of saying anything? If it pleased him to do this, if this was what he thought best, why, let him do it. Let every one act as it seemed good in his own eyes.

'And by-the-by, Clara, one thing more,' he said—'Ned's address. Where is he now? I must telegraph at once for him.'

Then some faint semblance of the tigress guarding her young appeared in Mrs Burton.

'Ned! Why should Ned be brought home? Why should he be involved in trouble he has nothing to do with? He is out of it; he, at least, is safe. No, papa; I will not have him brought back.'

'Clara, you are mad, you are incomprehensible!' cried her father. 'Give me the boy's address.'

'I will not,' she answered, looking at him.

The woman had come to light in her at last—the woman and something of the mother. As a daughter she had neglected none of the observances of respect. She had been dutiful, though she had long been an independent agent, and had forgotten the very idea of obedience. But never had she defied her father before. She did it now calmly, as she did everything. She had upheld her family and its importance as long as mortal strength could do it; and now when that had failed, she could at least defend her boy.

'Clara, you astonish me. I could not have believed it of you,' said her father severely.

But he had no time to remonstrate or to command. He had to hurry away for his train. And she stood and looked after him, her breath for the first time quickened with excitement, her resolution bringing a certain colour to her cheek. Ned was safe, and out of all this trouble. It was the only gleam of comfort in her clouded sky. He who should bring her boy back to undergo all this shame and suffering was her enemy, though it were done on the specious pretence of serving her. To bring her son back to support and help her would be to do her the last and cruellest wrong. She could do without the help and support. She was ready to bear anything, since it must be borne. What relief could it afford her to know that another suffered too, and that other her son? She went back to the house with quickened steps under the sway of the thought, that Ned, at least, was safe and out of it. She was not the kind of woman who would complain of bearing anything alone.

Breakfast was a very late and straggling meal that day at Dura; but Mrs Burton was the first at the table—before even the young man who had proposed a bath and a walk instead of sleep. The breakfast was as sumptuous, as well served, as usual, and there were the same number of servants about, the dogs, as usual, on the lawn, the man with the post-bags, as usual, visible, coming up the avenue. The ordinary eye would have seen no indication of any change. But Mrs Burton made a calm little speech to every new group, which had the most curiously disconcerting effect upon her guests. She said to them that family circumstances compelled her to make preparations at once for leaving Dura; that some things had happened which she need not tell them of—family events—which had changed all her arrangements. She hoped, under these circumstances, they would pardon her, if she said plainly—

'Oh, yes, certainly. Not another word,' the visitors cried, dismayed. They all gazed at each other, and whispered over their teacups when her back was turned. They heard her say the same thing to one party after another—even to the Marchioness herself, who had come down fully primed, meaning to overwhelm Mrs Burton with a theatrical leave-taking.

'Why, why, why!' she cried in her wrath, 'you mean that you want to—get rid of us, Mrs Burton!' and her hair stood on end upon her noble head.

'I am afraid, without making any mystery of it, that is what I do mean, Lady Upshire,' said the woman, who was only the wife of a rich City man—a parvenue, one of the nouveaux riches—fixing her blue eyes calmly upon her splendid guest.

'What pluck she has!' the young men said to themselves. They almost cheered her for her dauntless front. And they were all gone by two o'clock—Marchioness and maid, guardsman and public servant—every visitor, gentle and simple. They disappeared as if by magic. What questions they asked each other, what speculations they entertained among themselves, Mrs Burton neither knew nor cared. The first thing was to be free of them; and when the afternoon came, she was alone with the startled servants and her two aunts, to whom as yet she had given no explanations, and whose private opinion, stated a hundred times that morning, was, that at last beyond all controversy Clara must be mad.

CHAPTER X

Mr Baldwin came back to Dura in the afternoon, worn out and disappointed—foiled by the simple fact, which had never occurred to the old man as possible, that Clary—his innocent Clary—had wittingly or unwittingly given a false indication, and that St James's, Piccadilly, knew nothing of any such marriage. Mr Baldwin drove to all the hotels, to all the churches, he could think of, from St James's, Camberwell, to St James's, Kentish Town, but in vain. Just when it was too late to follow them further, he discovered an anonymous little chapel which he must have passed a dozen times in his journeys, where the ceremony had actually taken place. Charles Golden to Clara Burton. Then he had gone to the Northern Railway Station, and discovered that they had left by the eleven o'clock train. All he had done had been to verify their movements. The poor old man aged ten years during this running to and fro. He went back to his daughter worn out and miserable. Little Clary, the pride of the family, with all her beauty, her youth, and the possibilities that lay before her! 'Now I know that we may go too far in carrying out the precepts of Christianity,' he groaned, when his sympathetic sisters came to console him. 'We thought he had repented, and we took him back to our hearts.' In this, however, poor Mr Baldwin deceived himself.

Golden had been received back into their hearts, not because he had repented, but because the scandal against him had died into oblivion, and because in their souls even the honest men admired the consummate cleverness of the rogue. And in this point, at least, Mr Golden had not been mercenary; he had actually fallen in love with Clara Burton, knowing the desperate state of her father's affairs—affairs which were so desperate, when he was called on to help in regulating them, that he had been 'obliged to decline' the task. Golden had a little Sybarite 'place' of his own on the shores of the Mediterranean. So many scraps of money had adhered to his fingers in his various commercial adventures, though these adventures were always unfortunate, that he could afford himself that crowning luxury of a beautiful wife; and then Mr Baldwin was a rich man and a doting grandfather, who after a while would be sure to forgive.

As for Mrs Burton, she had expected her father's failure, and was not surprised or disappointed. She had given her daughter up, not with any revengeful or vindictive intention, but simply as a matter of fact. 'Oh, don't curse her, Clara!' Aunt Louisa sobbed in the midst of her tears. And then indeed Mrs Burton was surprised. 'Curse her! I have no intention of cursing her,' she said. Clary had taken her own way; she had pleased herself. What she had done was quite easily to be accounted for; it was human nature. Mrs Burton was not subject to passions herself, but she recognised them as a motive-power; and though perhaps in her inmost heart there was a sense of shame that her child should be violently moved by those lowest, almost brutal, forces (for so she deemed them), yet her intelligence understood and allowed the possibility. Clary had acted according to her nature; that was all that was to be said. She had laid an additional burden upon her family—or rather upon her mother, the only one of the family left to bear it; but then it was not natural to Clary to take account of what other people might have to bear. Thus Mrs Burton accepted it, making no complaint. If it gave her any additional individual pang for itself, and not merely as part of the whole, she at least said little about it, and made no individual complaint.

But there came a moment when actual feeling, emotion not to be disguised, broke forth in this self-possessed woman. She had decided to remain at Dura till further news, and until her husband's affairs could be fully examined into; and though her aunts went home, her father remained with her. Two long days passed over without news. On the third, Tuesday, Mr Baldwin went to town to make what inquiries were possible. As yet there had been but vague hints in the newspapers—rumours of changes affecting 'a well-known name in the City'—and the old man had hesitated to show himself, to ask any questions which might, as he said, 'precipitate matters.' 'While we are in ignorance, quiet is best,' he had said; but when the third day arrived, though Mrs Burton still bore the suspense like a stoic, Mr Baldwin could not bear it any longer. When he was gone, she showed no signs of impatience; she went about her business as usual, and she had a great deal to do. She had begun at once to wind up the accounts of the house, to arrange with her servants, to whom she was a just and not ungenerous mistress, when they should go, and what would be done to find them places. But when the languid afternoon came, her energy flagged a little. She did not allow, even to herself, that she was anxious. She went into the great drawing-room, and sat down near a window from which she could see the avenue. Perhaps for the first time, the impulse came into her mind to prefer a smaller room, to take refuge somewhere else than in this waste of damask and gilding; but if such was the case, she restrained and condemned the thought. She was herself so small, almost invisible, in the great, silent place, full of those mirrors which reflected nothing, those chairs where no one sat. No marble statue with a finger on its lip was ever so complete an embodiment of silence as she, seated there all alone, motionless, looking out upon the road. It might have been hours before any one came. A summer afternoon, slow, languid, endless, one vast blank of drowsy calm and blazing sunshine, the wind too listless to blow, the leaves too heavy to wave, everything still, even the birds. But at last, at last some one came—not Mr Baldwin's slow, heavy old steps, but rapid young ones, light and impatient. She gazed at the speck as it gradually approached, and became recognisable. Then her heart gave a great unexpected, painful throb. Ned! Her last little gleam of satisfaction, her last comfort, then, was not to be. He was not out of it, safe, as she had hoped, but here to bear all the brunt, to share all the shame. She tried to get up, to go and meet him, but sank back, faint and incapable, in her chair, trembling, sick to the heart; overwhelmed for the first time.

He came in, bringing a gust of fresh air (it seemed) with him. He was dusty, and pale, and eager.

'Mother!' he cried, as he came up to her.

She held up her hand with a gesture which was almost passionate, repelling him.

'Oh, Ned, Ned! why have you come here?'

'Don't you want me, mamma?'

He kissed her as he spoke, and put his arm round her. If she had been another kind of woman, he would have sobbed on her breast, for the lad's heart was very sore.

'No, I do not want you,' she said. 'I thought you were safe. I thought you were out of it all. I was ready to bear anything—it cannot hurt me—any more. But you, a boy, a lad, with all your life to come! Oh, Ned, Ned, why have you come here?' She had never done it before in all her life. She did not embrace him, but clutched at his arm with her two hands, and shed passionate, hot tears. 'I do not want you! I do not want you!' she cried, and clung to him. 'I wish you were at the end of the world!'

'Oh, mother!' cried the boy.

He was fond of her, though perhaps she had never done anything to deserve it. And she—loved him. Yes. All at once she found it out, with a mother's passion. Loved him so that she would have been glad never to see him again; glad to be cut in pieces for him; glad to suffer shame, and pain, and misery, and ruin alone, that he might be out of it. This, which she had scarcely suspected, she found out at last.

But when this moment was over, and the fact that he had come was indisputable, and had to be made the best of, Mrs Burton recovered her usual calm. She was ashamed of herself for having 'broken down.' She said it was fatigue and want of sleep which had made her weak, and then she told him all the circumstances dispassionately, as was natural to her. He himself had been summoned by a telegram from Golden. He had been at Dresden when he received it, and he had travelled night and day. But why from Golden, he asked, a man whom he hated? 'Your mother wants you here. There has been a great smash, and your presence is indispensable,' was what the telegram had said. But I will not attempt to describe how the little, pale, dispassionate mother told the tale, nor how the young son, full of youthful passion, indignation, rage, and grief, heard of his family's downfall, and the ruin of all its prospects and hopes.

When Mr Baldwin came back, he brought news still more overwhelming. The fact which had made further concealment impossible, and had driven Burton to flight, was the winding up of a trust account for which he had been responsible. The property had been invested by him, and he had paid the interest regularly; but it was found that not a penny of the original capital remained; he had appropriated all. When it was known that he had disappeared, other inquiries had been at once set on foot, but kept carefully out of the papers, lest his escape might be facilitated; and then such disclosures were made as

Mr Baldwin could only repeat bit by bit, as his strength permitted. The old man cried like a child; he was utterly broken down. It had even come out about Rivers's, he said. One of the missing books, which poor Drummond had been accused of destroying, had been found in a private safe, along with other damning accounts, which the unhappy man had not been able to destroy or conceal, so quickly did his fate overtake him. The unhappy man! Both Mr Baldwin and Mrs Burton remembered the time when Robert Drummond had been thus described—when all the newspapers had preached little sermons about him, with many a repetition of this title—articles which Burton had read, and shaken his head over, and declared were as good as sermons, warning the ignorant. This flashed upon Mrs Burton's mind, and it came more dimly to her father. Fortunately, Ned's misery was not complicated by such recollections; he had enough without that.

'But the general impression is that he has escaped,' said Mr Baldwin; and he repeated to them the vague account which had been given to him of the two futile detectives, who had watched the fugitive into a house, and kept in front of it, putting the inhabitants on their guard, while he was smuggled out by a side-door. No doubt he had escaped. And it was known that he had money; for he had drawn a large sum out of the bank the day before.

'I am glad you have come back, Ned,' the grandfather added. 'It is you who ought to manage all this, and not your mother. Of course she has her settlement, which nobody can touch. And I think now, my dear, that you should leave Dura, and come with me to Clapham. You will have your aunts' society to make up a little, and it will be more convenient for Ned.'

Mrs Burton looked at her son almost wistfully.

'Ned, is there any sacrifice I can make that will induce you to go away?'

'None, mother,' he said, 'none. I will do anything else that you ask me. But here I must have a will of my own. I cannot go away.'

'Go away!' said Mr Baldwin. 'I don't know how he has got here; for your mother would not let me send for you, Ned; but of course this is your proper place. It will be very painful—very painful,' said the old man. 'But you have your settlement, Clara; and we must hope everything will turn out for the best.'

'My mother will give up her settlement, sir, of course,' said Ned. 'After what has happened, she could not—it would be impossible—What! you don't see it? Must not those suffer who have done the wrong?'

'Ned, you are a fool,' said Mr Baldwin, 'a hot-headed young fool. I see your sense now, Clara. That scoundrel, Golden, has sent for him only to increase our vexation. Give up her settlement! Then pray how is she to live?'

'With me,' said Ned, rising up, and standing behind his mother's chair. He would have taken her hand to sustain him, if he could; but she did not give him her hand. He put his on the back of her chair. That, at least, was something to give him strength.

'With you!' Mr Baldwin was moved by this absurdity to something of his former vigour. 'It would be satisfactory, indeed, trusting her to you. I will have no Quixotical nonsense brought in. This is my affair. I am the proper person to look after my daughter's settlement. It is the only comfort in a bad business. Don't let me hear any more of such childish folly.'

'It is not folly,' said Ned firmly, though his voice trembled. 'I am sure my mother feels like me. We have no right to keep anything while my father has been spending other people's money; or if we have a right in law—'

Mrs Burton put up her hand to stop him. It was the first time in her life that she had allowed herself to be discussed, what she should or would do, without taking any share in it. The fact was, the question was a new one—the problem quite strange to her. She had considered it as certain up to this moment that her settlement belonged to her absolutely, and that her husband's conduct one way or other could have no effect upon her undoubted right. The problem was altogether new. She put up her hand to interrupt the discussion.

'I have not thought of this,' she said. 'Ned, say no more. I want time to think. I shall tell you to-morrow what I will do.'

Against this decision there was not a word to say. The old man and the boy gave up their discussion as suddenly as they had begun it. Let them argue as they would, it was she who must settle the question; and just then the great bell rang—the bell which regulated the clock in the village, and warned all the countryside when the great people at the great house were going to dine. The ears which were accustomed to it scarcely noted the sound; but Ned, to whom it had become a novelty, and as great a mockery as a novelty, started violently, put up his hands to his ears, and rushed out into the hall, where Simmons stood in all the splendour of his evening dress.

'Stop that infernal noise!' cried poor Ned, in a sudden outburst of rage and humiliation. He felt tempted to knock down the solemn spy before him, who already, he saw, had noted his dusty dress, his agitated face.

'Happy to see you home, sir,' said Simmons. 'Did you speak, sir? Is there anything as I can do for you?'

'The bell is not to be rung any more,' said Ned, walking gloomily off to his room. It was the first sign to the general world that the grandeur of Dura had come to an end.

A mournful dinner followed, carefully cooked, carefully served, an assiduous, silent servant behind each chair, and eaten as with ashes, and bitterness, and tears, a few faint remarks now and then, a feeble attempt, 'for the sake of the servants,' to look as if nothing was the matter. It was Mr Baldwin chiefly, a man who never could make up his mind that all was over, who made these attempts. Mrs Burton, for her part, was above all pretences. Her long stand against approaching ruin was over; she had laid down her arms, and she no longer cared who knew it. And as for Ned, he was too miserable, too heart-broken, to look anything but overwhelmed with sorrow and shame, as he was.

In the evening he strolled out, feeling the air of the house insupportable. His mother had gone to her room with her new problem which she had to solve, and Mr Baldwin was tired, and fretful, and anxious to get to bed early, feeling that there was a certain virtue in that fact of going early to bed which might redeem the unusually disturbed, excited life he was leading—a life in which he had been fatally entangled with ruins, and elopements, and sitting up half the night. Ned, who had no mind for sleep, and no power of thinking which could have been of any service to him in the circumstances, went out disconsolately, saying to himself that a stroll in the woods might do him good. But when he had reached the top of the avenue, where the path diverged into the woods, some 'spirit in his feet' led him straight on. Why, he asked himself, should he go to the village? Why should he go to the Gatehouse? Yes, that was where he wanted to go—where his foolish heart had gone before him, courting slight and scorn. Why should he go? If she had sent him away then with contumely, how much more now? At that time, if she had but looked upon him kindly, he had thought he had something to offer her worthy her acceptance. Now he had nothing, and less than nothing—an empty purse and a dishonoured name. Ned slouched his hat over his eyes. He would go and look at the house, look at her window. If he might see her face again, that would be more than he hoped for. Norah could be nothing—nothing to him now.

So saying, he wandered down the leafy, shadowy way. The sun had set, the gray of the evening had come on; the moon was past the full, and rose late; it was one of those soft, tranquil, mournful summer evenings which fill the heart with wistfulness and longings. The water came unbidden into poor Ned's eyes. Oh, what ruin, what destruction had overwhelmed him and his since last he walked down that path! Then everything that life could offer to make up for the want of Norah (though that was nothing) lay within his grasp. Now, though Norah was clearly lost, everything else was lost with her. He saw no hope before him; his very heart was crushed; a beggar, and more than a beggar; a man who did not know how to dig or how to work; the son of a father who was disgraced. These were miserable thoughts to pour through the mind of a young man of twenty-one. There have been others who have had as much to bear; but they, perhaps, had no Norah to complicate and increase the burden. As he drew near the Gatehouse, his heart began to beat louder. Possibly she would not care to speak to him at all, he thought; how quickly she had dismissed him last time, when he had no stains upon him, as he had now!

He drew his hat still more over his brows. He walked quickly past the Gatehouse. The windows were all open, and Stephen Haldane sat within, in an interior faintly lighted up by the candles which Miss Jane had just set down upon the table.

'Don't shut my window yet,' he heard the invalid say. 'My poor window! My chief pleasure!'

It was strange to Ned to hear those words, which seemed to let him into the very secret of the sick man's life.

'And a capital window it has been too,' said Miss Jane briskly, thinking of the book, and the money it had brought in.

Ned slackened his steps when he had passed. There had been something at one of the windows on the other side—something, a shadow, a passing gleam, as of a pale face pillowed upon two arms. The poor boy turned, and went back this time more slowly. Yes, surely there was a face at the window. The arms were withdrawn now; there was no light inside to reveal who it was; only a something—a pale little face looking out.

Back again—just once more, once more—to have a last look. He would never see her again, most likely. As far away as if she were a star in heaven would she be henceforward. He would pass a little more slowly this time; there was no one about to see him. The road was quieter than usual; no one in sight; and with his hat so over his eyes, who could recognise him? He went very softly, lingering over every step. She was still there, looking out, and in the dark with no one near her! Oh, Norah! If she could but know how his heart was pulling at him, forcing him towards that door!

He thought he heard some sound in the silence as of an exclamation, and the face disappeared from the window. A moment after the door opened suddenly, and a little figure rushed out.

'Ned!' it said, 'Ned! Is it possible? Can it be you? And, oh, what do you mean walking about outside like that, as if you knew nobody here?'

'Oh, Norah! I did not know if I might come,' said abject Ned.

'Of course you may come. Why shouldn't you come? Oh, Ned, I was so lonely! I am so glad to see you! I did not know what to do with myself. Susan would not bring in the lamp, and I am so afraid of this room when it is dark!'

'How you once frightened me about it!' he said, as he went in with her.

His heart felt so much lighter, he could not tell how. Insensibly his spirits rose, and with a sense of infinite refreshment, and even of having escaped from something, he went back to the recollections of his youth. Such an innocent, simple recollection, belonging to the time when all was pleasure, when there was no pain.

'Did I? But never mind. Oh, Ned! poor Ned! have they brought you here because of all this trouble? I have so much to say to you. My heart is breaking for you. Oh, you poor, poor, dear boy!'

This was not how he had expected to be spoken to. He could scarcely see her face, it was so dark, what with the curtains at the windows and the shadows of the lime leaves; but she had put her hand into his to comfort him. He did not know what to say; his heart was torn in twain, between misery and joy. It was so hard to let any gleam of light into that desperate darkness; and yet it was so hard to keep his heart from dancing at the sound of her soft, tender voice.

'Norah,' he said, 'oh, Norah! it will not be so very bad if you are sorry for me. You would not speak to me last time. I thought I might, perhaps, never see you again.'

'Oh, Ned! I was only a child. How foolish I was! I hoped you would look back; but you never looked back; and we who have been brought up together, who have always been—fond of each other!'

'Do you? do you? Oh, Norah! not just because you are sorry? Do you care—a little for me? Speak the truth.'

'Ned, Ned!—I care for you more than anybody—except mamma.'

There was a little silence after this. They were like two children in the simplicity of their youth; their hearts beat together, their burdens—and both the young shoulders were weighed down by premature burdens—were somehow lightened, they could not tell how.

After a while, Norah, nestling like a little bird in the dark, said softly, 'Do you mind sitting without the lamp?' and Ned answered, 'No.' They sat down together, holding each other's hands; they were not afraid of the dark. They poured out their hearts to each other. All his sorrows, all his difficulties, Ned poured into Norah's sympathetic bosom; and she cried, and he consoled her; and she patted his hand or his sleeve, and said, 'Poor boy! Poor, dear Ned!' It was not much. She had no advice to give him, not many words of wisdom; but what she did say was as healing as the leaves of that tree in Paradise. Her touch stanched all his wounds.

'I have something to tell you too,' she said, trembling a little, when all his tale had been told. 'Ned, you have heard of poor papa, my father, who died before we came here? Oh, Ned! listen. Stoop down, and let me whisper. Ned, he did not die—'

'Norah!'

'Hush. Yes; it is quite true. Oh, don't be frightened. I can't help being frightened staying here alone. Mamma went to him yesterday. Oh, Ned! after seven years! Was there ever anything so strange?'

'Poor Mrs Drummond!' said Ned. 'Oh, Norah, thank God; my father has not done so much harm as I thought. Are you all alone, my own darling? I suppose she was happy to go.'

He said this with a strange accent of blame in his voice. 'For her own selfish happiness she could leave Norah—my Norah—all alone!' This was what the young man, in his haste, thought.

'I think she was frightened too,' said Norah, under her breath. 'She did not understand it. It is as if he had been really dead, and come alive again. Mamma did not say anything; but I know she was frightened too.'

'Norah, most likely he hates us. If he should try to keep you from me—'

'Oh, Ned, do you mean that this means anything? Do you think it is right? We are all in such trouble, not knowing what may happen. Do you mean,' said Norah, faltering and trembling, 'do you mean that this means—Is it—being engaged?'

'Doesn't it, dear? Oh, Norah, what could it mean else? You would never have the heart to cast me off now?'

'Cast you off! Oh, no, Ned! Oh, never, Ned! But then that is different. We are so dreadfully young. We have no money. We are in such trouble. Oh! do you think it is right?'

'It can't be wrong to be fond of each other, Norah; and you said you were—a little.'

'Yes; oh, yes! Oh, Ned! do be satisfied. Isn't it enough for us to care for each other—to be the very best, dearest friends?'

'It is not enough for me,' he said, turning his head aside, and speaking sternly in the dark.

'Isn't it, Ned?' said Norah timidly. 'Ned, I wish I could see your face. You are not angry? You poor, dear boy! Oh! you don't think I could have the heart to cross you? and you in such trouble. Ned, what must we do?'

'You must promise me, Norah, on your true and faithful word, that you will marry me as soon as we can, whatever anybody may say.'

Norah in her alarm seized at the saving clause which staved off all immediate terrors.

'When we can, Ned.'

'Yes, my own darling. You promise? I shall not mind what happens if I have your promise—your faithful promise, Norah.'

'I promise you faithfully, Ned—faithfully, dear Ned!—when we can—if it should not be for years.'

'But it shall be!' he cried; and then they kissed each other, poor children! and Norah was sitting by herself crying when Susan brought in the lamp.

CHAPTER XI

Mrs Burton took her new problem away with her into the quiet of her room. It was a question which had never occurred to her before. Some few first principles even an inquiring mind like hers must take for granted, and this had been one of them. She had no love for money, and no contempt for it—it was a mere commonplace necessity, not a thing to be discussed; and though she had a high natural sense of honour and honesty, in her own person, it had not occurred to her to consider that in such a matter she had anything to do but to accept the arrangement which was according to law and common custom, an arrangement which, of course, had been made (theoretically) in view of a calamity such as had just happened. It was the intention of her settlement, and of all settlements, she said to herself, to secure a woman against the chances of her husband's ruin. She, in most cases, was entirely irresponsible for that ruin. She had nothing to do with it, and was unable to prevent it. She had married with the belief that she herself and her children would be provided for, and the first duty of her friends was to make sure that it should be so. Up to this point there was no flaw in the argument. Mrs Burton knew that she had brought her husband a good fortune; and her future had been secured as an equivalent. It was like buying a commission—it was like making an investment. She had put in so much, she had a right to secure to herself absolutely the power of taking it out again, or recovering what had been hers. Mr Burton had not incurred his liabilities with her knowledge or consent; he had never consulted her on the matter. He had never said or even hinted to her that her expenditure was too great, that he could not afford it. True it was possible that fastidious persons might blame her for proceeding so long on her splendid course, after hints and rumours had reached her about her husband's position; but these were nothing more than rumours. She had no sort of official information, nothing really to justify her in making a sudden change in her household, which probably would have affected Mr Burton's credit more than her extravagance. She was in no way responsible. She had even protested against the re-introduction of Golden into his affairs. She could not blame herself for anything she had done; she had always been ready to hear, always willing to give him her advice, to second him in any scheme he propounded to her. She put herself at the bar, and produced all the evidence she knew of, on both sides of the question, and acquitted herself. The money she could have saved by economy was not worth considering in the magnitude of Mr Burton's affairs. She had done nothing which she could feel had made her his accomplice in his wrong-doing.

And she had no right to balk her father in his care for her—to establish a bad precedent in regard to the security of marriage settlements—to put it in the power of any set of creditors to upbraid some other woman whose view of her duty might be different. She had no right to do it. She had to think not of herself only, but of all the married women who slept serenely in the assurance that, whatever happened, their children's bread was secure. She reflected that such a step would put an end to all security—that no woman would venture to marry, that no father would venture to give his child to a man in business, if this safeguard were broken down. It would be impossible. It would be a blow aimed at the constitution of the country—at the best bulwark of families; it would be an injustice. Of all a commercial man's creditors, surely his wife was the one claimant who had most right to come first. Others might be partially involved; she had put everything in his hands. Without this safeguard she would not have married him, she would not have been permitted to marry him. Going over the question carefully, Mrs Burton felt, beyond a shadow of a doubt, that she had right on her side.

She had right on her side—but she had not Ned. This was a very different matter—an argument such as she had scarcely ever taken into consideration before. Mrs Burton did not disdain the personal argument. She knew that in the confused state of human affairs, in the intricate range of human thoughts, it was often impossible to go upon pure reason, and that personal pleas had to be admitted. But she had never consciously done this before. She was almost scornful of her own weakness now. But she could not help herself. She had to suffer the entrance of this great personal argument, if with a mental pang yet without resistance. She loved her son. All that reason could do for her, all the approbation of her own judgment, the sense of right, the feeling that her position was logically unassailable, would not be enough to console her for the illogical, unreasoning disapproval of her boy. For the first time in her life, with a great surprise, this certainty seized upon her. Up to this time she had gone her own way, she had satisfied herself that she was right according to her own standard, and she had not cared what any one said or thought. But now all at once, with wonder, almost with shame, she found that she had descended from this high eminence. A whole host of foolish, childish, unreasonable principles of action, inconsequences, and stupidities were suddenly imported into her mental world by this apparition of Ned. Not the most certain sense of right that reasoning creature ever had, would neutralise, she felt, that pained and wondering look in her son's eyes. If he disapproved it would be a cold comfort to her that reason was on her side. If this indignant, impatient, foolish young soul protested against her that what she did would not bear comparing with some fantastic visionary standard which he called honour, what would it avail her that by her own just standard of weight and measure she was not found wanting? Thus all Mrs Burton's principles and habits, her ways of thinking, the long-exercised solitary irresponsible power of her intelligence, which had guided her through life for forty years, were all at once brought to a sudden stand-still by the touch, by the breath of that thing called Love, which, she knew not how, had suddenly come in upon her like a giant. This new influence paralysed the fine, delicate, exquisite machinery, by which hitherto all her problems had been worked out. She tried to struggle against it, but the struggle was ineffectual. It was the first time she had felt herself, acknowledged herself, to be acting like a fool! What then? She could not help it. Even in the clear, cold daylight of her mind the entrance of this new force, all shadowy, mysterious, wonderful, could not be contested. She threw down her arms once more. She had been beaten terribly, miserably in the battle of her life—she was beaten sweetly, wonderfully now, in a way which melted her hardness and made the disused heart beat and tremble strangely within her, in the other world where reason hitherto had reigned supreme.

But nothing more was said on the subject for some time. Next morning brought letters, which roused the little party once more into excitement. There was one from Mr Burton, informing his wife that he had got safely to France by a way little used, and was now in the small seaport of St Servan, awaiting letters from his family, and their advice as to what was best. He had not meant to go there, but a chance encounter with Golden at the station had driven him to take the down-train instead of the up-train. He would remain there if he could, he added, until he heard from home; but if any alarm came would hasten across the country to Brest, from whence he could get off to America. Mr Burton did not say a word of apology or explanation, but he begged to have news 'of all,' to be told 'how people were taking it,' and to have the newspapers sent him. He added in a P.S. the following question: 'By the way, what could Golden be doing at Turley Station, seven miles from Dura, at four o'clock in the morning? And who could the lady be who was with him? If you hear anything on this subject, let me know.'

Clara's letter was from Windermere. It was full of effusiveness and enthusiasm, hoping that dearest mamma would forgive them. Papa, Charles had told her, was not likely to be in a position to forgive any one, but would want it himself, which was very dreadful; but was it not beautiful of Charles, and showed how generous and true he was, that papa's ruin made no difference to his feelings? This reflection, Clara said, made her so happy, that she felt as if she could even forgive papa—for if he had not been so rash and so wicked she never would have known how much her dear Charles loved her. They were coming back to London in a fortnight from this heavenly lake, and would start then on a roundabout journey to Charles's delightful 'place' on the Mediterranean. And, oh! Clara hoped with effusion, dearest mamma would see them, and forgive them, and believe that she never had been so happy in her life as when she signed herself dear mamma's ever affectionate Clara Golden. These were the letters that came to the little party at Dura on the morning after Ned's arrival. They were received with very different feelings by the three. Mr Baldwin, on the whole, was pleased. He was pleased with the 'love to grandpapa,' with which Clara wound up her letter; and he was glad the child was happy at least. 'What is done cannot be undone,' he said; 'and that is quite true about there being nothing mercenary in it, you know.' Mrs Burton gave a faint smile as she laid the letters down one after another. They were just such letters as she expected. Had she been alone, perhaps, she would have tossed them from her in scorn, as she had done with the previous notes; but that had been in a moment of strong excitement, when she was not full mistress of herself; and what was the good, Mrs Burton thought, of quarrelling with your own whom you cannot alter; or of expecting sense and good taste where such qualities did not exist? From these two, her husband and her daughter, she did not expect any more.

But poor Ned was utterly cast down by these epistles. He asked himself, as Norah had done when Mr Rivers left her at the door of the Academy's Exhibition, was this natural? was this the way of the world? and, like Norah, felt his own distress doubled by the horrible thought that to think of your own comfort first and above all, and to be utterly unmoved by the reflection that you have caused untold misery to others, is the natural impulse of humanity. He was so sad, and looked so humbled, that his mother's heart was penetrated in her new enlightenment by a strange perception of how he was feeling. She was not so feeling herself. The sight of selfishness, even on so grand a scale, did not surprise nor shock her; but she felt what he was feeling, which was as strange to her as a new revelation. The family at Dura during these days were like a beleaguered city—they lived encircled in a close round, if not of enemies, yet of observant, watchful spectators, who might become enemies at any moment, who might note even the postmark on their letters, and use that against them. Whenever a step was heard approaching the door, a little thrill went through them. It might be some one coming to announce deeper misfortune still. It might be some one who dared to be insolent, some one who had a right to curse and denounce. The tension of their nerves was terrible, the strain of watchfulness, and the pain of standing secretly and always on their defence.

'Let us go, let us go, Clara, I cannot stay here any longer; now that we know where to write to them, let us go,' cried Mr Baldwin after the letters had been read and discussed; and then the old man went out to take a melancholy walk, and ponder what it would be best to do. Should they go back to Clapham? or should he take his poor child away somewhere for 'change of air'? If ever any one wanted change of air surely Clara must.

'Ned, come here,' said Mrs Burton, when they were left alone. He went and sat down by her, listless, with his hands in his pockets. Notwithstanding the joy of last night, the letters, the shame and ruin and misery, had overwhelmed Ned.

'I have been thinking over what you said yesterday about my settlement,' said his mother. 'Ned, in one way your grandfather was right. It is the equivalent to my fortune. It was the foundation of our family life—without that I should not have been permitted to marry; I should not probably have chosen to marry. To give up that is to make an end of all the securities of life—I speak as arguing the question.'

'How can we argue the question?' cried Ned. 'What have the securities of life mattered to the others, who had no connection with—with my father? He was nothing to them but a man of business. They trusted him, and they have nothing left.'

'Yes, Ned; but if one of them had been a secured creditor, as it is called, you would not have expected him to give up his security, in order to place himself on an equal level with the others. The most visionary standard of honour would never demand that.'

'We are not secured creditors. We are part of him, sharing his responsibility,' cried Ned bitterly, 'sharing his shame.'

'But we are the first of all his creditors, all the same, in justice; and our debt is secured. Ned, I do not say this is what I am going to do; but I think, according to my judgment, your grandfather is right.'

'Then, mother—' He had risen up, his face had grown very pale, his nostrils dilated, his eyes shining. She who had never been afraid for anything in her life was afraid of her son—of his indignation, of his wrath. She put out her hand, half appealing, half commanding, to stop him. She caught at him, as it were, before he could say another word.

'Ned, hear me out first! I approve of it as a matter of justice. I think we have no right to set up a new standard to make a rule for other women in my position. There will always be such, I suppose. The settlement itself was simply a precaution against this possible thing—which has happened. But I do not say I mean to act according to my opinion. That is different. I have—thought it over, Ned.'

'Mother,' he said, melting almost into tears, and taking her hand into his, 'mother! you who are so much wiser than I am—you are going to let yourself be guided by me?'

'Yes,' she said. 'I don't quite make myself out, Ned. I have always taken my own way. Mine is the right way, the just way; but perhaps yours is the best.'

'Mother, mother dear! I am awfully miserable; but I feel as if I could tell you how happy I am, now.'

And, without another word of preface, without a pause to hear her out, without even observing the bewildered look as of one stopped in mid-career with which she regarded him, Ned dashed into the story of his own love, of his despair and his joy. She listened to him with her blue eyes dilating, looking out of her pale face like stars out of a winter sky—suddenly stiffened back into a little silent stone-woman. She was bewildered at first and thrown off her balance. And then gradually, slowly, the new impatience and faith that had been born of love died in her, and the old, cold, patient toleration, the faint smile, came back. It was natural. His own affairs, of course, were the closest to him. He thought of his private story first, not of hers. She had never subjected herself to such a shock before, and did not know how hard it was to bear. Well! but what of that? That was her own folly, not any one else's. She had put aside her armour, thrown open her breast, for the first time; and if an arrow, barbed and sharp, was the first thing that came to it, that was but natural—it was her own fault. She sat, therefore, and listened with the faint smile even now stealing about her lips—a smile that was half at herself, half at human nature, thus once more, once again, proving itself. And Ned, who had felt so bitterly the absorption of his father and sister in their own affairs, their indifference to the feelings of others—Ned did the same. He slurred over the sacrifice which his mother, at no small cost, was bending her own will to make, and rewarded her by the story of his own boyish happiness—how Norah had cast him off once, how she loved him now. This was the best, the only return he could make to her. From her own serious, weighty purpose, which involved (she felt) so much, he led her aside to his love-tale, of which, for the moment at least, it was madness to expect that anything could come.

'But you don't say anything?' he said at last, half offended, when he had done—or rather when her failure of response had stopped the fulness of his speech.

'I don't know what I can say,' she answered, with a coldness which he felt at once. 'This seems scarcely the time—scarcely the moment—'

'Of course,' he said hurriedly, 'I do not expect nor hope that it can be very soon.'

'No one, I should think, would be so mad as to expect that,' said his mother; 'and these long, aimless engagements, without any visible end—'

'I do not see how my engagement can be thought aimless,' he said, growing hot.

'Not in your own mind, I suppose; but, so far as anything like marriage is concerned, considering the state of affairs generally, I do not see much meaning in it,' said Mrs Burton coldly. 'Your prospects are not brilliant. It was only last night, for instance, that you proposed to burden yourself with me.'

'Mother!'

'It is quite true. In answer to your grandfather's sensible question how I was to live, you answered: with you. Did you mean, upon some hypothetical engagement, whatever you may happen to get, to support a wife—and me?'

He made no answer. A hot flush of mingled anger and pain came over him; he was wrong somehow; he did not quite see how. He had missed the right way of making his announcement, but still it was not his fault. He could not see how he was to blame.

'You must not be surprised in these circumstances if I cannot make any very warm congratulations,' she added. 'Make your mind easy, however, Ned. I never intended to be a burden on you; but even without that—'

'What have I done, mother, that you should speak to me so?' he cried. 'You were so different just now. It is not for Norah's sake? No one could dislike Norah. What have I done?'

'Nothing,' she said; and then, with that faintest smile, 'you have acted according to your nature, Ned— like the rest. I have no reason to complain.'

Then there was a pause. He was a generous, tender-hearted boy, full of love and sympathy; but he had never so much as imagined, could not imagine, the state of feeling his mother had been in—and, accordingly, could not understand where he was wrong. Wrong somehow, unknowingly, unintentionally—puzzled, affronted, sore at heart—he went away from her. Was it mere caprice on her part? What was it? So it happened that the boy put his foot upon his mother's very heart; and then strained all his faculties, anxiously, affectionately, to find out what had made her countenance change, and could not, with all his efforts, discover what it was.

The smile remained on Mrs Burton's face when she was left alone. He had declined to hear her decision about the settlement. Was it not natural that she should reconsider it, now that she found how little interest he took in the matter? But it is easier to let that intruder Love, who disorders reason, into a woman's heart than to turn him out again. She did again another novel thing; she made a compromise. She sent for her father at once, and entered into the matter with him. 'I allow that all you say is perfectly just,' she said; 'but this is, partly, a matter of feeling, papa.' She smiled at herself as she said it, but yet did say it, without flinching. 'I will keep a portion of my settlement—say half. It is, as you said, the only thing I have to depend on.'

'My dear,' said poor Mr Baldwin, 'of course you have always me to depend on. You are my only child. What I have must come to you, Clara.'

'But I don't want it to come to me, papa.'

'No, that I am sure you don't; but what is the use of my money to me, but to make my child and her children comfortable—that is excepting, Clara—always excepting what I feel bound to do—what I have always done—in the cause of—God. But, all the same, I cannot approve of any sacrifice of your rights.'

'I would rather not say any more about it,' she said.

And thus for the moment the discussion terminated. Ned went down to the village again, and was made happy, almost quite happy, by a talk with Norah; and they went over together to the Rectory, and told Mrs Dalton, as a substitute for the absent mother, and were very wretched and very happy together over their miserable prospects and their rapture of early love. Norah, however, was sorry that he had told his mother so prematurely. 'She will think it heartless of us, Ned, to think of being happy when she must be so miserable. Oh, I would have broken it to her very gently. I would have told her how it happened—by accident—that we did not mean anything. Oh, Ned, boys are always so awkward. You have gone and made her think!'

'If you were to come and talk to her, Norah—'

'No, indeed. What am I to her? A little upstart thing, thrusting myself in, taking away her son. Oh, Ned, how could you? Go and give her a kiss, and say we never meant it. Say I would never, never think of such a thing while everybody is in such trouble. Say we are so sorry—Oh, Ned! how can you, you who are only a boy, be half sorry enough?'

With which salutary bringing down Ned went home, and was very humble to his mother and very anxious to win back her confidence—an attempt in which he partly succeeded; for, having once begun to open her heart, she could not altogether close it; and a new necessity, a new want, had developed in her. But he never made his way back entirely into that place which had been his for a moment, and which he had forfeited by his own folly. He never quite brought back the state of mind in which she had considered that matter of the settlement first. Next day Mrs Burton left Dura with her father, 'on a visit,' it was said; and Ned went to town, 'to see after' his father's affairs. Poor boy! there was not much that he could see after. He worked hard and laboriously, under his grandfather's directions and under the orders of the people who had the winding-up of Mr Burton's concerns in hand; but he had not experience enough to do much out of his own head; and it was in this melancholy way that his knowledge of business began.

And poor little Norah, alone in the Gatehouse, went and poured out her heart to Mr Stephen, who listened to her with a heart which throbbed to every woe of hers. A great woe was hanging over the Haldanes, a trouble which as yet they but dimly foresaw. Burton had ruined them in his prosperity, and now, in his downfall, was about to drag them still lower. Already the estate of Dura was in the market, with its mansion, and grounds, and woods, and farms—and the Gatehouse. They had got to feel that the Gatehouse was their home, and all Stephen's happiness was connected with that window, with the tailor and shoemaker who took their evening walks on the other side of the way, with the rector and his morning discussions, even with old Ann in her market cart. And how was he now to go away and seek another refuge? Heavy were the hearts in the Gatehouse. Norah, when Ned had gone, was overwhelmed by terrors. Fears lest her mother should not approve, wondering questions about her unknown father, doubts of Mrs Burton, fears of Ned and for Ned, came upon her like a host, and made her miserable. And then Mr Rivers came down, who had already made several attempts to see her, and this time made her wretched by succeeding and telling her another love tale, to which she could make no reply. But for that incident at the Exhibition, and the pain it had brought about, things might have ended otherwise. Had Cyril Rivers made up his mind in May instead of delaying till July, the chances were that Norah, flattered, pleased, and not unwilling to suppose that she might perhaps love him in time, would have given a very different answer. And then she asked herself in dismay, what would have happened when poor Ned came? So that, on the whole, it was for the best, as people say. The pain and shock of that discovery which she had made when Lady Rivers drew her son away—and he went—had been for the best; though it would be hard to believe that Cyril thought so, as he went back mortified to town, feeling that it had cost him a great deal to make this sacrifice, and that his sacrifice had been in vain.

Thus Dura changed in a moment, in the twinkling of an eye. The great house was empty and desolate; the great bell pealed no more through all the echoes; the noisy comings and goings of the Burtons, the sound of them as they moved about, the dash of Mr Burton's phaeton and his wife's fine horses, had all died out into the silence. Miss Jane plodded wearily about the village, trying to find some cheap cottage where Stephen could find refuge when the property was sold. And Norah, anxious and pale, and full of many terrors, lived alone in her end of the house, and watched for the postman every morning, and wondered, wondered, till her heart grew sick, why no letters came.

Where was Helen? She had disappeared from them into the unknown, as her husband had done. Was it into Hades, into the everlasting darkness, that she had followed her lost, as Orpheus followed Eurydice? A week passed, and the silent days crept on, and no one could tell.

Helen Drummond had a tedious voyage from Southampton to St Malo. She was not a good sailor, nor indeed a good traveller in any way. She was not rich enough to procure for herself those ameliorations of the weariness of journeys which are within the reach of everybody who has money. She had to consult cheapness more than comfort, and when she arrived at last in the bay, with all its rocky islets rising out of the blue, beautiful sea, and the little fortress city reigning over it, and all the white-sailed boats skimming about like so many sea-birds, she would have been unable to observe the beauty of the scene from sheer weariness, if anxiety had not already banished from her every thought but one.

Where was he? How should she find him? Was it real? Was it possible? Could it be true?

The boat was late of arriving; it had been delayed, and was not expected at the moment when the passengers were ready to land. Helen looked, with a beating heart, upon all the loungers on shore, wondering could he be among them; but it was not till almost all her fellow-passengers had left the vessel that a tattered, grinning Commissionaire came up to her, and asked if she were Madame Drummond. When she answered, a voluble explanation followed, which Helen, in her agitation, and with ears unaccustomed to the voluble Breton-French mixed with scraps of still less comprehensible English, understood with great difficulty. Monsieur had been on the pier half the night; he had been assured by all the officials that the boat could not arrive till noon. Monsieur had charged himself, François, to be on the watch, and bring him news as soon as the steamer was in sight; in place of which he, the delighted François, would have the gratification of leading Madame to Monsieur. Half dead with excitement and fatigue, Helen followed her guide. He led her along the rocky shore to where a little steam ferry-boat puffed and snorted. Then she had to embark again for a five minutes' passage across the bay. She landed on the other side, so stupified with suspense, and with the accumulated excitement which was now coming to a climax, that she felt incapable of uttering a word. Her body was all one pulse, throbbing wildly; a crimson flush alternated with dead pallor in her face; her heart choked her, palpitating in her throat. Whom was she going to meet? What manner of man was it who said he was her Robert, who wrote as Robert wrote, who had called her to him, with the force of absolute right? For was not Robert dead, dead, buried under the cold river, seven years ago? She was not happy, she was frightened, as Norah said. Her position was incomprehensible to her. She, Robert's spotless wife, his faithful widow—to whom was she going? She did not know what the words meant that were being poured into her ears. The figures she met whirled past her like monsters in a dream. Her own weary feet obeyed her mechanically; she moved and breathed, and kept command of herself, she knew not how.

There is a little cottage on the very edge of the cliff, in that village of Dinard on the Breton coast, which looks across the bay into which the Rance rushes impetuously meeting the great sea-tides—and from which St Servan opposite, St Malo with its walls and towers, all the lip of the bay lined with houses, with fortifications, with bristling masts and sails, show fair in the sunshine. Coming into it from the dusty road, so small is it, so light, so close to the water, the traveller feels that he must have come suddenly into the light poop cabin of some big ship, lifting its breast high from the sea.

Here it was that Helen came in, her frame all one tremble, breathless, stupified, carried along in the wild whirl of some dream. She saw some one get up with a great cry—and then—she saw nothing more. The excitement, the weariness, the strangeness and terror that possessed her, were more than she could bear. She fell down at Robert's feet, as she had done at the foot of the picture in the exhibition. It was perhaps the easiest, gentlest way of getting over the great shock and convulsion of the new life that had now to begin.

Helen was conscious after a while of a voice, of two voices talking vaguely over her, one which she did not know, one—At the sound of that her brain tried to rally; she tried to recollect. Where was she?—in St Mary's Road, in the old days before the studio was built? that was what it felt like. She could not see anything; a whirling, revolving cloud of darkness went round and round, swallowing her up. She tried to raise her hand to grasp at something. Now she was sinking, sinking into that sea which had gleamed upon her for a moment, through the window—a sea full of ships, yet with no saviour for her. If she could only move her hand, raise her head, see something beside this blinding blackness. And then again that voice! She had fallen, fallen somewhere, and something buzzed loud in her ears, something coming that was about to crush her—on the steps at St Mary's Road.

'Helen! don't you know me? Look at me, if you can, my own love!'

She gave a long, sobbing cry. She opened her eyes heavily. 'Yes, Robert,' she said. The wonder and the terror had gone away in her faint, with the seven years that created them. When the soul loses the common thread of time and place it comes back to its primal elements, to the things in it that are everlasting. She answered out of her unconsciousness as (God send it!) we shall answer our friends in heaven out of the death-trance, not wondering—restored to the unity of love which is for ever and ever, not for a time.

She was lying on a little sofa, that window on one side of her, with its glorious sea and sky and sunshine. On the other, a man, with hair as white as snow, with Norah's eyes, looking at her in an agony of tenderness, with a face worn and lined by suffering and toil. The sight of him startled her so that she came to herself in a moment. It startled her into the consciousness that she was his wife, and in a manner responsible for him, for his well-being and comfort. She started up, wondering how she could think of herself, indignant at herself for taking up the foreground for a moment. 'Oh, my dear, my dear!' she cried. 'What have they done to you, Robert?' and drew him to her, taking him into her arms.

Not frightened now, not wondering, not strange at all. The strangeness was that he had been kept away from her so long, cruelly kept away, to make him like this, whitened, worn, old. All at once strength and calm and self-command came back to Helen. Except for his looks, the harm some one had done to him, this interval crumpled away like a burnt paper, and disappeared, and was as if it had never been. She put her arms round him, drew him to her with an indignant love and tenderness. 'My poor Robert! my poor Robert! how you have wanted me,' she said, with the tears in her eyes.

'Ah! wanted you!' he cried; and he too gave in to this impulse of nature. He was not an impassioned man claiming his own, but a weary one come back to his natural rest. He put his white head down upon hers, and in the relief and sudden ease and consolation, wept like a child. It was more than joy; terrible fears had come to him at the last, terrors that his appeal might be unwelcome—that his recollection might have died out of her heart. He knew that she was in the sight of the world faithful to him; but whether her heart was true, whether the surprise would be a joy, he did not know.

Let us leave them to tell their mutual story. The reader knows one side of it. The other had come about thus. It took a long time to tell it so as to satisfy Helen; but it may be put here into fewer words.

On the night when Robert, as he said, died, he had been picked up by a tug steamboat, which was on its way down stream to take a vessel going to America down to the sea. He had been all but dead, and with the addition of the care, distress, and anxiety through which he had passed before, partial drowning was no joke to him. How it was that he managed to get transferred from the little steamer into the ship, he had never very clearly discovered. Whether he had passionately entreated to be taken on board, or whether he had dashed himself once more into the river and been rescued this time by the sea-going vessel, he could not tell. But, anyhow, he had been taken on board the American; and there, amid all the discomforts of a merchant ship, where there was no room for passengers, and where his presence was most unwelcome, he had an illness, which made his slow passage across the Atlantic look like a feverish dream to him. He knew nothing about it, except as a horror and misery which had been. When the ship arrived, he had been transferred to an hospital, where he lingered until all hope of life had gone out of him, if indeed any ever existed. And then, all at once, and unaccountably, he had got well again, as people do over whom no anxious nurses watch, who are of importance to no one. When he came to life again he was one of the poorest of the poor, unknown, penniless, an object of charity. In that position he could never go home, never make himself known to those whom (he felt) he had ruined, whom he had already made up his mind to leave free at the cost of his life. Forlorn, hopeless, and miserable, poor Robert had still the necessity upon him of maintaining the worthless life which Providence had, as it were, thrust back upon his hands. He went to the studio of a painter in New York—that same John Sinclair whose name had been attached to the 'Dives.' He had told his story fully and truly. When a man asserts in a painter's studio that he is himself a painter, the means are at hand for the verification of his assertion; and when Robert took the palette in his hand, Mr Sinclair believed his story. He had begun humbly, under this kind stranger's help; he had become a portrait-painter, a branch of art which, in his youth, he had followed for the sake of bread and butter, as so many do. But Robert, friendless and hopeless, driven out of everything but art, had, by a mere instinct of self-preservation, to keep himself alive, taken to his work in a way which made it a very different thing from the paint which is done for bread and butter. A very little bread and butter sufficed him. But man does not live by bread alone; and all the better aliment, the food of his soul, he had to get somehow out of his portraits. The consequence of this was, that gradually these portraits became things to talk of, things that people went far to see, and competed to have. He cared so little for it—was that why the stream of fortune came to him? But when his languid soul awoke after a while to a sense of the work he was doing, Robert ceased to care little for it. He began to care much; and as his portraits kept their popularity his gains increased. He became hungry for gain; he grew a miser, and over-worked himself, thinking of his wife, thinking of the child to whom he was dead, he managed to get some news of them incidentally through his friend and former patron Sinclair; he heard where they were, and that they were well. At length, when he had scraped so much money together that he thought he might venture upon some communication, his heart went back to the agony of his parting, and the subject of his last sketch returned to him. Ah! was he not Dives now, stretching out vain hands, not daring to cry! He could not summon courage enough to write, but he could paint—he could put all his despairing soul, which yet had a faint hope in it, into that imploring face, those beseeching hands. He worked at it night and day, throwing his whole heart and soul into the canvas. And, with a heart trembling at his own temerity, after he sent his picture to England he himself had come back, but not to England—he had not courage for that; he was not even sufficiently instructed to know whether it would be safe for him to go back—whether he might bring the law upon him with fresh bugbears and troubles in its train—but he went to France. He had come to Brest, and he had wandered to this the nearest point from which communication with England was easy. He had arrived at St Malo in May, at the very time when Helen saw the picture in the Exhibition, and received its message into her very heart. But he had not ventured to send his letter till months after—not till now.

'Helen!' he said, trembling; 'will you stay with me here? will you go with me, back to New York? What shall we do?'

'Robert, let us go home.'

'Can I go home? I do not think so. I have a little money, for the child and you. I made it hardly—after I died. I should not like to give it once again to satisfy people who suffered no more than we did.'

'Oh, Robert,' she said. 'I have my story to tell you too.' And her story took as long in telling as his did; for it was difficult to her to remember that he knew nothing—that he did not know what he had been accused of; as difficult as it was for him to understand the allusions she made to the lost books and the censure which had been passed upon his name. He would stop her and say, 'What does that mean?' a dozen times in a single sentence. And then, as the story advanced to its climax, impatience seized him, and a growing excitement. He got up from his seat beside her, and paced about the little room. Then she saw, for the first time, that he was lame. How he had suffered! The seven years had not made much difference to her; her peaceful life had smoothed out the lines which sorrow had made in her face. There was not a white thread in her brown hair; she had almost grown younger instead of older, having upon her wherever she went a reflection of Norah's youth, which somehow she shared. But Robert was lame, and walked with difficulty, a consequence of his almost suicide; he was old, thin, white-haired, with furrows of anxiety and longing and heart-hunger in his face. All this had been done by the man who had beguiled him into the doomed bank, who had looked on calmly at his ruin, who had willingly countenanced the destruction of his good name. Mrs Drummond had lived through it all, had got over her hot fits of rage and indignation, and at this moment had her heart softened towards Reginald Burton, whom she had saved. She was not prepared for the excitement, the suppressed fury, the passionate indignation of her husband, to whom all this was new. She told him of the paper she had extorted from her cousin that last night, 'which clears you entirely—' she said.

'Clears me!' he cried, gnashing his teeth. 'My God! clears me! I who have done nothing but suffer by him. Clears me!'

'I do not quite mean that, Robert. You were cleared before. No one believed it. But we thought Golden only was to blame. Now this paper is formal, and explains everything. It makes it all easy for you.'

He did not stop, as if this was anything consolatory; he kept moving up and down, painfully, with his lameness. 'And that scoundrel has got off,' he cried between his teeth—'got off! and has the audacity to clear me.'

Poor Helen was disconcerted. She had forgotten her own fury of indignation when she first saw the accusation against him. She had long, long grown used to all that, and used to the reflection that nobody believed it whose opinion was worth anything. She had insisted upon Burton's confession and explanation, she scarcely knew why—more as a punishment to him than as a vindication of Robert. She was confused about it altogether, not quite knowing what she meant. And now, in the light of his indignation, she felt almost as if she had done her husband an injury—insulted him. She faltered, and looked at him wistfully, and did not know what to say. She had not lost the habit of love, but she had lost the habit of companionship; she had told her story wrongly; she did not know how to bring him to her state of feeling, or to transport herself into his. And this too was the fault of the man who had driven Robert to despair—the man whom she had saved.

'He has got off,' she said humbly, 'by my means. Robert, I tried revenge once, but I will never try it again. I could not give him up, however bad he had been, when he was in my power.'

The sound of trembling in her voice went to his heart. 'My poor Helen! my sweet Helen!' he cried, coming to her. 'Do you think I blame you? You could not have done otherwise. For you there was but one course—but if I had the chance now—'

Just then there was a commotion at the door, and sounds of many voices. A great many exclamations in French, with one or two broken questions in English, came to their ears. 'You has you papiers. Domm you papiers. You say you is Jean—Jean Smiff, et pas—'

'Je me fie à monsieur ici. Monsieur est-il chez lui? C'est un Anglais. Il nous expliquera tout ça,' said another voice. It was the voice of the maire, whom Robert had made friends with in his hunger for human companionship. The parley at the door went on for a few minutes longer, and then there entered a band of excited Frenchmen. One, a gendarme from St Malo, carried an open telegram in his hand; another, in a blouse, kept his hand upon the shoulder of a burly Englishman in a light coat. The maire brought up the rear. They seemed such a crowd of people as they entered the little, light room, that it was some moments before the three English people thus brought face to face recognised each other. Helen with difficulty suppressed a cry. Robert stood confronting the party with the flush of his indignation not yet subsided, with a wonder beyond words in his eyes. As for the other, he showed no sign of surprise. He was driven back to his last stronghold, forced to use all his strength to keep himself up and maintain his courage. His eye dilated and gave a flutter of wonder at the sight of Helen. It was evident that he did not recognise her companion. He kept his arms folded, as if for self-preservation, to keep within him all the warmth, all the courage possible, physically to keep up and support himself.

The three men rushed into explanation all at once. A telegram had been received at St Malo, describing an Englishman who was supposed to have gone there, and whose description, which the gendarme held out, in the telegram, corresponded exactly with that of the prisoner. The prisoner, however, called himself Smith. Smiff—or Smitt, as his pursuers pronounced it—and produced papers which were en règle; but he could not explain what he was doing here; he showed no inclination to be taken to the English consul. On the contrary, he had crossed to Dinard as soon as he heard that inquiries had been made about him at his hotel. While all this was being told the stranger stood immovable, with his arms folded; he did not understand half of it. His French was as deficient as the French of untravelled Englishmen usually is, and the tumult around him, at the same time, confused his mind and quickened his outward senses. He could not make out what his chances of liberation were; but his eyes were open to any possibility of escape. They were bloodshot and strained those eyes; now and then that flutter of wonder, of excitement, of watchfulness, came into them, but he showed no other sign of emotion. At such a terrible crisis all secondary sensations perish; he had no time to wonder what Helen, whom he had left behind him in England, should be doing here. Rather it was natural that everybody connected with his fate should be here, gathering round him silently to see the end.

Thus this encounter had but little effect upon Burton; but it would be impossible to describe the effect it had upon the man who stood opposite to him, whom he had not recognised. Robert Drummond had suffered as few men ever suffered. He had died—he had come alive again—he had lived two separate lives. For some years up to this day his existence had been that of a man deprived of all the hopes and consolations of life—a man miserably alone, dead to every one belonging to him. Even the return to life which he had tried to realise this morning was no more than an experiment. He might never be able to conquer, to forget those seven ghosts which stood between him and his wife and child. He could not take up his life again where he left it—that was impossible. And all this had been done by the influence of the man before him, who was in his power, whom he might if he would give over to prison and trial and punishment. A gleam of fierce joy shot through Drummond's heart, and then—

They stood facing each other, with the Frenchmen grouped about them. But Burton had not, beyond the first glance, looked at his judge. His face confronted him, but his eyes did not; he had escaped as yet the knowledge who it was.

A thousand and a thousand thoughts whirled through Drummond's mind; he had only a moment to decide in; he had the past to satisfy, and the burning, fiery indignation of the present moment, in which for the first time he had identified and comprehended the past. Give him up! punish him! Should such a scoundrel get off, when innocent men had so bitterly suffered? Let him fall, and bring down in his train all who were concerned—all who made a prey of the ignorant and the poor! This wave of thought possessed him with a whirl and sweep like the rushing tide—and then there came the interval of silence, the moment when the waters fell back and all was still.

Revenge! 'I tried revenge, once, but I will never try it again!' Who was it that had said this close to him, so that the very air repeated and repeated it, whispering it in his ear? He had himself been dead, and he had come alive again. His new life, which had commenced this morning, was spotless as yet. He had to decide, decide, decide in a moment how it should be inaugurated, by mercy or by judgment—by the sin (was it not a sin?) of helping the escape of a criminal, or by the righteous deed (where was it said that this might be a sin too?) of handing him over to punishment. How his soul was tossed upon these waves! He stood as in the midst of a great battle, which raged round him. Fierce arrows tore his heart, coming from one side and another, he could not tell how. Give up the accursed thing—punish the unworthy soul—be just! be just! But then that other, 'Neither have I condemned thee; go, and sin no more.' And all had to be done in a minute, while those voluble explanations interlaced each other, and each man expounded his case. Drummond glanced at his wife for help, but she dared not look at him. She sat on the sofa against the light, with her hands tightly clasped in her lap. Was she praying? For so long, out of the depths of his hell, Dives, poor Dives, had not dared to pray.

He did not know what he said when at length he spoke; it was some commonplace, some nothing. But it attracted at once the attention of the prisoner. Burton turned round, and gazed at the man whom he thought dead. He did not recognise the voice, except that it was a voice he knew; he did not even recognise the face, which had grown prematurely old, framed in its white hair, at the first glance; but there crept over him a shudder of enlightenment, a gleam of perception. His senses were quickened by his own position. He shook where he stood as if with cold or palsy. He looked at Helen, he looked at the man by her side. Then an inarticulate cry came from him; terror of he knew not what deprived him, fortunately, of all power of speech. He fell back in his fear, and his attendants thought he meant to escape. They threw themselves between him and the door. It was then that Drummond spoke in his haste, scarcely knowing what he said.

'I know him,' he said in French. 'It is a long time since we have met, and he has just recognised me, you perceive. We are not friends, so you may trust me. His papers are quite right, and it is a mistake about the telegram. Look here; this is not his description. "Nez ordinaire;" why, he has a long nose. "Teint brun;" he is quite fresh-coloured, and his hair is grey. This is a great mistake. Monsieur le Maire, I know the man, and I will be responsible for him. You must let him go.'

'I thought so,' said the maire, pleased with his own discrimination. 'Je l'ai dit. Monsieur nous expliquera tout ça. Voilà que j'ai dit.'

'Mais, monsieur—' began the gendarme.

Helen sat against the light, seeing nothing, and closed her eyes, and clasped her hands in her lap. Burton, bewildered and terror-stricken, looked on without showing any emotion. Perhaps the passiveness of his face was his best safeguard. Five minutes of expostulation and explanation followed, and then gradually the Frenchmen edged themselves out of the room. Fortunately Monsieur le Maire had taken this view from the beginning; he had been sure it was a mistake. When they were got rid of at last, the three who were left behind looked at each other in a silence which was more significant than words. Burton dropped into a chair; he was not able to stand nor to speak, but kept gazing at Drummond with a pitiful wonder and terror. At last—

'Are you Robert Drummond?' he asked hoarsely. 'Have you come back from your grave—'

'I am Robert Drummond,' said the other; 'and you are—John Smith, who must be got out of here as soon as possible. Have you money?'

'Yes.'

'Then I advise you to go away at once. Go up to Dinan by the river-side, or walk to St Brieuc to get the train. In the one case you are on your way to Brest, where there are ships always sailing; by the other you can get to Paris or wherever you please. You may wait here till the evening, if you choose; but then go.'

'I will go to Brest,' he said humbly.

'I would rather not know where you went; but go you must. My wife and I met to-day for the first time for seven years; we do not wish for company, you may suppose.'

Drummond's voice was very stern. He had no compassion for the man who stood thus humbled and miserable before him; not for him had he done this. And Burton was too much stupefied, too much bewildered, to make any direct reply. He looked at Helen with dull wonder, and asked under his breath—'

'Did you know?'

'No,' she said. 'It came upon me almost as suddenly as upon you.'

Then he pulled some papers out of his pocket.

'These are English papers. I don't know if it is long since you have left. But you might like to see them.' When he had done this, he made a few steps towards the door, where the old French bonne was waiting to show him where to go. Then he paused, and turned round again, facing them. 'What a man says in my position is very little to anybody,' he said; 'but—I want to say to you, Forgive me. I have helped to do you dreadful harm; but I—I did not mean it. I never meant it. I meant to get gain myself; but I never wished to harm you.'

And then he disappeared, saved again, saved at his uttermost need—surely this time finally saved—and by those whom he had injured the most. When he reached the clean little room where he was to stay all day, it appeared to Reginald Burton that he must be in a dream. The same feeling had been in his mind ever since he escaped from England. All was strange to him; and strangest of all was the fact that he could no longer command or regulate matters by his own will, but was the sport of circumstances, driven about he knew not how. His bewilderment was so great that he was not able to think. Saved first by a helpless woman, whose powers he would have laughed at a month ago; saved now by a ghost out of the grave!

That night he left Dinard under cover of the darkness, and walked to St Brieuc, where he got the train for Brest. He arrived there in time to get on board of a vessel about to sail for America. And thus Reginald Burton escaped from the immediate penal consequences of his sins. From the other consequences no man ever escapes. The prison, the trial, the weary round of punishment he had eluded; but his life was over and ended, and everything that was worth having in the world had abandoned him. Love was not his to carry away with him; reputation, honour, wealth, even comfort were gone. He had to make a miserable new beginning, to shrink into poverty, obscurity, and dependence. It would be hard to say whether these were more or less easy to bear than the prison work, prison life, prison garb from which he had escaped.

CHAPTER XIII

This was the end of Mr Burton of Dura—Mr Burton, of the great City firm, he who had been known as one of the greatest of commercial magnitudes, he who had ruined as many people as if he had been an emperor. For some time there was a very great deal about it in the newspapers, and his concerns were exposed to the light of day. He involved many others with him in his downfall, and some in his shame. If he had been taken, he would have joined in prison those men whom in our own day we have seen degraded from a high position in society down to the picking of oakum in gaol—men whom we all pour our loathing upon at the moment of their discovery, but of whom we say 'poor souls!' a few months after, when some clever newspaper correspondent has a peep at them, disguised in the prison garb, and known as numbers 300 and 301. Burton missed the prison and the pity; but he did not miss the punishment. In spite of various attempts that were made to stop it, the investigation of his affairs was very full and clear. It became apparent from his own private books, and that one of Rivers's which had been found in his safe, that the bank had been in reality all but ruined when it was made into a joint-stock company. Burton and his colleague had guaranteed the debts, and put the best face possible upon things generally; and Mr Golden's management, and an unexpected run of good luck, had all but carried the labouring concern into clear water. It was at this period that Burton, thanking his stars or his gods, withdrew from the share in the management which he had held nominally, and left it to Golden to complete the triumph of daring and good fortune. How this failed is already known to the reader. The mystery of the lost books was never cleared up; for Golden was out of the way, enjoying his honeymoon, when the private affairs of the other conspirator were thus thrown open to the light of day. But there was enough in the one book found among Mr Burton's to show how very inconvenient to him the finding of the others would have been. Thus daylight blazed upon all those tortuous, gloomy paths, and showed how the desire of self-interest guided the man through them, with an absolute indifference to the interests of others. He had not meant any harm, as he said; he had meant his own gain in the first place, his own recovery when his position was threatened, his own safety when danger came. He had not set out with a deliberate intention of ruining others; but this is a thing which nobody ever does; and he had not cared afterwards how many were ruined, so that he could hold on his way. Such cases happen now and then, and human justice cannot touch them; but most generally Nemesis comes sooner or later. Even at the worst, however, his material punishment was never so hard as that of some of his victims. The loss of the trust-money, which had been the immediate cause of his ruin, took the very bread out of the mouths of a family of orphans; but Mr Burton, at the lowest depths of his humiliation, had always bread enough, and to spare. He was never even thrown into such mental anxiety, such stress of painful calculation, as that into which the inhabitants of the Gatehouse were cast by his downfall. Miss Jane went painfully all over Dura, looking at the cottages, to see if by any means something could be found or contrived to suit Stephen; and her heart sank within her as she inspected the damp, low-roofed places, which were so very different from the warm old wainscoted rooms, the comfort of the Gatehouse. When the property was sold, however, it was found that the Gatehouse had been made into a separate lot, and had been bought, not by the rich descendant of the old Harcourts who had got Dura, but by some one whose name was unknown.

'Somebody who is going to live in the house himself, no doubt,' Miss Jane said, with a very long face; 'and I am sure I wish him well in it, whoever he may be,' she added with a struggle. 'But oh, Norah! what a thing it will be for us to go away!'

'If I knew him, I would go to him, and beg for your rooms for you. He never would have the heart to turn you out, if he was a good man,' cried Norah. 'For us it does not matter; but oh, Miss Jane, for you!'

'It cannot be helped, my dear,' said Miss Jane, drying her eyes. 'We have no right to it, you know. It does seem hard that we should be ruined by his prosperity, and then, as it were ruined again by his downfall. It seems hard; but it is not anybody's fault. Of course when we accepted it we knew the penalty. He might have turned us out at any time. No, Norah; we have no reason to complain.'

'That makes it worse,' cried impulsive Norah. 'It is always a comfort when one can think it is somebody's fault. And so it is—Mr Burton's fault. Oh, how much harm he has done! Oh, what a destroyer he has been! He has done as much harm as a war or a pestilence,' cried Norah. 'Think of poor—papa!'

She had always to make a pause before that name, not believing in it somehow, feeling it hurt her. By this time she had heard all about the meeting between her father and mother, and the day had been fixed when she was to join them; but still she had a sore, wounding, jealous sense that the new father was her rival—that he might be almost her enemy. Fathers on the whole seemed but an equivocal advantage to Norah. There was Mr Burton, who had ruined and shamed every one connected with him; and there was poor—papa, who might, for anything she knew, take all the gladness out of her own life.

'Oh, hush, my dear!' said Miss Jane. 'Mr Burton has been a bitter acquaintance to us; but he is Ned's father, and we must not complain.'

Just then there was a knock at the door, and Ned himself came in. He came from town, as he did often, to spend the evening with his betrothed. Their days were running very short now, and their prospects were not encouraging. He had not even time to look for any employment for himself, so much was he occupied with his father's affairs; and Norah was going away, and when should they meet again? These evenings which they spent together were very sweet; but they were growing daily sadder as they approached more closely to the shadow of the farewell. But this time Ned came in with a flush of pleasure in his face. His eyes were so brightened by it, and his colour so much improved, that he looked 'quite handsome,' Miss Jane thought; and he walked in with something of the impulsive satisfaction of old days.

'My grandfather is a brick,' he said, 'after all. He has given me my fortune. He has helped me to do something I had set my heart on. Miss Jane, don't think any more of leaving the Gatehouse. So long as I live nobody can turn you out.'

'What do you mean, Ned?'

'I mean that dear old grandpapa has been awfully good to me,' said Ned, 'and the Gatehouse is mine. I love it, Miss Jane. Don't you say anything. You may think it will be bitter for me to come here after all that has passed; but I love it. Since ever I was a boy, I have thought this room the dearest place in the world—ever since Norah sat and talked rubbish, and frightened me out of my life. How well I remember that! She has forgotten years ago! but I shall never forget. What are you crying about, Miss Jane? Now this is very hard upon a fellow, I must say. I thought it was good news.'

'And so it is—blessed news, you dear, dear, kind boy!' cried Miss Jane. 'Oh, children! what can I say to you? God bless you! And God will bless you for thinking of the afflicted first, before yourselves.'

'I had nothing to do with it—I knew nothing about it,' cried Norah proudly; and all at once, without any warning, she threw herself upon Ned, and gave him a sudden kiss on his brown cheek. For five minutes after none of the three were very coherent; for to do a good action when you are young makes you feel very foolish, and ready to cry with any one who cares to cry. Ned told them all about it between laughing and sobbing—how his grandfather had given him his portion, and how it was the best possible investment to buy the Gatehouse. 'For you see,' said Ned, 'when Norah makes up her mind to marry, we shall have a house all ready. As for everybody here knowing what has happened, everybody all over the country knows,' he added, with a hot flush on his cheek; 'and at Dura people like me—a little, and would not be unkind, as in other places. And how could I let the place Norah had been brought up in—the place I love—go to other people? So, Miss Jane, be happy, and set your brother's mind at rest. Nobody shall disturb you here as long as I live; and if I should die, it would go to Norah.'

'Oh, Ned, hush!' cried Norah, putting up her hand to his lip.

And then they went out into the garden, and wandered about and talked. Nothing but this innocent and close association, with no one to think it might be improper or to call them to account, could have made exactly such a bond as that which existed between these two innocent young souls. They were lovers, and yet they were half brother and sister. They talked of their plans with the wistful certainty and uncertainty of those who feel that another will may come in to shatter all their purposes, though in themselves they are so unalterable and sure. There was this always hanging over them, like the sword in the fable, of which they were conscious, though they would not say a word about it. To-night their spirits were raised. The fact that this familiar place was theirs, that Ned was actually its master, that here they might spend their days together as man and wife, exhilarated them into childish delight.

'I always think of you as in that room,' he said to her, 'when I picture my Norah to myself; and there is never half an hour all day long that I don't do that. I always see the old curtains and the funny old furniture. And to think it is ours, Norah, and that we shall grow old here, too!'

'I never mean to grow old,' said Norah. 'Fancy, Ned, mamma is not old, and she is nineteen years older than me. Nineteen years—twenty years! It is as good as a century; it will never come to an end!'

'Or if it does come to an end,' said wise Ned, in the additional discretion of two years' additional age, 'at least we shall have had our day.'

With this chastened yet delightful consciousness of the life before them they parted that evening. But next time they met Ned was not equally bright. He had been very sorely tried by the newspapers, by the shame he had to bear, by the looks askance which were bestowed on 'Burton's son.'

'I never shall be able to stay there,' he said, pouring out his troubled heart to Norah. 'I cannot bear it. Fancy having to hear one's father insulted, and not being able to say a word. I cannot do it; oh, Norah, I cannot! We must give up the thought of living here. I must go abroad.'

'Where, Ned?'

'Oh, I don't know. America, Australia—anywhere. I cannot stay here. Anywhere that I can earn my bread.'

'Ned,' said Norah, her happy voice all tuned to tones of weeping, 'remember I am mamma's only child. She has got—some one else now; but, after all, I am her only child.'

'Do you think I forget that?' he said. 'It is because I am afraid, because I feel, they will never, never trust you to me—so useless as I am—my father's son. Oh, Norah, when I think it all over, my heart is like to break!'

'But, Ned, you were in such good spirits last night.'

'Ah, but last night was different. My own Norah! if they said no, dear, if they were angry—Oh, Norah! don't hate me for saying it—what would you do?'

'What could I do?' she said, with her brown eyes blazing, half in indignation, half in resolution. 'And what do you think they are made of, Ned, to dare to say such a thing to me? Was mamma ever cruel? I would do just what I will do now; I would say, 'Ned, please don't! dear Ned, don't!' But if you would, notwithstanding all I said to you, of course I must go too.'

'My own Norah! But now they are going to take you away from me, and when, when shall I see you again?'

'People go to St Malo by the boat,' said Norah demurely. 'It sails from Southampton, and it gets there in I don't remember how many hours. There is nothing against people going to St Malo that want to go.'

And thus once more the evening had a more cheerful termination. But none of the party were cheerful when Norah picked up all her little belongings, and went up to town to Dr Maurice who was to be her escort. Probably, of all the party, she herself was the most cheerful; for she was the one who was going away to novelties which could not but be more or less agreeable to her imagination, while the others, in the blank of their daily unchanging existence, were left behind. Miss Jane cried over her, Mrs Haldane bade God bless her, and as for Stephen, he drew her close to him, and could not speak.

'I don't know what life will be worth, Norah, without your mother and you,' he said, looking up to her at last with the patient smile he had worn since ever Norah could remember—the one thing in the world which was more pathetic than sorrow itself; for he loved Helen, and missed her to the bottom of his heart—loved her as a disabled, shipwrecked man may love a woman altogether out of his reach, most purely, most truly, without hope or thought of any return—but as no man may justly love a woman who has her husband by her side. This visionary difference, which is yet so real, Stephen felt, and it made him very sad; and the loss of the child gave him full warrant to look as sad as he felt.

'But, oh, Stephen! let us not complain,' said Mrs Haldane; 'for has it not been shown to us beyond all question that everything is for the best.'

All for the best! All that had happened—Mr Burton's ruin, the tragical overthrow of his family, the destruction of poor Ned's hopes and prospects, the shame and humiliation and misery—had all been so 'overruled,' as Mrs Haldane would have said, that their house was more firmly secured to them than ever, and was theirs, most likely, as long as Stephen lived! It was a small matter to be procured at such a cost; but yet it was a satisfaction to her to feel that so many laws had been overthrown on her account, and that all was for the best.

As for Ned's parting with Norah, it is a thing which must not be spoken of. It took place in the cab in which her young lover conveyed her from the station to Dr Maurice's door. Ah, what rending of the young hearts there was as they tore themselves asunder! What big, hollow eyes, with the tears forced back from them, what gulps of choking sorrow swallowed down, as Ned, looking neither to the right hand nor the left, stalked away from Dr Maurice's door!

To tell the truth, Dr Maurice himself was not very comfortable either. He had got a great fright, and he had not recovered it. His brain was still confused; he felt as if he had been beaten about the head; a dull, hot colour dwelt upon his cheeks. He tried to explain to himself that he was feverish; but he was not feverish—or at least it was only his mind, not his body, which was so. It was partly wonder, but chiefly it was fright, on account of his own marvellous and hairbreadth escape. At the time when he had made that proposal to Helen, he believed, as she did, and everybody else, that her husband had died years ago. And, good heavens! what if she had not refused? Dr Maurice grew hot and cold all over, he actually shuddered, at the supposition. And yet such a thing might have happened. He went reluctantly, yet with curiosity, to see his old friend. He wondered with a confused and troubled mind whether Helen would have said anything about it—whether Drummond would take any notice of it. The doctor was impatient with Drummond, and dissatisfied altogether as to his conduct. A man, he reflected, cannot do that sort of thing with impunity. To be for seven years as though he had never been, and then to come to life again and interfere with everybody's affairs! It was hard. Drummond had got his full share of sympathy; he had turned his whole world upside down. Seven years ago he had been mourned for as few men are mourned; and now it was a mistake, it was almost an impertinence, that he should come to life again, as if nothing had happened. But nevertheless Dr Maurice volunteered to take Norah to St Malo. He was glad to do it—to rub out the recollection of that false step of his—to show that he bore no malice, and that no thoughts were in his mind which were inconsistent with his old friendship for Robert and respect for Robert's wife.

Robert's wife! She had called herself so when she was but Robert's widow. But nobody understood, nobody thought, what a change it was to Helen to fish up her old existence again, and resume its habits as if there had been no break in it. Love had conquered the strangeness at first; but there were so many strangenesses to be conquered. She had fallen into so different a channel from that into which his thoughts had been diverted. They were both unchanged in their affections; but how different in everything else! They were each other's nearest, closest, dearest; and yet they had to make acquaintance with each other over again. Nothing can be more strange than such a close union, accompanied by such a total ignorance. It was not even as if Helen had remained as he had known her—had received no new influences into her life. Both had an existence unknown to the other. Robert in the joy of his recovered identity, in the happiness of finding that there was still love and companionship for him in the world, took the reunion more simply than Helen did, and ignored its difficulties, or did not feel them. He had always taken things more simply than she. His absolute faith in her, his simple delight in finding her, his fond admiration of her, revived in Helen some of her old feelings of suppressed wonder and half doubt. But that doubt was humbler now than it had been once. In the old life a ghost of impatience had been in her; she had doubted his powers, and chafed at his failures. Now she began to doubt whether she had ever understood him—whether she had done him justice. For once, at least, Robert had risen to that height of power which passion sometimes forces almost beyond the reach of genius. He had made alive and put upon a dead piece of canvas, for all the world to see, one face which was a revelation out of the worlds unknown. Helen's heart had never wanted any additional bond to the husband whom she had chosen and clung to through good and evil; but her mind had wanted something more than his easy talent, his exquisite skill, the gentle, modest pitch of imagination which was all that common life moved him to. But on that point she was satisfied now. The only drawback was, she was no longer sure that it was Robert. He was himself, and yet another. He was her own by a hundred tender signs and sureties; and yet he was strange to her—strange!

And it was thus, with a suppressed excitement, which neither told, that the re-united pair awaited their child's coming. She breathless with curiosity and anxiety to know what Norah would think of her unknown father; he eager to make acquaintance with the new creature whom he knew only as a child. 'The child' he called her, till Helen smiled at his pertinacity, and ceased to remind him that Norah was no longer a child. Their excitement rose very high when the steamboat came in. Helen's feelings were, as usual, by far the most complicated. Norah was her own creation, if we may say so, framed by her, cultivated by her—not only flesh of her flesh, but heart of her heart, and mind of her mind; yet the influence of Norah's opinions, Norah's ways of thinking, was strong upon her mother, almost more strong than Helen's were on Norah; for the latter had all the confidence of youth, the former all the hesitation of middle age. What if Norah should not 'take to' the new father—the stranger who yet was so truly her own Robert of old? Neither the one nor the other even so much as recollected Dr Maurice— the poor man who was bracing up his courage to meet them, wondering what they might think. And they thought of him simply not at all.

And Norah approached that rocky shore with an unconcealable, almost avowed, jealousy of her father. A shade of that emotion, half shame, half pain, with which a young woman regards her mother's second marriage was in her mind. It was a partial desecration of her idea of her mother, and she was jealous of the new companion who naturally must be more to Helen than even she herself could be. She was jealous, though she had long given her mother a rival more dangerous still in Ned; but in such feelings no one is reasonable. Dr Maurice had stolen into her confidence, she knew not how, and, partly out of pure perversity, was very strenuous in Ned's favour, and had promised to plead his cause. The wretched man was almost glad that there should be this new complication coming along with Norah, to perplex from the very beginning her father's relations with her. Had things been as he once hoped—had he been able to make Norah his own child, as he had tried to do—then he would have resisted Ned to his last gasp; but as she was not his, he was wickedly glad that she should not be altogether Robert's, but that from the first his should be but a divided proprietorship.

'I will do what I can to make things easy for you, Norah,' he said, as they drew near St Malo, half out of love, half out of spite. 'I will give you what I meant to leave you, and that should get over part of the difficulty.'

'Oh, Dr Maurice, you have always been so good to me!' cried heedless Norah. 'If it had been you instead of papa—'

She was angry with herself when she had made that foolish, hasty speech; but, oh! how sweet it was to her companion! What balm it shed upon those awkward sorenesses of his! He drew her hand through his arm, and bent over her with the tenderest looks.

'It would be strange if I did not do my best for my little Norah,' he said, with something like a tear in his eye. Hypocrite! If she had been his little Norah, then heaven have mercy upon poor Ned!

They landed, and there was all the flutter and agitation of meeting, which was more confusing, more agitating, than meetings generally are, though these are always hard enough to manage. They went together across the bay to the little cottage on the cliff. They took a long time to settle down. Robert hung about his child as if she had been a new toy, unable to keep from gazing at her, touching her, recalling what she used to be, glorying and rejoicing over the possession of her; while Helen, on her side, watched too with a painful closeness, reading the thoughts in Norah's eyes before they had come. She wanted to jump into certainty at once. But they had to eat, and drink, and rest; they had to talk of all that had happened—of all that might yet happen. And so the first days passed, and the family unconsciously re-united itself, and the extraordinary sank, no one knowing how, into the blessed calm of every day.

And then there occurred an event which took all the company by surprise: Norah fell in love with her father. She 'took to' him as a girl might be expected to take to a man whose image she was. She was more like him a great deal than she was like her mother. Her hasty, impulsive ways, her fresh simplicity of soul, were all his. She had been thought to resemble her mother before; but when she was by her father's side, it was apparent in a moment whom she most resembled. She discovered it herself with a glow of delight. 'Why, mamma, he is like me!' she cried, with a delightful youthful reversal of the fact. And poor Helen did not quite like it. It is terrible, but it is true—for the first moment it gave her a pang. The child had been all hers; she had almost ceased to remember that there could be any sharing of her. She had been anxious about Norah's reception of her father; but she was not quite prepared for this. Dr Maurice, for his part, was simply furious, and went as near to hating Robert Drummond as it was possible to do; but then, of course, that feeling on Maurice's part was simply ludicrous, and deserved nothing but to be laughed at. This curious event made the most tragi-comic convulsion in the cottage on the cliff.

CHAPTER XIV

And now all the threads are shortening in the shuttle, and the web is nearly woven out. If any one has ever supposed for a moment that Robert Drummond and his wife would make a last appearance as cruel parents, interfering with their daughter's happiness, it does not say much for the historian's success in elucidating their characters. If Norah had wanted to marry a bad man, they would no doubt have made a terrible stand, and made themselves very unhappy; but when it was only their own prejudices, and poverty, and other external disadvantages that had to be taken into account, nothing but the forecasting imagination of two timid lovers could have feared for the result. When two people have themselves married upon nothing, it is so much more easy for them to see how that can be managed over again; and, heaven save you, good people! so many of us used to marry upon nothing in the old days.

But a great deal had to happen before this could come to pass. The Drummonds went home to England late in the autumn, and Robert was received back by the world with such acclamations as perhaps have not greeted a man of his profession in England for ages. Of itself the picture of 'Dives' had made a great impression upon the general mind; but when his strange story became public, and it was known that the picture of the year had been painted by a man risen, as it were, out of the grave, warmer still became the interest in it. The largest sum which had been given for a picture for years was offered for this to the resuscitated painter. Helen, always visionary, revolted from the very thought of selling this picture, which had been the link between herself and her husband, and which had so many associations to them both; but Robert had too much practical good sense to yield to this romantic difficulty. 'I am no longer Dives,' he said, as he drew his wife's arm through his own, and took her out with him to conclude the bargain. It increased the income which Robert's American gains brought him, and made them a great deal more comfortable. But Helen would never visit at the great house where 'Dives' was, and she would have given half her living to have possessed the greatest work her husband ever produced—the only one by which, all the critics said, he would be known to posterity. This was one of the disappointments of her new life, and it was without doubt an unreasonable disappointment, as so many are that sting us most deeply. The Drummonds were so fortunate, after some waiting and bargaining, as to secure their old house in St Mary's Road, with the studio in which such happy and such terrible hours had been passed. It was beyond their means; but yet they made an effort to purchase this pleasure for themselves. And here for two years the family lived together unbroken. Now and then they went to the Gatehouse, and made the hearts of the Haldanes glad. And painters would throng about the studio, and the old life came back as if it had never had a break. By times Helen would sit in the familiar room, and ask herself was it now—the present—or was it the past which had come back? The difference was, there was no child curled against the window, with brown hair about her shoulders, and a book in her arms, but only that slim, fair, brown-eyed maiden, who wore a ring of betrothal upon her finger, and had thoughts which travelled far by times after her distant lover; and that the master of the house, when he came into the room, was not the light-footed, youthful-browed Robert of old, but a white-haired man, growing old before his time. These were the changes; but everything else was unchanged.

Robert Drummond, however, never painted another picture like that 'Dives;' it was the one passion flower, the single great blossom, of his life. He painted other pictures as he used to do, which were good Drummonds, specimens of that master which the picture-dealers were very willing to have and collectors to add to their treasures, but which belonged to a world altogether distinct from the other. This Helen felt too with a gentle pang, but not as she had felt it of old. Once he had risen above that pleasant, charming level of beautiful mediocrity; once he had painted, not in common pigments, but in colours mixed with tears and life-blood. At such a cost even she was glad that no more great works should be produced. She was satisfied; her craving for genius and fame had once been fed, almost at the cost of their lives; and now she was content to descend to the gentler, lower work—the work by which men earn their daily bread.

Ah! but even then, even now, had it been—not Raphael, perhaps, who was one of the Shaksperian men, without passion, who do the work of gods as if they were the humanest, commonest of labourers—but such a fiery soul as that of Michelangelo whom this woman had mated! But it was not so. She could have understood the imperfection which is full of genius; what she was slow to understand was the perfection in which no genius was. But she was calmed and changed by all she had gone through, and had learned how dearly such excellence may be bought, and that life is too feeble to bear so vast a strain. Accordingly, fortified and consoled by the one gleam of glory which had crowned his brows, Helen smiled upon her painter, and took pleasure in his work, even when it ceased to be glorious. That was over; but the dear common life—the quiet, blessed routine of every day—that ordinary existence, with love to lighten it, and work to burden it, and care and pleasure intermingled, which, apart from the great bursts of passion and sorrow and delight that come in from time to time, is the best blessing God gives to man—that had come back, and was here in all its fulness, in perfect fellowship and content.

Norah lived at home with her parents for two years—the reason of which was, not that they objected to poor Ned, but that Ned was so sick at heart with all that he had suffered, that he was not capable of settling down to such work as could be procured for him in England. He was 'Burton's son;' and though even the people who looked cold at him on account of his parentage would soon have forgotten it, Ned himself could not forget. There was even a moment of despair in which he had declared that he would not share his disgrace with the girl he loved, but would carry it with him to his grave as soon as might be, and trouble no one any more. This state of mind alarmed Norah dreadfully, but it did not alarm the more experienced persons, who were aware that the mind at one-and-twenty has a great many vagaries, and is not always to be taken at its word. The despair came to a sudden end when Ned found himself suddenly appointed to a vice-consulship in an Italian seaport, where his chief made him do all the work, and where he received very little of the pay. When this serious moment came, and life had to be fairly looked in the face, Ned came to himself—he became a reasonable creature. Of course, after his despair, his first idea was to be married instantly; but finally he consented to wait until something better—something they could live on—could be procured for him. He bore his banishment valiantly, and so did Norah. And it did him good; he began to forget that he was 'Burton's son;' the whole terrible story began to steal out of his mind with that blessed facility which belongs to youth. His sky brightened from those early clouds; his mind, which was a very good, clear, capable intelligence, developed and strengthened; and finally, the exertions of his mother and grandfather, and those of Drummond, who had some influence too among great people who were lovers of art, procured him an appointment at home. Ned would have nothing to do with business; he shuddered at the very name of it, and rejected the plans his kind grandfather had formed for him with a repugnance which was almost horror. Mr Baldwin did not understand how the boy could be so foolish; but his mother understood, and subdued all opposition. Instead of taking his chance, therefore, of commerce, with the hope of becoming in his turn a millionnaire, Ned made himself very happy in the public service on a few hundreds a year. If he lived long enough, and nobody was promoted over him, and nothing happened to him or the office, the chances were that after thirty years or so he might find himself in enjoyment of a thousand a year. And all the family said to each other, 'That is very good, you know, for a young man without much interest,' and congratulated Ned as if he had the thousand a year already which was thirty years off, and subject to all the chances of good and evil fortune, of economical ministers, and those public crises which demand the sacrifice of junior clerks. But notwithstanding all these drawbacks, Ned was very happy in his new appointment, and his marriage day drew nigh.

Mrs Burton had lived for some time with her father and her aunts at Clapham—as long, indeed, as she could bear it; then she took a little house in town. She had given up half of her settlement to her husband's creditors; and whether she measured her sacrifice by her own knowledge of human nature, or did it simply in the revulsion of her heart, after Ned's careless reception of the larger offering which she was willing to have made for him—certain it is that she got much more honour from her public renunciation of the half than she would have done had she let the whole go as she once intended. Her magnanimity was in all the papers, and everybody commended the modest, unexaggerated sacrifice. And she had still a very good income of her own, derived from the half she retained. Her life in London, she thought, was happier than at Clapham. Yet, perhaps, a doubt may be entertained on this subject; for a life so limited was hard to her, however luxurious it might be. She did not care for luxuries; but she did care to watch the secret movements of life, to penetrate the secrets of human machinery, to note how men met the different emergencies of their existence. She gathered a little society round her who were as fond of this pursuit as herself; but unless they could have provided themselves with cases on which to operate, this association could not do them much good, and it was dry fare to be driven to scrutinising each other. She thought she was happier in her tiny house in Mayfair, where she kept three maids and a man, and was extremely comfortable; but I believe that in reality her time of highest enjoyment was also her time of greatest suffering, when she was ruling her own little world at Dura, and seeing her house tumble to pieces, and holding out against fate. She had had a chance for a moment of a better life when her son came back, and touched with a careless, passing hand those chords of her heart which had never vibrated before. But the touch was careless, momentary. Before that vibration had done more than thrill through her, the thoughtless hand was lifted, and the opportunity over, and Mrs Burton, with her soft cynic smile, her perfect toleration for the wants and weaknesses of humanity, her self-contained and self-sufficing character, had returned to herself. She was proud, very proud, in her way, and she was never betrayed into such weakness again. Which was to blame, the mother or the son, it would be hard to say; and yet Ned could hardly be blamed for failing to perceive an opportunity which he never guessed at nor dreamed of. Some exceptionally sympathetic natures might perhaps by instinct have felt the power that had been put into their hands; but it is impossible to say that he was to blame for not feeling it. Of all human creatures in this chilly universe, Ned remained the one who most deeply interested his mother. She made no opposition to his marriage; she even made a distinct effort to like and to attract Norah, who on her side did her best to be affectionate and filial to the woman whose cold gentleness and softness of manner were so unlike her own. It was an experiment which mutually could not be said to have failed. They were always, as people say, on the best of terms; but so far as any real rapprochement went, it cannot be said that it succeeded. Ned's life, however, such as it was, was the one point in her family to which Mrs Burton could turn without that emotion of calmly-observant contempt—if the sentiment could be described as anything so decided or warm as contempt—with which she regarded human nature in general. Her husband, when he reached America, at once wrote home to claim a share in the income secured by her settlement, which she accorded him without hesitation, moved by a certain gentle, unexpressed disdain. He received his allowance, as she termed it, or his share, as he called it, with unfailing regularity, and made a hundred ventures with it in the new field of speculation he had entered on with varying success. He gained money and he lost it as he moved about from one town to another; and sometimes in his letters he would tell her of his successes— successes which made her smile. It was his nature, just as it was Mr Baldwin's nature to take the chair at meetings, to devote himself to the interests of the denomination. The one tendency was no more elevated than the other, when you came to look into them, the student of human nature thought. Perhaps, on the whole, the commercial gambling on a small scale which now occupied the ruined merchant was more honest than the other; for Burton thought of nothing but his own profit or gain, whereas Mr Baldwin thought he was doing God a service. But this was not a comparison for a daughter, for a wife, to make.

And then Clara came back from her southern villa, a young mother, with a husband who was no longer her lover, and of whom she had become aware that he was growing old. The villa was situated on the shores of the loveliest sea, in the most beautiful climate in the world; but Clara tired of it, and found it dull, and with her dulness bored her husband so that his life became a burden to him. He brought her home at her urgent desire, with her baby, and they lived about in London for a short time, now in an hotel, now in a lodging, till it occurred to Clara that it was her duty to go and live near 'dear grandpapa,' and delight his old age with the fourth generation of his descendants. It suited her very well for a time. 'Dear grandpapa' was abject to her; her aunts became slaves to herself and her baby; she became the centre of all their thoughts and plans. Clary, who loved all pleasant things, and to whom luxury and ease were life, made herself at home at Clapham; and Mr Golden relieved her of his presence, paid visits here and there, lived at his club—which, strangely enough, had not expelled him—and returned to all the delights of his old bachelor life. What was to be the final end of it was hard to prophesy; but already Clary had begun to be bored at Clapham, and to make scenes with her husband when he paid her his unfrequent visits. And this was the love-match so romantically made! Clary, amid all her jealousies and all her dulness, kept so firm a hold upon the rich old people who could not live for ever, and who could restore her at their death, if they so pleased, to much of her old splendour, that her mother derived a certain painful amusement from this new manifestation of her life. Amusement, I cannot deny,—and painful, I hope; seeing that the creature who thus showed forth to her once again the poor motives and self-seeking of humanity was her only daughter. But with such evidences before her eyes of what human nature could be, was it wonderful that Mrs Burton should stand more and more by herself, and harden day by day into a colder toleration, a more disdainful acquiescence in the evils she could not fight against. What was the good of fighting against them? What could she do but render herself extremely unhappy, and spoil the comfort of others without doing them any good? It was not their fault; they were acting according to their nature. Thus Mrs Burton's philosophy grew, and thus she spent her diminished life.

It was in the midst of all these varied circumstances that the joy-bells rang for Norah's wedding. Mrs Burton did not go; for even her philosophy was not equal to the sight of Dura, where, according to the wish of both bride and bridegroom, the bridal was; but Clara, eager in the dulness of Clapham for any change, was present in a toilet which filled her aunts with compunction, yet admiration, and which one of them had been wheedled into giving her. Clara took great state upon her as the matron, the only one of the party who had attained that glory, though she was the youngest, as she reminded them all. 'But if I don't do better than Clary has done, I hope I shall never marry at all,' Katie Dalton cried with natural indignation. The pretty procession went out of the Gatehouse on foot to the church behind the trees, where Norah, as she said, had been 'brought up,' and where Mr Dalton blessed the young pair, while his kind wife stood holding Helen's hand and crying softly, as it were, under her breath. Helen herself did not cry; and Norah's tears came amid such an April shining of happiness, that no one could object to them. The whole village came out to watch the pair whom the whole village knew. A certain tenderness of respect, such as the crowd seldom shows, was in the salutations Dura gave to the son of the ruined man who had so long reigned among them. No one could remember, not the most tenacious rural memory, an unkind act of Ned's; and the people were so sorry for him, that their pleasure in his joy was half pathetic. 'Poor lad!' they said; 'poor fellow! And it was none of his fault.' And the friendliness that brought him back to hold his high festival and morning joy of youth among them touched the kindly folks, and went to their hearts. Stephen Haldane sat at his window, and watched the bride come and go. Tears came into his eyes, and a pathetic mixture of gladness and sorrow to his heart. He watched the procession go out, and in his loneliness folded his hands and prayed for them while they were in church. It was summer once more, and the blossomed limes were full of bees, and all the air sweet with scent and sound. While all the goodly company walked together to the kirk, Stephen, who could not go with them, sat there in the sunshine with his folded hands. What thoughts were in his mind! What broken lights of God's meaning and ways gleamed about him! What strange clouds passed over him through the sunshine—recollections of his own life, hopes for theirs! And when the bride went away from the door, away into the world with her husband—in that all-effectual separation from her father's house which may be but for a few days, but which is more or less for ever, Stephen once more looked out upon them from his window. And by his side stood Helen, escaped there to command herself and to console him. The father leaned out of the window, waving his hand; but the mother stood behind, with her hand upon the arm of the invalid's chair. When Robert turned round, it was with wonder that he perceived in Stephen's eyes a deeper feeling, a more penetrating emotion, than he himself felt, or had any thought of. He held out his hand to his friend, and he put his arm round his wife.

'Well, Helen,' he said, with his cheery voice, 'she is gone as you went from your mother; and there are two of us still, whatever life may have in store.'

'If there had not been two of us,' the mother cried, with momentary passion, 'I think I should have died!'

Stephen Haldane took her hand in his, in sign of his sympathy. He held it tightly, swaying for a moment in his chair. And he said nothing, for there was no one whose ear was his, to whom his words were precious. But in his heart he murmured, God hearing him, 'There is but one of me; and I never die.'

Margaret Oliphant – A Short Biography

Margaret Oliphant Wilson was born on April 4th, 1828 to Francis W. Wilson, a clerk, and Margaret Oliphant, at Wallyford, near Musselburgh, East Lothian.

She spent her childhood at Lasswade, near Dalkeith, Glasgow before moving to Liverpool.

Her youth was spent in establishing a writing style so much so that, in 1849, she had her first novel published: Passages in the Life of Mrs. Margaret Maitland based on the Scottish Free Church movement. It met with some success and was a good start to her career.

Two years later, in 1851, her third book Caleb Field was published. It was also now that she met the publisher William Blackwood in Edinburgh and was asked to contribute to his well-received Blackwood's Magazine. It was to be a lifetimes endeavor. Over the course of the relationship she would have well over 100 articles published.

In May 1852, Margaret married her cousin, Frank Wilson Oliphant, at Birkenhead, and they settled at Harrington Square, Camden, London. He was an artist working primarily in stained glass. With the marriage she became Margaret Oliphant Wilson Oliphant.

Their marriage produced six children but three tragically died in infancy.

When her husband developed signs of the dreaded consumption (tuberculosis) they moved, on the advice of doctors, to warmer climes. In January 1859 it was to Florence, and then to Rome where, sadly, he died.

Margaret was naturally devastated but was also now left without support and only her income from her writing. She returned to England and took up the task of supporting her three remaining children by her literary activity.

By now she was being published both as an established novelist and regularly in Blackwood's Magazine, amongst others. Her incredible and prolific work rate increased both her commercial reputation and the size of her reading audience.

Against this her domestic life continued to be tragic, full of sorrow and disappointment.

In January 1864 her only remaining daughter Maggie died and was buried in her father's grave in Rome. Her brother, who had emigrated to Canada, was shortly afterwards involved in financial ruin. Margaret generously offered a home to him and his children, adding another demand to her already heavy responsibilities.

In 1866 she settled at Windsor to be closer to her sons, who were being educated at near-by Eton School. That year, her second cousin, Annie Louisa Walker, came to live with her as a companion-housekeeper. Windsor was now to be her home for the rest of her life.

Her literary career for three decades was one of constant delivery and success. Whether she wrote historical works or across several genres in fiction: domestic realism, historical, romance or supernatural she was successful.

For more than thirty years she pursued a varied literary career but family life continued to bring problems.

The literary ambitions she wished for her sons were unfulfilled. Cyril Francis, the eldest, died in 1890, leaving a Life of Alfred de Musset, incorporated in his mother's Foreign Classics for English Readers. The younger, Francis, who she nicknamed 'Cecco', collaborated with her in the Victorian Age of English Literature and won a position at the British Museum, but was rejected by Sir Andrew Clark, a famous physician. Cecco died in 1894.

With the last of her children now lost to her, she had but little further interest in life. Her health steadily and inexorably declined.

Margaret Oliphant Wilson Oliphant died at the age of 69 in Wimbledon on 20th June 1897. She is buried in Eton beside her sons.

At her death, Margaret was still working on Annals of a Publishing House, a record of Blackwood's Magazine with which she had enjoyed such a successful relationship.

Her Autobiography and Letters, which present a thoughtful picture of her domestic anxieties, was published in 1899. Only parts were written with a wider audience in mind: she had originally intended the Autobiography for her son, but he died before she could finish it.

Opinions on Oliphant's work are split, with some critics seeing her as a 'domestic novelist', while others recognize her work as influential and important to the Victorian literature canon. Critical reception from her contemporaries is also divided. John Skelton took the view that Oliphant wrote too much and too quickly. Writing a Blackwood's article called 'A Little Chat About Mrs. Oliphant', he asked, "Had Mrs. Oliphant concentrated her powers, what might she not have done? We might have had another Charlotte Brontë or another George Eliot." However not all of the contemporary reception was negative. The esteemed M. R. James admired Oliphant's supernatural fiction, concluding that "the religious ghost story, as it may be called, was never done better than by Mrs. Oliphant in 'The Open Door' and 'A Beleaguered City'. Mary Butts lavished praise on Oliphant's ghost story 'The Library Window', describing it as "one masterpiece of sober loveliness".

More modern critics of Oliphant's work include Virginia Woolf, who asked in Three Guineas whether Oliphant's autobiography does not lead the reader "to deplore the fact that Mrs. Oliphant sold her brain, her very admirable brain, prostituted her culture and enslaved her intellectual liberty in order that she might earn her living and educate her children."

Whatever the merits of their cases Margaret Oliphant has been shamefully neglected in modern years. She is now becoming more widely recognised as a leading writer of her day.

Margaret Oliphant – A Concise Bibliography

A canon of more than 120 works, including novels, travel books, histories, and volumes of literary criticism.

Novels

Margaret Maitland (1849)
Merkland (1850)
Caleb Field (1851)
John Drayton (1851)
Adam Graeme (1852)
The Melvilles (1852)
Katie Stewart (1852)
Harry Muir (1853)
Ailieford (1853)
The Quiet Heart (1854)
Magdalen Hepburn (1854)
Zaidee (1855)
Lilliesleaf (1855)
Christian Melville (1855)
The Athelings (1857)
The Days of My Life (1857)
Orphans (1858)
The Laird of Norlaw (1858)
Agnes Hopetoun's Schools and Holidays (1859)
Lucy Crofton (1860)
The House on the Moor (1861)
The Last of the Mortimers (1862)
Heart and Cross (1863)
Salem Chapel (1863)
The Rector (1863)
Doctor's Family (1863)
The Perpetual Curate (1864)

Miss Marjoribanks (1866)
Phoebe Junior (1876)
A Son of the Soil (1865)
Agnes (1866)
Madonna Mary (1867)
Brownlows (1868)
The Minister's Wife (1869)
The Three Brothers (1870)
John: A Love Story (1870)
Squire Arden (1871)
At his Gates (1872)
Ombra (1872
May (1873)
Innocent (1873)
The Story of Valentine and his Brother (1875)
A Rose in June (1874)
For Love and Life (1874)
Whiteladies (1875)
An Odd Couple (1875)
The Curate in Charge (1876)
Carità (1877)
Young Musgrave (1877)
Mrs. Arthur (1877)
The Primrose Path (1878)
Within the Precincts (1879)
The Fugitives (1879)
A Beleaguered City (1879)
The Greatest Heiress in England (1880)
He That Will Not When He May (1880)
In Trust (1881)
Harry Joscelyn (1881)
Lady Jane (1882)
A Little Pilgrim in the Unseen (1882)
The Lady Lindores (1883)
Sir Tom (1883)
Hester (1883)
It Was a Lover and his Lass (1883)
The Lady's Walk (1883)
The Wizard's Son (1884)
Madam (1884)
The Prodigals and their Inheritance (1885)
Oliver's Bride (1885)
A Country Gentleman and his Family (1886)
A House Divided Against Itself (1886)
Effie Ogilvie (1886)
A Poor Gentleman (1886)
The Son of his Father (1886)
Joyce (1888)

Cousin Mary (1888)
The Land of Darkness (1888)
Lady Car (1889)
Kirsteen (1890)
The Mystery of Mrs. Biencarrow (1890)
Sons and Daughters (1890)
The Railway Man and his Children (1891)
The Heir Presumptive and the Heir Apparent (1891)
The Marriage of Elinor (1891)
Janet (1891)
The Cuckoo in the Nest (1892)
Diana Trelawny (1892)
The Sorceress (1893)
A House in Bloomsbury (1894)
Sir Robert's Fortune (1894)
Who Was Lost and is Found (1894)
Lady William (1894)
Two Strangers (1895)
Old Mr. Tredgold (1895)
The Unjust Steward (1896)
The Ways of Life (1897)

Short stories
Neighbours on the Green (1889)
A Widow's Tale and Other Stories (1898)
That Little Cutty (1898)
The Open Door (1918)

Selected Articles

Mary Russel Mitford (Blackwood's Magazine, Vol. 75, 1854)
Evelin and Pepys (Blackwood's Magazine, Vol. 76, 1854)
The Holy Land (Blackwood's Magazine, Vol. 76, 1854)
Mr. Thackeray and his Novels (Blackwood's Magazine, Vol. 77, 1855)
Bulwer (Blackwood's Magazine, Vol. 77, 1855)
Charles Dickens (Blackwood's Magazine, Vol. 77, 1855)
Modern Novelists—Great and Small (Blackwood's Magazine, Vol. 77, 1855)
Modern Light Literature: Poetry (Blackwood's Magazine, Vol. 79, 1856)
Religion in Common Life (Blackwood's Magazine, Vol. 79, 1856)
Sydney Smith (Blackwood's Magazine, Vol. 79, 1856)
The Laws Concerning Women (Blackwood's Magazine, Vol. 79, 1856)
The Art of Caviling (Blackwood's Magazine, Vol. 80, 1856)
Béranger (Blackwood's Magazine, Vol. 83, 1858)
The Condition of Women (Blackwood's Magazine, Vol. 83, 1858)
The Missionary Explorer (Blackwood's Magazine, Vol. 83, 1858)
Religious Memoirs (Blackwood's Magazine, Vol. 83, 1858)

Social Science (Blackwood's Magazine, Vol. 88, 1860)
Scotland and her Accusers (Blackwood's Magazine, Vol. 90, 1861)
The Chronicles of Carlingford (Blackwood's Magazine 1862–1865)
Girolamo Savonarola (Blackwood's Magazine, Vol. 93, 1863)
The Life of Jesus (Blackwood's Magazine, Vol. 96, 1864)
Giacomo Leopardi (Blackwood's Magazine, Vol. 98, 1865)
The Great Unrepresented (Blackwood's Magazine, Vol. 100, 1866)
Mill on the Subjection of Women (The Edinburgh Review, Vol. 130, 1869)
The Opium-Eater (Blackwood's Magazine, Vol. 122, 1877)
Russian and Nihilism in the Novels of I. Tourgeniéf (Blackwood's Magazine, Vol. 127, 1880)
School and College (Blackwood's Magazine, Vol. 128, 1880)
The Grievances of Women (Fraser's Magazine, New Series, Vol. 21, 1880)
Mrs. Carlyle (The Contemporary Review, Vol. 43, May 1883)
The Ethics of Biography (The Contemporary Review, July 1883)
Victor Hugo (The Contemporary Review, Vol. 48, July/December 1885)
A Venetian Dynasty (The Contemporary Review, Vol. 50, August 1886)
Laurence Oliphant (Blackwood's Magazine, Vol. 145, 1889)
Tennyson (Blackwood's Magazine, Vol. 152, 1892)
Addison, the Humorist (Century Magazine, Vol. 48, 1894)
The Anti-Marriage League (Blackwood's Magazine, Vol. 159, 1896)

Biographies

Edward Irving (1862)
Francis of Assisi (1871)
Count de Montalembert (1872)
Dante (1877)
Cervantes (1880)
Life of Sheridan in the English Men of Letters series (1883)
John Tulloch (1888)
Laurence Oliphant (1892)

Historical & Critical Works

Historical Sketches of the Reign of George II (1869)
The Makers of Florence (1876)
A Literary History of England from 1760 to 1825 (1882)
The Makers of Venice (1887)
Royal Edinburgh (1890)
Jerusalem (1891)
The Makers of Modern Rome (1895)
William Blackwood and his Sons (1897)
The Sisters Brontë. In: Women Novelists of Queen Victoria's Reign (1897)

www.ingramcontent.com/pod-product-compliance
Lightning Source LLC
Chambersburg PA
CBHW052021020726

47501CB00004B/1173